MW00806926

July 21, 2022

Becky,

   Thank you so much for reading my novel. I hope you enjoyed it.

   thanks,

   Jody Herpin

RELATIVE CONSEQUENCES

A NOVEL BY

JODY HERPIN

I dedicate this novel to my daughter and English teacher extraordinaire, Jennifer, who helped me polish my manuscript and who graciously lent me her insight.

I'd like to add a "thank you" to Martha Simons and Peggy Pope Gunther of Bonita Springs, Florida. On a warm day in November 2015, these two lovely ladies took the time to reminisce about old Bonita Springs with me. Martha's sketch of the downtown area in the 1950s served as the basis for my hand drawn map, which I inserted at the beginning of Part Two.

Although I lived in Bonita Springs as a child, the story of Jessy Tate is a work of fiction. All the characters, events, and a few locales mentioned in this novel grew from my imagination. Although, I did incorporate actual past and present settings and business establishments. With that in mind, please forgive if my memory and research erred in any way.

"It is in pardoning that we are pardoned."

—Francis of Assisi

"Forgiveness is the final form of love."

—Reinhold Niebuhr

CONTENTS

PART ONE

PART TWO

PART THREE

PART ONE

CHAPTER ONE:
LEMONS IN MY WINE

My mother was always right. To this day, her words of wisdom and forecasts of doom remain inside my head, proving her infallibility. One of her favorite prophecies, *nothing good happens in the middle of the night*, rang true three nights ago on Monday, October 24, 2005. A sneaky aneurysm exploded in my sixty-three-year-old husband's brain. Sometime between one and two in the morning, I found Phillip lying face up on the floor staring at the ceiling, not breathing, not moving. I followed the ambulance that took him to the hospital while the paramedics kept him clinically alive. Unfortunately, my husband never woke up. Phillip Tate died alone.

Today I, Jessy Tate, sit in the back of a Lincoln Town Car, frowning at the withering mums and thinning pansies bordering the sidewalk and the jumble of orange and brown littering the grass in front of my North Atlanta home. My daughter, Gretchen, covers my hand with hers as the chauffeur steers into my driveway and parks. Leaning into the seat, the leather, cool behind the nape of my neck, I glance at Gretchen. "You know, on a day like today, your dad would spend the entire afternoon raking leaves into little piles."

"Come on, Mom. Time to go inside."

"Wait a sec." I rummage through my purse and find a zippered makeup bag holding a compact and a lipstick. The last thing I want is to look the part of the grieving widow, not to mention one who hasn't slept in several days. Opening the compact, a blatantly honest reflection glares back at me in the miniature mirror. "I've aged ten years." I smear the burgundy stain on my lips. "Why did I buy this color? It washes me out." I drop the tube into the makeup pouch, while Gretchen gently repositions the silver chain around my neck, shifting the clasp to the back.

The chauffeur offers to help me out of the car. I slide both feet into chunky black pumps. When I step onto the driveway, a chilly blast of autumn wafts through my hair. Mario Ricci, a towering man with a full head of gray, holds open my front door. He boasts a white carnation pinned to a navy lapel. As I pass by, his sympathetic dark eyes snag mine. "Jessy." He nods.

I can't believe he has the nerve to show up here. I turn away.

As Gretchen and I cross the threshold, she whispers in my ear. "Remember, Mom, you're not to lift a finger today. Mimi and I will take care of everything."

She needn't worry about that. I do not intend to do anything. If I could, I'd crawl into a corner and sleep forever. However, due to the eclectic array of mourners trickling into my home, I can't. I prop against the dining room table. That throbbing pain that originated at the base of my neck decides to shoot into my right temple. I'll bet Mario Ricci brought his wife.

A vaguely familiar woman comes to my rescue by handing me a glass of pinot noir. I graciously accept. Feigning politeness, I listen to her kindhearted words and say, "Thank you. I'm sure Phillip is glad you came." It quickly becomes my standard reply.

You can bet wherever he is, my Phillip is more than glad. He's reveling in the attention, everyone paying tribute to his life. He is, or rather was, a people person, an exceptional corporate attorney, and a salt-of-the-earth kind of guy, albeit bent toward the narcissistic. Friends breathe tributes into highball glasses, their mouthfuls crammed with guacamole and *queso* dip. Apparently, my husband aspired to be God's gift to Atlanta, Georgia. Isn't it funny how we often canonize the dead?

Nevertheless, I happen to know that Saint Phillip fell a little short of the title. Don't get me wrong, I loved and respected the man, but boy, could I enlighten this crowd by spouting a list of his sins. All of which I forgave, by the way.

When Gretchen announces the placement of crudités and chilled shrimp on the dining room table, I'm able to break away from a cluster of properly clad women and wander into the living room. My timing is perfect. The couch empties allowing me to seize the end seat adjacent to the fireplace. One shoe slips off, and another; all ten digits grip the rug. Why did I wear this skirt? It makes it hard to conceal my chubby knees.

"I ought to stoke the fire. It's…" My delivery trails off into a sigh. To my right, crackling embers hiss, emitting the aroma of burnt hickory. Candles. Yes, candles. Someone should light the ones on the mantel.

I'm supposed to mingle, but it's my party and I'll isolate if I want to. Instead, I people-watch while guests stray to and from the food in the dining room, reminding me of chattering squirrels stuffing their cheeks for winter's storage. I gaze from one side of the room to the next. There's Mario Ricci's wife. Damn, she's coming this way.

"Oh, Jessy. Mario and I are so sorry. We're going to miss Phillip. The neighborhood won't be the same without him."

I swallow. "Thanks, Phoebe. Uh, would you mind getting me a refill?" I hold up my empty glass with an unsteady hand. "It's the red." I sigh. What I really need is a Xanax.

"Glad to." She takes the glass and hurries toward the dining room.

A gaggle of noisy couples closes ranks across the room, the women yakking, the men hovering nearby slurping cocktails, tedium stamped across their faces. Near the entryway, another group of bereaved souls studies me as if expecting the fragile widow to faint or wail at a moment's notice.

Phoebe is at my side with a full glass in her hand. "Mario and I are heading out, but please let us know if there's anything we can do."

"Okay, thanks." I grab my wine and then turn to face the fireplace trying to swallow the lump in my throat. I wonder if she knows.

A group of ladies from my church, Our Lady of Lourdes, congregates behind the sofa. "Did y'all hear about Fred and Isabel?" One woman's intonation drowns out the others. "I understand he caught her red-handed. An instructor at her gym."

Another woman throws in her two cents. "And after the death of their son and all. Good Lord, it's nearly been a year. Remember, he hung himself in their garage?"

All of a sudden, I'm transfixed on an image in my mind—the Donaldson's teenage son, Gary, struggling for life, trying to pry the rope from his neck. It's hard to catch my breath. I set the wine down. Scurrying through the house, I pass through the kitchen and out the back door. The fresh air clears my head. "Boy, do I need Dr. Priest right now." My wristwatch says five-thirty. Two hours have passed since I loitered at my husband's graveside and placed a perfect lily on his coffin.

I left my shoes behind. My feet freezing, I hurry back inside. Since no one took my place, I sink into the sofa and sip wine. Before long, someone refills my glass again. As I reach for it, the cushions shift. Hanna Carter, a neighbor from three houses down, sets her ample backside next to me.

She pats my hand. "Oh, honey, we will miss your husband so much. Phillip was a marvelous Willow Tree Association president. He always managed to get things done around here."

The pasted expression on my lips begins to fade as I cringe at the woman's high-pitched inflection.

"But, it's always the ones left behind who suffer. Isn't it? If you need me, call and I'll be right over. I'm free during the week except Tuesday morning canasta, of course, and Wednesdays and Friday afternoons." The buxom woman takes a breath. "By the by, I brought you a gallon of sweet tea and my famous three-bean casserole. In spite of…you know…you must preserve your strength."

"Uh huh."

Hanna swallows a sip of straight bourbon over ice. "Your circumstances are dreadful right now, but what do they say? When life gives you lemons to put in your, no, wait a minute, that's not right."

"You make lemonade." I hold the pinot noir under my nose and inhale. Savoring the deep cherry aroma might help me forget why I'm here and what I did. I take a sip. Sheltering the liquid in my mouth for several seconds, I permit the warmth to coat the back of my throat before it goes down. I wish Dad were here. He'd say the right words. I fondle the necklace at my throat.

Hanna stands up. She pets me on the shoulder, not so much in a sorry-for-your-loss fashion, but more in line with a good-dog gesture. She wanders off, no doubt in search of bourbon.

Another half hour slips by. One by one, mourners approach me. Every condolence similar yet genuine, dripping with pity and declaring sorrow for my loss. I smile at the sight of my twenty-year-old granddaughter who blocks my view of the dining room. She comes closer and wedges between the elderly woman at the end of the couch and me. Mimi presses a kiss on my cheek; a hint of gardenias saturates the area around us.

"Gran, Mom and I can stay and help for a few more days if you want."

I examine her face—no wrinkles, no worry lines, skin as smooth as the inside of a seashell, and her eyes, incredibly expressive. "Mimi, have I told you that most of the Blanchard family members have been blessed with eyes the color of copper pennies?"

She smiles. "Yes, ma'am."

"Sweetie, you and your mother can go on home after the reception. It's time for me to be alone." Shivering, I fold my arms and squeeze my elbows. "Will you do me a favor though? Please go grab the pashmina off the end of my bed, and the black clutch, too." Bending both knees, I draw my feet under me.

Mimi disappears into the hallway. Within minutes, she reappears carrying my belongings. "Here you go." She covers my shoulders with the shawl.

I dig for the magic pills tucked inside my purse. Tapping the bottom of the prescription bottle forces the tablet into my hand. The Xanax goes down easily with the sip of wine. I pass the empty glass to my granddaughter.

* * *

At seven-thirty, laden with overnight bags and containers full of leftovers, Gretchen and Mimi tramp to their car. I open another bottle of red.

Gripping a half-full glass, I ramble from room to room counting the potted peace lilies—the perfect gift for the bereaved, I suppose. Someone scattered them throughout the house with no regard for order or place-ment. It's something I'll have to deal with tomorrow. In spite of the clutter, my home seems larger. The quiet ricochets off the walls.

Back in the kitchen, I set the glass on the counter and crack open the refrigerator. "I'm starving to death. Hey, Phillip, may I fix you a snack?" My hand quickly covers my mouth as if I could ram the words back inside. "Oh, my God, he's really gone." I clutch my middle and crumble to the floor crying gut-wrenching tears, the same tears I harbored all day long, the ones that refused to show up at the funeral.

* * *

I awaken on the kitchen floor. It's dark and eerily quiet. The only sounds I hear are my rumbling belly and the *hum* of an open refrigerator. How long have I been lying here? Hugging a barstool, I pull myself up and grasp a container of tiny fried chicken wings and drumsticks from the fridge's top shelf. Placing the food on the counter, I nudge the door shut with my foot. The light switch is to my right.

For a half hour, I devour the caterer's leftovers, licking my fingertips between bites of greasy poultry and swigs of wine. A bit lightheaded, I steady myself next to the counter and giggle. "Have you had a little too much wine today, Jessy Tate?"

After stripping off a wrinkled blouse and squirming out of a straight skirt, I shed tights, bra, and panties. I leave the funeral outfit in a heap on the floor. Tapping the wall along the hallway keeps me from losing my balance on the trek to the master bedroom. Somewhere in the house, a phone rings.

The marble-tiled floor in the master bath gives me pause. Ten years ago, Phillip searched months for the perfect stone. I step inside the shower stall and adjust the spray to the highest setting. Powerful jets batter burning neck muscles as I say a prayer that the hot water washes the last few days down the drain.

Shampoo drips down my face. I close my eyes and visualize the scene where I walk into the bedroom. I see Phillip lying on the floor, his body cold to the touch. His eyes are open, but he doesn't see me. I'm screaming.

The young paramedic's words spool inside my brain, his voice steady and unemotional, "Ma'am, if it's any consolation, your husband probably never felt a thing, never felt a thing, never felt a thing."

How ironic and so unfair. I feel every damn twinge, regret, and stab in my heart, and he felt nothing. The spray hits my face when I open my eyes. I plant my hands on the tile and let the water and the memories rain on me. In a flashback, I walk the sugar sands of a Gulf of Mexico beach with Phillip. Laughing, loving, the two of us planning a future, sharing dreams.

Gently at first, I run a soapy loofah over the imprints left on my skin, miniature reminders of college days—a butterfly tattoo gracing a shoulder, a tiny peace symbol adorning the back of my hip. Scrubbing reddens the skin while I scour myself to erase the guilt. The angry words I said to Phillip the day he died fill my head. Regret takes over. If I scrub harder, everything might disappear, even the images invading my dreams. Nothing makes sense anymore. Nothing.

The sponge slips from my hand. The water cleanses me until the spray runs cold.

CHAPTER TWO:
BLESS YOUR HEART

I punch the pillows at the headboard. "That's better." I lean backward pressing numbers into my cell. It's late, but I don't care.

An old friend answers. "Hello, Rhodes Residence." Rita's affected accent reveals no trace of any regional twang.

"I hope it's not too late to call. It's me—Jessy."

"Wait. It's bad news. I can tell."

"Phillip passed away." My voice catches. "We held the funeral today, and I'm having a rough time."

"What happened?"

I relay the details—how I found him, how empty the house is, and how much my insides hurt each time I walk into our bedroom.

"You'll get past this. Don't worry. Are you sleeping at all?"

"Some. I've been taking Ambien, but I'm going to stop because I wake up feeling like a zombie. I'm also having those nightmares again. Remember the last time we spoke, I mentioned the dreams about Bonita Springs."

"Yeah, grief is a bitch. When my late husband kicked the bucket, it was hard, but I muddled through."

"It's more than grief. Something or someone is haunting me."

"I doubt that. You experienced a life-altering trauma, and as we all know, time is the only cure. You will eventually move on. Hell, I'll bet you marry again someday."

"No. I don't ever want to get that close to anyone again. I couldn't imagine another heartbreak like I'm experiencing now." My gaze drifts to the empty side of the bed. "I really miss him. I know I'm blessed to have Gretchen and Mimi, who are always there for me, and Dad, but he's in Florida, and—"

"Uh, sorry, honey, but I'm going to have to cut this short. Early day tomorrow. Why don't you drop me a letter or an email? I'll write you back and fill you in on my life. You hang in there, you hear."

The connection dies.

"Thanks for nothing, Rita May." I press another set of numbers generating chimes at the other end of the line.

I expect Dad will answer with his usual cadence. He once explained the reason for the peculiar response. "Baby girl," he said, "I announce myself proudly, slowly, not fast and all jumbled together and insignificant, but one word at a time. Believe me. People remember my name."

Tonight there's a fragility in my aging father's speech. "Elijah. Lee. Blanchard here."

"Hi, Daddy. Are you in bed?"

"No way. I'm watching the news. Glad you called. I've been thinking about you today."

I picture the silver-haired man nestled in his beat-up recliner occupying an entire corner of an archaic-paneled den, his beloved books overstacked on maple-stained end tables framing a threadbare yet cozy sofa, and a Hi-Fi record player balancing on a rickety table near the window. On the far wall and totally out of place in the time-lapsed room, a flat screen TV, a gift from Phillip and me. The forty-six-inch rectangle angles perfectly so window glare won't obstruct the view of Brian McCann or any other Braves player smacking a homer over the wall at Turner Field.

"Today, we said goodbye to Phillip, Dad." I play with a fistful of hair, bringing the strands from behind my ear and awfully close to my lips.

"Oh, my Lord, was the funeral today? I'm sorry, sweetie. I should have realized. I blame Manuel. He forgot to remind me. Things sort of slip my mind now and again." He clears his throat three times, a grating habit camouflaging his memory lapses.

"It's okay." While recapping the events of the last few days, I can't hide the exhaustion in my voice.

"Bless your heart. I should have been there. You did have a priest, didn't you?" He pauses. "Is Gretchen there with you?"

"My late husband, a.k.a. Mr. Perfectly Organized, planned his own funeral service years ago, up to and including the *Amen*, and don't worry, the service was coated in Catholic. Gretchen and Mimi stayed here with me for several days, but I've already sent them home. I needed time alone. If I'm not mistaken, didn't you feel that way when Delilah died?"

"You're right. I wanted the solitude of my own grief."

My father and I briefly discuss his health, and he reiterates the usual playback of his everyday life in Bonita Springs where he will live forever.

"I wish you were by my side, Daddy."

"Close your eyes, Baby Girl, and pretend I'm there."

Snatching a tissue from a nearby box, I dab the corners of my eyes. "By the way, I'm definitely coming for a visit soon, maybe in the summer. I'm in desperate need of a massive dose of Florida sunshine." That's not all. I need my dad—the one constant in my life. Closing my eyes, his bungalow comes to mind, windows wide open, and two squeaky overhead fans transporting muggy air from one side of the house to the other. Eli Blanchard doesn't believe in air conditioning.

"Can't wait. Love you, Jess." His voice quivers.

"Love you, too. Is Manuel nearby?"

He clears his throat. "Hold on a sec." The wheelchair whirrs in my ear. "Here, Manuel, my daughter doesn't trust me when I tell her I'm as healthy as a horse."

"Hey, Jess. Sorry about your husband." The young man's silky-smooth accent always surprises me.

"Thanks. Hope you're okay. If you're not within earshot, will you tell me how Dad is really doing?"

"We're good here, and Mr. Eli's pretty spry for eighty-nine. His doctor suggested he not become too sedentary, you know, so we stroll outside most mornings if it's nice out. At his last doctor's appointment, uh, two weeks ago, his blood pressure had stabilized, but his glucose levels hit the roof. Dr. Honeycutt increased his insulin and gave him a new prescription for a stomach complaint."

"Thanks. I'll give his doctor a call in a day or two for an update." I jot *call Dad's MD* on the notepad I keep on the bedside table. "By the way, I'm planning a trip to Bonita Springs in early summer. Are you up for a well-deserved break?"

"You bet I am."

I hang up and collapse into the pillows. After *clicking* off the lamp, I roll on my side facing the vacant side of the king size bed. You'd think I'd use the entire bed, but apparently, widows don't sleep in the middle.

While I wait for the pill that I ingested earlier to take its sweet time, my brain sets on simmer. Maybe if I lie still, I can hear Phillip's irritating deep-sleep breathing, the habit where he inhales through an open mouth, exhales by blowing out a puff of air, all ending with a subtle *pop*. If God grants my wish, I'll never complain again.

* * *

Sometime during the early morning, the nightmare returns, bringing with it the citrus fragrance I despise. I wake steeped in perspiration, my heart pulsating in my ears, the bedroom walls closing in on me. As I close my eyelids, I wait for the inevitable. The room begins to spin. I knot the rumpled sheets. Per my psychiatrist's previous instructions, I open my eyes and focus on one item, a lamp on the chest on the other side of the room. Slowly, the vertigo subsides. I lean forward, elbows on my knees. "One thousand, two thousand, three…" Done at fifty, the air in my lungs remains shallow. Dr. Priest's words resound in my ears, "Try belly breathing."

It works. The spell is over. Exhausted, I weep into the creases of Phillip's pillow until I fall back asleep.

* * *

The sign on the office entrance reads, Justin Priest, Ph.D., Family Therapist. Leaning against the ledge at the reception's sliding glass window, I scribble my name on the bottom line of the sheet attached to the clipboard. Chelsea, the frizzy-haired brunette behind the partition, who religiously burns a scented candle at her desk, waves at me.

"Morning, Mrs. Tate."

Slumping into a loveseat, I sniff. Today, the waiting room reeks of banana pudding. A recent issue of *Jezebel* piques my interest until Chelsea announces my turn.

Dr. Priest knows that I'm an excellent patient who listens to his advice, dutifully ingests the drugs he prescribes, and never misses a scheduled appointment. Eight years younger than me, the good-looking doctor wears his age like a soft, worn leather jacket, warm and gorgeous. I'd never admit the fact aloud to a soul, but my crush began at our initial session ten years ago. Surely, I'm not the only female patient who is secretly in love with him.

"How are you, Jessy?" His handsome face sports a scruffy beard today.

Wiggling into a pea green recliner, I alter the footrest lever. "Not so great."

The doctor sits in a nearby chair, legs crossed, a yellow legal pad poised on his lap. A thick masculine pen hooks at the neck of his navy pullover. He removes his glasses and frowns. "I'm sorry about your husband. I caught the blurb in the obits, and it mentioned he led a healthy, active life."

"Hardly sick a day. The attack occurred without warning. An aneurism." I don't plan on any tears, but I extract a tissue from my purse anyway. Folding the Kleenex in half and in half again, I tap my right eye. I should buy waterproof eyeliner.

Dr. Priest returns his glasses to his nose, unclips his pen, and jots a note on the pad. "Are you here to discuss how to cope with your loss? If so, I can recommend an excellent grief support group. Or are we venturing back into ancient territory?"

I fiddle with a loose ballet flat. "A little of both and then some." Smoothing a wrinkle in the fabric, I run my hand down the front of my charcoal-black tunic. Yes, the skinny jeans were definitely the right choice this morning. I always make a point to look my best when I see Dr. Priest.

"Tell me exactly why you're here today." His slight smile is off-center.

At first, I'm tentative, but within minutes, words spill out of me as if I'd sprung a leak. I grab more tissues, the eye makeup becoming a lost cause. Sobbing as I speak, it all pours out—the emptiness, the heartache, the anger, and a slight indication of guilt. However, I hoard the big secret. I can't admit all my sins; he already knows too much about me.

"It's expected. You're human. The two of you had an argument. It's okay. What you're feeling is normal. You are struggling with unresolved issues that you must let go. You didn't cause his death or put the aneurism in his brain."

"But Justin, I wasn't there. Earlier that evening, I met a friend for dinner. If I had been with Phillip, I could've called 911, and he might be alive today. Don't you see?"

"It's not unusual to feel guilt while grieving for a loved one. You must forgive yourself, but you already know that."

I decide to change course. A minute into a description of my night-time terrors, my voice weakens. "I'm physically exhausted, and those dreams are destroying what little sanity I have left." I wipe the perspiration at my hairline with a shriveled tissue.

Again, Dr. Priest scribbles on his pad. "In the state you're in, it looks to me like you've resuscitated dormant anxieties."

I straighten my posture causing the footrest to slap against the chair. "I'm sure you're right, but the nightmares are worse than before. I'm afraid to go asleep, and if I do, a pungent aroma awakens me. In one repetitive dream, I'm a frightened child and someone's chasing me, and in another, the banyan tree is center stage. The mere thought of it bothers me. In fact, the last time I paid a visit to Bonita Springs, even driving past that ridiculous tree made me nauseous." The tissues are in shreds in my lap. I ball the scraps inside my hand.

Dr. Priest crosses to his desk. "Your subconscious is protecting you, but at the same time, it's trying to evoke a memory of an event or trauma fixed in your past." Parking in his swivel chair, he opens a hefty textbook to a bookmarked page. He puts on his glasses and reads several paragraphs aloud from the medical journal. He closes the book. "You see. The anxiety you are experiencing is quite normal."

"Well, I certainly don't feel normal."

"Will you consider hypnosis again? Although the last time didn't spark a reaction, it's still worth another shot, especially since your dreams have escalated and are revealing clues from the past. You are close to the finish line, Jessy. I don't think it will be long before we learn what triggered your anxiety in the first place. Let's try hypnosis at your next session." He removes his glasses.

"If you think it will help." I swallow hard.

"At your last appointment, we discussed the old picture albums belonging to your parents. Have you had a chance to study the photos?"

"No, I, uh, forgot." My vision skews to a vent above me where a warm draft blows the bangs off my forehead.

"Take the time to examine them. The process will help you." He absently rubs the bridge of his nose where his glasses left an indentation.

"What if the photos upset me? Make matters worse?"

"Your memory needs a kick-start. Begin slowly examining one photo, then another." Dr. Priest checks the clock on his wall. "Time's up, but I'm recommending you return to a regular appointment schedule. Stop by and see Chelsea on your way out." He returns his glasses to his nose and studies my file. "And you're still taking Ambien?"

"On and off."

"And Xanax, I presume?"

"Couldn't live without it."

"We'll call your pharmacy and update your refills."

I stand up as he approaches me.

"Jessy, listen to me. Number one. Grieve your loss, however long it takes. Number two. Don't worry. We'll solve the nightmare mystery. I have no doubt."

On my way out the door, I drop tissue remnants into the wastepaper basket.

* * *

As I maneuver the Ford Explorer into my subdivision, Dr. Priest's advice sinks in. Of course, he's right—healing takes time. "But right now, the guilt is what's killing me. Okay. Okay. I'll be a good Catholic and go to Confession."

CHAPTER THREE:
A FISH OUT OF WATER

November 3, 2005

Dear Rita,

How are you? During our brief phone conversation, you didn't give me a chance to ask about your wedding. Please send pictures. According to the internet and the news, your husband is quite the statesman.

The past month is a blur. The house is way too quiet. It's as if I don't belong here anymore, like a fish out of water or something. I'm thinking of adopting a pet, but I don't know if I have the patience for a puppy; they're such messy little babies.

Gretchen keeps in touch and we often get together on weekends. Her decorating business keeps her busy though. By the way, she and Conner have finally separated. She caught him cheating again—the last straw. My granddaughter, Mimi, a sophomore at Georgia State majoring in journalism, has blossomed into a stunning young woman. I'm sure her parents' issues trouble her, but unfortunately, she doesn't share those parts of herself with me.

Oh, and I'm having anxiety attacks and nightmares again. If I didn't have my psychiatrist, Dr. Priest, I'd be certifiable. FYI, you now have a starring role in the crazy dreams. The doctor says it's my mind blocking a significant event from my childhood. Do you recall anything frightening or traumatic that I may have seen or endured when we were kids together in Bonita Springs?

Anyway, the doctor suggested I set goals to avoid wallowing in self-pity and grief. As a result, I've been riding Nutmeg on a regular basis, and I have plans to resurrect my jewelry business. I've also decided to visit Dad in the summer. When I spoke to him the other night, I realized how much I miss him.

Given that I have unintentionally become a free bird, I might surprise you by flying to D.C. and landing on your doorstep.

Jessy

I tuck the letter in an envelope, seal it, and stick a wildlife stamp at the corner to mail in the morning.

I met Rita May McAfee, now Rita Rhodes, at age eleven and she, thirteen. We instantly became best friends. We've kept in touch over the years, but life took us down dissimilar paths. I'm a retired eighth-grade teacher. She owns her own business and is a Nutrition Instructor at a college in Virginia. To this day, I cherish her friendship albeit a long distance one. We've only seen each other twice in the last thirty years—once when Phillip and I opted for a driving vacation along the Eastern coast to Virginia and another time when Rita came to Atlanta for a Health and Wellness Conference.

I used to confide in her, and she would share her secrets with me. Not as much anymore. These days, she simply brags about her wonderful life and closely guards the rest.

*　*　*

Another appointment with Dr. Priest in early November, which includes a session under hypnosis, fails to ignite any revelations. Sadness consumes me as I muddle through the remaining days of the month. When Thanksgiving announces itself, I refuse to let the holiday interfere with my misery. Nothing is normal—Gretchen struggling to end her marriage and mourning her father, Mimi dealing with her parents' separation and the loss of her grandfather, and crazy me, alone and burdened by guilt and grief.

On the first Friday in December, I phone my granddaughter and break the bad news. "I'm sorry, Mimi, but Christmas isn't coming to the Tate house this year."

She groans in my ear. "But Gran, no big tree?"

"Nope, can't do it. There's no holiday spirit here." I clear my throat. "How's school?"

Mimi lets go of a loud sigh. "I'm sorry you're so sad. But, yeah, school's pretty good. I've been writing articles for Georgia State's student paper, *The Signal*. Yesterday, my editor asked me to contribute an additional blurb for the February edition in honor of Martin Luther King and Black History Month. If approved, the paper might ask for a series of articles for future publication. I've never tackled anything so historically significant and timely."

"And the subject you've picked?" I run hot water in a sink full of suds.

"Civil Rights from my lily-white southern roots' perspective. I have to narrow in on a specific theme, but I've time to decide. I may beg your insight since you lived during the fifties and sixties."

"Happy to help." I grab a dishtowel. "I'm so proud of you. Be sure to keep me posted on your timetable. Oh, by the way, did I tell you I'm going to open up my jewelry business again?"

"That's great. Please let me set up your website."

"I learned my lesson. Of course, I will."

* * *

It's January and despite an attempt at positive thinking, I've shrunk into an existence of solitary confinement. Clinging to a dandy depression, I pride myself on the longevity of my extremely foul mood. I've neglected my neighbors and refused any social requests, with the onslaught of freezing weather suppressing any desire to do otherwise. Although ghosts from the past frequent my nights, I spend the days mastering a new toy—a laptop, a Christmas present from Gretchen and Mimi. So far, I've searched and googled everything from apathy in America to zebras and their mating habits.

On a dreary Tuesday morning, I binge *Cooking Channel* reruns on TV and drain a pot of coffee. At noon, a flicker of energy stirs in me. A much-needed shower and a turkey sandwich revive me enough to charge the attic stairs. I'm on a mission, and the marked boxes are easy to find. Since I packed away Phillip's collection of Coca Cola memorabilia weeks ago, I officially claim his home office for my own. Before unpacking the cartons, I reprise an old ritual and sip from an icy bottle of Snapple Peach Tea. "It's time to get cracking."

Four years ago, I adapted a stay-at-home business from a hobby I had fancied since childhood. Because I failed to market my creations, the business suffered a quick but natural death. Today, I'll discover if I still have the ability to craft jewelry out of what Mother Nature leaves behind.

I place ten clear plastic shoeboxes in a row at the back of my work-table. Each latched box safeguards a variety of shells, variegated or metal beads, pearls, or gemstones. Smaller tins store epoxy, tiny plastic bags full of earring jackets and studs, wire, and other magic-making supplies. Because the light must shine on my hands, I arch the lamp's gooseneck at a right angle and unwrap a few necessary tools. Taking a seat, I dig through my desk drawer and unearth a tablet of paper. In order to awaken any dormant creative juices, I must practice sketching several designs before diving into the process.

Primed with pencil in hand, the blank page stares back at me. My brain is chockfull of everything except inspiration. No lightbulbs. Not one artistic impulse. Allowing ten more minutes reveals little. Doodles and overlapping circles cover the page. As a result, my eyes pool with moisture. "There is nothing left in me. I'm empty, hollow like my seashells, no life inside." I rip the paper in two. "Damn it, Phillip Tate. Why did you have to die?" A ringtone coming from my pocket interferes with my outburst. I don't recognize the number. "Hello."

"Hi, this is Mario…Ricci."

At the sound of his sultry voice, my body tenses. "What do *you* want?"

"Thought I'd check on you. How are you doing?"

I stand then sit back down again. "I'm fine." Sweat dampens the back of my shirt.

"Good, good. Um, I think about you often and would love to see you again. Just coffee or a drink. I've missed you."

"Let me stop you right there. We won't be having coffee or a drink or anything ever again. In fact, in the future, I plan to avoid you at all neighborhood functions."

"Sorry to hear this. I thought we were having fun."

"Goodbye, Mario." I mash the red button on the phone and lean forward, my throbbing head in my hands. The cellphone's ring startles me. "Leave me alone!"

"Uh, Mrs. Tate. Mrs. Tate, are you okay?"

"Oh, I'm sorry. Who's there?"

"Chelsea at Dr. Priest's office. Did I catch you at a bad time?"

"Uh, a little under the weather." My bare foot encounters a rebellious loop in the sisal rug and I wiggle my big toe inside the weave. Why did Mario have to ruin my day?

"I'm sorry. I'm calling to remind you of your appointment tomorrow at two."

"Thank you." I disconnect and breathe. "Tomorrow?" I sigh at the prospect of conjuring up more demons for Justin Priest. "I need fresh air." I bound from the chair, slide on my loafers, and dash into the foyer where a sweatshirt hangs on the hall tree. I zip up, extremely thankful the jacket has a hood.

Trotting outside, I inhale a mouthful of frigid air as I glimpse smoke rising from my neighbors' chimney. The smell of burning logs lifts my spirits. A full mailbox reveals an absurd amount of junk mail, two belated sympathy cards, an electric bill, and a six-by-nine manila envelope from Alexandria, Virginia. An icy gust of wind whips across my face. Protecting the bundle, I jog back inside.

I peel off the sweatshirt, grab my glasses, and then perch on a stool at the breakfast bar. Two folded sheets of off-white monogrammed stationary and a stack of photographs lay inside the large envelope.

January 12, 2006

Dear Jessy,

Happy New Year! I know I took forever to write you back. Please forgive. Sorry about your husband's death. Hang tough, your mourning period won't last forever.

Now to my news! My wedding and reception were perfect, the most elegant affair making the front page of the society section in the Washington Tattler. Three local television stations interviewed Harrison and me, and we remain topics of gossip all over the internet. Snapshots enclosed. My brand spanking new husband, Congressman Harrison Rhodes, is the most handsome man alive, not to mention extremely sweet and kind. He's running for re-election and there's no doubt he'll win. Everybody in D.C. loves him. Being involved in politics, I've met so many influential men and women who have helped my business thrive. Life is good.

I'm in the best shape ever. I exercise or run every day, rain or shine, and of course, I'm careful of my diet. According to Harrison, I look amazing. I purposely keep my age a secret from him and everyone else. He believes I'm not much older than fifty-five or so.

I'm convinced your shrink is an idiot. Didn't another psychiatrist nearly fifteen years ago insist your parents were to blame for your problems—the rebellion in high school and your brief stint in rehab in college? I realize you've been gaga over that cute doctor forever, but he's a quack if he's encouraging you to relive your past. The nightmares will fade if you shake off your negativity. Focus on living your life to the fullest. Hell, why don't you find a lover? Best therapy to distract one from any stress, and for that matter, I know from experience that sex works wonders for the ego. I remember you mentioning a guy in your neighborhood, someone who had a crush on you. Why don't you go for it?

Now let's talk Bonita Springs. I have no recollection of any trauma or event during the short time I spent there as a kid. I remember attending school, babysitting my bratty siblings, and hanging with you. Nothing else. You take it from me. Dwelling on the past will bring you nothing but pain.

If you're lonely and bored, try an exercise class or yoga. The workouts will cleanse your spirit as well as your mind. Yes, ride your horse, create beautiful jewelry, and snap out of the funk you're wallowing in.

Got to run. Client waiting. She's the wife of a prominent DC lawyer. You should see her—dripping with diamonds.

Rita

Crumpling the pages, I throw the letter into the kitchen trashcan. "Rita May McAfee Rhodes, you're lying to me. You know more about Bonita Springs than you're admitting." My body tenses. Whether she likes it or not, Rita represents a major piece of the puzzle inside my head. I drift over to the wine rack and pick out a bottle of Merlot.

CHAPTER FOUR:
GOOD RIDDANCE

Rita Rhodes taps her laptop keyboard browsing the internet for health and wellness sites. On the other side of a king-sized bed, Harrison Rhodes fixates on a CNN news feed streaming across his own computer screen. The singsong tone of her cellphone disturbs the couple's weeknight ritual.

She squints at Caller ID and sighs. "Hello."

"Rita, sorry it's late, but I need to speak to you," says an out-of-breath Jessy Tate.

"What's the matter now, Jessy? Did somebody else die?"

"No, of course not. I read your letter and I'm mad at you. You don't get it, do you? I have no memory of a huge part of our childhood. You must know something that can help me."

Rita closes her laptop. She thrums well-manicured fingernails on its lid. "I truly believe you've ventured over to the dark side." She chuckles. "Your worrying is making you nuts. Let it go. It's the past, another lifetime." Rita chews on her bottom lip.

"I can't. Tonight, when I complied with Dr. Priest's request and looked through old photos, I barely got into the first album before I suffered a major anxiety attack."

Rita huffs. "Were there pictures of your parents in the albums?"

"Yes, of course."

"Then it's obvious."

"No, it's not. My parents don't make appearances in my nightmares. The fear is real and it has to do with you, me, and God knows who or what else, Rita May."

"Don't call me that." She sighs. "Listen Jess, it's late and I have a meeting in the morning. We'll talk again soon. Bye now." Since the conversation left a dull ache between her brows, Rita stores the laptop in its case on the floor. She lies down on her side, facing away from her husband. "Why can't she leave well enough alone? She makes my head hurt." Mumbling another complaint, she forcefully kicks the sheet to the bottom of the bed.

Harrison gently pats her thigh. "Are you all right? Who were you talking to anyway?"

She rolls to face him. "An annoying old friend who recently lost her husband. Apparently, I'm her sounding board."

He raises an eyebrow. "Who?"

"Jessy Tate." Rita stretches toward the bedside where a cup of water and a hefty bottle of Ibuprofen reside. "You don't know her. She lives in Atlanta." She gulps three tablets with a sip of water.

Harrison scans his laptop screen. "What were you saying about the past?"

"It's nothing. The woman is a nutcase. Night, honey."

* * *

On Tuesday morning, Rita gathers her carrot-colored locks into a bunch at the back of her head. Stretching a coated rubber band, she twists her hair into a fat ponytail. She smears sunscreen on her face and appraises herself in the bathroom mirror.

"Oops." Rita fingers a wisp of gray sprouting from her hairline. "At least the salon appointment is Friday." She grimaces at a twinge at the back of her neck. *Thanks a lot, Jessy Tate.*

Her running gear drapes a tufted stool in the walk-in closet. Dressed in underwear and a sports bra, she pulls on thermal tights and then a pair of ebony torpedo pants. Lastly, she dons a matching long sleeve turtleneck. Squatting on the stool, Rita completes the outfit adding sport socks and expensive running shoes.

Like a grating radio commercial, Jessy Tate's southern drawl inhabits Rita's mind. "The fear is real and has to do with you, me, and…" The red-head's jaw tightens. Using her right hand, she cracks the knuckles on the left; she repeats the gesture on the other hand. She touches her toes then lifts both hands above her head tilting to the left. With Jessy's voice swirling through her thoughts, Rita counts to ten and stretches to the right. *Get out of my head, you infuriating bitch.*

She hustles onto the landing, stopping at the top of the staircase. Bracing a foot upon the railing, her nose grazes a knee. She straightens her leg. "Harrison, I'm going on a run." She puts the right leg down and extends the left.

"Wait a minute," Harrison shouts from somewhere downstairs.

Her warmup complete, Rita darts back into the bedroom for earplugs and her new iPod Nano. While attaching the strap to her upper arm, she flies downstairs to the foyer where her husband waits next to the open coat closet.

He turns and wraps a gray scarf around Rita's neck. "I'll probably be gone before you return."

She hugs his waist. "I don't think it's a muffler kind of day."

"Yes, it is. Give me a kiss, stubborn woman."

Her mood lightens. "You bet." She relaxes in his embrace. "Have a magnificent day, Congressman Rhodes." She opens her mouth giving him the sort of kiss he adores.

He cups both hands under her bottom. She giggles.

Holding her at arms' length, Harrison swipes a stray hair from Rita's face. "By the way, I'm working late tonight. Dinner meeting. Love you." He climbs the stairs two at a time, his bathrobe flowing behind him like Superman's cape.

"Love you more." She stuffs her hands into running gloves. Clutching the doorknob, she calls for the housekeeper.

"Yes, ma'am." Dolores scurries into the vestibule.

"Be back in an hour." Rita reaches into her pocket for the earplugs as she opens the front door to a rush of cold.

Setting both fists at her hips, Dolores frowns at her boss. "Are you warm enough, Mrs. Rhodes?"

Rita nods and shuts the door behind her. She plugs into her iPod and then adjusts the headband that protects her ears. Sucking in a mouthful of ice-cold air, she conceals half her face with the scarf. A quick perusal of her surroundings precedes a hamstring stretch at the curb. Taking another deep breath, she takes off down the sidewalk. Her speed increases as she mentally constructs a letter to Jessy Tate.

* * *

Propped against the desk, Rita glances over her shoulder at the clock on the wall. "Eleven-thirty guys. Don't forget. Group projects are due in two weeks. I'm expecting excellent work from you. I'd like updates by Thursday."

The classroom empties and she stacks three file folders inside her leather briefcase. Rifling through her purse, she salvages a memo pad and scribbles *call the caterer for a 4/12 Open House*. A noisy belly reminds her that there's an insulated lunch bag in her desk drawer. Rita ingests five raw carrot sticks, four ripe strawberries, and a slice of turkey breast. She gulps from a water bottle, gathers her belongings, and dashes from the classroom.

As she weaves through a mass of college students, a colleague brushes against her arm. "Hey, Rita, how's it going?"

"Oh, hi, Pam. Can't talk. Running late." Shoving one arm and then the other into coat sleeves, she maintains her stride. Rita sprints to the faculty parking lot where a new black BMW X5, a generous wedding present from the congressman, awaits.

Traffic congestion hampers her route from George Mason University to the office. Groaning, Rita depresses the button on the steering column that scans the radio stations. "I'm going to be late." A Chuck Berry classic blasts from the speakers. "Maybelline" plays just long enough. "Ugh, I despise this song." She switches to an easy listening selection.

Rita wheels into one of the last remaining spots on the top level of the parking deck. Before exiting the car, she checks her image in the rear-view mirror, grabs her briefcase, and flings a cross body bag over one shoulder. A nearby elevator carries her down to the fourth floor.

Violet Winfrey, a statuesque African American woman in her mid-forties, stands erect at the office door. "You're late." The woman's lips spread into a narrow burgundy line.

"Afternoon, Mrs. Winfrey. Sorry you had to wait. Traffic was awful." Rita smiles at a whiff of a familiar scent. Predictably, her client smells as if she dipped herself in a vat of Calvin Klein's Eternity.

"Perhaps if you had left earlier or tried another route." The woman hugs an oversize designer purse up against a generous bust.

Rita unlocks the door and allows Mrs. Winfrey to go ahead into the intimate, yet tasteful, waiting room. A banana-yellow loveseat fits between a pair of antique cherry side tables, while a navy blue and white-striped wing chair occupies the space in the corner. The two women walk further into the cozy office. Mrs. Winfrey brushes the edge of the desk jarring a framed photo.

Rita watches Harrison's picture topple over. "So how've you been?" She removes her coat and hangs the overpriced wrap on the wall hook before settling into the swivel chair behind the desk.

Mrs. Winfrey sits with her knees and ankles together, her mink coat buttoned up to the neck, her lap hidden by the Michael Kors bag. She licks her lips. "I've come to the conclusion your food regimen is far too strict for me. Twice this week, I've been on the verge of fainting from lack of nourishment and low blood sugar."

Rita repositions the picture frame. "No problem. I'll modify your plan. Did you bring your food sheets?" She retrieves a red pen from the desk.

Mrs. Winfrey plucks a notebook from her purse and passes the journal to Rita. "I always do."

"Give me a minute to review your notes." Rita senses the woman's glare. *I wish I could kick her to the curb, but she's got friends in political high places.* "Considering your entries, I'm going to suggest—"

"Pardon me for interrupting, but I have to ask you a question. It's been gnawing at me for some time." The woman's chest heaves; her narrow, severely plucked eyebrows scrunch together.

Rita tilts backwards.

The woman sputters a fake cough. "I'm curious. Can you tell me how you were able to charm such a *fine* Black man into marrying you? I mean, you two certainly aren't a natural match. I can't possibly be the only person questioning your arrangement. How on God's green earth did you manage to snag Congressman Harrison Rhodes? I mean, I'm sure he could pick from dozens of young, professional African American women." She purses her lips as if she's sucking on a lemon.

Rita's mouth falls open. Taking a minute to compose herself, she bristles. With hands steepled together on top of Mrs. Winfrey's file, she clamps her jaw shut, breathing through her teeth before she speaks. "The answer to your question is simple. I'm the luckiest woman in the world. On the other hand, Harrison is also lucky. You see, when he chose me, he got the smartest, most beautiful woman around. Period." She *clicks* her tongue. "Now, I'm afraid you'll have to leave." Rita stands. "Here's your notebook. There are plenty of other nutritionists available, and no doubt, you'll find someone who will suit you better. By the way, you don't owe me a dime. Don't bother to contact me again, you narrow-minded bitch."

"I won't sit here and listen to your insults." Mrs. Winfrey storms out of the office.

Rita sighs. "Good riddance." She pumps a squirt from the hand sanitizer bottle that lives on her desk. Rubbing her hands together, she says, "I could sure use a massage and a three-olive martini chaser."

She marks the file *CANCELLED*. Placing a phone call to Harrison, she tucks the folder into a cabinet while leaving a voicemail message. "Honey, I can't wait to tell you about my day. A client verbally attacked me. I'll explain tonight. Love you."

With the workday ending at four, the afternoon sails by unlike the drive home, which takes an hour and a half. She presses the automatic opener and maneuvers her car into the garage where the housekeeper cracks open the door. Exiting the BMW, she walks into the kitchen. "Basil, garlic, and cumin. Something smells amazing. What's cooking, Dolores?"

"It's my mama's recipe." The petite woman trails her boss into the foyer. "Here, let me hang up your things." Dolores extends an arm to receive Rita's coat and scarf. "Did you have a nice day, Mrs. Rhodes?"

"Yes and no. Certainly not a boring one." She slides out of a pair of heels.

"I set the mail in Congressman Rhodes' office. Would you like me to serve the two of you supper tonight? I can stay if you wish."

"No, thanks. He's working late. You go on home to your family." Rita climbs the stairs carrying her shoes.

"Thank you, ma'am." Dolores retreats to the kitchen.

In the master suite, Rita changes into a George Mason University T-shirt and yoga pants. She plants her iPod into its charging station and presses play. A soft melody drifts throughout the room. While Rita poises barefoot on the carpet, her body postures into the first stance. At the end of a twenty-minute routine, the corpse pose eases her into a tranquil mood, unravelling taut muscles.

Rejuvenated, she skips downstairs and breezes into Harrison's den pausing briefly to examine the mail stacked on the corner of his desk. A letter from Beaufort, South Carolina addressed to him in a nearly illegible scrawl conspicuously peeks from the pile of bills. The upper left hand corner of the envelope reads Mary-Mary Anyika Rhodes.

"Hmm, the mother-in-law speaks."

Rita licks the corner of her mouth where a tiny bump has formed. She charges into the family room and checks the mini fridge under the wet bar. She smiles. "Dolores, you're a gem." Two chilled glasses sit adjacent to a pitcher of martinis. "Boy do I deserve this."

After pouring a drink, her bare feet slap the hardwood as she wanders into her office. Rita pulls a coaster for her glass from the top drawer of her desk. The second drawer stores writing supplies. She finds two ecru sheets of stationary, one possessing a demure fern green monogram.

Ten minutes later, she seals the envelope. "That ought to do it." She presses a stamp in place. After pinching an olive from the liquid in her glass, she drinks the last sip of her martini. She eats the olive whole.

* * *

An evening drizzle outside sets the mood as Rita steeps in a tub full of lilac-scented bubbles. Candles nearby flicker in the dark. When the temperature of the water turns cool, she steps out and wraps herself in an oversized terrycloth robe.

She enjoys a second martini and spends the rest of the evening sampling Dolores's concoction of stewed beef and vegetables as she reviews notes on sugar addiction, the premise of a book she intends to write once her husband wins re-election.

At eight minutes past ten, the garage door hums. Rita poses at the top of the stairs, hair flowing onto almost bare shoulders, a flimsy negligee exposing the body she works obsessively to maintain. A tummy-tuck eight years ago and a facelift two years later corrected any damage gravity bestowed on her. After all, she had no choice but to emulate her namesake, Rita Hayworth, the redheaded glamour girl of the 1940s, whom the press nicknamed *The Love Goddess*.

Clutching two brimming martinis, she leans against the railing. Harrison's footsteps *clack* across the tile floor in the kitchen.

"Hey, baby. We're waiting." Her declaration oozes with intent.

For a second, he hesitates at the bottom of the staircase, sporting a perceptive grin. Tossing his coat on the bannister, the three-piece suited congressman hurries up the stairs. "Did you say we?"

"Me and your extra-dry martini."

* * *

While Harrison brushes his teeth, Rita dons a robe and creeps downstairs. She returns cradling the piece of mail from South Carolina. She waits at the end of the bed fanning herself with the envelope. When he moseys into the bedroom, she says, "Surprise."

"I don't believe my heart can handle any more uh…surprises, baby." He swipes his chin with a hand towel.

Rita hands him the correspondence she pilfered from his desk. "Open it. I'm dying to hear the news from Beaufort." She pats the mattress.

Harrison tosses the towel back into the bathroom and flops onto the bed. Clasping the envelope, he tears one side and then blows into the opening. He removes the notepaper and reads aloud.

Tuesday

Dear Rabbit,

> *First off, sorry I couldn't make the wedding. Washington D.C. is too dang far to travel.*
>
> *I pray to the Lord you are well in body and in spirit.*
>
> *I've got news. I guess I'm not sucking in enough air into my lungs. Dr. Cook diagnosed emphysema and sent me to a lady doctor, Dr. Priscilla Reece, a pulmonary specialist. Nowadays, I need oxygen all the time so I have to wear a tank strapped to my back. I can't smoke anymore. Apparently, if I light one up, I'll blow myself to bits. The oxygen does help me breathe better though.*
>
> *I'm officially inviting you and your new wife to my birthday party. No excuses. I'm turning eighty-six on April 4, and I'm throwing myself a celebration. We're fixing all my Gullah favorites. I invited the relatives, plus the whole damn neighborhood. Let's pray for sunny weather, no skeeters, no bugs, nothing but a sand gnat or two. Everyone misses you and really wants to meet the new Mrs. Harrison Rhodes.*
>
> *Love, Mama*
>
> *P.S. Bring wedding pictures.*

Harrison creases the letter. "She's given me no choice." He retrieves his phone from the dresser. "Roger will have to rearrange my schedule. Two days is all I can spare."

"Wait a second. Why does your mother call you Rabbit? More importantly, does she have any idea that you married a White woman?"

CHAPTER FIVE:
BEAUFORT BOIL

On April 4, an early morning flight puts Rita and Harrison Rhodes into Charleston by ten. The congressman rents a Cadillac XTS sedan and makes a stop at Magnolias, his restaurant of choice for brunch. Cruising slightly above the speed limit, he propels the car down US-21 toward Beaufort allotting Rita an hour and a half to quiz him on his family.

She angles the visor at her image before applying another coat of bright pink to her mouth. Slipping the lipstick into a makeup bag, she surveys the landscape. Two spindly-legged egrets dip their beaks in the marshy water by the side of the highway. "Wow. These wetlands go on forever. Who is responsible for them? Who takes care of the alligators, for instance?"

"South Carolina Fish & Game, I suppose, but the South Carolina Department of Natural Resources protects these wetland and marsh sites here along the coast. The federal government also manages some wetland areas in the Low Country."

She bites the hangnail on her thumb. "Harrison, you have to give me more background info if I plan to have any sort of intelligent conversation with your mother. I don't want her to think I'm an idiot." Clearing her throat, she attempts to camouflage the slight edge in her speech. "I'm begging you. The place will be infested with your relatives, and here I come all White and shiny. They'll hate me."

"You're being silly. Besides, I'm sure the family spotted the announcement in the paper or saw pictures of the wedding on the internet."

"But your mama doesn't own a computer, and obviously, your constituency doesn't quite reach South Carolina. If she has no idea whom you married, won't she be angry?" She corrects the direction of the air conditioning vent permitting a steady stream of cool air to hit her face. "I sure would be."

"You don't understand. I'm Mama's pride and joy and can do no wrong." His smirk exposes his perfectly straight whitened teeth.

"Okay, *Mr. Pride and Joy*, give me a clue how to force your relatives to fall in love with me."

"My advice. Relax. You have nothing to worry about because you're gorgeous and smart, and mine."

"I can't relax, Harrison. If I had my way, I'd jog alongside this car." She cracks her knuckles.

"I promise. My family will love you."

"Won't I offend some of the more conservative members by merely being there?"

"I don't know, but if so, they'll just have to deal with it. Anyway, when haven't you made a first-rate impression? You're always the life of the party. Tonight, you'll meet everybody. Because my Gullah ancestors settled in the Low Country, most of my relatives still live in or near Beaufort and congregate at Mama's house on special occasions. Family parties consist of drinking, dancing, and storytelling."

"Storytelling?"

"Yeah, mostly superstitions passed on from one generation to another. It's a lot of mumbo jumbo."

Rita raps her French manicured nails on the console. She readjusts her sunglasses. "Can't wait."

The car whizzes by a figure sitting under a lean-to on the side of the road. An elderly Black woman in a large sun hat sits encircled by baskets of varying sizes.

"Is she a Gullah?"

"We say the Gullah people, and yes, she is. She's selling sweet-grass baskets."

"Ooh, I've got to have one of those." Rita lowers the window.

"No problem. Mama has way too many. She'll give you one."

At the end of an oyster-shelled driveway sits a colonial-style house—the home Harrison purchased for his mother five years ago. Rita scratches an itch on her hand as she gazes through sunglasses at a rocker-crowded veranda that hugs the entire front of the refurbished white two-story clapboard structure. Four sleek ceiling fans orbit in harmony over the colorful rag rugs scattered on the wide-planked floor.

Harrison leads the way towing both pieces of carry-on luggage.

She steps from the car feeling the Low Country sun bake her exposed shoulders. A bead of perspiration trickles the length of her breastbone. Slowly climbing the stairs to the porch, Rita passes a daisy-shaped ceramic ashtray, one of several placed at the corners of the wooden railing. *Why in hell did I quit smoking?*

She stops at the top of the stairs. "Harrison, did you notice? Most of the doors in the neighborhood are painted bright blue."

Ignoring the comment, he twists the brass doorknob and opens the door. "Mama, where are you?"

A faint voice with a distinctive southern drawl comes from the back of the house. "I'm in the kitchen. Get yourself on in here, Rabbit, and give us a hug."

Rita catches the screen door before it slams shut. She strolls inside where an unusual blend of aromas tickles her nose—boiled meat with a dash of Pine Sol. She trails Harrison down a hallway next to an arched entry to a living room. Rita pauses to take an inventory. On the far wall, woven baskets hang from iron hooks. An eclectic array of antiques and newly upholstered pieces inundate the room. Besides an excess of family photos, knickknacks sit on every table displaying a palpable affinity for bunnies.

The up-to-date kitchen is a surprise, its modern oak cabinetry extending from counter to ceiling. Mary-Mary Anyika Rhodes straddles a stool in front of the sink with a bright pink backpack strapped onto a pair of boney shoulders. Midway into peeling a bowlful of potatoes, she places a naked spud in a colander on the counter and twists the water nozzle to the off position. Taking a moment, she dries her hands on a nearby dishtowel. "Hello, son."

Harrison places the suitcases in the hallway. "Hey, Mama. It's good to see you." With Rita a few steps behind, he rushes to the elderly woman. He leans down to kiss her sagging cheek. When he straightens, Harrison puts his arm around Rita's shoulders pulling her close. "This is Rita."

His mother takes her time adjusting the clear plastic oxygen prong tucked into her nostrils before she slides off the stool. Gradually lifting threadlike brows above a pair of wire-rimmed glasses, she checks out her new daughter-in-law. "Nice to finally meet you." Her dark eyes teem with judgment.

"Back in a minute." Harrison exits the kitchen with the luggage.

Rita inches a step toward her mother-in-law, inspecting the woman's sandaled feet. "How do you do, Mrs. Rhodes."

A slight simper bows the woman's lips. "Call me Mary or Ani, either one will do. So, my dear, how was the wedding?" Her fixed stare bores a hole through to Rita's soul.

The old bat already hates me. "Uh, fantastic, but short and sweet. Small gathering." She scratches her hand. "Your home is lovely. It's so, uh, southern." Rita wanders over to where the window commands a view of a manicured backyard full of massive water oaks; putty-colored moss swings from the branches. "You have such a nice lawn. What's that yard ornament covered in blue glass bottles?"

"My bottle tree. Uh, would you please reach there in the cabinet and fetch three tumblers? Harrison's brother, Preacher, built me that tree. Toss in some ice cubes and pour us some tea from the pitcher there."

Obliging her new mother-in-law, Rita sets the full glasses of tea on the island.

"Thank you. I'm dry as a bone. Don't tell me you've never seen a bottle tree?"

"No, ma'am." *Where is my husband?*

"I've never been without a bottle tree. It's sort of expected around these parts. My gramma used to tell us stories of evil haints waking folks, whistling and a-groaning all night long. She said if a person was lucky, the bottles would trap the demons inside. First light of a new day was supposed to kill them dead. It's the blue color that keeps one safe."

"Do you actually believe that?" *Ah, the blue door explanation.*

"It's one of them better-safe-than-sorry situations." Clasping a glass, Ani worms off the stool and shuffles to the stove where the ingredients in two portly stockpots bubble on simmer. She checks under each lid before she limps across the kitchen to a long wooden table at the far end of the room. "Blasted arthritis." Lowering herself into a padded ladder back chair, she inhales a lungful of oxygen. "Bring your iced tea and set yourself right beside me. Let's chew the fat a little."

Rita plants herself on the bench at the side of the table.

Ani takes a swig of tea. Wiping her mouth with the back of her hand, she says, "Have some. It's pure heaven in a glass. You got to get the sweetness just right, so you dump the simple syrup in before the brew has a chance to cool. I add sliced lemons to the pitcher after it's chilled in the fridge for about three hours."

Rita winces at the blister on her lip. *Harrison better get in here.*

Her mother-in-law alters the oxygen prong's position. "Now start talking, missy."

Rita examines the ceiling fan above her. Although the breeze keeps the kitchen temperature acceptable, moisture accumulates between her breasts. She takes a big sip of tea. Shocked at the degree of sweetness, she presses her lips together when swallowing. "I grew up in Charlotte, North Carolina, and graduated with a B.S. at UNC Charlotte, where I also earned a Master's Degree. When my late husband died, I resumed a teaching career at the college level in Virginia and opened my consulting business." She does not intend to give Mama Rhodes any more so-called history. She scratches the palm of her hand.

Coughing several times, Ani shields her mouth with a forearm. The reverberation in her lungs reminds Rita of the *clacking* of a freight train. Ani removes the backpack and puts it on the table. "So how old are you, dear?"

This witch is baiting me. Rita fakes a smile and hopes her eyes don't betray how she really feels toward her mother-in-law. "How old do you think I am?" She clenches her teeth.

Ani chuckles. "Not falling for that one." She coughs again. "Do you work outside the home or do you take care of my boy?"

Rita takes a deep breath and speaks through her exhale. "I'm a certified nutritionist. I teach classes at George Mason University and have my own business in Alexandria."

"A business, huh? You're in retail?"

"No, I counsel clients on eating properly to improve their health. I recommend specific diets for certain illnesses or conditions."

"Give me an example." Ani downs most of the liquid in the glass.

Chatting about her profession, this Rita can do. "Um, let's assume you're having an allergic reaction, say hives on your skin, and your doctor is unable to pinpoint the source. The reaction is often a response to a food allergy or possibly your environment. At first, I recommend a detox program where you embark on a fast. Then you gradually reintroduce foods back into your diet to find the allergy's source. Eating organic or natural foods leads to a healthier and less toxic lifestyle." She scratches. Rosy bumps speckle her palm.

"Uh huh." Ani plays with a defiant strand of hair that has escaped from the bun at the base of her skull. She ogles her daughter-in-law's hand. "What are *you* allergic to?"

"Nothing." In an instant, Rita places her other hand on top of the rash.

Ani rattles the ice in her glass. "Do you have any children, Rita?" Harrison cruises into the room. "Join us, son. I'm acquainting myself with your new wife. You always did fancy redheads, didn't you?"

"Ah, no, no children," Rita's speech is barely audible.

Harrison sips from the other glass of tea on the counter. He gapes at his wife. "Honey, are you okay?"

"Is there any bottled water?"

He shakes his head and sits next to her on the bench.

Ani coughs and checks the clock over the stove. "It's time we got on the stick. Folks will start showing up in three hours. Let's see. Ribs are nearly ready, Preacher's been smoking a pork butt, and there's a side of beef on the spit." Harrison's mother waggles a finger at her son and points to the desk in the corner. "Rabbit, go dig in the junk drawer and fetch me a tablet and an ink pen."

Rita chomps on a piece of ice. "Ani, why do you call him Rabbit? He won't say."

The old woman draws in a sharp mouthful of air. She takes a minute to exhale. "You see, Rabbit is my first. Lordy, before he was even three years old, I was chasing him everywhere, so we called him Rabbit. It became his Gullah community or basket name. In our culture, names have meaning."

Rabbit's given name is John and his Gullah name is Kudima. Mutomba is the family name. His great, great grandpa adopted the name *Rhodes* from the plantation owner who freed him. My son's full name is John Kudima Rabbit Mutomba Rhodes. His daddy, John Kudima Crabby Mutomba Rhodes, rest his soul, was a crab fisherman who worked every day of his life."

Rita licks the edge of her bottom lip. "What does Kudima mean in the Gullah language?"

"To work. Our people have always been a hard-working folk."

"So where did the name, Harrison, originate, Ani?"

The woman nods at her son. "That there was his choice."

Harrison rummages through the contents of the drawer. "I never liked my given name. John is what I would call unremarkable, but Harrison, now that's unique enough to stand out both socially and politically. I changed my name when I received my scholarship to Annapolis."

Ani coughs again, deeper this time. She swallows another gulp of tea. "He'll always be Rabbit to me. In high school, he was the absolute best football player ever. The Navy gave him that scholarship. Such a smart boy and mighty handsome in his uniform. Mmm, mmm. He was the first Rhodes to finish college, much less serve in the U.S. Navy and be a congressman. I'm a very proud mama. Around here, we all think that Rabbit will end up being President of the United States one day."

Rita tries another sip. "I agree with you. Uh, do your other children also have a string of names?"

"No. You see, ten years came and went until I birthed another baby. By then, everybody settled on just nicknames and given names. My other boys—Joseph, we call Jo-Jo, and William's nickname is Preacher. That boy was yelling at everybody when he was born. My daughter, Odessa, we named Baby Sister. Enough about that. We gotta get busy."

Harrison strolls back to the bench clutching writing utensils. Ani raps her bony knuckles on the wooden table. "Write, boy, write. First, the food. The meat is set, except the grilling part."

Rabbit scrawls on a pad. "I'll give Preacher a hand, don't worry."

His mama huffs another snort of oxygen. "I'm making fried corn cakes. Pearly, she's bringing gumbo and red rice. Baby Sister's toting mashed yams, and Jubilee is fixing a mess of greens. And, of course, we're having a Beaufort Boil." Ani nudges Rita's arm. "I'm hoping you can handle that job."

"Glad to help, but I've never made a Beaufort Boil."

"It's an easy Frogmore Stew. I'll show you. Rabbit, the folding tables are in the shed. Set them up in the grass. Newspaper is stacked in the garage. Your brothers are bringing the smoker. Oh yeah, dig out my Christmas lights. They're in a box in the basement with all the other holiday stuff. Y'all can string them on the front porch."

Harrison salutes his mother. "At your service, ma'am."

* * *

Rita showers in an upstairs bathroom and then slathers the inside of her arm with Calamine Lotion. "Darn, this rash keeps spreading." She dons a red long-sleeved cotton shirt, pulls on a pair of white Capri pants, and reapplies her makeup. Due to the South Carolina humidity, attempts at taming her unruly curls are fruitless.

At six-thirty, when Ani announces, "Supper's ready," Rita watches Harrison and his youngest brother, Jo-Jo, drain the boil's scalding liquid in the side yard. The men spill mixtures of spicy crab legs, shrimp, sausage, onions, red potatoes, and corn over the rectangular tables papered with the Beaufort Gazette. Baby Sister and Jubilee, Ani's sister, place other delectable creations on another table. Holding fast to sturdy paper plates, family members and neighbors pile on the local fare. Romping children snake between adults seated in lawn furniture or on blankets in the grass.

Rita and Harrison dine on the veranda enjoying the evening weather, which doesn't disappoint. Temperatures cool down a bit, courtesy of a front coming in from the east. Once the scraps from dinner go into the trash, the Rhodes' brothers make room for dancing. A boom box playing favorites incites couples to move and groove on the porch, the yard, and the driveway.

The redhead does her best to keep her distance from Ani, but forces herself to mingle with the rest of the clan. After several hours of dancing with the males in the crowd and downing too many glasses of Jubilee's potent St. Cecelia punch, Rita lands next to her husband on the veranda.

By that time, the crowd's party mood had tempered and families had begun to leave. Someone lowers the music volume and the remaining guests gather on the porch, several in rockers, and others content to roost on the cool wooden floor.

Preacher crows, "Who's got a tale to tell?" A few audience members raise their hands.

Several stories of the good old days fill the night air. An older gentleman wearing a red plaid bow tie educates the intimate gathering with a Doc Buzzard yarn. Apparently, the infamous root doctor could remove curses and spells generated by the ghosts and witches that roamed the islands off the South Carolina coast.

Rita nudges Harrison. "Curses and spells? Yeah, right."

"Uncle Preacher," a teenager calls out. "Tell us the one about Mundy Mike."

Rita blinks. *Mundy Mike?*

Harrison's brother tips back in his rocker and swigs from a beer bottle. "Now that's a true story. Mama's brother, Mike, or Mundy Mike, was a gentle soul, but he had his faults. He drank a little too much, loved to shoot craps and smoke a little weed, but all in all, he was a good father and a trustworthy man."

An older woman lifts her hands toward the heavens. "Oh, yes, Lord, a mighty fine man."

Another mumbles, "Amen."

Preacher rocks back and forth. "One night an unlucky streak cleaned him out. Mike staggered home to an empty house. Seems his no-good wife, Blossom, took off and left town. She'd run away with another man and taken Snapper, Mike's five-year-old son." Preacher drains his beer.

Rita absent-mindedly squeezes Harrison's hand.

"You see, Mundy Mike worked for the railroad, laying ties and track, but he lost interest in everything when his wife and kid left. At fifty-six, he quit his job. He told everybody he decided to leave Beaufort to ride the rails. He took his best pal, Blue Boy, with him. I hear tell that dog was the ugliest hound you ever saw. Now and again, Mike would send letters home to Mama filled with information about each town he'd come across. In his last letter, sounding heartbroken, he wrote of Blue Boy's passing. Mike went on to mention of a yearning to ride a train to the tail end of Florida where vegetables and fruit grew year round just ripe for the picking. He said that's where he could work a lot or a little, whatever he had a mind to do. Mama never heard from her brother again.

"Now a couple years later, I think it was in 1956, there were rumors in Beaufort regarding a man resembling Mundy who died in a nasty train wreck. Another one described Mike shooting dice and losing everything he owned including his soul to the devil."

A woman hollers, "Lord have mercy."

Preacher eyes his mother. "Mama, do you have anything to add?"

Ani rocks backward then forward. "I'll never forget my brother's big ole smile and those three teeth missing in front. Mike Mundy Limba Patterson was a loving man and a first-rate father."

A quiver darts up Rita's spine brushing the back of her hairline.

Harrison leans close to her. "Honey, you're squeezing so hard you're going to break my hand."

Rita releases her grip. "Uh, I don't feel well. I'm going to call it a night." She slinks into Ani's house and runs upstairs. Standing in front of the bathroom mirror, she splashes water on her face with unsteady hands. "Oh, my God. Harrison is related to that damn hobo."

* * *

On the flight home the next morning, Rita nurses a headache and shades bloodshot eyes behind oversized sunglasses.

Harrison glances over at her. "I'll summon the flight attendant for a cup of ginger ale. You can take an ibuprofen." He stretches to press the call button.

"Okay." She loosens her seatbelt and reaches for her earbuds. "I'm fine. I just need some peace and quiet." After adjusting her iPod to play smooth jazz, she closes her eyes. Rita can't afford to let anyone discover any of her secrets, especially the one haunting her childhood friend, Jessy Tate.

CHAPTER SIX:

SOMETHING THE CAT DRAGGED IN

The receptionist greets me as I stroll into the waiting room. "Hi, Mrs. Tate."

First on Dr. Priest's after-lunch schedule, I sit alone sniffing a whiff of cinnamon. No doubt, a leftover Christmas candle burns on Chelsea's desk. Opening my trusty compact, I regard my likeness. Two truths are crystal clear—reality is a bitch and the overpriced makeup I wear, which claims to hide age lines, deep-set wrinkles, and shadows around my eyes, is a waste of money. An uneasy sigh escapes my lips and I tuck the compact inside my purse. I'm halfway into a *People* magazine article on Meryl Streep, who by the way looks pretty good for her age, when the receptionist announces my name. I toss the magazine aside.

Dr. Priest crosses his office to the doorway. "How are you today, Jessy?" He guides me to the couch.

I meet his blue-eyed gaze. "No change."

He eases himself into an oversized desk chair, the one sporting rolling castors. The fiftyish man wrinkles his brow. "So no progress since our last session?" When he sits up straight, the chair leather creaks.

"Nope." I fiddle with a strand of hair behind my ear. "The stupid dreams are repetitive, but sometimes one will surprise me. I awoke from a doozy last night where I kept counting umpteen pairs of shoes and boots. Weird, huh? Of course, there's the banyan tree and Rita May." I place my handbag on the floor. "Are you going to hypnotize me again?"

"Yes. If it's all right with you, we can begin right away. Please lie back."

"Don't know why I'm nervous today." I prop on a pillow and clasp my hands together at my abdomen.

The doctor rolls over to the sofa. "Slow deep breaths, Jessy, and listen to my voice. Let go of your thoughts." His intonation is low, flat, and repetitive. "Close your eyes. Visualize yourself at the edge of a mountain stream, the cool water flowing over smooth stones. You are at peace. Nothing can harm you." Dr. Priest's soothing voice lulls me into a tranquil state. "Let's go back in time. You are a child around ten years of age, perhaps older. Where are you?"

"Inside the layered roots at the base of the banyan tree."

"Is that a special place?"

"It's our clubhouse. No one can see us."

"Us?"

"Rita May and me."

"Are you comfortable? Are you safe?"

My breathing becomes rapid. "Yes...and no."

"Why are you unsure?"

"Wait. Someone's coming."

Dr. Priest's tone changes. "Tell me who it is."

"I want to run, but I can't move."

"Why are you afraid?"

"I hear men coming. I'm afraid they'll find me. There's laughter and a girl is crying. I'm scared."

"Who is crying?"

My body stiffens. "It's me." Breathing in spurts, I'm sobbing and clawing at the sofa cushions.

The doctor's hand rests on my shoulder. "Open your eyes, Jessy. You're safe."

I sit up swinging both feet to the floor. Perspiration dampens my blouse. "Oh, my God. I can't stop shaking."

Dr. Priest offers a box of tissues as he strides to the desk. He presses the intercom button. "Chelsea, please bring Mrs. Tate a bottle of water." Sitting in his swivel chair, he scribbles a note on a pad. "Can you explain what frightened you?"

When I clutch both hands together, my knuckles become white. "Not really. It was like one of my nightmares. The tree and that horrible sickly smell. Shadows but no faces. Men shouting."

"Take a few deep breaths."

"Muddy boots were everywhere." My heartbeat slowly decelerates.

"I'm proud of you, Jessy. Your mind is beginning to open small windows into your past."

Chelsea breezes into the room and hands me a cool bottle, and I down several gulps before she leaves.

Dr. Priest jots an entry in a spiral notebook. He stops writing and waves at a nearby chair. "Please, come sit."

For the next half an hour, the doctor offers an extensive assessment of my progress to date. Clearing his throat, he taps the face of his wristwatch. "I'm afraid our time has run out." He rises, his chair skidding backward. "You've accomplished quite a lot today." Seizing my hand, he gently pulls me to my feet. "Your homework is to examine the photos we discussed. After today's experience, I'm betting those pictures will trigger a new response. I guarantee it."

"But…but what if they stir up some unbearable memory, something shocking?"

"Yes, there's always that chance. On the other hand, your fear could be as nonthreatening as an overheard quarrel between your parents, an argument blown out of proportion. Remember, when we are children, frightening events can originate in our imaginations."

* * *

Dressed in a cotton nightshirt, I gently smooth night cream on my face and examine the image in front of me, the weary, sleep-deprived widow in the bathroom mirror. "Oh, my God. I look like something the cat dragged in." I pause. "A cat. That's it. The perfect pet to keep me company. Easy, clean, and no trouble, except for the litter box thing." Teeth brushed, I flip off the bathroom light on the way to the bedroom.

Photo-packed albums live in the thick drawers of an antique chest once belonging to my late mother, Margaret English Blanchard. Three faded cloth-covered volumes illustrate my transformation from baby to pig-tailed tomboy to boy-crazy teen. I select the one on top of the stack and crawl into bed.

Braced against king size pillows, I stroke the fragile corner-worn scrapbook resting on my lap. My heartbeat escalates. "Why am I so worried? These dumb photos won't make a dent in my memory."

I open the book. The scent of time itches my nose. My mother's handwriting is visible on the inside cover—Elijah and Margaret Blanchard, 1951–1955. In the first few pictures, my father, a lanky young man, and my mother, a beauty with wavy black hair, stand side by side in front of a restaurant. I turn the page, and a sequence of beach scenes tumbles out, the glue on their brittle edges long gone. Bits of yellowed paper, not unlike the memories the album protects, disintegrate between my fingers. At the back, a handful of snapshots remain intact—one of the twosome on a pier—Mother giggling at Daddy, he grinning back at her, love in their eyes, the blissful couple holding hands. There's another picture of me, a toddler digging in the sand. I let the chronological photos guide me through the years.

Tension knots my back between my shoulders. I close the album. "It's too hot in here." I slide off the bed and shuffle into the hallway. The thermostat requires tweaking. On my way back, I remove another scrapbook from the chest.

Sitting on top of the covers, I flip to the first page full of pictures, revealing various shots of me again at age nine, and my parents standing in front of my dad's diner—the perfect, happy family. Back then, we moved from Miami to Bonita Springs because of his aging parents, Grandma Betty and Grandpa Caleb, who at the time lived in the cottage where my father currently resides.

Toward the end of the album, I encounter an entire page devoted to a children's party at the beach. I keep going back to one picture where I'm standing with a troop of swim-suited children. Although most of the summer of 1956 remains a mystery to me, I do recall the birthday. Using my index finger, I outline the tallest girl. "Rita May and her mop of ginger curls."

On the next page, there is a photo of Skip Goodman with two other boys. For a moment, my vision shifts to an image of the monstrous banyan tree standing in front of the Bonita Springs Community Pavilion. My pulse quickens as I fixate on the sepia-tinted photo. The tree's roots, like tentacles, hook onto a smaller, withered tree, snaking toward the ground, strangling its prey, forming large cavities at its base. A memory bursts into my brain like a flashbulb from an antiquated camera. "I recognize the odor in my dreams. It's from the shrubs that grow in front of the pavilion— the Allamanda bushes dotted with the citrus-smelling yellow flowers." My hands tremble. "I'm done." After shutting the book, I hurry into the bathroom. The Ambien goes down effortlessly with a handful of cool water. I don't care how late it is, I'm going to phone her.

* * *

After a useless debate with Rita, I get into bed and tug the sheet to my chin. An hour later, I ease into a restless fog of dreams.

It's five-fifteen the next morning, and I lie in the middle of the bedroom floor, curled in a fetal position, crying hysterically, my nightgown drenched in sweat.

The night had exhumed the dead.

PART TWO

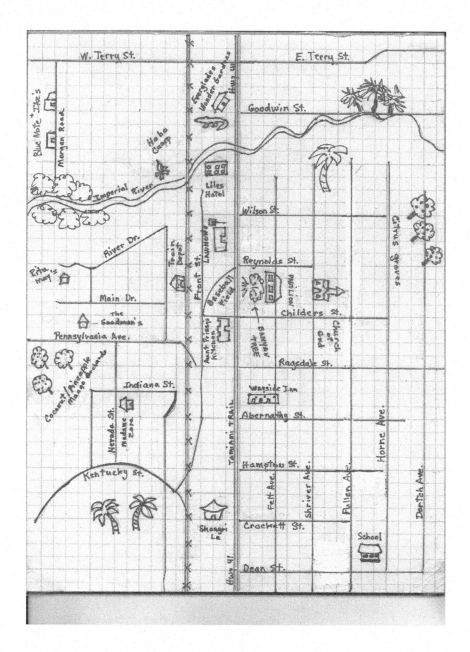

BONITA SPRINGS (1955-56)

CHAPTER SEVEN:
NEXT TO GODLINESS

In 1955, Jessy's mother spoke the gospel truth, at least that's what Jessy believed. The bleak sayings and adages Margaret Blanchard chose to dole out to her daughter stuck to the eleven-year-old's brain as if inscribed with an indelible felt-tip marker. The latest saying—*bad luck comes in three's*—weighed on the girl. Although she had no choice but to listen to the venom spewing from her mother's lips, she didn't always agree. Then again, Margaret Blanchard was always right.

Over the past few days, Jessy experienced a trilogy of personal misfortune. Monday afternoon, while attempting a tricky hopscotch maneuver in front of the school, she tumbled onto the sidewalk and chipped a front tooth. The spill resulted in unbearable embarrassment and an upcoming dental appointment. The second disaster unfolded on Tuesday morning. Jessy's teacher, Miss Rydell, stunned the fifth-grade class with a pop quiz in arithmetic. Not her best subject, Jessy hoped for a C. The third calamity came to pass on Wednesday evening, October 12.

"No. We're not getting a dog." Margaret took a slow drag from a cigarette.

Although Jessy's father was initially on her side of the argument, his expression proved he yielded to her mother's veto.

"Not going to happen, Jessica Rose. We have a cat. Enough said." Margaret removed her eyeglasses. "Elijah, don't you give in to this child. The discussion is closed."

Eli Blanchard shook his head, a signal for Jessy to surrender. Clutching two platefuls of fried chicken, mashed potatoes, and the buttery green peas his daughter adored, he set supper on the kitchen table. "Eat up. I'll see you two later. I had to let Camilla go home early so I'm pulling double duty tonight."

"Why on earth?" Gripping a cocktail, Margaret groaned as she stood up. She scuffed across the linoleum floor and landed in a chair at the end of the table, her terrycloth robe skimming the floor.

Eli dried his hands on a dishtowel. "Her youngest has a fever." After placing the towel on a wall hook, he left through the red door in the corner that connected their apartment to the back of Aunt Prissy's Kitchen, the diner he owned and managed.

Jessy lay on her tummy on the living room rug, sketching the final touches of a masterpiece, an adorable beagle with floppy ears. Being a wiz with a willow stick, she applied one last stroke completing the picture to her satisfaction. She stored the shoebox full of art supplies and the pad of paper in her bedroom closet, and then washed her hands.

When she sat at the table with her mother, the two bowed their heads.

"Go ahead and say the blessing, Jessica, and sit up straight." Margaret stiffened in her own chair.

Jessy placed a cloth napkin in her lap and made the sign of the cross. "Bless us, oh Lord, and these Thy gifts which we are about to receive from Thy bounty through Christ our Lord. Amen." Keeping with tradition, she gestured another crisscross sign of reverence. Afterward, she bit into a fried chicken leg and eventually dug into a mound of potatoes. "This is so good. I think Daddy is the best chef in the whole world."

"Please chew and swallow before you speak. No one wants a glimpse at what's lurking inside your mouth." Margaret nibbled on a piece of white meat she pulled from a juicy breast. Tilting her glass, clear liquid dribbled into her mouth.

"Mama, aren't you hungry?"

"Not really." Margaret stabbed at a slippery green pea.

Jessy finished her last drop of milk. "Can I be excused?"

Her mother took a bite. "Yes."

Jessy scraped her plate into the trashcan, and she set the dishes and silverware in the sink. "Can I watch TV?"

"Yes, but it's *may* I be excused, and *may* I watch TV." A swath of Margaret's jet-black hair fell into her eyes. She brushed a wave off her face and curved a strand behind her ear. "Please take my plate, too. Um, have you seen that new pack of cigarettes?"

"By the toaster," said Jessy as she cleared the table.

Margaret grabbed the pack of Winstons on her way to the living room where she wilted into olive green sofa cushions.

After turning the TV dial to the correct channel, Jessy sprawled on top of the rug. "Guess what, Mama? We have three new kids in our school."

Her mother plucked a book of matches from her housecoat pocket. When she lit the cigarette, her hands shook. "Uh huh." She flicked the scorched match into the ashtray on the coffee table.

The child inched closer to the table. "A girl named Rita May McAfee and her two younger brothers." Aware of her mother's habit of letting ashes gather at the end of a cigarette, Jessy nudged the ashtray forward. "She's thirteen and taller than most of the other kids in my class, even the boys. Her brother, Gregory, is eleven. Another brother, Clark, is nine and in the third-grade classroom across the hall from me."

A stream of smoke leaked from Margaret's open lips.

"And the kids didn't wear any shoes to school."

Margaret paused before bringing her cigarette to her mouth. "No shoes?" She sucked in another drag.

"Yeah. Isn't that cool?"

The woman placed the butt on the rim of the ashtray. At the beginning of a speech on the dangers of going barefoot, Margaret encased her legs in a creamy beige afghan. "There are germs in the dirt and if you cut your foot, the wound might become infected. Besides, there's ringworm, impetigo, to name a few skin afflictions one could catch. It's not sanitary. Remember, young lady, cleanliness is next to Godliness." She angled her glass to her lips letting an ice cube tumble into her mouth. After crunching, she swallowed. "Are the parents ignorant? I don't understand how decent folk could send their child to school without shoes."

Jessy clenched her teeth.

Margaret continued the outburst. "Evidence of a family with no class." She inhaled one last time and smashed the butt in the ashtray. "Yesterday when I stood in line at the pharmacy, Mrs. Atkins mentioned that a new batch of drifters recently rolled into town. Mark my words, Jessica, your barefooted friends belong to a migrant family who pick vegetables and fruit for a living."

Trying to ignore her mother and focus on the TV screen, Jessy twirled the strands of hair she had earlier pinched between her fingers.

"And I imagine the family lives in a Sherwood shack down behind the depot or in a migrant camp near Estero. Those orange and tangerine pickers disappear when the seasons change. Honey, they're low-rent trailer trash, gypsies who wander the country searching for jobs. They'll leave Bonita as soon as they harvest the fruit and the work dries up. Uh huh. No class." Margaret pointed at the television. "Can you fix the picture on the tube?"

As Jackie Gleason danced from side to side into fuzzy, horizontal lines on the screen, Jessie crawled to the set. She jiggled the rabbit ears, a gesture that usually did the trick. For the time being, the picture remained clear. It wasn't long before Margaret raised her empty glass and rattled the ice cubes left in the bottom. Jessy sprang to her feet. On her way to the kitchen, she nicked the glass from Margaret's hand.

Jessy could reconstruct the cocktail blindfolded. First, she dropped a fresh cube from the ice tray into the lowball glass and then measured a jigger full of Smirnoff's. She drizzled the vodka on top of the ice. A splash of Florida's freshly squeezed finest topped the liquor. She stirred the mixture until the cat vaulted onto the counter.

"Get down, Muffin. Mama will fuss," she whispered and nudged the tabby to the floor. Clutching the finished product, she offered it to her mother. "You'll love Rita May. She's beautiful and has the most gorgeous red hair, loads of freckles, and sad green eyes."

Margaret smirked at her daughter and accepted the drink. "I'm not sure I want you to befriend those children. You might inadvertently pick up all sorts of nasty habits."

Jessy didn't relax until her mother fell asleep on the sofa. Margaret snored right through the last minute of the Honeymooners.

* * *

"Daddy, it's hot today, way too hot for shoes. Don't you agree?"

Eli opened his mouth to answer, but Margaret called from the bedroom. "Jessica, we discussed this last night. No daughter of mine is going to school barefooted. Not another word on the subject."

"But it's not fair."

Her mother sauntered into the kitchen, her nightgown barely obscuring a delicate frame. "I gave you my reasons. Don't talk back."

"The subject is closed. You're wearing shoes." Eli's lips formed a straight line.

"But, Daddy." Appealing her case, she shared details of her shoeless friend. "Please."

He wrinkled his brow. "It doesn't matter what anyone else does. Go fetch your shoes. Now." He poured a cup of coffee for his wife who roosted in a kitchen chair, the newspaper spread out in front of her on the table.

In a huff, Jessy stomped down the hall. Minutes later, she returned to the room wearing white ankle socks and saddle oxfords. "Okay, I'm ready."

"No, you're not. Come closer."

Jessy took one giant step toward her mother.

Margaret bent over and re-tied the girl's shoes. "You're a mess, Jessica. At your age, you should know how to fix your hair. Please go get me a brush, a comb, and two matching barrettes."

Jessy dashed down the hall. Reappearing at Margaret's side a few minutes later, she noticed the dark circles around her mother's violet eyes. "Did you sleep okay, Mama?" She shifted her weight from one black and white shoe-clad foot to the other.

"Yes, quit wiggling." Margaret meticulously parted her daughter's chestnut-colored hair to the side. Clamping two barrettes into place prevented unruly strands from dipping too close to Jessy's mouth. Both parents detested their daughter's nasty habit of chewing on her hair. In fact, Margaret threatened to trim Jessy's locks short as a boy's if she didn't curtail the practice. "Now twirl and let me see if you pass inspection."

Jessy obeyed. Upon Margaret's approval, she kissed her parents on the way through the room. With a lunchbox under one arm, she pushed against the back door, making sure to avoid the tiny tear at the side of the screen. She held the door ajar surveying the street running parallel to the diner. "I'm gonna kill Skipper Goodman. He's late again."

She stepped down and without warning, a gust of wind caught the door and slammed it shut behind her, the resonance scattering a flock of gulls feeding in the parking lot. Jessy listened for her mother's inevitable declaration.

"Jessica Rose Blanchard! We are civilized people. We do not slam doors."

She giggled and wiped the sand off the top stoop. Careful not to dirty her new Sears and Roebuck Catalogue dress, Jessy sat down. To kill time, she monitored a trail of ants marching to and fro from one pebble to the next. Finally, she caught sight of a winded boy barreling toward her.

Skip halted at the base of the concrete steps. He grabbed his knees, his breathing shallow.

"What do you know? It's the slowest boy in the world. You'd be late for your own funeral. Here." Jessy shoved her lunch box into his hands.

"Sorry." He straightened and swept blondish bangs from his eyes.

The route to school, which never varied, expended twenty to twenty-five minutes, depending on the children's pace. Jessy and Skip meandered to the end of Childers Street and veered right in front of Aunt Prissy's Kitchen. Walking five long blocks, the kids edged the sandy shoulder on Highway 41 (also known as the Tamiami Trail) south to the corner at Dean Street.

That intersection was Pinky Grizzle's territory. The crossing guard, whose body shape matched the Stop sign she waved, stood her post every weekday morning, and again each afternoon. Rain or shine, the jovial woman with the frizzy gray hair, who donned pink ankle-length skirts and coordinating sneakers, guided schoolchildren safely across the highway. Wearing a contagious smile, she chanted a melodious "Have a blessed day."

Skip and Jessy sprinted the last two blocks to the Bonita Springs Elementary School. The historical brick building incorporated grades one through eight, the least populated classes housing two grades apiece. Jessy retrieved her lunchbox from Skip who shadowed her into the fifth-sixth room. Asthma had kept her in fifth grade. The new girl, Rita May McAfee, sat at a desk in the sixth-grade section near the window, her hands clasped together on top of a book. Jessy signaled a hello and settled into a desk on the other side of the room behind Rita May's brother, Gregory. He and his orange hair stood out like a buoy in a sea of unremarkable children.

Their teacher, Miss Rydell, a pencil-thin young woman, strutted into the classroom wearing her beige every-other-day jumper and white puffy-sleeved blouse. She paused at her desk in front of a chalkboard where she had listed the daily assignments. Despite her slight frame, her voice projected significant authority. "Settle down." Her tiny left hand rested on top of a replica globe of the world allowing her to spin the sphere using one finger. Squinting, she placed her right hand on a bony hip. "I'm waiting." Once the students hushed, the teacher scanned the room. "Class, please stand." Her voice stayed in monotone, flat as the bodice of her jumper.

Everyone rose to attention and faced the far corner of the room. Eighteen children placed their right hands over eighteen hearts and recited "The Pledge of Allegiance" to the American Flag. For the next three and half hours, both grades endured a vocabulary quiz, a lengthy reading lesson, and three mimeographed arithmetic handouts, which consisted of two pages of fractions, and one with ten mind-boggling word problems.

Two pedestal fans located at opposite corners of the classroom propelled lukewarm air toward the children as they scarfed down their lunches. Between sips of milk from a thermos, Jessy gobbled up a peanut butter and jelly sandwich in record time. She extracted a wax paper-wrapped cookie from her Annie Oakley lunchbox and consumed half on route to the sand-scattered lot at the back of school property.

Rita May sat cross-legged in the grass at the base of a giant oak, one of two shady spots on the playground.

Jessy squatted nearby. "How'd you do on your arithmetic test?"

"Easy-peasy. At my last school, I got all A's." Rita May's accent hinted at a Midwestern twang.

"How come you're…uh…wearing shoes today?"

The redhead casts her gaze downward. "These are Mama's flats, but they're too big and slide off my feet."

Jessy did her best to mask her disappointment. "Here's half a sugar cookie. Camilla baked it."

Rita May's green eyes narrowed when she smiled. "Thanks. Who's Camilla?" She bit into the luscious pastry.

"She and Daddy do the cooking at his diner, Aunt Prissy's Kitchen. Uh, where did you used to go to school?"

"Is Aunt Prissy your relative?"

"Nope. The old owner named the diner before Daddy bought it."

"Oh. I bet I've been to more schools than you have. Six schools total. Last year in Druid Hills, Illinois." She swallowed the last of the cookie.

"Me, I spent first, second, and third grades in Coral Gables, fourth and fifth in Bonita Springs."

Rita May stretched her legs out in front of her. "We came here because of my papa's new job. He's one of the bosses; he oversees the workers who pick oranges, grapefruit, and tangerines in the nearby groves."

Jessy sighed. Her mother's assumptions were correct.

At one o'clock, Miss Rydell rang the bell ending recess. The girls hustled to the far side of the building, but Jessy's stubby-legged pace proved no match for Rita May's long-limbed strides. Assuming the rear of the line, Jessy envied the teenager's attributes—milky-white skin, sprinkled with exactly the right amount of freckles. Rita May's gingerbread curls cascaded onto her shoulders reminding the younger girl of a movie star she'd seen in *Photoplay*. On the other hand, Jessy's straight-as-a-fishing pole hair resembled the color of a muddy tide pool.

After two more hours of constant schoolwork, Jessy stared at the clock on the classroom wall as if she could make its hands move at will. Clutching empty lunchboxes and spelling books, the kids waited in their seats like caged animals anticipating freedom from a captor.

Miss Rydell also eyed the clock. "Don't forget class, spelling unit test tomorrow. Both grades." At two fifty-five, the teacher opened her mouth but hesitated a minute; a slight sneer spanned her face. At last, she announced, "Class dismissed." The herd trampled from the room.

Jessy ran to catch up with her new friend. "Where do you live?"

"Past the ballfield and on the other side of the railroad tracks." A shoe accidentally slipped off Rita May's foot. She stopped to empty the sand from its instep.

"We're almost neighbors. I live on the side street near the ballfield. We could walk home together."

Rita May slid her foot back into the shoe. "Sure, but I have to wait here until my brothers show up. I'll meet you at the highway."

Jessy glanced at the boy behind her. "Come on, slowpoke."

Skip caught up to Jessy, and soon the duo joined Rita May and her brothers where Dean Street intersected the Tamiami Trail. Grouping together at Pinky Grizzle's corner, the children paraded single file with Pinky guiding them across the highway. Once on the other side, the line of children hugged the edge of the road going north. The redheaded teen stooped to pick up a rock, her thin frame curving forward, revealing a crescent-shaped birthmark on her right shoulder. She hurled the stone into the street. "I can't dillydally today. Gotta babysit so Lynette can help Davis in the groves until dark."

Jessy mimicked Rita May and tossed her own rock. "Who are Lynette and Davis?"

"My mama and papa. Wow, you've got a good arm." Rita May bowed scooping two palm fronds from a pile under a tree bordering the street. She gave one limb to Jessy.

"You call your parents by their first names?"

"It's no big deal." Rita May dragged her limb in the dirt.

Jessy's piece broke in half. "How many people are in your family?" She lobbed part of the stick into the grass and twirled the end piece as if it was a baton.

Rita May gestured at the boys behind her. "You've met Gregory and Clark. There's also Doris, age five, and Debbie, she's three and a half, who's nothing but trouble, and the baby, Marilyn. She's almost one, cute but a handful."

"You're a lucky duck. It's just me, Mama, Daddy, and Muffin, our cat. It's a family of six if you count my Grandpa Caleb and Grandma Betty."

Rita May let go of her limb. "A lucky duck? You're full of it." Sweat trickled from her hairline along the sides of her face. "It sure is muggy today. It's not even summer yet."

"It's hot most of the time around here."

All five kids, two girls and three boys, came to a halt at the corner of Childers and Highway 41. Jessy made her move. "Rita May, do you want to come over to my place on Saturday? Or just do something together?"

"Sure, but I have chores in the morning. I'll meet you at the ballfield. Noon tomorrow. We'll go exploring." She joined her two brothers who already crossed to the other side of Childers Street.

Jessy bounced on the balls of her feet. "I'm going exploring."

Skip elbowed her. "You're going where?"

"None of your beeswax." She poked him with the palm branch.

He rubbed his arm. "Cut it out."

Jessy and Skip walked the few steps to the entrance to Aunt Prissy's Kitchen. The two hopped up on the brown planter in front of the diner. He scooched close to her.

Jessy moved away. "Quit crowding me."

"Come on, Jess. I like you." He slanted to his right, eyes closed, lips puckered.

She folded her arms across her chest. "Stop that. I've told you before. Quit the lovey-dovey stuff. Why can't I crack a dent in your thick skull? I'm never going to let you kiss me. You might as well quit trying."

"But you're my girlfriend."

"Skipper Goodman, I'm not anybody's girlfriend and I never will be."

"Too bad. I'm not giving up. I'll wear you down." He shifted several inches to the left. "Why don't we go inside and ask your daddy to fix us each a cherry smash?"

"Nope. I'm going home. It's almost time for my shows." Jessy jumped to the ground and brushed off the back of her skirt. Carrying a lunchbox and a speller, she trotted around to the side of the diner.

Skip tailed her into the back parking lot. "See you later, alligator." He darted into Childers Street.

Jessy paused to watch him sprint down the road. *Maybe someday I'll let him kiss me.*

CHAPTER EIGHT:
PICK YOUR PLEASURE

Jessy planted her feet in front of two side-by-side screened doors at the back of the diner—the left one painted brown, the right one the color of a ripe avocado. Leaving her book and lunchbox on the stoop, she chose the brown door that opened into the diner's storeroom. Inside, she threaded herself between rows of stocked metal shelving until she entered the steamy kitchen. Camilla stood at the stove dipping a ladle into an oversized stockpot. Perspiration covered the cook's face.

When Jessy shoved saloon-style doors into the heart of Aunt Prissy's Kitchen, a rush of cool air from a window unit stroked her cheek. A soda fountain counter and eight red-vinyl topped stools occupied half the diner's service area, with matching booths and chrome-edged Formica tables inhabiting the rest. Top-forty tunes played from a jukebox in the far corner.

A broom-wielding waitress swept under a booth at the back of the restaurant. At the sight of Jessy, Mary Louise Blakely halted her efforts. No makeup embellished the young woman's oval face, but when Mary Louise managed a shy smile, her dark eyes brightened, revealing a natural beauty. "Hi, Jess."

"Hi. Have you seen my daddy?"

"Nope. He's gone off somewhere." Mary Louise resumed sweeping the floor, her stringy brown ponytail moving with each pass of the broom. She wiped her brow on her sleeve. "I think he told Camilla where he was going though."

Jessy backed into the swinging doors, nearly slamming into the cook.

The round woman placed a fist upon her chest. "I do declare, child, you scared the living tar out of me."

"I'm sorry." Jessy gulped air. "Where's Daddy?"

Camilla dried her wet hands on her apron. "Mr. Eli's gone to Fort Myers to pick up supplies. Don't you fret none. He'll be back in time for the supper rush."

Jessy trailed the cook to the back of the kitchen. "What's the special tonight?"

Camilla wrinkled her nose and sniffed. "Can't you guess?"

"Um, too many things smell good. I can't tell."

"Tonight we's got chicken potpie, roast beef, uh, spaghetti and meatballs, fried pork chops and gravy, and of course, your favorite, macaroni and cheese. Pick your pleasure, child."

"I can't. I love all the food you fix, especially your biscuits."

Camilla's toothy grin shined almost iridescent against her dark complexion. She opened her inviting arms. Without hesitation, Jessy fell into the woman's embrace and basked in the scent of vanilla and almonds. Everyone in town knew Camilla's husband, Toby, kept his wife well stocked in Ambush cologne.

Camilla put Jessy at arm's length. "You run on home. I've got work to do."

"May I have a drink first? Maybe a Coke?"

The sturdy woman hung onto the left side of the swaying doors. "Mary Louise, this child wants a Coca Cola."

Jessy ducked under the cook's arm squeezing through the space between the doors. Claiming a stool at the counter, she waited for Mary Louise to set the broom aside. The waitress breezed behind the soda fountain. She dribbled cola syrup and carbonated fizz into a tall glass filled with ice. To finish, the waitress stuck a straw into Jessy's favorite beverage. "Here you go."

The child drank her Coke in fifteen minutes, simultaneously quizzing Mary Louise on the subject of Sally, the waitress' four-year-old daughter. Her glass now empty, Jessy slid off the seat, hurried through the kitchen, and then the storeroom. She pushed open the back door where she scooped up her belongings. Her wristwatch read quarter to four. Cars and pickup trucks would soon crowd both front and back parking lots.

Hesitating, she peered through the screen on the green door. Once inside the dark apartment, Jessy stole into the living room where the radio on the bookshelf crooned a mellow Sinatra tune. Margaret lay on the sofa as limp as the washcloth shading her eyes; all signs indicated a migraine headache.

Jessy slipped into her room undetected and changed into shorts and a matching sky blue top. Stretching out across her bed, she retrieved the library book she kept under her pillow. She thumbed to page twenty-five of *The Ringmaster's Secret*, resuming the adventures of Nancy Drew.

The shuffle of Margaret's slippers across the linoleum floor broke Jessy's concentration. She noticed that the hands on her turquoise alarm clock pointed to four fifty-five. The Mickey Mouse Club came on at five. Jessy marked the beginning of Chapter 6 leaving the mystery on the bedspread. When she gradually opened the bedroom door, the hinge squealed.

"When did you get home?" Her mother's unsteady voice gave Jessy all the information she needed.

The girl strolled into the kitchen. "A while ago."

Margaret, her hair in disarray, wrestled with a stubborn ice tray until she dislodged a few cubes. "Honey, I'm having a terrible day. No TV this afternoon. Please go to your room and play. I need peace and quiet. Anyway, don't you have homework?"

"No, ma'am, it's Friday." Jessy gritted her teeth. Under her breath, she mumbled, "And my show is on," and plodded back to her room. *Why does Mama always have to be sick?* Jessy flopped on the bed. Luckily, a clump of hair broke free from the clutches of the barrette. Tucking the strands between her lips, she escaped into her book for another hour.

There was a soft knock on her bedroom door. Eli cracked it open. "Hi, Baby Girl. Your dinner's on the kitchen counter. Chicken potpie and biscuits. Stay awake tonight. Don't forget. We have a date."

"I won't forget." She bookmarked her place leaving Nancy Drew and her pal, George, in mortal danger. Following the delicious scent of her father's cooking, she found two warm plates draped in tinfoil on the kitchen counter near the stove. Because Margaret remained in her room, Jessy dined alone on a TV tray with the television volume turned low. She gave her full attention to *My Friend Flicka*. An hour later, after a boring western on the *Zane Grey Theater*, she switched off the set, slipped on her pajamas, and got into bed. She waited for her father while immersing herself in the next chapter of her book.

When Eli's footsteps creaked the linoleum in the hallway, Jessy stuffed the captivating mystery under her pillow. The highlight of her week, their Friday night date, involved playing cards for an hour. She won five out of six hands of gin rummy that night.

"Okay, champ, let's call it a night."

Jessy covered her legs with the bedsheet. "Daddy, is Mama getting worse?"

The space between Eli's brows indented into a small crevice. "I'm not sure. Why do you ask? Did something happen?"

In an instant, Muffin pounced on the bed. Jessy scooped up the cat in her arms. "No. She just acts sicker. Why can't she go to another doctor?

One who works in Fort Myers or Naples?" Flipping on her side, she curled the kitty to her chest. A satisfied purr vibrated in Jessy's ear.

"I'm trying to find her some help. Please don't worry." He rubbed the lines on his forehead.

"I'll pray some more. Night, Daddy."

Eli stalled at the foot of the bed. "Couldn't hurt." He flicked off the overhead light when he left the room. "Goodnight, Jess."

She tossed the sheet aside and knelt next to her bed, beginning the customary "Now I Lay Me Down to Sleep" prayer. After blessing a repertoire of players, she ended with a special request. "And please, God, don't forget. Make Mama feel better so she and Daddy can stop arguing. Amen." When she returned to bed, she fell asleep with a soggy tuft of hair in her mouth.

* * *

Eli's harsh words leached through the walls. "Damn it, Margaret. I've had enough."

"I'm doing the best I can." His wife's voice trembled.

"I don't believe you. It's a mystery how you claim to be deathly ill and can't crawl off the sofa for anything, but you can walk two blocks to the liquor store to buy booze and cigarettes. I'm about to throw in the towel. If not for Jessy, I'd…"

"You'd what, Elijah Blanchard? Leave me? Go ahead and say it. I don't care. Anyway, you have no idea how much I hate Bonita Springs and your precious diner. I can't stand it here. I want my old life back."

"You can't mean that."

"Yes, I do. In Miami, before Jessica came along, we used to go dancing. You'd show me off to your friends. We had no responsibilities. We were free."

"You're crazy, woman. You're living in the past. If you don't start acting like a real mother, your daughter will grow to resent you."

"You're the one who's crazy. Jessica Rose loves me."

"Listen to me. I'm giving you an ultimatum. If you can't find a way to help yourself, I'll do it for you. There are plenty of sanitariums or rest homes for people who share similar problems. Something's got to give, Margaret. I've lost patience. It's now or never."

Jessy buried her head, her tears staining the pillow. A door slam ended the spat and spooked the cat. The child lay awake until Muffin resumed the position next to her.

CHAPTER NINE:
LIKE A STUCK PIG

Jessy awoke to an unmistakable aroma. "Camilla's making biscuits." Her bare feet hit the floor. In a matter of minutes, she made her bed, brushed her teeth, dressed in navy shorts and a T-shirt, and put on a pair of old sneakers. Not wishing to disturb her mother, the child slowly opened the red door that entered into the storeroom. She almost bumped into Eli, who stood balanced on a stepstool stacking an extra-large can of tomatoes on top of another one.

"Whoa, where's the fire? You're not supposed to run in here or any other part of the diner. It's dangerous."

"Sorry. Oh, hi, Delilah."

Halfway hidden behind the door, the blonde gripped a supersized can of green beans. "Hi, yourself, doodlebug. I bet you're ready for breakfast. Let's get you fed." The waitress transferred the container to Eli. Taking Jessy's hand, Delilah smacked a mouthful of gum.

Customers adored Delilah Duncan, particularly the men. "Like flies to sorghum," Jessy's Grandpa Caleb often said, his words explaining the phenomenon to whomever would listen. The overall atmosphere in the diner on any given day depended on which waitress worked the floor. During Delilah's shift, patrons remained in a collective agreeable mood.

Even Skip fancied the blonde waitress. "She's pretty and her parts jiggle," he confessed to Jessy one afternoon back in the spring.

Blowing a pink bubble through glossy red lips, Delilah pulled Jessy into the bustling kitchen. They charged through the waving doors, and the waitress nodded toward the end of the counter. "There's a seat. Hurry now. Go grab it."

Jessy zipped behind the strip of stools. She mounted the empty seat and spun once to marvel at the diner's activity. She loved Saturday mornings at Aunt Prissy's Kitchen. The restaurant hummed. Recurrent laughter competed with the clink of silverware on heavy duty porcelain plates. Weekend regulars who hunched over steaming plates of eggs and bacon debated the latest gossip, their southern drawls thicker than the bowl of creamy grits that accompanied their breakfast orders.

As Jessy spun on the top of the stool, the jukebox played "Heartbreak Hotel" while Delilah trotted out from the kitchen clasping the edges of a loaded tray. She sashayed to a booth in the corner where two good ole boys slurped coffee and perused the morning paper.

"Here you go, gentlemen." The waitress placed hot food in front of the men, and then made her rounds with the coffee pot. "Now, who needs a refill?"

"Hey, honeybun, how's about a little sugar…in my coffee, of course?" The redneck from the booth beamed as if he'd won a prize for idiot of the year.

Delilah went about her business ignoring the table full of cackling men, turning her attention to a couple with a young boy.

Jessy absorbed all the interactions in front of her. She only became distracted when Eli slid behind the counter. "Miss Blanchard, have you made your decision?"

"Too many choices."

"Let me suggest fried eggs over easy, country ham, grits, and a hot biscuit."

Her tummy growled. "Yes, thank you."

Eli dashed back to the kitchen.

Jessy killed time counting the cities on the map-of-Florida placemat until Delilah covered Orlando and half of the state with a plate of steaming food. The child stabbed her fork into a piece of ham. For the next fifteen minutes, she wolfed down her breakfast. Using the nub of a biscuit to sop up the last bit of egg yolk, she reassessed the morning crowd.

..Initially, Jessy tuned out the noisy quartet of men at the neighboring table, but while nibbling on a second biscuit, she swiveled in the direction of a deep southern accent. The brawny man stood next to his table, both thumbs hooked onto the purple suspenders that yanked his dungarees an inch above his ankles.

Someone said, "Sit down, Bubba."

Bubba didn't budge. Employing a homegrown vernacular, he boasted to the others. "I swear the big boy fought me the whole time. It was the fattest Snook this side of Estero Island. It could've been Ole Stinky. You know I'm dying if I'm lying, boys."

A customer remarked, "Well, you best keep the light on tonight. Wouldn't want you to croak in the dark." His friends hooted and hollered. Another man chimed in. "You couldn't catch a Snook if I threw one at you."

Jessy giggled until someone stroked the back of her neck. She recognized the scent. Caleb Blanchard always kept a stash of raw peanuts in his shirt pocket.

"Hello there, munchkin, give me a peck." Straddling the vacant stool beside Jessy, the man's weathered face beamed.

Jessy kissed the crusty man's stubbly cheek. "Morning, Grandpa."

Delilah appeared behind the counter gripping the handle of a coffee pot. "Hi there, Caleb. What's your pleasure?" She poured coffee into a mug and set the fresh brew in front of the old man.

"You shouldn't ask me such a thing in front of this here child." He winked at the waitress. "Instead, I'll have the special."

"Orange or tomato juice?"

"Just coffee, sugar." He winked at Delilah again.

Caleb Blanchard maintained a legendary reputation. "The old man can charm a she-crab out of its shell," Margaret remarked more than a few times.

Jessy nudged her grandpa. "Why didn't you bring Grandma Betty?"

The man tugged at his waistband, his broad shoulders resembling her father's frame. "Honey, your grandma's got too much energy for me. Damnation! Excuse my French. The old woman wakes me at the butt-crack of dawn and afore I can say, 'Where's my coffee,' she's giving me chores to do." He slurped a swig from a mug, his copper-colored eyes squinting at his grandchild. "By the time I left, she was getting ready to mop the kitchen floor and the clock on the wall hadn't even struck eight yet. She started giving me a list of honey-do's, one of which was to ready another flowerbed. I got the hell out of Dodge right quick."

Holding her grandpa's undivided attention, Jessy described her new friend. "And Rita May is real smart. She's a teenager."

"You don't say." Her grandpa sipped his coffee.

In no time, a tall, slender customer sprouting a neatly trimmed salt and pepper beard perched on the other side of Caleb, drawing him into a more stimulating dialogue. The older man generously offered his opinion. "No doubt, Leroy. Ain't no way the Brooklyn Dodgers should've beaten the Yanks. This World Series sure is disappointing."

* * *

Jessy entered the apartment careful not to slam the back door. She tip-toed up to her mother, who sat at the kitchen table. "How are you feeling today?" The child hugged her neck.

Engrossed in the Miami Herald, Margaret bit into a piece of toast. A smoldering cigarette teetered on the edge of a saucer not far from her arm. She petted her daughter's hair. "Not too bad. Did you enjoy your breakfast?"

"Of course. Grandpa Caleb sat next to me." Jessy darted into her room to retrieve her Mickey Mouse wristwatch, a gift from her grandparents on her tenth birthday. It was eleven o'clock when she buckled the band around her wrist and drifted into the living room. She waited on the sofa scanning the funny paper until eleven fifty-five. Jessy knew the ropes. Kids never asked permission too soon; one waited to the last possible minute. After all, you're doomed if parents have too much time to think on the request. "Mama, I'm going to the ballfield to meet my friends. We're going exploring. I promise I'll be home by dark."

Margaret blew on the match she'd used to light her cigarette. "Remember don't go past the railroad tracks or anywhere near the hobo camp. Nothing but evil can come from such a place."

"Yes, ma'am."

Once outside, Jessy trotted across Childers Street into the ballfield where a Junior Little League game was in full swing behind the fence—a pitcher on the mound, a batter and a catcher at the plate. Seven other players speckled the bases and the outfield, their chatter tossed around like the ball from player to player. She climbed the bleachers positioned left of home plate. Landing on the third row, Jessy checked the dilapidated scoreboard at the far end of the field. The Tigers had taken the lead over the Orioles.

Although the teenage boys in red and white uniforms had previously scored five runs, the scoreless team, which was up to bat, appeared ready to pounce. A boy in blue swaggered to the plate. On the top row of the bleachers, two overzealous preteen girls cheered on their hero. People in the stands hushed. The player swung at the first pitch. Strike one. On the next pitch, the lanky boy watched the ball zip past him. Strike two. He stood in position waiting for the next pitch. This time, he hammered a double into the outfield at the exact moment three blasts heralded the arrival of a freight train rolling into the depot behind the field. Applause from a small group of vocal fans rivaled the rattling boxcars and squealing brakes.

A figure galloping parallel to the fence caught Jessy's attention. Within minutes, a flush-faced Rita May scaled the bleachers.

"Sorry I'm late. Chores." Attempting to catch her breath, Rita May sat in front of Jessy.

"No big deal. Let's do something fun. I don't have to be home until dark."

"Me neither. I'm thirteen for heaven's sake." She stretched both legs onto the empty row in front of her. "Why don't we find a hideout or a clubhouse?"

"That's a great idea. A clubhouse just for us. No boys allowed. There's a spot behind the Church of God, an old grove of trees at the edge of the lot. No one uses it. There's also a pasture behind the cemetery or we can look around back of the Everglades Wonder Gardens. Ever been there?"

Rita May shook her head.

"Come on, I'll show you."

First Jessy, then Rita May, vaulted the bottom row of bleachers and tore out of the park. Due to Saturday's traffic, the girls hesitated at the corner of the Tamiami Trail. Rita May soon took the lead. "Before the day is over, I want to go down by the hobo jungle."

Jessy scuffed her sneakers against the road. "I'm not allowed to."

"Your parents treat you like a baby, don't they? I've been at least a hundred times. Anyway, what adults don't know won't hurt them. Right?"

"Yeah, I guess." Jessy's heartbeat quickened at the notion of disobeying her mother.

Heading north, the girls trekked past the Liles Hotel and the River Court cottages. The road narrowed at the bridge over the coffee-colored Imperial River. One at a time, cars waited their turn to cross from either side.

At the end of the bridge, the girls swung left toward the town's only real tourist attraction since the Shell Factory burned down in 1952. The graveled parking lot in front of the Everglades Wonder Gardens contained only one car—a shiny, green and white Chevrolet convertible, a Miami decal visible on its back bumper.

Two rockers sat on either side of the window on the Wonder Garden's narrow front porch. Jessy peered through the glass pane. "It costs fifty cents to see the exhibits and tour the entire place, but sometimes I get in for free."

"Why?"

"On Saturday nights, my father hauls the diner's leftovers to Mr. O'Brien who feeds the scraps to the reptiles. If Daddy lets me ride along, I get to watch the gators in the pit fight each other for food. It's crazy."

"Cool."

"It's gross, but yeah, way cool."

"It'll take me months to save fifty cents. Lynette only gives me a measly nickel once a week for babysitting and chores."

Jessy moseyed to the other side of the porch. "Come on. Let's go back where the woods meet the river." She swatted at the mosquito on her shoulder.

The girls hiked the depth of the fenced property. They slowed their gait when Rita May pointed to a speckled hawk circling above them. Suddenly, a loud *growl* startled the kids.

"Sounds like a wildcat." Jessy clamped onto Rita May's arm.

The redhead flinched at the younger girl's touch. "So what really lives in there?" She pointed to another high-paneled fence beyond the chain-linked one.

"All kinds of dangerous animals."

Rita May put her fists on her slender hips. "Give me a break. Nobody would let wild animals simply roam free. We're not in the jungles of Africa. Anyway, if that's really a wildcat, he could leap right over any fence." She lifted both hands over her head.

"Maybe so, but I do know there's a gigantic black bear named Old Slewfoot living there."

"No way."

"Uh huh. I saw him in a cage once. My dad told me Slewfoot starred in a Hollywood movie years ago."

"Ouch." Rita May clasped her foot. "I stepped on a piece of glass." She lifted a bloody heel.

"You're bleeding like a stuck pig. Come on. I'll bet Miss Mamie has a Band-Aid."

Jessy headed back to the Gardens' entrance with Rita May hobbling close behind. The injured girl rested in a rocker, while Jessy rambled inside expecting to see Miss Mamie, the elderly woman who worked the cash register at the attraction for the past twenty-five years. Instead, a fleshy-faced man with a protruding gut sat behind the counter. Jessy couldn't help but stare at the man's lopsided hairpiece.

"May I help you?" He reached up and centered the black toupee.

"Is Miss Mamie in the back or something?"

He sniffed. "No, I'm in charge today." His nasal tone indicated an immediate need to blow his nose.

"Uh, do you keep Band-Aids here? My friend injured her foot and the cut won't stop bleeding. She's right outside."

He sniffed. "Yeah, I've got a first aid kit just for such emergencies." He opened a nearby closet and snared a cigar box. "Let's see—bandages, tissues, and a bottle of mercurochrome. Go fetch your friend. I'll fix her up." He set the box on the glass cabinet stocked full of souvenirs and pamphlets.

"Thanks, Mister." Jessy held the front door open, while Rita May hobbled over the threshold.

The odd little man snorted, pulled a stained handkerchief from his pants pocket, and wiped his nostrils. He returned the handkerchief to its home and then patted the back of a nearby wooden chair. "Take a seat right over here." He grinned at Rita May. "My, my, you're a striking young lady with those magnificent curls. My name is Mr. Edson, but you can call me Oliver. And your name is?"

She scanned the tile floor and sat down. "Rita May."

Oliver Edson glanced at Jessy, but promptly reset his sights on Rita May who propped her foot against the display case. He stooped to observe the injury, his horn-rimmed glasses sliding to the end of his nose. "How old are you, Rita May?"

"Thirteen."

"Perfect."

Jessy wandered away from the examination leaving Mr. Edson attending to her friend's foot with his pudgy hands. She stooped to look through a glass cabinet at reptile relics and then browsed the wall of photographs depicting a hunter capturing wild animals and a few photos of a man airboating in the Everglades. As usual, she petted the tri-colored stuffed fox lurking in the corner.

"Try and sit still. I warn you. This might sting a teeny-weeny bit," said Oliver.

The comment drew Jessy back to check on her friend. Using a tissue, the man blotted the teenager's heel. He dribbled mercurochrome on her instep. When the reddish-orange liquid seeped into the gash, Rita May winced.

Oliver blew on the injury. "Now for a Band Aid." His mouth bowed into a bizarre smile baring tiny-yellowed teeth. "There you go." Supporting her ankle, he stroked her foot. "My, my, you are a beauty. I could just eat you up."

Rita May yanked her foot from his grasp and limped to the door.

"Y'all can visit the exhibits any time. Won't cost you a dime." He sniffed.

"Uh, thanks, Mr. Edson." Jessy rushed out the door finding her friend standing in the parking lot.

Rita May stared straight ahead. She cracked the knuckles on both hands. "Let's go."

"Why are you in such a hurry?"

"That man gives me the creeps."

"Yeah, he is a little weird…are you hungry? I'm dying of starvation."

"I guess so."

"If we go by the diner, Camilla might give us a snack." She checked her watch. "It's past two. The lunch crowd is almost gone."

The trek from the Everglades Wonder Gardens to the back of the diner took fifteen minutes. Jessy pointed to the grass behind the lot. "Wait over there." She disappeared into the restaurant reappearing five minutes later clutching two bottles of Coca Cola. Two packs of Lance crackers peeked from her shorts' pocket.

Settling on one of the picnic table benches, Rita May took a gulp of her Coke. "Didn't you mention something about a grove behind a church?"

Jessy stuck the entire peanut butter cracker inside her mouth. "Uh huh." Her mouth full, she mumbled, "Rows of trees…lots of bushes."

"Okay, we'll check it out, but first I'm going home to put on some shoes. I'll hurry back." Rita May set the empty Coke bottle on the table.

Jessy studied Rita May as the girl crossed the street. In spite of the slight hitch in her stride, the redhead sprinted the length of the ballfield. Her frame evaporated into thin air once she jumped the railroad tracks.

Crunching on a cracker, Jessy climbed onto the table, reclined on her back, and scanned the clear blue sky, the expanse similar to the color of her mama's favorite dress. A gust of wind rustled the lush pines at the back of the lot. October weather was close to perfect unless Mother Nature graced southern Florida with tropical storms, but at that moment, no menacing clouds lurked anywhere on the horizon. Jessy squirmed upright in time to see Rita May sprinting toward her.

The older girl scaled the table. "My foot hardly hurts anymore. By the way, from now on I'm wearing shoes whenever we go exploring." She slipped off a faded blue sneaker to check the bandage. "When we were at that Wonder Gardens place, did you notice Oliver Edson's beady little eyes, and did you catch a whiff of his breath? Like a dead fish. When he held my foot, he looked just like my baby sister does when she spies an ice cream cone." Rita May slid her sneaker back on. "I hope I never run into that creep again."

CHAPTER TEN:
AND THE CREEK DON'T RISE

Rita May let Jessy lead the way, hiking north for three blocks before altering their course. The short trek ended at the Bonita Springs Church of God. Behind the church sat an overgrown lot filled with age-old avocado trees, encircling rows of an exhausted orange grove. Jessy brushed away the debris off a patch of sand then sat down.

Rita May plopped down next to her. "If these flies would go away, this place might not be half bad." She swatted at a bothersome insect hissing near her face.

For an hour, the duo discussed club names, favorite movie stars, and a list of the cutest boys in school. The conversation eventually skewed personal when Rita May began counting the freckles littering her legs. "I hate these ugly spots. You're lucky that you don't have many." She rubs her legs up and down. "I was born in Elaine, Arkansas. What about you?"

"Miami."

The older girl gathered a few twigs at her feet. "But the last place I lived, um, was Hamilton County, Illinois. From there, we drove four days to get to Bonita Springs for Papa's new job. Did I tell you he's a foreman?" She crisscrossed the sticks constructing a triangular box on a bare patch of ground. "According to Davis, it won't be long before White people can't find any jobs. He says the Mexicans and the Negroes are stealing them all. He's lucky to have a friend in North Carolina who might find him an even better job where he'll have more responsibility, like a warehouse supervisor. If that happens, we'll have to move again."

Jessy scratched her legs. "Uh, do you like it here in Bonita?"

"Sure. At least, we got a decent size house. At our last place, all eight of us shared only one room. Families took turns at the water pump, and there were bugs everywhere." She kicked the structure she created.

Jessy squinted. "I don't understand. Why did you have to live there?"

Rita May twisted her face and scoffed. "You can't help it, can you? Dumb just leaks right outta your mouth." She collapsed backward in the grass. "Listen to me, stupid. We are poor. Fruit pickers barely earn sixty to seventy cents a box full. Papa does earn a nickel extra for every box his workers can pack, plus the ones he picks himself. It's more money than he usually makes. I guess it's nothing compared to rich folks like your daddy. My papa's got a lot of mouths to feed so he's always trying to make more money."

Jessy hugged her knees bringing both to her chest. She pulled a piece of Juicy Fruit from her pocket. "Here. Take half."

Rita May sat up and accepted the gum. Peeling off the wrapper, she broke the stick in half, shoved a piece in her mouth, and handed the rest back to Jessy. "We won't be here a long time. Probably leave in the fall." She stared at the ground as she dismissed the heaviness in her chest.

"You can't move away."

"There you go again. Grow up. Life ain't always the way you want it to be, but it can change in a second." Rita May glared at the younger girl. "That's why I don't depend on nobody else to make it better. It's all up to me."

Jessy lifted a squished orange off the ground. "When can I come to your house to meet your little sisters?"

"Mama doesn't like me to have visitors because our place smells funny. Lynette scrubs and scrubs, but the mildew sticks to the walls. Despite that, we've got it a little better than most pickers. Only ten families live in Mr. Sherwood's shacks. Other families live in tents at the camp in Estero where there ain't no privacy and the commodes stink. At least we got running water."

Jessy slapped at a horsefly resting on her elbow. "Our apartment is connected to the back of the diner. Mama hates it because it's too little. She says the customers make too much noise, and the smell of the food upsets her stomach." She rubbed where the insect bit her. "What are you gonna be when you grow up?"

"Me? I'm going to college, gonna find a good job, and a rich husband." She chuckled.

"Why are you laughing?"

"Papa told me he'd never let me leave home. He says mean things when he's drunk."

"Does he drink vodka?"

"Nah, beer mostly." She blinked at the sky.

Jessy stared at the sandy clay. "My mama *loves* vodka. She drinks so much, she makes herself sick." Unearthing a stick from a pile of leaves, she wrote her name in an undisturbed area of ground. "You're the only person I've told." Jessy smeared her name with sand.

Yeah, poor Jessy Blanchard. Her mama's a drunk. Big deal. Rita May rose to her feet dusting grass off her shorts. "Think of a name for our club. How about the Girl's Only Club?"

"The Mystery Club."

"Nah. We'll think of something better later. What do *you* want to be when you grow up, Miss Jessy Blanchard, who lives in a nice apartment, and gets whatever she wants?"

Jessy sprang to her feet. "I don't get everything I want. That's a silly thing to say." She twirled on her tiptoes. "I want to be a dancer and a movie star."

Rita May jumped up. Simulating an airplane, she spread her arms. "I might be a pilot and fly a jet plane around the world." She dipped downward angling her body toward the ground. "I'll never be an ordinary housewife like my mama and I'll never have any kids. *B o r i n g*. Boring."

"Yeah, boring."

"Tell me about your parents, Miss High and Mighty." Rita May knelt on the ground.

"Stop saying things like that." Jessy swallowed hard. "Eli, my dad, works at his diner. My mother, Margaret, lies on the sofa glued to the TV, smoking cigarettes and drinking screwdrivers."

"A screwdriver? Wait a minute. Are you kidding me? You got a TV?"

"Daddy bought us an RCA last year." Jessy popped her gum. "A screwdriver is simple to make. You pour vodka in a half-glass of orange juice and add ice."

Rita May squatted and dug into a clump of leaves until she found a patch of green. "I found a four-leaf clover. It's good luck." She stuck the notable weed of good fortune into her shirt pocket.

Jessy mimicked her friend by rummaging through the grass. "There's no more left." Her palm brushed over a rotting orange. "Yuk." She pitched the chunk across the yard.

Rita May applauded her friend's toss. "Wow, you throw like a boy. You should grow up to be the first lady baseball pitcher." She patted her pocket, insuring her luck stayed put. "On my sixteenth birthday, I'm gonna find me a job. Don't waitresses make lots of money? What about the ones at the diner? Are they nice and what do they look like?"

"We have two. Mary Louise doesn't talk much, but she's nice. Her hair is straight like mine, and is the color of root beer. She's got the cutest little daughter named Sally. My mama doesn't like her much. She pokes fun at Mary Louise behind her back, says she has the personality of roadkill and a figure as flat as an ironing board."

"Your mom is funny."

"No, she's not. She says mean things about people sometimes. Wish I had a Kleenex. I'm sticky."

"Isn't there another waitress?"

"Delilah. She's the pretty one who's always joking around. Customers love her. She has blonde wavy hair and wears dark red lipstick. She could be a movie star. Mama calls her a hussy."

Rita May giggled. "De-li-lah. Sounds like the name of a song."

Having spit on the palm of her hand, Jessy smeared the gooey substance on her shorts. "If you stop by the diner, I'll introduce you. Is a hussy somebody who is crazy?"

Rita May smirked. "I think you get more stupider by the minute. No. A hussy is a big flirt, and she don't care if the man she likes is married or not." She jumped on top of a protruding root.

"Hey, you're not limping at all anymore."

"I told you my foot is all well." Rita May shooed the flies buzzing around her head. "This place sucks. These nasty flies are eating me alive. Let's look somewhere else." She circled the tree and stopped. "I've got it. The name of our club will be the RJ Secret Club—R for Rita, J for Jessy."

* * *

Palm tree silhouettes dotted the western skyline as Rita May and Jessy tramped onto Front Street, the narrow road behind the baseball field. The street ended near the depot where the girls jumped over the tracks. Rita May shepherded Jessy into the woods to the edge of a gradual ravine. A campfire light flickered in a clearing below.

"Rats. The jungle's not crowded tonight." The teenager's eyes sparkled. "One time, I saw a guy playing a fiddle, and twenty or more tramps drinking booze and dancing around the fire having a high ole time."

Jessy ducked behind a bush, her light brown eyes as round as Camilla's biscuits. "How many times have you been down there?"

"Like too many to count. Our shack is a stone's throw on the other side of the woods. Sometimes, me and Gregory sneak out late at night and spy on the hobos." Rita May nudged Jessy. "They won't see you. It's okay."

"It'll be dark soon. I should probably go. Anyway, won't we get in trouble? Hobos might not like it if we just barge in on them."

"You're such a baby and a scaredy cat. It's not their property, but you best keep your voice down, just to be on the safe side." Rita May chuckled to herself.

The girls carefully crept down into the ravine toward the campsite until the ground leveled off and then hid behind a huge hibiscus bush. Four men circled a thriving fire, the men's faces exposed by the glow. Moving in a constant side-to-side motion, one man supped from a bowl balanced on his lap, scooping up his food with a wooden spoon. An older fellow lay on the ground, a threadbare jacket shrouding his shoulders. The other two crouched in the dirt. They stared into the flames.

"I'm kinda scared." Jessy reached for Rita May's hand.

The older girl shoved the girl's hand away. "Knock it off. If we're gonna stay friends, you've got to grow up some. I ain't your mama." She had enough clingy siblings at home.

A whistle broadcasted a train's arrival, the one that coasted through Bonita Springs around seven o'clock every day. The monster's brakes squealed as it drew closer to the depot, the noise distracting a nearby flock of gulls.

"Daddy says hobos are sometimes just men down on their luck." Jessy sucked on the clump of hair she'd pulled from behind her ear.

"He's right. A lot of bums or hobos used to be broke farmers, but then there's the deadbeats, the lazy ones who won't work."

Jessy whispered, "It's getting dark. I've gotta go. See you Monday."

"Whatever." Rita May shrugged. *She's such a wimp.*

* * *

The moonlight aided Rita May's short journey down the dirt road. When she neared the shack, she slowed her pace and kicked an empty tin can off the path. "I'm sick of babysitting those brats." She dawdled a moment in front of the place she temporarily called home. Through the front window, she spied her mama balancing a toddler on her hip.

The teenager sighed and opened the door. She sidled up to Lynette who stood against the stove, stirring the contents of an iron skillet.

"Where in God's green earth have you been, girl? Here, take this baby."

Rita May held open her arms for Marilyn. She lifted the toddler up and twirled around until the child laughed aloud. "Me and my friend, Jessy, sort of lost track of time. Sorry." She posed in a kitchen chair jostling the baby on her knees. "Something smells good."

"Beef and potato hash. Your daddy won a few dollars shooting dice. Brought us home almost half a cow."

"Where is he now?"

"He polished off a sandwich, and before I could turn around, he high-tailed it off to some God-awful place." Lynette dried her hands on a rag. "He'll walk through the door soon. Lord willing and the creek don't rise."

Cursing Davis in a whisper, Rita May chewed the inside of her cheek. She knew firsthand where her papa snuck off to most nights.

Lynette unconsciously patted the ponytail sitting high on her head. Auburn tendrils framed her face. "Never you mind. I need your help. The boys are about finished bathing in the tub in back. You go on and clean up the girls. Those young'uns have been playing in the dirt the better part of the day. There's warm water on the stove."

"Yes ma'am."

* * *

By nine o'clock, her brothers lay sleeping on a pallet in the front room, the girls on a mattress next to them. Nearby, floorboards creaked in a soft, repetitive rhythm. Rita May lingered at the threshold of her parents' room. Sitting with her eyes shut, Lynette cradled the baby in her arms in a rocker handed down from one generation of the McAfee family to the next. Rita May studied her mama. *She's the most beautiful woman I've ever seen.*

The teenager clutched a broom handle. Using her body to prop open the front door, she swept sand and dust onto the narrow front stoop. The last time Rita May checked, the clock said ten twenty-four. There was no sign of her papa.

Back inside, she waited in a chair beside the wooden dining table, her chin on top of folded arms. At the first inkling of Lynette's subtle snore, she snuck out the door. Of the two beer joints in Bonita Springs, Davis McAfee preferred Ike's Bar. The rundown dive accepted anyone who could pay a quarter for a watery beer. On the other hand, the Blue Note Club, a slightly classier establishment where the beer cost a penny more a pint, catered only to white folks. Both honkytonks sat a half-a-mile apart on Morgan Road between West Terry Street and the sandy banks of the Imperial River.

By this time, the shrunken moon, hung on the other side of the sky. Though its brilliance had faded, the moon still furnished Rita May with enough light to see where she was going. The racket provided by the frogs, katydid's, and other unseen creatures of the night kept the redhead alert. When she rounded the corner near the Blue Note, she hesitated when she heard a bluesy piano tune. Seductive and mellow, the notes drifted through the trees. Next to a lone lightbulb, a sign advertising Cold Beer swung above the door. Two men and a dark-haired woman huddled against a black Oldsmobile parked on the side of the building. Rita May ducked behind a tree.

Just then, a stocky man burst through the exit. He stumbled at first, but managed to compose himself, his pasty face outlined by the lightbulb's glow. Rita May recognized the devil at once.

Deputy Sheriff Billy Grizzle, in full Lee County uniform, waddled onto the strip of dirt road. Flanking the officer, a curvy, butter blonde dressed in a crimson halter dress stepped into the light. The deputy stole her hand and pinned her against the car door, kissing her mouth.

He pulled away. "Okay, okay. Run along now, Sylvia. Can you catch a ride? I'm late and Pinky will have my ass if I don't get on home." Billy climbed inside his official vehicle leaving his date standing next to the car.

The woman scrambled to the passenger's side and knocked on the window. "No. You need to give me a ride. Open the door."

"All right. But if I take you home, I can't come inside tonight." He leaned over and opened the door. "Anyway, ain't your kid at home?"

"I thought I told you. He's spending the night at a friend's house. I'm free as a seagull. Don't you want to see how I look in that red negligee you bought me?" She squirmed into the car, and the pair blurred together in the dark.

When the patrol car passed by, Rita May scowled at the couple inside. *I hope his wife finds out.* The teenager possessed a valid reason for hating Billy Grizzle. The first time the McAfee family stepped foot into downtown Bonita Springs, the officer belittled Davis and Lynette in front of their kids and a handful of customers at Lawhon's Meat and Grocery. When Davis ignored the police officer, Billy let him know where he stood on the subject of newcomers. "This is my town, and I keep the peace in this part of the county. You people really don't belong. As long as you're here though, you better stay out of trouble. I'll be watching you." Once Davis paid for Lynette's groceries, the family left without incident.

.The teenager continued down the road hiding in the shadows until she reached Ike's Bar, where the honky-tonk music enticed her. Closing in on rock-throwing distance, she hunkered down. Two men loitered next to the entrance. Taking a chance, Rita May trod into view.

The lanky one spied her first. "Isn't it a little late for you to be out, young lady?" He waved a lit cigar in the air.

She coughed inhaling a whiff of the man's smoke trail. "Um, I'm looking for Davis McAfee. Have you seen him?"

"Nope, not for a while," said the puny one. "He might've gone on home."

Her heart beat like a jackhammer in her chest. "No, he didn't." She pointed to the side of the building. "That's his car right there. Can you go fetch my papa? If you can't, then I'll just have to go inside and get him myself."

"No, no. You stay put. I'll go."

When the shorter man opened the door into the bar, the *clinking* of piano keys grew louder. A soulful tune ricocheted through the water oaks that hovered over Ike's Bar. Rita May cracked her knuckles while she waited.

Soon Davis McAfee erupted from the bar. He faced his daughter, his deep-set eyes showing signs of fear, his face the color of the Coca Cola sign nailed to the side of Ike's front window. "What's the matter? Is there an emergency? Who's ill?"

Rita May muttered an icy retort. "Everyone is fine. I just wondered when you were coming home."

His demeanor changed. Widening his stance, Davis straightened to his six-feet-four frame. "Ain't none of your business, gal. Needed to unwind a bit. It's been a long, hard day." Digging into his pocket, he withdrew a handkerchief and wiped the sweat from his forehead. "Go on now. I'll be home when I'm good and ready."

Her mission accomplished, Rita May did an about-face. She strolled back down the dirt road marveling at the millions of stars overhead and allowing them and what was left of the moon to chaperone her the rest of the way home. Hesitating at the crossroads, the row of shacks to her left, Rita May scanned the sky. "So, God, if there is a heaven and you're in charge of the big picture up there, I'd appreciate some help down here. You've gotta fix things. It ain't fair that Jessy lives in a real home and gets to watch TV, and I don't. I want my family to live in a big house where I can have my own room." Rita May marched up to her door. "But since I've seen a lot of poor folks pray and get nothing out of it, you go on about your other business. I'll just figure it out all by myself."

CHAPTER ELEVEN:
PRETTY AS A PEACH

Jessy sprinted all the way home. Out of breath, she leaned against the green door and removed her sneakers before tiptoeing into the apartment. She was careful not to rouse Margaret who lay asleep on the couch. Once in her room, she shut the door, flicked on the lamp near her bedside, and spent the next hour absorbed in one of Nancy Drew's harrowing adventures.

A soft knock brought her back to the present. Eli cracked open the door and whispered, "Wash your hands and I'll fix you a sandwich."

Jessy bookmarked page sixty-two, tucked her book under a pillow, and shadowed her dad into the kitchen where she washed her hands. Poised in a chair at the table, she scrutinized Eli's preparation of a peanut butter and grape jelly sandwich. He set his creation on a paper towel.

"Thanks, Daddy. Um, why did Mama go to bed so early?"

He straddled the chair next to her. "I guess she didn't feel too well. How was *your* day?"

She gulped from a glass of cold milk. "Me and Rita May searched everywhere for a clubhouse."

"Did you find one?"

"No luck yet." She used her tongue to unstick peanut butter from the roof of her mouth. Another sip of milk left a mustache on her upper lip.

"I'm sure you'll find something soon, exactly what you're looking for." He yawned. "It's Saturday night, and you know what that means."

"You've gotta make a run to the Wonder Gardens. Can…may I come?"

He nodded as she crammed the last bite in her mouth. "Why doesn't Miss Mamie work there anymore?"

"She doesn't?"

"Nope. We stopped by today. A man named Oliver Edson was the only one there."

Eli pushed himself from the table, his long legs similar to the gangly frog Skip accidently stepped on one day last spring. Jessy's dad rubbed the back of his neck. "Miss Mamie is probably part time now. She's no spring chicken, you know. I've seen Mr. Edson at the diner once or twice. Was he polite to you?"

Jessy took her napkin and wiped her mouth. "Yes, but he's weird."

"What do you mean?" Eli frowned, his brows almost obscuring his eyes.

"Rita May cut her heel and Mr. Edson fixed her up with mercurochrome and a Band-Aid. Afterwards, he rubbed her foot with his eyes shut and kinda smiled. He acted like one of those rednecks in the diner who flirts with Delilah. He kept telling Rita May how pretty she was and all."

Eli gently cupped Jessy's chin in his hand. "Listen to me. From now on, you're to stay away from the Wonder Gardens unless we're together. Got it?" He kissed her on the cheek.

"Yes, Daddy." She swiped a napkin across her mouth once more eliminating any trace of a milky residue.

"Go get your sneakers. I'll meet you in the back in five minutes. Deputy Grizzle is lending a hand tonight. The slop can is full to the brim."

He hustled into the diner. "Hey, Billy. When did you get here? Uh, do you know that new guy in town, Oliver Edson?" Eli's voice bounced off the walls of the empty restaurant.

"Yeah. I know him. He might have only one oar in the water, but he's right friendly. Volunteered to help me do a bit of community work. Why do you ask?"

Jessy set her plate in the sink. Grabbing her sneakers, she hurried outside in time to observe her father and the officer wrestle the heavy can onto the truck bed. Eli offered his hand to Billy. "Thanks for the help."

The deputy sheriff shook her father's palm. "No problem. It's how we do things in this here town. I scratch your back and so forth." Billy grinned, exposing his famous gold tooth. Everybody in town knew the story. Pinky, Billy's wife, knocked his eyetooth loose during a family squabble. The way the deputy told it, she apologized by paying a Miami dentist to plug the gap with a solid gold replacement. Pinky promised never to strike him again.

Because Jessy, and more than likely everyone else in town, knew Pinky Grizzle couldn't hurt a fly, Eli's version of events made more sense. "Billy lost his tooth in Fort Myers in a bar fight. When both men sobered up and the other guy apologized, he offered Billy a bribe to let him off the hook. The deputy took the cash and bought himself a gold tooth."

Deputy Grizzle homed in on Jessy. "How are you tonight, little lady?"

"Fine." She climbed into the cab of the truck and put on her shoes. When Billy turned his head, Jessy stuck out her tongue at him. Fortunately, no one saw the indiscretion.

"So, Elijah, can I depend on you or not?" Billy's query hung in the night air.

Eli snapped back. "Stop bugging me. I'm drowning in work. I lost another dishwasher today."

"Most folks manage to do their part. Just saying."

"You heard me."

Billy smacked his gum. "All right, all right. I'll switch subjects. By the by, I have a favor to ask. Can I borrow your truck this Saturday night?"

"Nope."

"Come on, man."

Jessy's father locked the tailgate in place. "Why do you need my truck?"

"It's private. Don't tell no one but I'm seeing Sylvia Goodman on the sly."

Eli smirked. "Private? Billy, every warm body in Bonita Springs has heard about you and Sylvia. Everybody except Pinky."

Billy stiffened. "I guess I need to be more discreet." He crossed his arms at his belly, which folded over his waistband like the crust on the edges of Camilla's chicken potpie. "Anyway, I'm taking Sylvia to Naples for the weekend. Pinky thinks I've been asked to give a speech at a law enforcement conference in Miami." His snicker ended in a snort. "Hell, the woman is dumber than a sack of cement. She'll believe anything I tell her."

"Can't, Billy. I have to take the slop to the Gardens like I do every Saturday night."

"Meet me at the Blue Note at ten-thirty. I'll stick the patrol car around back and then take you home. You'll have the pickup back by Sunday morning. Deal?"

"Okay, but just this once." Jessy's father stepped to the driver's side of the truck.

"Thanks, old friend." Billy walked away and climbed into the patrol car.

Inside the cab of the truck, Eli switched on the ignition. He drove down Highway 41, the identical route the girls took earlier that day. Approaching the Everglades Wonder Gardens, he deviated onto a dirt road that dead-ended at the gate. The single streetlamp's glare directed them to the delivery entrance. Eli swerved the truck, easily backing into the opening. Shifting into gear, he honked the horn.

Gil O'Brien appeared from a nearby building and tore across the lot jangling a loaded keyring. The long-limbed night manager unlocked the gate. When he spread the enormous chain-link doors apart, he stumbled causing a shiny metal flask to fall from his pocket. Gil brushed himself off and retrieved the whisky.

Eli killed the engine. Pulling on work gloves, he leapt from the truck. "Jess, stay put until I call you."

On her knees and doubled over the driver's side window, Jessy observed the men transfer the trashcan from the truck to the pavement and finally out of sight. She tapped her fingers on the Chevy's side door while combing the heavens for any sign of the Big Dipper. A howl from inside the property spooked her. *I'm not scared. I'm not scared.* With her eyes shut, she said a prayer, just in case.

Within minutes, her father scuffed across the gravel to the truck. "You ready?" He muscled open the heavy door.

"You bet." Jessy jumped to the ground. Walking next to Eli, her heart fluttered. She'd witnessed this spectacle several times; she knew what to expect.

Primed to take-in the experience, the child stretched on tiptoes at the four-foot concrete wall. On top of the structure, another two to three feet of interwoven wire safeguarded onlookers who might lose their balance. In the pit below, ravenous gators, too many to count, feasted on Aunt Prissy's tasty leftovers. Mesmerized, Jessy clutched her father's hand. "I could stay here all night. Skip couldn't do this; neither could Rita May. I'm the brave one."

Eli squeezed her hand.

Gil appeared from behind a door adjacent to the pit and ambled over to Eli and Jessy. Removing his ball cap, the man scratched the top of his head where a slight clump of greasy hair remained. Twice, in between chomps of what appeared to be a hunk of chewing tobacco, he opened his mouth, spat on the ground, and attempted yet failed to converse. At last, he uttered, "Uh, how's tricks, Elijah, I mean, at the diner?"

Dropping Jessy's hand, her father stepped back from the fence. "Running smooth as clockwork. You ought to stop by more often."

Gil, who usually spoke in an easy manner, strained to raise his voice above the chaos resonating from the pit. "Yep. I really should. Uh, tell me, how's that good-looking waitress? The yeller-haired one, uh, Delilah?"

"She's fine." Eli's tone sobered. "I suppose."

"I've been meaning to ask her to the picture show. She's as pretty as a peach, that one. She's got gumption, too." Gil's grin broadened enough to reveal both rows of tobacco-stained teeth. "I like girls with lots of gumption. Yes, I do."

Eli straightened his posture. "Yep, she's a looker all right. Hear tell she's got a boyfriend though. Um, lives in Naples."

Jessy rotated toward her dad's voice. *Delilah has a boyfriend.* Her stare locked in on Eli.

"Ah, now that's a pity. A real pity." Gil turned his head, spat a wad right on the concrete, and then reached into his pocket for a pouch labeled Red Man. "Hell, I'm always a day late and a dollar short."

"Thanks a lot, Gil. We've got to get on home. Remember what I said. You come on by the diner. Coffee's on the house."

"Will do, Elijah. The gators and crocs thank you. They sure do love your table scraps."

Father and daughter climbed back in the pickup. He wheeled through the gate opening while Jessy knelt on the seat watching Gil O'Brien through the back window. "Daddy, does Mr. O'Brien like his job?"

Gil pulled the gate together and shut off the floodlights. He waved at the truck, his obscure figure standing behind the chain link fence.

Eli swerved onto the main road. "I have no idea."

* * *

Jessy's dad sat on the edge of her bed. "Night, Baby Girl. Thanks for coming with me tonight."

"You're welcome. I overheard you and Mr. O'Brien talking about Delilah. I didn't know she had a boyfriend. What's his name?"

"Don't know him." Eli's gaze strayed from her scrutiny.

"But you told Mr. O'Brien that he lived in Naples."

"It's not polite to eavesdrop. Night, Jess." He switched off the light.

CHAPTER TWELVE:
BARKIN' UP THE WRONG TREE

During the month of October, Miss Rydell's fifth and sixth graders used their bi-weekly hour of art class to construct paper cutouts of bats, pumpkins, witches, and ghosts, producing a classroom drenched in black and orange. Crepe paper streamers dangled from the ceiling, and the teacher thumbtacked a life-sized picture of a disagreeable witch to the outside of the classroom door.

At ten minutes until three on the twenty-eighth of the month, Miss Rydell made an announcement. "There's no homework this weekend, but you must bring a yummy treat to school on Monday. We'll share our goodies at the Halloween party, which will begin at exactly two o'clock. I promise we'll have a spooky good time."

On the journey home, the kids couldn't stop yakking about the party. All conversation ceased though as they strolled onto the baseball field. Skip saw him first. The rumpled man sat on the ground slumped against the fence behind home plate, his hat concealing most of his face. He made no sound or movement.

Clark bent over to pick up a stick. "Maybe he's dead. I'll poke him and see."

Recalling her mother's cautionary words, Jessy whispered, "You better not. If he's asleep, you'll wake him. He might be dangerous."

The man's foot wiggled. The shocked children shuffled backward. The vagrant then extended his arms above his head and stretched. Gazing into the sun, he lifted the brim of his hat and opened one eye then the other. "Uh, can I help you kids?"

Rita May inched closer. "Just checking to see if you were breathing. You looked deader than a mackerel."

The hobo chuckled. "No, missy, I ain't dead. I's hongry and wore out is all."

Jessy took a step forward. "My daddy owns the diner over there. I'm sure he'll give you something to eat, if we ask him."

"You're mighty kind." The bear of a man clung to the fence struggling to gain his footing. His dark skin shined like highway asphalt on a rainy day, and his cheery expression revealed two chipped teeth on top with several vacant spaces throughout. A straggly salt and pepper mustache masked his top lip and tufts of hair protruded from under a shabby hat.

"Don't go anywhere. I'll be right back." Jessy sprinted from the ball field. Skip followed, leaving Rita May and her brothers squatting at the fence, not quite ten feet from the vagrant.

At the Childers Street curb, Jessy stopped to check both ways. She overheard the hobo say, "I answer to Mundy Mike or Mundy or plain Mike."

Skip arrived at the diner first and heaved himself onto the edge of the planter near the front door. "Don't take forever."

Jessy rushed inside and sauntered past the counter, her cheeks pink from the heat. Mary Louise, the lone person in the service area, sat slouched at a center table meticulously filling tabletop shakers from a large container of Morton's Salt.

The waitress smiled at the girl. "Hey there."

"I have sort of an emergency. Is Daddy in the back?"

"Yep. I'll fetch him." Mary Louise abandoned her task and barged through the swinging doors into the kitchen.

Before the panels stopped flapping, Eli came through and sidled up to his daughter. "An emergency, huh?"

"Kind of. May I have a couple of leftover biscuits and a Coke? Please."

He tilted his head to one side. "Starving again? Are your friends starving, too?"

"No, it's not for me or my friends."

"Jessy?"

"I can't tell you. Mama won't approve."

He stooped to her level. "Jessy."

"Promise you won't tell her." She swallowed. "There's a hobo at the ballfield who's weak and hungry. He can hardly stand. In fact, at first we thought he was dead."

Eli's eyebrows scrunched together. "I see."

"His name is Mundy Mike. He's a big old colored man. He means no harm. It's likely he's simply down on his luck."

"Send him to the backdoor. I'll fix him up."

"Terrific." Leaving her lunch box and library book on the soda fountain counter, she flew out the exit, almost running into Skip. "Daddy's gonna feed him."

His eyes widened. "But Mundy's colored."

"So what if he is?" She ran ahead of Skip and crossed the street.

Rita May and her brothers gathered on the top row of the bleachers. "Did you get him a biscuit?" she asked.

"Daddy's fixing him a whole meal." Jessy pivoted toward the soft-spoken giant of a man. "Mr. Mundy, if you follow me, my father's gonna feed you." She glanced to her right. "Are you coming, Rita May?"

"Nah. We're running late. Bye, Mr. Mundy." Rita May hopped down the bleachers until she reached ground level. She tore across the field catching up with Gregory and Clark.

Mundy squinted at Jessy. "What's *your* name, little lady?"

"Jessy Blanchard. He's Skip Goodman."

The boy by her side stuck out his chin. "I'm her boyfriend."

She gritted her teeth. "No, he's not." The two kids and the hobo dawdled at the street corner.

Skip tugged at the man's sleeve. "Um, do you ride the freight trains?"

Mundy ran a finger over his mustache. "I do. In fact, I used to ride them rails twice a month. Not as much anymore. Mostly I'd catch a cow crate now and then. See, I twisted my leg a couple of months back. It's troublesome when I try to hop on and off, especially when the train is on the fly." He stooped to tie his right shoe at the curb, the one with the frayed hole in the toe of the leather. "See, I's got these buddies—Pleasin' Pete and Gator Breath."

Skip giggled. "Gator Breath? That's a funny name."

"Hush, Skip. So, Mr. Mundy, where are your friends now?"

"Haven't seen them boys for a week or two, but they'll turn up sooner or later."

The man fascinated her. "Do your friends take care of you?"

Mundy bristled. "Nah, don't need them to. I do mighty fine on my own."

The afternoon sun weighed on the threesome cutting across Aunt Prissy's back lot. Mundy shed his hat and yanked a sun-bleached red bandana from his shirt pocket. His face glistened; he dabbed his brow. "Is there water nearby? I'd like to clean up a bit, if you don't mind."

Skip gestured to his right. "Follow me."

The kids showed Mundy the faucet protruding from the side of the building. He rinsed his hands at the spigot. The tramp paused to take a drink. Then he squatted close to the ground, and the cool water splashed his head. On the way back, he used his bandana to dry his face.

Jessy headed to the backdoor of the diner. "Skip, you and Mundy wait here." She charged through the storeroom into the sweltering kitchen where a window fan whirred at high speed. The device blew warm air at Eli as he leaned over a wooden table cutting wide ribbons out of flattened pieces of dough. "Daddy, he's waiting out back."

Eli turned toward the cook who stood at the stove. "Camilla, will you finish these dumplings for me, please?" Jessy's dad set the knife on the table.

"Sure, Mr. Eli." The woman toddled from the other side of the room. "Hello, little one. You home from school already?"

"Yes, ma'am. I brought Mundy Mike with me. He's starving to death."

"Is he now?" Camilla's eyes twinkled when she spoke. "Who is this fella you've done brought home? A new boyfriend?"

"Gosh, no. Mundy Mike is a hobo. We found him asleep over by the ballfield fence. We thought he was dead."

The woman's response came from behind pursed lips. "Humph." Her head bobbed. "Let me steal a peek at this here hobo man."

Eli wiped his hands on his apron as he trailed Jessy through the storeroom, Camilla at his heels.

Jessy stepped outside first. "Daddy, this is Mundy Mike."

Eli let the screened door shut behind him. He extended his hand. "My name is Eli Blanchard. I understand you're hungry."

Camilla seized the edge of the screened door cementing her feet to the threshold. With one fist resting on her hip, her black eyes glared at the unkempt man.

Mundy arose and removed his hat. His chin rested on his chest. "Yessir." He shook Eli's hand. "I'm grateful for any food you can spare." The man bowed at the sight of Camilla. "How do, ma'am."

"Humph." The cook let go of the door. "Well I never…no count… old fool." Shaking her head, she mumbled another inaudible phrase and trudged back into the storeroom.

Eli managed a smile. "Take a seat out there at the picnic table, and I'll bring you a plate. Jessy, you and Skip thirsty? How about a root beer?"

"Yes, thank you."

"Yes sir, Mr. Blanchard."

Eli zipped back inside. Mundy and Skip followed Jessy to the shady spot behind the diner's parking lot where Camilla and the waitresses often took their breaks. The kids and the ragged man chatted until a police vehicle drove by on Childers Street. The Lee County Sheriff's Department patrol car, bearing green and gold stripes, came to screeching halt at the corner.

"Rats," said Skip. "It's Deputy Grizzle. He'll spoil everything."

No one liked Billy Grizzle, much less respected him. A regular at Aunt Prissy's Kitchen, he maintained a reputation for bragging about his meager attempts at preserving the peace in Lee County. Most people merely tolerated the man. In spite of everything, he still represented the law.

Emerging from his parked cruiser, the pudgy officer adjusted his waistband and plodded into the grass. He slowed his gait at the picnic table. "Haven't you brats got better things to do than hang out with him?" Billy nodded at the hobo.

Jessy clenched her jaw. "We're having a snack with our new friend, Mundy Mike."

The vagrant tipped his fedora at the deputy sheriff.

A toothpick dangled from the corner of Billy's mouth. When he *clicked* his tongue, Jessy anticipated the forthcoming lecture. With hands fisted on his hips, he spouted an unwelcomed opinion. "You shouldn't be socializing with his kind, and you're old enough to know better." The sound of a slamming door cut the deputy's sermon short.

Eli sauntered out of the diner. "Billy, leave the kids alone."

The officer bounded toward Jessy's dad, meeting him halfway across the lot. "Elijah, tell me what in the Sam Hill those kids are doing? If the bum's causing trouble, I'll run him off." Billy pinched his toothpick and began an archaeological dig between two bottom teeth.

Eli slowed his pace. "No, you won't. You're barking up the wrong tree. The man is hungry. He'll eat and be on his way." He continued walking toward the picnic table.

The deputy headed for the steps at the back of the diner. "We'll see, but I think I'll stick around a spell, if it's okay."

"Suit yourself." When Jessy's father reached his destination, he set a feast in front of the famished man and handed cold drinks to the children. "Eat up, Mr. Mundy." Eli nodded and headed back.

The seasoned hobo, who looked to be in his fifties, opened his mouth, ogling the plate of food. Pure delight spread across his face. He yanked off his crumpled hat, inhaling the bouquet of the hot meal—stewed chicken and dumplings, green beans, a generous scoop of creamed potatoes, and two of Camilla's supersized biscuits.

Mundy bowed his head. "Dear Lord, thank you for Mr. Eli and these young'uns who's giving me a hot and a flop. Amen." He lifted a buttered biscuit and dunked the bit of heaven into the gravy. Savoring a mouthful, the man curtained his eyes.

Jessy studied Mundy's every move. In between sips of root beer, she satisfied her curiosity. "A hot and a flop?"

"A hot meal and a place to lay my head."

"Oh, and is your name Monday, like the first day of the week?"

He patted his mouth using the cloth napkin Eli furnished. "Yup, but it's spelled different. I got born on a Monday. My poor mama couldn't write good so she spelled my name M U N D Y. Mike's my other name." He scooped another forkful of potatoes into his mouth.

Skip slurped his drink. "Do you have a last name?"

"Patterson. Mike Mundy Limba Patterson is my full Christian name."

"Limba? Another weird name."

Jessy glared at the boy. "Pay no mind to him, Mr. Mundy. He's a stupid kid."

"Am not."

"Are too."

Mundy devoured every morsel on the plate, but wrapped the last biscuit in his bandana. Tucking the treasure inside his shirt pocket, he sighed. "Lordy me, I'm as full as a tick. If it's not bothering nobody, I'm gonna set a spell." He dipped to the ground and buckled against a tree trunk employing his hat to conceal his face.

Skip handled trash duty while Jessy carted the tray of dishes to the diner's backdoor where Eli and Billy stood face to face involved in a serious discussion. She waited until the policeman stopped babbling. "Here, Daddy. Mundy's taking a nap in the grass."

Eli opened the screen door. Holding it ajar with one hand, he seized the tray with the other. "Billy, if you want to take this further, why don't you come on by tonight? The special is country-fried steak."

"Maybe I will, Elijah." Billy spun around and gazed in the direction of the sleeping man lying in the shade. In a futile attempt to pull his pants up over his belly, the deputy yanked on his waistband before he took off across the parking lot.

Skip dumped the trash in the outside can, then sat next to Jessy on the top step. "I'll bet you money Grizzle's gonna make Mundy leave. Wait and see."

"He better not hurt him." She chewed on her lip.

The deputy sauntered up to the hobo. He nudged the man's leg applying pressure with the toe of his boot. Mundy Mike lifted the edge of his hat. Billy leaned over, barking vague profanities at him. Mike slowly got to his feet. He snatched off his hat, but the fedora slipped from his hands, landing on the ground. Deputy Grizzle promptly squashed the hat under the heel of his boot.

Heat rose in Jessy's face. "Grizzle is such a jerk."

Skip went mute, his mouth hung open like a hooked red snapper.

Mundy's posture braced, yet his focus on the hat didn't waver until Billy removed his foot. The deputy poked the hobo in the chest. "Are you hearing me, boy?"

Mundy Mike nodded before he bent over and hooked the brim of his property with his index finger. Not uttering a word, he slapped the hat against his thigh shaking off any dirt. He squatted in the grass, resuming his position next to the tree. The hobo repositioned the fedora to protect his face from the sun.

The overweight Lee County Deputy muttered to himself as he clomped toward the diner, pausing in front of the children to continue his vocal condemnation of Mundy Mike. Jessy elbowed Skip's side. She stared at the front of Billy's uniform where the fate of a middle button lay in jeopardy. When the deputy exhaled, his beer gut ballooned, straining the lone thread that kept the button in place. The kids hid their faces. Behind their hands, the pair snickered at the prospect of an impending disaster.

The deputy snarled. "What's so funny?"

"Nothing," said Skip, trying hard not to burst into laughter.

Billy's meaty paw landed on the boy's sandy blonde hair. "By the way, kid, how's your pretty mama? I haven't seen her lately."

"She's busy working." Skip's mood suddenly changed along with his posture.

"Son, you be sure to tell her that Billy says hello. Won't you?" The rotund man withdrew his hand, rubbed his belly then belched.

Skip balled his fists before he spoke again. "Yeah, sure." His blue eyes shot daggers at the deputy. "That ain't never gonna happen," he said under his breath.

The officer then leaned close to Jessy, his nasty breath grazing her cheek. She scooted away, but Billy seized her wrist. "Jessy Blanchard, you think you're such a smart girl, don't you? But even smart girls have to obey the rules." The shrunken toothpick poked out between his fleshy lips.

Jessy wrenched free, Billy's sneer reminding her of a villainous comic book character. The deputy lacked only one thing—the swarthy mustache.

Crackling static from the patrol car's two-way radio diverted Billy's attention. "Deputy, Deputy Grizzle. Armed robbery on McGregor Boulevard, Fort Myers. Officer needs assistance. I repeat. Needs assistance...crowd control." He hurried to his vehicle, ducked inside, and gunned the engine.

Hunched together, the kids giggled at Billy's extra wide U-turn effort, the patrol car's tires shrieking as they scraped the curb. Lights flashing and the siren wailing, the car finally swerved into traffic on the highway.

"I hate Deputy Grizzle." Jessy folded her arms on top of her knees.

"Me, too, and he had to go and touch me. I bet I got cooties in my hair. Yuk!" Skip stuck his finger in his mouth and pretended to gag. "Everybody in the county is afraid of him, but not me."

"Me neither." Jessy suddenly broke into a singsong rhyme. "Grizzle, Grizzle is a blubber fat fizzle. His dog eats steak but Billy eats kibble. The man can't shoot and he ain't smart. All he can do is belch and fart."

The boy joined in. "He can't run fast, he can't run far, he can't even squeeze into his car. Grizzle, Grizzle is a blubber fat fizzle." The kids laughed until their sides ached and their eyes watered.

Skip wiped his face on his shirttail. "Where'd you learn that song again?"

"Susie Turner, a seventh grader last year, made it up right after the deputy gave that dumb safety presentation to the whole school." Jessy straightened her legs. "I heard a priest at St. Anne's say you're not supposed to hate people. It's a mortal sin, and you'll go to hell. You're just supposed to hate their sinful deeds, but I'm sure if the priest ever met Billy Grizzle, he'd agree with me. Grizzle is a horrible man. I don't see why some folks think he's such a big scary deal. I don't care if he is a deputy sheriff."

Skip yawned. "Look, Jess. Mundy Mike is still asleep in the grass. Whoa, it'll be dark in a minute. I better run on home."

Jessy never saw it coming. Skip leaned in and laid a sloppy kiss on her mouth. "Gotcha."

"Oooh, that's disgusting. I warned you, Skipper Goodman." She punched him below his left shoulder.

"Ouch." Frowning, Skip squeezed his bicep.

She wiped saliva off her mouth. "Can't we just be friends who don't ever kiss?"

"I guess, but I think one day you'll want to kiss me. But by then, I'll have lots of girlfriends, and I'll be too busy kissing them to give you the time of day." He flipped his bangs off his eyebrows and jogged into the street.

Jessy counted several older boys as potential boyfriend material. Regrettably, poor Skipper Goodman hadn't made the cut. On the other hand, Skip sat high on the top rung of the friendship ladder. She pitied him; he didn't have a dad. Skip and his mother stuck by the story of his father dying in the Korean War. However, a different version buzzed around town like the mosquitoes in the middle of August. Hearsay claimed a gigolo deserted Sylvia Goodman while she was in the family way, leaving her to raise a son alone. Although the term gigolo escaped her, Jessy knew that a woman could have a baby by *going all the way*, but she wasn't exactly sure what that entailed.

Skip's mother, an attractive blonde with baby blue eyes and porcelain skin, wore her hair teased into a bouffant style and donned waist-cinched dresses emphasizing her curvy figure. Besides working part time during the week at Bealls Department Store in Fort Myers, she conducted jewelry-making classes in her dining room every other Friday afternoon during the school year and weekday sessions in the summer.

Skip and his mom lived on Pennsylvania Avenue over the tracks and about four blocks down from Aunt Prissy's Kitchen in a two-bedroom ranch-style home. He was a good son who helped his mom whenever he could. In return, she trusted him by giving him his own house key, which dangled from a metal clasp at the end of a green lanyard he wore around his neck. Depending on Sylvia's schedule, Skip frequently walked home from school to an empty house.

Since Jessy assumed the role of secret keeper, she appreciated why Skip despised Billy Grizzle. His hatred began one day last April. Due to a canceled after-school Scout meeting, Skip arrived home early. Approaching his yard, he spied his mother and the deputy locked in an embrace behind the front screened door.

The day he confided in Jessy, he cried, "And I saw them kissing and hugging." On three other occasions, Skip encountered the empty Lee County vehicle curbed near his home. Each time he sought refuge behind a neighbor's hibiscus bush until the deputy drove away.

Skip swore Jessy to secrecy. "I'm only telling you because you're my girlfriend. Pinky-swear you won't blab." To seal the deal, the children hooked their pinky fingers together.

"I'm not your girlfriend, but don't worry. I won't say a word." Due to Skip's slip of the tongue, Jessy felt it was still necessary to flick him on the side of his head.

Sad to say, the information he had divulged confirmed the gossip that constantly made the rounds at Aunt Prissy's Kitchen.

CHAPTER THIRTEEN:
EVERY DOG HAS A FEW FLEAS

Before she dressed that Saturday morning, Jessy checked on the hobo. To her disappointment, he vanished before she had the chance to offer him one of Camilla's biscuits for breakfast.

After killing a good hour dining on pancakes and bacon at Aunt Prissy's, she strolled back home. Repeatedly checking the hands of the clock in her family's kitchen, she dusted her dresser, then changed the sheets on her bed, and lastly, scrubbed the bathroom from top to bottom. She devoted what time remained of the morning to her favorite television programs.

During a commercial break, Margaret broached the subject Jessy wanted to avoid. "I understand you have a new friend."

The child caught her breath, but continued to fixate on the TV screen. "Yes, ma'am, but he's long gone now."

Margaret sat at the kitchen table perusing the local newspaper. "You're not to make a habit of talking to strangers. There are wicked people in this world." She reached for her cigarettes and lighter.

"Yes, ma'am."

At twelve fifty-five, she tore outside at the same time Rita May stepped off the Childers Street curb. The two girls met halfway. Before they raced to the diner's front entrance, the kids discussed what they would order for lunch. Dressed in shorts, exaggerating the length of her freckled limbs, the ginger-haired girl strolled in first. Jessy suffered a slight stab of jealousy, her own legs resembling the chunky pilings supporting the Naples Pier.

Inside Aunt Prissy's Kitchen, most of the laughter stemmed from the end of the counter where Eli joked with a customer. Chuckling to himself, he cruised toward the girls who stole two stools in the center of the row. "Afternoon, ladies. What'll it be?"

"Daddy, this is Rita May, my new best friend."

"How do you do?"

Rita May nodded. "Hi, Mr. Blanchard, your restaurant is really neat."

"Thank you."

Jessy said, "We'd each like a cherry smash and a grilled cheese sandwich, please."

"Coming right up." Eli prepared the order while Jessy gave her friend a quick visual tour of the diner.

"And over there is the jukebox."

Jessy's dad set the beverages and the sandwiches on the counter. Without hesitation, the girls noisily slurped down the coveted ice-cold liquid through their straws in between gooey bites of melted cheese on toast. The lively diner patrons and busy waitresses kept the girls entertained.

Both kids observed Delilah parading back and forth by way of the swinging doors from the kitchen to the service area. The waitress paused behind the counter, her hands full of dirty dishes. Cornering Eli, she whispered in his ear bringing a sparkle to his eyes and a smile to his lips. Shoulder to shoulder, the pair pushed through the doors to the kitchen and disappeared.

By the time Rita May finished her drink, the lunch crowd had shrunk. "Listen. Don't you just love this song?" Chuck Berry's rendition of "Maybelline" wailed from the far side of the diner. She twisted around on her stool. "I'm guessing the blonde waitress is Delilah. Right?"

"Uh huh. Isn't she pretty?"

"I love her hair." She crunched a few pieces of ice. "She likes your dad, doesn't she?"

Her glass empty, Jessy sucked air through her straw. "Everybody does." She wiped her mouth with a napkin. "Want to go play a game in my room? I've got Monopoly. My mother won't mind."

"Nah, not today."

"Why don't we go to your house?"

"Nope."

"I'd love to see your room."

Rita May chewed on her bottom lip. "I don't have a room, dummy. I sleep with my sisters on a mattress in the front room, the boys close by. The baby sleeps in the one and only bedroom with my parents."

"I wish I had brothers and sisters. You're lucky."

The teenager locked her jaw. "Damn, you're stupid, girl. I'm not lucky at all. I don't have any privacy. When I grow up, I'll have everything I want, and it won't have anything to do with luck." She spun halfway around.

Waiting for Rita May's mood to mellow, Jessy remained quiet until another rock n' roll record dropped onto the jukebox turntable. She snapped her fingers to the beat of the song. "Can you jitterbug?"

"Yep." Rita May shimmied off the stool taking both of Jessy's hands. "Do what I do."

The eleven-year-old caught on right away by mimicking the teenager's moves. The kids jived and twirled in front of the soda fountain. At the end of the song, the handful of customers remaining clapped at the performance, encouraging the girls to bow to the audience.

Minutes later, Rita May and Jessy skipped out of the diner, each one chewing on a toothpick they nicked from a cup near the register. Because no sidewalk existed, the kids stayed close to the curb along the highway. The majority of the traffic faced south, the unseasonably warm weather inspiring the cars to turn west on Bonita Beach Road.

On route, Jessy repeated the events of the previous evening to Rita May. "...and then dumb ole Grizzle cussed at Mundy and stomped on his hat. The poor guy didn't do a doggone thing."

The pair wandered across Wilson Street. North of Benson's Grocery, Doc Baird's Cabins sat cattycornered on the other side of the Imperial River across from the Everglades Wonder Gardens. The campground offered rentals and tent sites to vacationers towing campers, which the locals called tin cans, behind cars displaying license plates from faraway states like Michigan and Ohio.

Yankee tourists escaping winter's chill might spend a night or two at the Liles Hotel on their way to and from Naples or Miami. The grand two-story white structure backed up to the river, adding to the hotel's popularity. The neighboring Imperial River Court cottages, which bordered on the sandy riverbank, offered another lodging option.

That day, the sunshine's warmth lured families outside. Six fishermen holding outstretched poles in their hands dotted the riverbank, their lines idling in the water. Downstream, a straw-hatted man in a rowboat strummed a hillbilly tune on his guitar provoking a meager applause.

Jessy and Rita May lingered near the end of the bridge to wave at a canopied boat crammed full of sightseers before continuing to the other side. The girls inched onto the muddy sand, removed their shoes, and flung the sneakers backward onto the dryer bank.

Jessy was first to wade into the cloudy water. "If you stand still, you can see your feet. The minnows think your toes are other tiny fish."

"Wow, you're right." Rita May used her foot to churn the cool water. "They're too fast to catch."

"You have to use a net."

Towering pines and ageless oaks shaded the riverbank while generous mangroves flanked the shoreline. With their serpentine roots submerged in the Imperial River, knob-kneed cypress trees flourished wherever they pleased.

Rita May eased into the cool river, rippling the water with her fingers. "I wish we could find a raft or a boat. I'd float forever."

Cautiously advancing into the muck, Jessy's feet sank for a minute and then skimmed over the underwater rocks. "Whoa. It's slippery." She slushed back to the bank. Cozying up to an oblivious box turtle, she rested on a weathered stump of a rotted cypress, the last of its branches scattered across the mud. She cupped both hands on her mouth and hollered to an angler several yards up river. "Catch anything today?"

"A couple mullets and a rebellious jack."

She attempted to clean her feet. "Darn, the mud won't come off."

Rita May sloshed through the water until her feet found dry ground. "I forgot to tell you. Last Sunday, when Lynette, me, and the girls went walking downtown, we saw a sign advertising a psychic on Nevada Street. The clerk at the drug store gave me directions."

"You mean like a fortune teller? In Bonita Springs?" Jessy forced a dirty foot inside her shoe.

"Her name is Madame Zora, and she foresees the future. One session only costs a dollar per person." Rita May slipped on her sneakers. "How much money do you have?"

"Right now I have twenty cents, but on Friday, I'll get my allowance." Jessy glanced down at her feet. "I'm a mess."

"I've got a nickel. Why don't we try to save enough money, pool it together, and go get our fortunes read?"

"Sure. So what are you going to be for Halloween? I'm gonna dress up like a hobo."

Her friend struggled with the laces on her shoes. "Simple. A ghost. I don't really like Halloween all that much. My parents make me drag my sisters and brothers out trick-or-treating. Lynette catches the better part of the deal. She gives candy to the trick-or-treaters and takes care of the baby. Davis doesn't stick around. He goes drinking at the juke joint."

"Never heard of a juke joint."

Rita May dusted off the back of her legs and wet shorts. "Don't you know anything? Bonita Springs has two of them. One for just White people and one for everybody else. Davis loves to drink beer, especially at Ike's Bar. The music is loud and the people are drunk, mostly men and gussied-up women whose lips are painted bright red and have rouge on their cheeks, the sort Lynette calls floozies."

Jessy climbed halfway the distance to the top of the riverbank. "Is a floozy the same thing as a hussy?"

"Uh huh." Rita May met her at the top.

"Why don't we sneak out one night? I want to see what a floozy looks like."

A grimace spanned Rita May's face. "You're a daredevil, Jessy Blanchard."

"Mama goes to bed early. Daddy, much later. Once they're asleep, it's like they're dead."

The older girl paused to stamp the gunk from her shoes. "My parents sleep like that, too."

Jessy patted her grumbling belly. "I'm starving to death. Come on, I'll race you."

On the way back to the diner, Jessy broached the prospect of the two becoming best friends forever.

Rita May agreed. "We'll say a vow and do a ritual. Yeah, and we'll be blood sisters. We can make it a special ceremony, sort of an RJ Club initiation."

"What kind of sisters?" Jessy blinked several times. "How do we do that? You're not talking about real blood, are you?"

"Are you scared of a little icky blood?" Rita May sneered at Jessy. "Grow up. All we got to do is pledge an oath, stick our finger with something sharp, and squish our blood together. Nothing to it."

When a streak of light flashed on the south side of the sky, Jessy scanned the charcoal clouds. "I'm not afraid of blood." She swallowed.

A clap of thunder boomed.

"Don't forget the party at school on Monday. I'm bringing candy." Rita May strayed to the curb.

"Cool. Chocolate candy?"

The older girl trotted to the other side of Childers. "No. Hard candy, soft centers. Lynette stockpiles bags of it. She has a sweet tooth and rewards the little kids when they're good."

Another thunderclap struck closer. Jessy shook off her shoes and beat the soles against the concrete step at the back of the diner. She sighed. "Mama's gonna kill me." She tiptoed into the apartment, one mud-crusted sneaker in each hand. Jessy was sure she heard Nancy Drew calling her name.

* * *

Margaret sat engrossed in an evening variety TV program. She tapped her foot to the rock n' roll music blaring from the set. Dressed in pajamas, Jessy pretended to have a partner and danced in front of the television.

"Look, Mama, my friend, Rita May, taught me how to jitterbug."

To the child's amazement, Margaret sprung from her seat and pulled the coffee table against the sofa. She kicked off her slippers, flung her bathrobe to the side, and gripped Jessy's hand. Mother and daughter jitterbugged until "Rock Around the Clock" ended.

Jessy laughed while trying to catch her breath. "Wow! You're a really good dancer."

Margaret dragged the table back in place. Lolling back on the cushions, she strained for her glass. "Honey, there's more to me than meets the eye. I used to be a fun person, quite creative, too. I loved to paint and dance, you name it. Wish I could go back in time…before…"

"Before what?"

"Why don't you give me a kiss goodnight?"

Jessy placed a peck on Margaret's cheek. Unable to temper the mood, she pirouetted down the hall and into her room. She nodded off to sleep with the lamp on, her face stuck to page twenty-six of her latest mystery.

Another deafening squabble woke her in the middle of the night, ruining Jessy's spectacular Saturday.

* * *

On Monday morning, Sylvia Goodman drove the kids to school in her shiny new Oldsmobile. The first to arrive, Jessy and Skip offered their delicious contributions to the teacher. Miss Rydell, dressed in an appropriate black cape and pointy hat, grinned with delight.

"Happy Halloween, children. Everything smells delicious. Please put your goodies on the table at the back of the room." The teacher gestured behind her.

As the morning crept along, Jessy's mind wandered with thoughts of Camilla's jack-o-lantern sugar cookies. Lunchtime couldn't come soon enough. At twelve-thirty, she caught up with Rita May on the playground.

"You and me and, of course, Skip can go trick-or-treating tonight until our bags are so full we have to drag them home. What do you say?"

"Maybe. I'll ask Lynette one more time."

"If you can, meet us at the picnic table at six-thirty."

After recess, the children waited another excruciating hour while eyeing the treats on the long rectangular table. In addition to Skip's pumpkin pie and Camilla's cookies, the alluring sweets included a spider-topped vanilla frosted cake, a container of jellybeans, orange and black iced cupcakes, and two additional plates of spooky cookies. Rita May's candy-filled coffee can sat adjacent to the pie. On another table sat stacks of paper cups and plates, a wicker basket full of plastic forks, a mound of paper napkins, and a large bowl of orange punch. At precisely two o'clock, Miss Rydell instructed the students to put their desks in a circle. Sampling the goodies, playing a Halloween-themed version of Bingo, and dunking for apples kept the energetic sugarcoated children entertained until the end-of-the-day bell.

* * *

Although the weatherman predicted heavy rain for the thirty-first, a fine mist settled in the low-lying areas of Lee County. With no moon in the early evening sky, the light affixed to the side of Aunt Prissy's Kitchen, the two dim bulbs over the back doors, and the blurry streetlight on the corner of Highway 41 and Childers Street would have to be enough to provide enough illumination behind the diner. Jessy paced beside Skip who sat cross-legged on top of the picnic table, his elbows on his knees.

She checked the time on her watch. "Where is Rita May? It's past six-thirty."

"Why are you asking me?"

"We can't wait any longer or the other kids will scarf up every last piece of candy in town."

Skip's eyes narrowed. "So you're supposed to be a hobo?"

"Yes. These are Daddy's old clothes."

"Mom said I'm a playboy, whatever that is."

Jessy inspected his attire. "Mmm. Let's see, striped shirt, bow tie, and matching black pants and vest. I guess a playboy is a boy pretending to be a man." She giggled.

"Ha, ha. You think you're funny, don't you?"

"Dadgummit! Where is that girl? It's almost seven…Ah, forget it. We're leaving."

The hobo and the playboy paraded down Childers Street clutching empty pillowcases. The fog rolling in off the Gulf punctuated the eerie Halloween vibe as the pair passed an array of ghosts, four Superman-caped boys, one Davey Crockett, five witches, three Frankenstein's, and other spooky characters on their journey throughout the town's neighborhoods. Charitable adults slipped Hershey Bars, Double Bubble, Lifesavers, and Tootsie Rolls into the children's sacks before Jessy and Skip wandered into an unfamiliar part of Bonita Springs. As if orchestrated, one by one, porch lights dimmed.

Skip yawned. "I'm pooped. Let's go home."

Suddenly, the tepid night air snared an echo of a man's guttural cackling.

"Did you hear that?"

"Ooh, is it a ghost?"

"Shh. You're so droll, you dumb boy."

"Droll?"

"Were you hatched or something? Droll means funny. Listen."

Skip cocked his head. Jessy put a finger to her lips.

An abrasive twang sliced into the fog. "Damn, Tiny, haven't you ever been coon-hunting?" More laughter ensued.

The children directed glances at one another, their mouths agape.

Skip glowered. "It's Grizzle."

Not waiting to confirm their suspicions, the kids sprinted all the way back to the baseball field. They parted ways when Jessy crossed the street. "Bye, playboy."

He saluted his friend. "See ya, hobo." Tucking his sack of candy under his arm, Skip vaporized into the fog.

Jessy entered the apartment and found Margaret in her usual spot sipping on a nightcap, patches of her hair curled in pink foam rollers, feet propped on the coffee table. "Glad you're home safe and sound. My, my, you've quite a haul there. I don't believe there's an ounce of room left in your pillowcase."

"I know." Jessy dumped her bounty in the center of the living room rug.

"Are you going to share?"

"Sure." Jessy handed her mother a Milky Way bar. "Where's Daddy? He should be home by now."

"I have no idea where he is. May I have a pack of M&M's, too?"

Jessy obliged her mother. "It's late. Aunt Prissy's is dark. Where could he be?"

"Don't know. Don't care." Margaret followed bites of candy with swigs from her cocktail. "Anyway, every dog has a few fleas. Even your goody-two-shoes daddy."

"Fleas? Daddy has fleas?"

"Never mind." She grimaced.

While flitting into the kitchen, Jessy opened a Snickers bar. She returned carrying a glass of milk and an empty cereal bowl. She bit into the chocolate as she sprawled on the rug in front of the candy. "Are you going to wait up for him, Mama?" The girl rummaged through the stash until she filled the bowl with Eli's favorites.

"Nope." Margaret crumpled an empty wrapper. Covering her shoulders with a throw, she bent to kiss her daughter. "I'm off to bed."

Jessy grabbed handfuls of the candy still on the rug and stuffed the pieces back into the pillowcase. "I'd like to wait up."

Her mother shuffled into the kitchen. She set her empty glass on the counter. "Go to bed. Tomorrow is a school day. Your father will turn up sooner or later."

On the way to her room, Jessy set Eli's bowl of candy on the kitchen table.

CHAPTER FOURTEEN:
HALF-COCKED

Jessy checked the bleachers, dusting bits of dirt and a dead bug off the wooden planked seats. She settled on the row in front of Rita May. "Today was the longest school day ever. It was like Miss Rydell was trying to see how much work she could give us in one day."

Rita May cautiously put one foot in front of the other. Mimicking a tightrope walker, she negotiated the top row of the ballpark bleachers. "Yeah, I know."

"Aren't you glad tomorrow is Thanksgiving? There's no school for four whole days so we can look for our clubhouse on Friday."

"I can't on Friday. I gotta babysit all day. We'll have to do it on Saturday."

"I've been thinking we should try looking behind the banyan tree in front of the pavilion. A row of bushes hides the back of the tree where the roots form deep holes. Oh, and I'll bring a safety pin, uh, for the blood sister thing."

"No need. My pocketknife will work better than any old pin." Rita May hopped down onto each row until she landed on the ground. She shielded her eyes from the sun when she said, "Catch ya later, gator."

As the McAfee boys caught up with their older sister, Skip finished his run around the bases landing at home plate. He trotted toward the bleachers, climbed up, and parked himself next to Jessy. The children strained to make out the hazy outlines of their friends as they faded into the backdrop of the late autumn afternoon. When a whistle signaled an incoming train, the carrot-topped MacAfee siblings vaulted the railroad tracks just in time.

As the Atlantic Coast Line towed its cargo past the depot, a disheveled man jumped from a slow-moving boxcar. "Is that Mundy Mike?" Jessy rubbed her nose, the train leaving distinct odors of oil and steel in its wake. The powerful engine growled as it chugged on its way to another small town.

"Mundy doesn't wear overalls, and that guy is too skinny." Skip stretched. "I've got to go. I promised Mama I'd help her bake six pies. I don't know why we're making so many."

The pair strolled into the street, Skip veering down Childers and Jessy heading straight to the diner. At the back stoop, she pulled off her saddle oxfords.

"Jessica, I'm glad you're home." Margaret stood behind the apartment's screened door clutching a drink.

"Oh, hey." Carrying her lunchbox, shoes, and socks, Jessy stalked her mother into their kitchen.

"May I get you a glass of milk or something?"

"No, ma'am."

"Go sit on the sofa."

Jessy obeyed, recognizing her mother's no-nonsense tone. The child avoided eye contact.

Margaret eased into the end cushion on the couch. "Honey, I'm going away for a month or so."

"Where?" She twisted her watchband twice.

"Your daddy and I agree that I should take a much-deserved rest. There's a place in Miami, like a hospital, where I can relax and work on getting healthy."

Jessy studied her mother's face. "But you'll come back. Right?" With tears coating her face, she snatched some hair from behind her ear.

Margaret took a gulp from her drink. "I should be home by Christmas, but I'll probably have to go back for another month after that." Spotting the ashtray on the coffee tray, she removed the smoldering butt that teetered on the edge. Margaret brought the cigarette to her lips. She stopped short of inhaling. "Jessica, quit sucking on your hair."

The girl parted her lips, the soggy tresses sticking to her cheek. "I wish you didn't have to go." She squirmed closer to her mother.

Halfway through a lukewarm hug, Margaret patted her daughter's shoulder. "You're going to have to grow up a bit, young lady. Your father will need you. Though lately, I do believe he's getting plenty of tender loving care."

The cool breeze from the air conditioner swept over Jessy's tear-stained face. "When are you leaving?"

"Sunday. Now go play, sweetie. I need to lie down." Clutching her cocktail, the inebriated woman stood up too fast. She staggered and lost her balance, falling into the sofa. Jessy jumped up and then guided her mother to bed.

Afterward, Jessy flew into her room collapsing on the bed next to a soft mound of Creamsicle-tinted fur. "Muffin, she's going away. I don't understand why Doc Barnes or some other doctor in Bonita Springs can't make her well." She cuddled the cat in her arms to muffle the sobs.

* * *

Jessy woke up to the sound of water running. She lumbered into the kitchen. "I didn't mean to fall asleep. It's dark already." She sank into a chair.

"That's okay, Baby Girl. Are you hungry? I brought you and your mama the special tonight—meatloaf and mac and cheese." Although Eli grinned, the weariness in his eyes gave him away.

"May I carry my plate to my room?" She wasn't very hungry.

"Sure, sweetie. I'll check on you when I get home later on and make sure you're all tucked in."

* * *

At eleven o'clock on Thanksgiving night, Jessy hugged her bed pillow and listened to Margaret's voice bleed through the apartment walls. "Answer me. Do you plan on firing the girl or not?"

"Probably not."

"You better change your mind. Even though waitresses in Lee County are a dime a dozen, I suppose *she's* indispensable. I'm not kidding, Elijah. She's gone by Christmas or else."

Jessy pulled the covers over her head.

"Or else?" Eli's tone sent a chill down Jessy's spine.

She prayed, "Please, God, make them stop fighting."

* * *

At five-thirty on Saturday afternoon, Jessy and Rita May discovered the ideal clubhouse behind the gigantic banyan tree. The enormous roots braided in all directions creating several cubbyholes and a larger cavity at the rear where at least two kids could hide.

"It's perfect—nice and private." The redhead wiggled into a gap next to Jessy, but struggled when trying to cross her legs. "Can you swipe stuff from your house, you know, for the clubhouse?"

Jessy poked a few strands of hair into her mouth. "Sure."

"Why are you so mopey today?"

"I'm in a lousy mood that's all." She curved the damp pieces behind her ear.

Rita May surveyed the space around her. "Well, snap out of it and listen. Every time we have a meeting, we should bring stuff. First thing we need is a flashlight."

"Daddy has an extra one."

"And a blanket. It's sort of damp in here." Rita May yanked a pocket-knife out of her pocket and unfolded a sharp blade. "I'm ready if you are."

Jessy blinked. "That might have germs on it."

"I'm not an idiot. I washed the knife off already." Rita May bit her lip and forced the tip of the blade into the pad of her thumb. A scarlet bead trickled down onto her palm. She used a leaf to blot the puncture and to wipe the blade's sharp edge.

The younger girl grabbed the knife. With teeth clenched, Jessy nicked her own finger. Blood pooled at the source. The two girls clasped hands while Rita May dug into her pocket and retrieved a folded scrap of paper. As they pressed bloody fingers together, the girls read the oath aloud. "I, Rita May McAfee..."

"And I, Jessica Rose Blanchard..."

In unison, the girls stated, "...Being of sound mind and body, we are hereby members of the RJ Secret Club and promise to be best friends forever. Our clubhouse is private, and things we do and say are private, too. We promise to keep our secrets until we die."

Rita May abruptly pulled her hand away. "It's official. We're blood sisters and club members forever and ever."

Jessy stared at the tip of her finger. "We should wash up. The public restrooms are on the side of the building." She was first to crawl out of the tree cavity.

The girls trooped to the far side of the pavilion where two water fountains sat against the wall between the men and women's restrooms—one marked *White*; the other *Colored*.

Rita May scowled. "Adults make the dumbest rules, and there's always some big shot telling people how to act, what to say, and what to do."

"I never understood why there are separate fountains." Jessy stood still as the older girl surveyed her surroundings, bowed, and rinsed off her finger with water from the *wrong* fountain. Then she took a big gulp. The water sprayed Rita May's curls as they fell onto her face. When she finished, Jessy took her turn.

The girls headed for home. By the time they tapped the fence at the ballfield, the sun had set in Bonita Springs. Rita May circled Jessy. "Guess what? After the holidays, I'm moving to Mrs. Cook's class. Miss Rydell and Principal Newsome said I should be in the seventh grade."

"That's great. Uh, I've got a secret, but I'll tell you. After all, you're my blood sister now." Jessy's expression soured.

Rita May slowed her stride at the curb.

The younger girl wiped the sand off her sneakers. "Mama's going to a rest home because she drinks too much. I don't remember a time when she didn't need a screwdriver to feel good." She kicked the ground using the heel of her shoe. "We're taking her to Miami tomorrow."

"That's rough. Yeah." Rita May scanned the sky. "Look up there. It's the first star. Make a wish for your mom."

Jessy heaved a sigh. "Star light star bright, first star I see tonight, I wish I may, I wish I might, have the wish I wish tonight."

* * *

At nine thirty-five, the parking lot remained empty except for Eli's Chevy pickup. Jessy and Skip sat cross-legged on top of the stoop engrossed in a fierce game of checkers, the porch light illuminating the board. Skip's hand hovered over his red checker. He grinned then jumped two of Jessy's black game pieces. A repetitive tap on the doorframe caused the kids to turn their heads.

Eli stood behind the screen. "Y'all want to ride to the Wonder Gardens?"

Jessy's face beamed. "Sure."

"How about you, Skip? Do you need to ask your mother's permission?"

"No, sir. She doesn't worry when I'm with y'all."

"Okay then, come on inside, you two. I could use your help before we go."

Jessy collected the checkers and the board. "Skip, go on and I'll meet you in a minute." She opened the green door and tiptoed into the apartment. Her parent's bedroom door was ajar. Margaret stood folding a nightgown into an open piece of luggage.

"I miss you already." Jessy ran into her mother's arms.

Margaret clutched the girl's hand. "Did you injure yourself?"

"It's just a little cut."

Margaret stroked the child's finger. "Did you cleanse the wound? Did you use soap? It needs mercurochrome."

"Yes, ma'am, but I'll do it again." She scurried to the bathroom. Jessy scrubbed her hands. To appease her mother, she dabbed disinfectant on the incision and placed a Band-Aid on the miniscule puncture. "Bye, Mama. I'm going with Daddy on a run to the Wonder Gardens."

She hurried into the diner's kitchen and pushed through the swinging doors. Jessy found Skip leaning up against the jukebox, checking on the tune choices.

Within a few minutes, Eli called out, "I need you guys in the storeroom."

The kids discovered him straining to move the slop can, the amount of table scraps proving too heavy to handle by himself. Together, the children pushed and Eli dragged the heavy aluminum trashcan across the linoleum floor.

A raspy voice startled the threesome. "Is anybody there?"

The kids dogged Eli to the back door where he expressed surprise at the huge silhouette behind the screen. "Hey there, Mundy Mike."

The hobo took two steps backward, his hat in his hand. "Hope I didn't bother you, Mr. Eli. Well, hello. It's them sweet young'uns."

"Hi, Mundy." Jessy greeted the hobo. Standing close to the screen, she looked the man up and down.

Eli cracked the door. "Sorry, but I'm afraid the kitchen is closed for the night."

"I know it's late and all, but I don't suppose you have any leftovers just hanging around. I was just passing by, saw your lights, and you know, y'all treated me so kindly last time I came a-calling."

"The kids and I are getting ready to run an errand, but I tell you what. If you'll do me a favor, I'll rustle up a couple of cheese sandwiches for you."

"I be glad to. Thank you, sir."

Eli dashed back inside. The kids hustled outside on the steps, and Jessy immediately began to quiz Mundy on how long he intended to stay in town. For fifteen minutes, Mundy entertained the kids with bits of information about his chosen career.

A few minutes into the conversation, Skip nudged Jessy and pointed to the street. Two men idled under the streetlamp in a haze of cigarette smoke.

The taller fellow whistled to gain Mundy's attention. "Hey, did you git any grub?" Not waiting for any reply, both men wandered into the parking lot.

Mundy waved his buddies over. "Miss Jessy, these are my friends—Pleasin' Pete, who can't help the way he talks." The man smiled. "And that there is Gator Breath Jones." The scruffy-bearded older man next to Mundy took a step toward the kids.

Jessy nodded at the men. "How do you do?"

Pleasin' Pete, corrugated and brown, a timeworn Yankee baseball cap masking one eye, shuffled his shoes across the concrete. He whispered an inaudible comment.

Jessy blinked twice, her nose crinkling. "Pardon me?"

The man's eyes peered into hers. "Pleasin' Pete says mighty fine, thank you."

Gator Breath peeled off a straw hat revealing a balding head. He reshaped his hat's brim several times, his thin-skinned hands resembling Camilla's roll of Saran Wrap, the kind of cellophane she used to protect her biscuits. A faded denim shirt swallowed up the bum's emaciated frame.

"Howdy do, kids." His mouth lacked several teeth on both rows.

Eli emerged from the diner toting a paper bag and an opened bottle of Fanta Grape. He smiled at the eclectic group lurking at the stoop. "Mmm, whom have we here?"

Mundy cleared his throat. "Uh, Mr. Eli, these are my friends, and they ain't had nothing to eat in two or three days."

Eli passed the sack and bottle to Mundy. "Okay, I'll fix a few more sandwiches, but it's the best I can do tonight." He turned to go inside, but hesitated. "Damnit." The patrol car idled abutting the curb, its red lights flashing on top of the vehicle.

Jessy elbowed Skip and nodded at the Lee County vehicle.

The driver's side door sprung open; Billy Grizzle spurted from the car. Waving his nightstick in the air, he traipsed across the gravel. "You boys get on outta here. Quit mooching food off Mr. Blanchard."

The hobos scattered.

Eli shouted at the deputy. "Don't go off half-cocked, Billy. They're not bothering me."

Billy huffed, pausing in front of the stoop. "Panhandling is a crime, Elijah. You ain't obliged to give them anything."

"Mind your own business." Eli's lips formed a scowl. "Go keep the peace somewhere else."

The deputy's chubby cheeks resembled two ripe tomatoes. "I'll leave when I'm good and ready."

Jessy's father gestured to the kids. "Hop in the truck and lock the doors. I'll be along shortly."

"Yes, Daddy." She grabbed Skip's hand and the children dashed to the pickup, while Eli and the deputy sheriff marched into the storeroom.

The kids scrambled into the cab. "I've got dibs on the window seat," said Skip.

Flashing him a dirty look, Jessy locked the Chevy doors. The amber streetlight at the corner flickered, its light exposing the hobos that had gathered at the picnic table. Mundy gnawed on his sandwich, Gator Breath reclined on his back on a bench, and Pleasin' Pete rested in the grass, his cap bonded to his skull.

Jessy's body tensed. "I hate Fizzle Grizzle. I wish Daddy would punch him in the nose."

Skip chuckled. "I'd pay to see that. When I'm old enough and tall enough, I'll beat him up. I'll hit him so hard he'll bleed all over the place."

Kneeling on the seat, both kids curved their bodies over the edge of the opened window. To their disappointment, the Lee County Deputy stormed outside and bolted to the curb, not a scratch on him.

In a few minutes, Eli came out clutching two paper sacks and headed straight for the hobos who thanked Jessy's father for the food. Before he left, Eli nodded at Mundy. Together, the two men tramped across the lot into the storeroom. Around that time, Billy crawled back into his patrol car.

Jessy and Skip observed Mundy and Eli drag the slop can out the door, over the concrete steps, and onto the parking lot. They heaved the container up on the truck bed.

"I appreciate your help, Mike." Jessy's dad shook the vagrant's hand. After securing the tailgate, he ran back to the diner and locked the door.

When Eli got behind the steering wheel, he took a hard look around before shifting into first gear. The hobos had disappeared.

For a time, sightings of Mundy Mike and his friends were scarce. Jessy wouldn't catch a glimpse of him again until spring, when the weather in south Florida could be just as temperamental as Billy Grizzle, the Deputy Sheriff of Lee County.

CHAPTER FIFTEEN:
ANY FARTHER THAN I CAN THROW 'EM

Jessy ate the majority of her meals at the soda fountain counter. During the breakfast rush and between the hours of five and six in the evening, the waitresses saved the end stool on the row, the one closest to the kitchen, for Eli's daughter. The key position granted the child an excellent view of kitchen activity, and if she rotated to her left, she could observe the entire service area.

The dinner menu on that early December evening featured fried shrimp, hush puppies, and grits. Jessy patted the grease off her lips with a napkin while eavesdropping on the voices from a nearby table. These were the regulars—men who made it a habit of dining at Aunt Prissy's Kitchen every Friday night. She idled at her vantage point. The lanky man at the head of the table talked with his mouth full of her daddy's delicious fried chicken. His line of dialogue piqued Jessy's interest.

"Did you fellas hear what happened in Montgomery yesterday?"

His tablemates shook their heads. One redneck stopped chewing. "What in tarnation are you talking about, Tom?"

"Hell, boys. It was on the radio last night, and they ran the story again this morning. The world could be coming to an end, and you'd all be left in the dark." He snorted. "There was this colored woman in Montgomery who refused to give up her seat to a White man on a loaded city bus. Can you believe it?"

Jessy caught the gist of the banter, but the subject soon lost its appeal. Anyway, she didn't comprehend why anybody cared about some random woman. The chatter wasn't describing a gruesome car wreck or a shooting or anything terrible. Taking intermittent sips of iced tea, she asked Delilah for an ice cream sundae.

"Let me check with your dad." The waitress pushed her way into the kitchen.

Eli waltzed back into the dining area and stood behind the counter. "Craving a sundae, Baby Girl?"

"Yes, please."

Jessy monitored every aspect of her father's work. First, he scooped vanilla ice cream into a parfait glass. Then Eli drizzled the right amount of chocolate syrup on top. He topped it off with a dollop of whipped cream before adding a spoonful of chopped nuts and a maraschino cherry.

"Here you go. When you're done, run home and put on your PJs. You may watch TV until bedtime." Eli wiped the countertop using a wet cloth.

The first mouthful of ice cream triggered a slight brain freeze causing Jessy to wince. "Uh, those men over there were talking about a lady in Alabama who didn't give up her seat to someone on a bus. What's the big deal?"

"It's complicated. I'll explain later."

Her lips formed a pout. "Phooey. I wanted to know." Sometimes, she disliked being a kid. If she was a grown up, she wouldn't have to wait for an explanation.

Jessy dug her spoon into the creases of the parfait glass until the bowl appeared empty. She licked the sticky residue from her mouth and slid off her stool. Instead of heading straight to the apartment, she wandered into the diner's kitchen where Camilla stood bent over a wooden table kneading a ball of dough. Flour covered the floor at the cook's feet. With a quick swipe of the back of her hand, white specks now powdered Camilla's face. She looked up when she saw the girl.

Jessy sidled up next to the woman. "I've got a question."

"What's on your mind, child?" Camilla sprinkled a handful of flour across the table and some on top of the creamy white lump in front of her.

"Did you hear the news about a colored lady who didn't give up her seat on a bus in Alabama?"

Camilla flattened the dough, her rolling pin squealing each time she pushed the wooden cylinder back and forth. "Nope. Ain't got the foggiest notion what you're talking about. My radio's been on all day, but I only listen to the spirituals on the gospel stations. Don't care for the news. It's always bad."

* * *

Eli sat on the edge of her bed. "Move over, honey." He curved his arm around his daughter. "You're not going to let it go. Are you, Jessy?"

"No sir."

"The incident on the bus was unprecedented."

"Huh?"

"The first time in the history of that city, possibly in the entire state of Alabama."

"But why?"

"Coloreds and Whites don't sit together on city buses."

"Dumb, dumb, dumb."

"It's the law, and it's been that way forever. Anyway, four coloreds hopped on the bus and sat on the fifth row. The White folks sat in the first four rows, but one man didn't have a seat. The bus driver asked the colored people to transfer to the back so the man could sit up front. Three out of the four did what the bus driver asked and quietly moved to the back of the bus—all but Rosa Parks. She refused and got arrested."

"Arrested? In jail?"

"Yes, for civil disobedience."

Jessy sat up. "Wait a minute. Aren't gentlemen supposed to give ladies their seats? Still, why did she cause trouble?"

"I told you, very complicated. The woman took a stand claiming she deserved to sit wherever she wanted no matter the color of her skin."

"I wouldn't have gotten out of my seat either." She flopped back on the pillow and sniffed. Tonight, her daddy smelled like fried fish.

"There is no easy solution to the Civil Rights issue. If there's one thing I'm sure of, people can't handle change. Honey, when you're grown, things will be better. I'm sure of it. Good night. Sweet dreams." He kissed her on the cheek.

"And the woman's name again?" Jessy scrunched under the covers, the sheet pulled to her chin.

"Rosa Parks," he said as he closed the bedroom door behind him.

* * *

During the next few weeks, diner customers kept up to date on the most gossip-worthy news topic of the day—the persuasive and outspoken Negro Baptist preacher named Martin Luther King.

* * *

On Friday afternoon, the last school day before Christmas break, as she waited for the bell to ring, Jessy tapped a rhythm out on her desk using all ten fingers. Miss Rydell looked in her direction. She stopped fidgeting; she checked her watch again. Two forty-five. Earlier that day, Eli travelled to Miami to collect Margaret, designating Camilla to be in charge of the diner. At three o'clock, Jessy abandoned her friends and raced home from school. She burst into the apartment calling for her mother.

Margaret, who resumed her position on the sofa, propped her feet on top of the coffee table. She held a lit cigarette between two fingers on her right hand. "Come give me a hug, sweetie."

The child darted to her mother's side. "You look beautiful, Mama." The two embraced as Jessy scanned the room for telltale signs. The counters lay bare, not a cocktail or a Vodka bottle in view.

* * *

Jessy and Margaret made the most of their time together. They baked holiday cookies, shopped for wrapping paper, tinsel, and two wreaths— one for the backdoor and one for the diner's entrance. Two nights before Christmas, the family trimmed a small but perfect spruce, the colored lights warming the compact apartment.

Jessy awoke on Christmas morning to the scent of warm cinnamon buns and the fragrance of pine. After breakfast, the family gathered around the tree. Jessy's loot consisted of two Nancy Drew books, a genuine sterling silver scarab bracelet, and a pearl white cardigan with a detachable lace collar. The set of art supplies under the tree came from her grandparents. Eli gave Margaret a turquoise pendant and clip-on earrings to match, and in return, received a multi-striped silk necktie. He opened his present from Jessy, a *Best Dad in the World* plaque. Eli showed his appreciation with a bear hug.

Jessy handed a small box wrapped in red paper to her mother. "Hope you like it."

Margaret tore off the wrapping. After opening the lid, she unfolded a white cotton handkerchief with miniature red poinsettias painted at the corners.

"I made your present at school." The child waited for a reaction.

"It's lovely and so thoughtful." Margaret held the handkerchief a moment before placing it back in its box. "I'll save it for special occasions."

During the rest of the school break, Jessy spent most mornings with her mother. In the afternoons, she and Skip played games or she met Rita May at the clubhouse. Margaret continued her sobriety causing everyone in the apartment to sleep peacefully, even the cat. Because no arguments occurred during the night, Jessy clung to the hope that her mother would remain as content as one of Gil O'Brien's gators after a meal of Aunt Prissy's leftovers.

On Sunday, New Year's Day, Eli drove the family to Miami to drop Margaret off at the rest home. Heading back down Highway 41, he surprised Jessy by making an unscheduled stop at the Howard Johnsons in Naples. Father and daughter sat in a booth while she licked a double-dipped ice cream cone. She studied her dad, his body sagging against the red vinyl seat. The object of his gaze unclear, he gripped a navy blue mug of coffee.

"Daddy, you don't have to worry. When Mama comes home to stay, she'll be healthy, and we'll be a family again."

Eli chugged coffee. "Honey, I'm going to tell you the truth. Yes, your mother is better, but she has a ways to go yet. If and when she becomes healthier, our situation…might not be the same. She loves Miami. She always has." His shoulders drooped; his eyes clouded.

She patted his hand. "Daddy, I'll take care of you until Mama comes home." She bit her lip. If she cried, he might cry, too.

He squeezed her hand. "We'll take care of each other."

* * *

Due to the McAfee's work schedules, Rita May's babysitting responsibilities increased, which left Jessy with fewer afterschool options. Homework came first followed by hanging with Skip and watching her favorite television shows. Jessy also found the dark clubhouse an ideal location to dive into her mysteries by the glow of a flashlight. On Saturdays, Jessy and Rita May conducted clandestine RJ Club meetings. Jessy saved Sundays for Eli.

One particular Sunday morning in late January, father and daughter skipped church. Instead, Eli picked up Grandpa Caleb before the sun peeked above the horizon. The day before, Jessy agreed to go to Little Hickory Pass with them. Big mistake. Having joined the men on several outings before, she brought Nancy Drew along to arrest the inevitable boredom. The cool temperatures of late also made a sweater necessary.

Caleb never failed to recite his mantra at the onset of any fishing trip. "If you want to bring home a cooler of fish or merely attempt to catch Old Stinky, the famous Snook and the shrewdest son of a gun in Lee County waters, you must sit your ass in a boat at dawn and not budge until dark when you can't see your hand in front of your face."

The hour-long drive on the highway and over the bridge to the Pass afforded Jessy plenty of time to read and pray for a downpour. Eli parked the truck in the dirt behind a lagoon surrounded by dense mangroves. The men lugged Caleb's rowboat from the pickup to the water's edge. Eli trudged back to the truck to retrieve the cooler, and Jessy carried the bait bucket.

As the boat idled in shallow water, Caleb and Jessy claimed their seats. Then Eli shoved the vessel deeper into the lagoon. He climbed inside next to Jessy who scooted over as far as she could. For the time being, she held her nose. It would take about an hour for her senses to adapt to the smell of the murky lagoon plus the live bait—a putrid combo of rotten eggs and fish. Gripping a cane pole, she peered into the bait bucket where anxious shrimp and minnows swam for their lives in briny water. Eli and Caleb cast their lines, the whiz of their spinning reels slicing into the calm around them. Jessy wanted to comment on the pod of brown pelicans that flew overhead, but refrained. Noises spooked the fish.

Eli whispered reminders. "Keep an eye on the bobber, Jess. If the cork dips under the water, a fish is nibbling on your bait."

Although she'd heard similar rhetoric on other excursions, Jessy politely nodded and concentrated on her fishing line, the red and white ball dancing on top of the water. Jessy obeyed her father for nearly thirty minutes before monotony set in. She clutched the pole with one hand, and cradled her book with the other. Caleb and Eli didn't bother Jessy except to offer her a sandwich and lemonade at lunchtime, after which her eyes focused on her book not the lagoon. Nancy Drew and George were in danger. Only when the men's occasional low-key conversations piqued her interest did she halt any effort to solve the mystery.

Soon the sun sank behind the mangroves, which prompted her grandpa to root inside the cooler. "It's time to chuck the puny littles and the trash fish that don't belong on anyone's table." He threw one after another into the brackish water. "Fish sort of remind me of people. Some folks aren't suitable like the fish we throw back. Some folks we call friends. They're good people we can depend on. There will come a time when we'll have to rid ourselves of the bad and keep only the good."

Eli frowned. "Dad, that's enough of that kind of talk."

Caleb grinned at his granddaughter. "Jessy understands me, don't you?"

"Sure, Grandpa."

"Let's pack up and head home," said Eli. The catch—six medium-sized Snook, four speckled trout and two huge redfish—proved enough to advertise on the upcoming menu for Aunt Prissy's Monday Lunch and Dinner Specials.

At the end of Jessy's long day, she soaked in a bath full of bubbles and gobbled up a bowl of vegetable soup and a leftover hunk of buttery cornbread. The tired child fell asleep once her head indented the pillow.

* * *

On Monday, at six in the evening, Jessy sat on a diner stool, bestowing her full attention to a page of difficult fractions. After a while, however, the chitchat of nearby customers became interesting. The servers strutted from the kitchen to the patrons, bringing far more than delicious food. At approximately six forty-five, Delilah carted the last two plates of fried fish, hushpuppies, and coleslaw from the kitchen into the service area. By five after seven, everyone in the place had heard the latest news from Alabama. Someone bombed two residences—one house belonging to E.D. Nixon, leader of the Montgomery Chapter of the NAACP, and the other one, the home of Reverend Martin Luther King.

Jessy spread butter on a warm hushpuppy and popped the tidbit in her mouth. What if someone bombed Aunt Prissy's Kitchen? Chugging cold milk, she squelched the outrageous notion. If she rushed to finish the last three problems on her homework, she might not miss the beginning of *American Bandstand.*

* * *

The aroma of bacon woke Jessy from a pleasant dream about her mother. Once dressed, she meandered into the diner's kitchen unnoticed. Eli poked sausages while they charred on the griddle. Bacon sizzled in a skillet on the other side of the stovetop. Camilla, resting on a stool, cut biscuits on a floured worktable. She pressed the open end of a hollow-out tin can into the fresh dough creating three-inch rounds. Humming a gospel tune, a melody Jessy could sing by heart, the cook arranged the discs in rows on an extra-large cookie sheet.

The woman glanced up from her task and waved a dismissive flour-covered hand at the girl. "Child, why is you in my kitchen? You gonna burn to a crisp in here."

"I'm going. I'm going." Jessy shoved the doors into the dining area. She hopped up on the stool at the end of a long string of customers perched at the soda fountain, the line reminding Jessy of a row of starlings gathered on a telephone wire.

Down at the other end of the counter, Mary Louise poured coffee into a customer's cup. When the waitress spied Jessy, she strolled over. "Morning, young lady. Ready to order?"

The girl touched a finger to her mouth. "Morning. May I please have pancakes and sausage? Oh, and orange juice."

"It'll be ready in two shakes." Mary Louise bent over in front of a slot cut into the wall labeled *DIRTY DISHES*. She shouted through the opening. "A short stack and a couple of rollers." The waitress poured freshly squeezed juice from a carafe and then set the glass on the child's placemat.

Jessy grasped the beverage admiring the miniature oranges and leaves painted on the outside of the glass. Within minutes, Mary Louise waltzed into the dining area balancing breakfast on a tray along with a miniature pitcher of syrup and three butter pats stacked in a ceramic bowl of ice chips.

Jessy inhaled her breakfast in fifteen minutes. Swiveling a quick 180 degrees, she licked syrup from her lip and visually swept the packed dining area. Groupings of four to six occupied the corner booths. Billy Grizzle and his cronies seized the largest table in the middle of the room. The loudmouth good-ole-boys stuffed their faces at the same time lobbing sarcasm and one-liners back at each other.

Eli offered a coffee refill to a woman sitting in the booth next to the jukebox. Next, he paused at the deputy's table. "Does anybody need coffee or extra biscuits?"

Billy stopped slurping from a mug of coffee long enough to display an extra-wide smile causing his flabby jowls to obscure the corners of his mouth. "Nope. We're full. As usual, Elijah, you done yourself proud." The officer pressed his palm to his gut and birthed a vulgar belch. "Ah, excuse me. By the by, you ain't seen any more of them colored hobos, have you? I warned them boys not to bother you no more." The deputy pulled a toothpick from his pocket and stuck the sharp end in between his two front teeth, excavating remnants from his meal.

Eli set his jaw. "No, but it's really my business, now isn't it?"

The deputy examined the hidden gem he mined before placing the pick back between his lips. "Yeah, well, I don't trust freeloaders any farther than I can throw 'em." Although Billy's snarl exposed his prized gold tooth, the toothpick somehow remained in place.

Most of the men left the table, their shoes depositing dried mud underneath, dirt Mary Louise would have to sweep up later. Billy was the last person in the group to hoist himself from a chair. He moseyed up to the cash register wearing the same boots that crushed Mundy's hat, the ugliest brown boots Jessy had ever seen.

CHAPTER SIXTEEN:
TOAD CHOKER

February snuck into Bonita Springs bringing a chilly rain. All during dinner on Thursday evening, the steady downpour hit the front windowpane of the McAfee home. Although Lynette and Rita May cleaned up the dinner dishes, the smell of ground beef, kidney beans, and stewed tomatoes lingered about the room.

Davis McAfee inched forward in a chair, his powerful forearms resting on the table in front of him. While still handsome, his skin displayed signs of premature aging with wrinkles surrounding his eye sockets, profound for a forty-two-year-old man. For those who worked outdoors every day, the sun showed no mercy. Davis swept both hands into his reddish-brown hair. "Four days, and the rain keeps on a-coming. Damn! When is this toad choker gonna end?" The man's contagious foul mood infected everyone in the family, everyone except Lynette.

Wearing a gentle smile, she drifted toward her husband. "Honey, you've got to have a little faith."

Davis slammed his fist on the table rattling a bowl of fruit. "Woman, you know that if the pickers can't work, there ain't no money coming in this week." His body drooped.

Lynette squeezed his hand. "Don't fret none, honey. There's emergency cash in the coffee can. The Lord will provide. Perhaps it'll stop raining tonight. I'll pray on it."

"You go right ahead." He grumbled to himself. "Lot of good it'll do."

Lynette eased into a chair next to her husband and bowed her head. "Dear Lord, we appreciate the rain, but we really could use some sunshine. You see, my man has to work. Thanks for listening. Amen." She stroked her husband's calloused hand. "There now. You wait and see."

* * *

Due to the previous week's weather, Mr. Sherwood's grove sat four days behind schedule. Consequently, when the showers ended, Davis insisted Rita May and her mama help him out. He demanded that the teenager skip school in order to mind the three youngest while Lynette picked tangerines from first light in the morning until two o'clock in the afternoon. As soon as her mama finished her shift, it was Rita May's turn to work in the groves until dark.

On Friday, February 8 at six in the morning, Lynette nudged the teenager awake. "I gave Marilyn a bottle and she's gone back to sleep. Wake the boys in an hour. There's oatmeal in the double boiler on the stove." At the slight beep of a car horn, her mama tiptoed out of the room and shut the door gently behind her. Tires spun in the gravel outside as Rita May fell back into a dream. She was a movie star and lived in a Hollywood mansion. The baby's cry roused her into reality.

Her brothers went to school, but Rita May stayed home, keeping the little girls and the baby fed and out of harm's way. She washed dishes, swept the kitchen, and soaked a pot of beans for supper, all before noon. Rita May's sisters, all except Marilyn, entertained themselves with baby dolls outside in the grass. Around two-thirty, while nibbling on a sandwich, the teenager flinched at the squeal of brakes. Lynette opened the front door, her face scarlet from the heat, her dress soiled. "You best make it quick. He's right disagreeable today."

Rita May dawdled, taking her time to fetch her sneakers. She strolled to the car and then climbed into the passenger side of the station wagon. The teenager glared at her papa. "I hate you for making me work."

A scowl veiled his face, his eyebrows melding together. "Watch yourself, girl. Don't be getting an attitude with me. I ain't in the mood for your sassy mouth today."

Rita May switched on the radio in the midst of a news bulletin. "The first Negro student to attend the University of Alabama, Miss Autherine Juanita Lucy, checked in for her first class today alongside the rest of the students. Miss Lucy, the youngest of nine children, was born in Shiloh, Alabama, the daughter of a sharecropper."

"If she can do it, so can I." Rita May hadn't meant to speak aloud.

"Daughter, that girl in Alabama ain't got nothing to do with you. Shut off that thing." At a fork in the road, Davis wheeled the station wagon closer to the gate.

Most mornings except Sunday, Davis and his boss, Mr. Sherwood, each hauled a truckload of men and woman, a mix of races and nationalities, to the groves where laborers nabbed canvas bags to strap on their shoulders. Pickers lined the rows of tangerine trees on a ten-acre block. Functioning in tandem, they filled the sacks with ripe fruit from trees three times the height of an average man. The men and women dumped the contents of the weighty bags into crates stacked under each tree. As each crate filled, the workers loaded the harvest onto the larger trucks, which made delivery at the packing plant the next day.

The cessation of the rain left brutal heat, oppressive humidity, and acres of mud. Rita May joined the workers, the blazing sun scorching the girl's exposed fair skin, her shoulders and arms catching the worst of it. Thank goodness, her mama's wide-brimmed hat protected her face and neck. She didn't need another freckle on her nose.

For Rita May, culling tangerines didn't take much concentration even as each piece of fruit she picked represented a hatred for her lot in life. *Why doesn't Papa have a better job? Why did Lynette have to have so many babies?* Whenever she crammed a tangerine into a sack, the resentment festered. She gnawed in the inside of her cheek until she felt a painful twinge.

By six that evening, Rita May's head throbbed, and the smell of citrus and sweat made her nauseous. Her tummy queasy, she pushed herself to fill five more crates working beside a group of Spanish-speaking men at the northeast corner of the grove. When she strayed to the west side, she joined several young women and made use of a bucket of water and ladle nearby.

A girl climbing the ladder to Rita May's left signaled a hello. "I'm Tanya Crowder. I'm not a regular." Perspiration soaked the girl's white blouse; her dark brown arms gleamed in the sun.

"Me, neither. I'm Rita May McAfee." She drank more water.

Tanya placed a tangerine into her sack. "McAfee? Your daddy's one of the bosses." She pulled another piece of citrus from the tree. "I'm only working here so I can save enough money to run away from this crappy town." The girl let the tangerine slip from her hand. The fruit landed under the ladder.

"Be careful. Mr. Sherwood won't pay you for busted fruit." Rita May tossed the fallen citrus in the trash bucket and ascended her own ladder. "Why do you want to leave?"

"I want to find a different life, I guess. I'm going to New York City where people of color get more respect. Gonna find me a job singing in a nightclub. Granny says when I sing "The Man I Love," she hears the voice of Billie Holiday. Can't earn no money singing in this dead town."

Rita May plucked more fruit from a large branch. "Did you already finish high school?"

"I'm fourteen and almost grown so I don't need school no more. I got to earn money for Granny and save up for a train ticket."

After the sun sank into the horizon, a purple haze tinted the sky above the trees. The ringing of a loud cowbell signaled the end of the workday. As if someone flicked a switch, the workers scrambled down the ladders, emptied their sacks, and ran to the water buckets. Within minutes, the men and women climbed into the trucks like escapees scaling a prison wall.

Tanya tagged along with Rita May, who found Davis leaning against his station wagon. "Papa, are you driving a truckload back to the camp?"

He blotted his face using his handkerchief. "Not tonight. Mr. Sherwood asked Hector to make the run over to Estero. Let's you and me go on home."

She turned her head. "This is Tanya."

"Hey, Mr. Mac."

Davis muttered a hello.

"Papa, can we give her a ride to the bridge? Please?"

He slid inside the driver's side of the Woody and squinted at Tanya and his daughter. He cranked the ignition. "She can crawl in the way back."

"Okay, we'll both ride back there." Rita May and Tanya scrambled inside.

Side by side facing the back window, the girls chatted about boys, movie magazines, and their favorite color of lipstick. Noticing the bulging middle button on the front of Tanya's sleeveless blouse, Rita May tugged at the front of her own shirt, which was flat as the bottom of an iron skillet.

"Hey, I've got candy." She fingered the bottom of her pocket and handed a sticky butterscotch to Tanya. "Does your daddy pick fruit, too?" Rita May tossed another piece of candy in her mouth.

The girl tore off the wrapper. "Don't got no daddy." Sucking on the sweetness, Tanya leaned backwards, her hands behind her neck. "Hey, Mr. Mac, can you let me off up here?"

Davis slowed the station wagon. "Yep." When he idled at a Stop sign near the Imperial River, both girls jumped out.

"Thanks for the ride," said Tanya.

Rita May walked up to the driver's side window. "Tanya and me are walking part way home together."

Davis huffed. "Suit yourself, but I wouldn't dillydally. There ain't gonna be much of a moon tonight."

The station wagon rambled over the bridge leaving Rita May and Tanya on the side of the road. The teenagers crossed over the river as the sky turned dark. The slamming of a nearby door caused the girls to turn toward the noise.

Oliver Edson, who appeared to be locking the entrance to the Everglades Wonder Gardens, squatted near the door. He looked to be searching for something. When he straightened, his leer fell on the girls. While rearranging his toupee, he shouted, "Hello there. Do you lovely young ladies need a lift? It's awful dark out tonight."

Tanya didn't blink. "Oh, no. Not him. That guy is bad news. I ain't letting no crazy White cracker put his hands on me. Later, Rita May. I'm taking a short cut." Tanya sprinted down a dirt path leaving Rita May frozen in her tracks.

Startled at Tanya's words, Rita May took a second to collect her wits. The teenager began slowly, taking one step at a time, her heart vibrating throughout her body.

"Hold on there, honeybunch. You're Rita May, that gorgeous redhead. Please, let me give you a ride. I promise I won't bite. We could just get acquainted a little bit. You know what? I'll give you a hundred-dollar bill if you'll get in my car."

At the sound of Oliver Edson's southern drawl, the redhead ran for her life.

CHAPTER SEVENTEEN:
SINNER IN A CYCLONE

Rita May paused at the shack's door for a second, grabbing the piercing pain at her waist. When she bounded inside, she bolted the flimsy lock behind her.

Her mother rushed to her side. "What's wrong?"

The teenager slumped into the empty chair closest to her papa, the one saved for Lynette. The rest of the family sat around the table, their mouths full of pork chops and sautéed apples.

Davis clasped her shoulders. "Girl, what's the matter with you? What happened to make you act like this?"

She answered between quick breaths and swelling sobs. "A man… was…chasing me."

Davis puckered his brow. "Who was chasing you?"

The reply spewed from her mouth. "Oliver Edson stalked me from the bridge. He wouldn't leave me alone." She wiped her sweaty forehead. "He said he wanted to run his hands through my red hair."

Gregory asked, "Who is Oliver Edson?"

Clark held the baby on his lap. "Did he hurt you, Rita May?"

Lynette stood behind her daughter. "Boys, hush now. Let me tend to her."

Davis stood up, his chair sliding backward. He paraded around the room, murmuring to himself, one hand fisted inside the other. "Oliver Edson, huh?"

"Honey, let me handle this for now, please." Lynette dashed to the sink. She soaked a dishcloth in cool water and squeezed the rag several times. "Rita May, come here."

The teenager obeyed. Lynette gently placed the cloth on the girl's splotchy face. Then she dabbed both of her daughter's wrists before she set the compress at the nape of Rita May's neck. She leaned close to the girl's ear and whispered, "You're safe now. Nobody is going to hurt you." The woman pitched the rag on the counter and then ran water into a clean glass. "Here, sip this and go on back to the table."

Once seated, Rita May hunched forward. Using her shirttail, she wiped both eyes.

Davis set a box of tissues in front of her and sat down. "Daughter, calm down and tell me everything."

She sipped water and composed herself. "He works at the Wonder Gardens. When I cut my foot the other day, he put a bandage on it. The man was weird, but not scary. Not like he was tonight."

"He chased you in his car?"

"Yessir." She slurped from her glass. "He drove a vomit-green convertible real slow next to me, and he kept trying to get my attention. I told him to leave me alone, but he wouldn't go away." She sucked in air and exhaled. "I started running and turned into the woods. That's where I thought I'd lost him, but I didn't. He came closer and closer. I kept on going at full speed, and I guess he got tired and quit. When I reached our road, he was nowhere in sight." She cracked the knuckles on each hand. "Daddy, I want you to kill him or at least beat him up and toss him in the river. He should pay for scaring me like that." She stared at Lynette who sat next to Davis. "I don't understand. Why in hell did that weird little man want me?"

"Language, girl." Lynette lowered her voice. "We'll talk later."

Davis yanked the napkin from his collar and flung the cloth on top of a half-eaten plate of food. "Don't you worry none, Rita May. I'll fix the degenerate son of a bitch. It may take a day or two to handle it, but I promise you he won't bother you or anybody else again. In the meantime, the Everglades Wonder Gardens is off limits. And if you do happen to run into Edson again, you run like crazy to a crowded area on the double."

Lynette spoke in a soothing tone. "I'll heat some water. You could use a good soak, girl."

* * *

Once everyone went to bed, Rita May snuck outside and sank in an area of cool grass, her arms hugging her knees.

The door creaked. Lynette sat down beside her. "Can't sleep?"

"Nope. I keep wondering why Oliver Edson picked me."

Lynette swept a strand of hair from her daughter's face. "You are a nice-looking girl, and you're gonna be even prettier when you grow up. Boys will soon notice how special you are. Listen to me, honey. There will be all kinds of men in your life. The sad fact is it won't be easy to tell the difference between the good ones and the bad, but you'll learn soon enough. Mr. Edson, he's the worst of the lot—evil and dangerous."

"Yeah, he's a creep."

"Remember. If it doesn't feel right, it usually isn't. Always rely on your gut."

"Don't worry, I will."

* * *

Because Jessy invited Rita May to the diner for lunch, the redhead hurried to finish her chores by eleven o'clock. The girls agreed to make their Saturday afternoon special and dress up a bit. After all, Mrs. Goodman offered to teach them a free jewelry-making class at one-thirty that afternoon.

Rita May promptly arrived at Aunt Prissy's Kitchen at noon wearing her best dress, the lilac one with puffy sleeves and a scallop-edged collar. Lynette purchased the beauty at a Thrift Shop owned and managed by the Garden of Gethsemane Evangelical Church back in Druid Hills, Illinois. Rita May loved the dress. Though lately, the dress felt a little snug. She checked her feet, proud of clean white socks and a pair of Mary Janes, a recent secondhand store purchase.

Stepping into the noisy restaurant, she spotted Jessy, who was dressed in a pale-yellow dress, on a stool in mid-spin. There were no empty tables, and several people stood in line next to the cash register. Waitresses zipped back and forth from the kitchen transporting overloaded trays.

Rita May approached the soda fountain. "Hey."

Jessy's rotating came to a halt. "Hey, yourself. Oh, I love your dress. Hop on." She patted the empty seat to her right. "It's saved for you."

Rita May hoisted herself onto the stool and browsed the lunch options written on a chalkboard above the swinging doors. "I can't decide. You?"

"Easy. I'm ordering a hamburger, French fries, and a milkshake. Today's Special."

"Me, too." She tightened the bands at the bottom of the pigtails her mama meticulously braided, the plaits neat and silky-smooth.

"My daddy is a great cook. You'll love his burgers. Uh, how come you didn't go to school yesterday? Were you sick?"

"No." She bit her lip.

The blonde waitress appeared behind the counter. "Hi, girls."

Jessy nodded at her friend. "This is Rita May."

The ginger-haired beauty forced a shy grin. She quickly determined that Delilah was cute, but her mama was prettier.

"Pleased to meet you." Delilah withdrew a pencil stub from behind her ear. "Are y'all ready to order?" She pulled a notepad from her apron pocket.

Jessy stared at the chalkboard. "We'll both have the special and strawberry milkshakes."

Rita May spoke up. "I'll have chocolate, please."

"Okey dokey." Delilah charged into the kitchen.

The older girl twirled on her stool coming to a stop to face the lunch crowd. "Boy, this place is jam packed today."

"It's the Saturday regulars. Lots of people come for breakfast and don't leave until after lunch. I can name everybody here."

"Okay, smarty pants. Who are the guys sitting at that table over there?" Her finger indicating a booth in the far corner.

Jessy's demeanor smacked of confidence. "Gil O'Brien is the tall man in the green overalls; he works the night shift at the Wonder Gardens. To his right is Frank Tilton. He's the Tuesday and Thursday teller at the bank. He's always cracking jokes. That's Willie Staples, the druggist wearing the plaid shirt. I've never seen him smile. Not once. On the end, that's my Grandpa Caleb. The chubby guy at the other end of the table is Fizzle Grizzle. I forgot to tell you...uh, Skip and I saw some teenagers kissing behind the bleachers at the ballfield yesterday."

"I'll do you one better. The other night when I went to find Papa, I passed by the Blue Note. Grizzle was there."

"So?"

"When he walked out of the honkytonk, a blonde woman was on his arm. She got in his car, and they started making out, you know, playing backseat bingo. They drove off together in the patrol car. Isn't he married?"

"Yeah. He's married to Pinky, the crossing guard." She wrinkled her nose. "Did you say they were playing bingo? In the car?"

Delilah barged in on the girls' conversation. "Here you go."

Both girls swiveled to face their plates. In between bites, the kids discussed pertinent club business—whether or not to allow boys to join. It took fifteen minutes of discussion to agree to a *yes*.

After she had scarfed up every crumb on her plate, Rita May patted her tummy. "I'm so full I could pop."

A bell jingled and a draft of tepid air wafted across the soda fountain. Delilah greeted the customer, her words loud enough for everyone to hear. "Welcome to Aunt Prissy's Kitchen. There's a seat at the end of the counter or you're welcome to wait. I can grab you a table in about ten minutes."

"Thank you, I'll just set on down right here. My, my, you sure are a beauty."

The man's nasal intonation struck Rita May as familiar. She craned her neck as Oliver Edson squirmed onto the far stool. A chill tore through her. She poked Jessy's arm. "I'm done. I'll meet you outside." She shimmied off her seat.

Jessy opened her mouth letting go of the straw. "But you haven't finished."

"Tell your dad I said thanks." Rita May darted through the exit, almost running into a woman and a little boy right outside the door. She jogged to the side of the diner, her heart quaking in her chest.

Five minutes later, Jessy called out to her.

"I'm over here," said Rita May squatting in the shade.

The younger girl ran to her side. "Why did you leave in such a hurry?"

"Oliver Edson came in and I didn't want him to see me. Let's get out of here."

During the girls' stroll down Childers Street, Rita May volunteered the particulars of her harrowing experience. "...and I told Papa to kill Oliver Edson."

Jessy swallowed. "He wouldn't really murder him. Would he?"

"He might if he got mad enough." The teenager kept watch over her shoulder all the way to the Goodman house.

Jessy rang the bell. Skip opened the door, his eyes probing hers. "Uh, I can't play today. I'm busy."

Jessy smirked. "We're here to take the jewelry class, dummy."

He hollered toward the back of the house. "Mom, my girlfriend and her string bean friend are at the door."

"For the one hundredth time, I'm not your girlfriend and quit calling Rita May names."

Sylvia Goodman arrived at the door dressed in a Kelly green blouse tucked into khaki pedal pushers. "Welcome, girls."

"Mom, I'm going over to Noah's house." Skip sauntered past the girls and down the front steps.

"Be home before dark."

Jessy took the lead and trailed Sylvia into a spacious dining room. Shoeboxes crammed full of craft materials and seashells sat on a vinyl daisy-patterned tablecloth protecting a sizeable mahogany table.

Sylvia tapped the table's edge. "Okay, girls. Why don't you sit across from each other?"

The redhead sat on the far side and folded her hands in her lap. "I love your bouffant hairdo, Mrs. Goodman, and the way your bangs sweep off to one side."

"Me, too," said Jessy.

"Why thank you. It's a new style I'm trying."

During the next hour, the lady of the house taught the girls how to create jewelry with seashells. When Rita May required guidance gluing a teeny cockle to an earring post, Sylvia hovered close emitting the scent of jasmine.

At the end of the session, Jessy placed a one-dollar bill in Sylvia's hand. "Daddy said I have to pay you no matter what you say. If it's okay, I'd love to take another class in a couple weeks."

"Of course. Call me and I'll put your name on my calendar. Follow me, girls. I've got refreshments."

The kids shadowed the striking woman into a bright blue and white kitchen where the threesome sipped pink lemonade and munched on warm chocolate chip cookies. Sitting in the breakfast nook, Rita May looked down at her lap. She soon felt Sylvia's stare.

"Honey, are you okay? You're as pale as a sinner in a cyclone. Do you feel ill?"

Rita May cracked the knuckles on her left hand. "No, ma'am. Um, you and Deputy Grizzle are friends, right?" She repeated the habit on the right hand.

"Yes, we are. Why do you ask?"

"Uh, a scary thing happened to me the other night." She took a deep breath. "When I was walking home, a man named Oliver Edson chased me. He wanted me to get into his car, but I outsmarted him and ran so fast he couldn't keep up. Papa says Mr. Edson is a pervert, and that Deputy Grizzle should stick the degenerate son of a bitch smack dab in jail."

CHAPTER EIGHTEEN:
THE FINAL STRAW

Eli slid a stack of grimy plates through the opening behind the soda fountain. Rafael, the recently hired kitchen help, accepted and rinsed off the dishes before loading them in the dishwasher. Balancing on the end stool, Jessy swallowed the last bite of a fried egg sandwich as her father wiped the counter behind the soda fountain.

"Daddy, have you heard from Mama lately?"

"Yes. In fact, I received a postcard from her yesterday. I meant to give it to you." He turned around and sighed. "We'll read it tonight at bedtime. I promise."

"So she's coming home soon?" Jessy held her breath.

"We'll see. The good news is that she's well enough to leave the rest home and she rented a furnished apartment. She's doing so well that she has her eye on a temp job. Before you were born, Margaret was a secretary and typed one hundred words per minute."

Jessy exhaled a puff of air. "I miss her."

"Of course you do, Baby Girl." He rinsed the dishrag in the sink. "If the warm weather continues, why don't we go to the beach on Sunday afternoon?"

"Can Rita May come with us?"

"Sure. Now, go on outside. Skip will be here any minute."

* * *

The open windows in the classroom did little to alleviate the stuffiness when the humidity reached its peak. Set on the highest speed, the corner fans barely stirred the air. Jessy's skin felt sticky. She licked her lips and tasted salt.

The restless children wiggled in their seats; several in the back whispered among themselves. Miss Rydell cleared her throat. "Quiet, class." Aiming the end of a rubber-tipped pointer at the extensive map of the United States, she tapped in the center of the State of Texas. "State and capital, please."

Jessy and several other children raised their hands.

The teacher glanced around the room. "Opal?"

"It's Texas and Austin is the capital. *A u s t i n.*"

She whisked the pointer northward. "Correct. This one? Skip?"

"Wyoming. Cheyenne is the capital. *C h e y e n n e.*"

"Yes, it's Wyoming, but you're incorrect about the capital. Does anyone else have the answer? Gregory?"

"It's Madison. *M a d i s o n.*"

"Excellent. Class, please close your books and tear out a piece of lined paper from your tablet. Also, you'll need a sharpened No. 2 pencil."

Jessy and her classmates groaned.

"Please put your name at the top of the page, and number your paper from one to forty-eight. List each state next to a number. Next to the state put a dash and the corresponding capital. An example would be *Florida – Tallahassee.* There, I've given you an answer already. You'll have twenty minutes to complete the list. Starting…now."

Miss Rydell, wearing shiny new penny loafers, clomped back to her desk. "Don't forget, spelling counts."

Over the holidays, the fifth-sixth grade teacher rearranged the classroom, switching Jessy's seat to the second to last desk on the third row. Now she sat in front of the most despised girl in fifth grade, Opal Grizzle. Jessy concentrated on her assignment until she felt a puff of hot, stinky breath on the back of her neck. She whispered, "Stop it."

Miss Rydell noted the verbal exchange. "Jessica, am I going to have to move your seat again?"

"No, ma'am." She pinched her nose using her left hand. She scribbled *Alabama – Montgomery* with her right.

Everyone in Jessy's class disliked Opal Grizzle. The girl failed to use deodorant and stunk to high heaven; but the real reason everyone hated her—Opal was a bully.

Opal commanded a small but effective crew—Pudge, a square-shaped girl who dressed in her brother's clothes and kept a pocket knife inside her shoe, and C.J., whose parents named her Cynthia Jane, a spindly girl who wore her toffee-colored hair in pigtails. The trio professed expertise at letting curse words roll off their tongues.

Although most kids feared the Grizzle Girls, Jessy managed to avoid all three. However, back in October, Opal went too far when she called Rita May poor *White trash in* front of the class. Jessy retaliated by drizzling playground sand into Opal's thermos one day when the intimidator wasn't paying attention.

* * *

Fifteen minutes had passed. On the first Wednesday in April, Jessy sat alone under the oak tree in the center of the playground. "Where is Rita May? Recess is almost over." When she looked up, Opal and her pals stood in front of her.

A grimace appeared on the leader's face. "So where's your skinny freckly friend today?"

Jessy shrugged and bit into a piece of apple she'd saved from lunch.

Pudge poked Jessy's shoulder. "She asked you a question."

Jessy leered at the girl. "Disappear."

Opal leaned in and spoke in a singsong voice. "We've got a secret. Somebody's daddy got tossed in jail last night. Now he's a jailbird." She snickered. "Amy Nash heard Principal Newsome talking to Mrs. Cook this morning. I guess my daddy speaks the God's honest truth when he says that the McAfee family is low rent."

Jessy gritted her teeth. "You're lying." She stood up, parted the three-some, and made a beeline back to the school building. She burst into the classroom, interrupting her teacher who was wiping the chalkboard. Jessy hesitated a second before she spoke. "Uh, Miss Rydell, why did Rita May go home early today?"

The petite woman's back was to the girl, both hands pushing the wet cloth back and forth over the blackish-green board. "Mrs. Cook mentioned a family emergency. That's really all I know. Lord, I hope it's not serious." Miss Rydell continued the seesaw motion of removing the morning's chalk dust.

"Don't worry. I'll find out." Jessy sank into her seat visualizing a number of disturbing scenarios.

* * *

It was twenty minutes past three, and Jessy couldn't find Gregory and Clark. "I'm going home. Come on, Skip. Keep up."

He trailed six feet behind her. "I'm trying to, but you're walking too fast."

"I'm in a hurry. I have something important to do today."

The kids stopped at the diner's entrance. Skip collapsed on the drive-way in front of the caladium-filled wooden planter. "Here, take your things. I can't move another inch. Need water. Dying of thirst."

"Oh, quit being such a weenie. Meet me in back." Jessy yanked her lunchbox and book from his hands and tramped inside.

Mary Louise, a wet cloth in her grasp, stretched to clean off the soda fountain counter. She swiped the surface twice. "Hi, Jess."

"Is Daddy in the back?"

"No, sweetie. He and Delilah drove to the Lee County farmers market, but they're due back shortly. Camilla wants to see you though."

Moving backwards into the hinged doors, Jessy tiptoed into the kitchen without making a sound. Straddling a stool at the back of the kitchen, Camilla mumbled while thumbing through a notebook full of recipes. Jessy embraced the cook from behind.

Startled, Camilla turned around and laughed out loud. "Hey there, little one. Now that you're home from school, I'm supposed to tell you to go on and put on your play clothes. When you get back, I'll fix you a bite." The cook re-positioned the navy bandana that concealed her hair.

"Can Skip have a snack, too?"

"Of course. I like that sweet boy."

Jessy darted through the storeroom to the screened door in the back. "Hey, Skip. Camilla's got snacks. Wait here."

In five minutes, dressed in olive green shorts and a white sleeveless blouse, she paused at the backdoor gripping a paper bag between her teeth and clutching two chilled bottles of Coca Cola. She grunted at Skip who opened the door and grabbed the drinks. Both kids devoured Camilla's sugar cookies while sitting on the top step.

Jessy wiped crumbs off her shirt. "I'm going over to Rita May's house. You coming?"

Skip slurped the last of his Coke. "Sure. Mama won't be home until after six." He threw away the trash and set their empty bottles near the back door before he scooped up his books and lunchbox.

The pair trekked to the baseball field. Because a pickup game was in progress, they bordered the fence to the corner before changing direction. Facing northwest, the kids scaled a damaged piece of chain-linked fencing close to the railroad tracks. Although no train was visible at first, an escalating rumble convinced the twosome to hesitate at the depot.

Skip jumped first. "The train's coming fast." Jessy followed him, but lingered on the grass near the other side of the tracks.

The whistle blew several times motivating the children to cover their ears. The noise, a high-pitched resonance of metal on metal, signaled the train's deceleration. Minutes later, the engine picked up speed proceeding down the tracks, leaving a duo of unrecognizable vagrants behind. A white-haired man and a ball-capped woman donning knapsacks scurried into the narrow gorge, disregarding the children.

Because Rita May had once alluded to the whereabouts of the shacks owned by Mr. Sherwood, Jessy felt comfortable leading Skip on a hike east down Main Drive. When they reached the dirt road, they took a sharp right. The kids turned left onto another road scarcely wide enough to fit a car and soon spotted a row of small rundown houses.

Jessy put her hands on her hips. "This must be the place, but I don't know which one it is."

Skip brushed damp bangs off his forehead. "We'll just have to knock on every door."

When no one answered at the first residence, Jessy and Skip fled to the next house where a baby's squeal prompted him to knock twice.

"Who's there?"

"Skip and Jessy."

Rita May opened the door.

Jessy stepped in front of Skip. "We're checking on you. May we come in?"

"I guess…for a minute." Rita May moved aside to let her guests pass. "I'm babysitting. Lynette and Davis aren't here right now."

Skip whispered in Jessy's ear. "Is she talking about her mom and dad?"

Jessy nodded and scanned the front room of the McAfee home, which was more of a dining room than a living room. She counted six straight-backed chairs and two benches, surrounding a long wooden table. A single light bulb swung from a wire over the table, and two lit candles adorned the windowsill above the sink.

Jessy and Skip found seats at the table, Skip setting his lunchbox and books next to him.

Before long, Clark bounded into the house with his little sisters in tow. A few minutes later, Gregory entered from the back of the house, a fussy one-year-old in his arms. "Hey, guys."

"Give me that baby." Rita May snatched the child from her brother. "And, Clark, you take the girls back outside. Jessy and Skip came to visit *me*." Grumbling to himself, the youngest brother seized his sisters' hands and stormed out. Gregory sat beside Skip.

Jessy opened her arms. "Oh, please let me hold her. She's adorable."

The teenager set the squirming baby on her friend's lap. "Jessy, meet Marilyn." She sighed. "I guess you're here on account of my emergency. I'm surprised you didn't hear what happened."

"Nope, not a thing." Jessy let the baby play with her watch.

"Well, last night my papa and his buddies attacked Oliver Edson when he left work at the Wonder Gardens."

Skip leaned in toward Rita May. "Who is Oliver Edson?"

The tall redhead stood up. "A pervert." She opened the refrigerator door and retrieved a baby bottle. She gave it to Jessy. "Feed her and she'll love you forever."

Jessy waved the milk in front of the baby. Easing backward into Jessy's lap, the curly-haired toddler hooked chubby hands around the bottle. Marilyn giggled and stuck the tip of the rubber nipple between her lips.

Jessy beamed. "She's so cute. Go on and finish, Rita May. Uh, what's a pervert?"

"A really bad man who likes teenage girls. Anyway, the men jumped the sicko, stuck him in the back of Papa's station wagon, and drove down the dirt road behind Ike's Bar. Papa beat him to a pulp and left him there thinking he might be dead."

Jessy's mouth fell open.

"But, some Good Samaritan found him and drove him to the hospital in Fort Myers. Papa said he was pretty beat up." Rita May bit her bottom lip. "When he woke from a concussion, the idiot blabbed to the Lee County sheriff. They arrested Davis early this morning. Lynette's gone to ask Mr. Sherwood for bail money."

"Wow," said Skip. "How long will your dad be in the slammer?"

Rita May shrugged. "Could be hours. Could be days. I don't think the sheriff should've punished Papa. Oliver Edson is the bad guy. Why isn't *he* in jail? The creep deserved everything he got. Isn't there a Bible quote about taking revenge, like an eye for an eye?"

"Yeah. Once at Mass, I heard a priest read where that was in an Old Testament verse."

Down at the end of the table, Skip and Gregory began a thumb-wrestling competition. In the midst of a maneuver, Skip paused. "What in the world did Edson do anyway? Something really terrible?"

Rita May answered by hitting the high points of her ordeal.

"You're lucky you're a fast runner." Skip spied the clock on the wall. "Holy cow! I gotta go."

"Bye, sweet Marilyn." Jessy kissed the baby's head.

Rita May lifted the baby out of her friend's arms and set the bottle on the table.

"Hope your daddy comes home real soon." Jessy shadowed Skip to the door.

* * *

On the way to the Goodman's house, Jessy gave Skip permission to hold her hand. However, when the kids spotted Skip's mom on the front porch, the two unclenched and slowed their pace.

"Skipper Theodore Goodman, you're late again." Sylvia's southern accent resonated throughout the neighborhood.

Jessy scurried in front of the boy. "Hi, Mrs. Goodman. Please don't be mad at him. It's my fault we're late. We stopped to visit Rita May. There was an emergency. You see, the sheriff threw Mr. McAfee in jail since he almost killed Oliver Edson. Remember when Rita May asked you to talk to Deputy Grizzle about that pervert?"

Sylvia licked her lips. "Of course, but Oliver Edson is the one who belongs in jail, not Mr. McAfee. I've heard rumors about that snake, Edson, ever since he slithered into our town. I reported your friend's run-in, and the deputy assured me he took care of the matter." She folded her arms in front of her. "Let me fetch y'all some lemonade. Then I'm gonna give Billy, uh, Deputy Grizzle a call and give him a piece of my mind." Sylvia marched inside.

Twilight brought a calm to the neighborhood as the kids sipped their lemonade under the porch light on Skip's front stoop. An official Lee County vehicle cut short the tranquility by skidding to a stop in front of the Goodman house. Billy Grizzle gushed from his patrol car. He loped across the grass until he reached the kids who made room for him to pass.

Billy charged into the house, the screened door thumping behind him. "Sylvia, are you okay?"

Jessy and Skip peered through the screen.

Standing in the entryway, Sylvia clamped onto the deputy's arm. "Why didn't you arrest Oliver Edson like I asked you to do?"

Jessy whispered, "This is going to be good."

The deputy sucked air between his teeth. He exhaled, his expression transforming into a scowl. "What the…Oliver Edson? Dispatch called this an emergency."

"It is an emergency to me." Sylvia pursed her lips.

"I promised you I'd check up on the situation and I did. You know damn well I can't put a man in jail on your word or the hearsay of a kid, especially one of them picker's kids. I chose to give Edson the benefit of the doubt. He's not such a bad guy, maybe a little hinky though. Anyway, I understood that the poor man got beat up pretty bad."

"Wait a minute. Did you say *picker's kids*? And *the poor man*? I am sick of you and your ways, Billy Grizzle. This is the final straw, mister. You let a menace go free, but you incarcerate poor Mr. McAfee for protecting his daughter from that evil, disgusting freak."

"The sheriff made that call. Not me."

"That's right. Pass the buck. I guess I can't count on you for anything. What a major disappointment you have become! We're done, finished, kaput."

"Shut up, Sylvia. The whole neighborhood can hear you."

"Get off my property. Right now!"

Sylvia barely shoved the deputy, but he stumbled into the screened door and onto the porch. Giggling at the commotion, Jessy and Skip scattered into the yard.

Billy stood on the front steps glaring at Sylvia, his face distorted, his cheeks splotchy red. Wormlike veins protruded at his temples. "Who do you think you're talking to, woman? I'm the Deputy Sheriff of Lee County. I don't need this shit. You're disrespecting me and I won't have it."

Sylvia lifted her chin and crossed the threshold out to the front porch. "Why don't you go on home to your stupid wife?" At that moment, she looked down and spied the children squatting in the nearby grass. "Skipper, come inside and go to your room. You stay in there until Deputy Grizzle leaves. Jessy, you run on home."

Skip obeyed, and Jessy set her glass on the bottom step. She moseyed to the left edge of the yard. Determined not to miss a moment of the argument, she saw her chance and doubled back, crouching in the bushes under the bay window.

The shouting match progressed into the middle of the Goodman's freshly mowed front lawn. The ruckus attracted Sylvia's neighbors who loitered in bunches in their own yards much like Georgia's fire ant population in the summertime. When in another fit of anger, Skip's mother swung at Billy, the punch landing on the side of his jaw. The deputy wasted no time; he poked his index finger inside his mouth.

Jessy, afraid of reacting, covered her mouth with both hands, knowing Grizzle's precious gold tooth could be in jeopardy.

Billy cupped his cheek and waggled his jaw. Easing closer to Sylvia, his nostrils flared. He shoved her and shouted, "Enough."

Skip's mother landed on her butt. "Ow!" The shock on her face vanished when she fingered the torn hem of her dress. "Look what you've done, you horrible man." She struggled to her feet, her ruby lips pinched together.

Jessy focused on the couple. She never saw the dark figure cross the lawn until he appeared at the deputy's side.

"What the…," Billy stuttered.

Mundy Mike's hands clinched the deputy's shirt collar. He lifted Billy clean off the ground, the officer's toes skimming the grass, his arms flailing at his sides.

Eye to eye, Mundy scowled at the deputy. The hobo's speech remained steady. "Shame on you, Mister Deputy. You hurt that pretty woman. You, of all people, should know better than to treat a lady like that, you being such a high and mighty policeman and all. How come you is acting more like a backwoods redneck? Too bad all the folks around here just saw you push her down." The hulking man, easily a head taller than his nemesis, gradually lowered Billy to the ground. With his unyielding stare, Mundy's tone was soft but firm. "You ain't never gonna do that again. Are you?"

Billy stammered a weak response. "Nnnn...no."

Sylvia inched next to the deputy. "Mister, don't worry. I'm fine. He didn't harm me one little bit. You can let go of him."

The hobo released his hold on Billy's lapels. Mundy Mike removed his hat. Bowing his head, he said, "Are you sure, ma'am?"

"Oh, yes. Anyway, he's going home right now." She sneered at Billy. "Aren't you, Deputy Grizzle?"

"Yes. Yes, I am." The officer, visibly shaken, took his kerchief, wiped his ashen face, and took three wobbly steps backward.

Sporting a satisfied expression, Mundy Mike lumbered toward his buddies. When the hobo reached the curb and put on his hat, Jessy sighed. She switched her focus to Billy, his face puffed and reddened.

In a flash, the deputy pulled a gun from the holster on his hip, aiming the weapon at the unaware trio in the street. Billy cocked the pistol. Two deafening *clicks* pierced the air.

Jessy couldn't breathe.

"No, you don't, Billy Grizzle." In an instant, Sylvia tugged at the deputy's arm knocking the gun from his hand.

Billy leaned over to retrieve the weapon, but it was too late. Mundy Mike and his friends were gone. Jessy inhaled a deep breath of fresh air, letting it out in tiny increments.

The porch light cast a glow on the couple, keeping them in Jessy's view. The deputy scowled at his mistress, his dark eyes seething with rage. "You and me, Sylvia. We're history." He plodded through the yard to his vehicle.

"You're not calling the shots, Billy Grizzle. I am, and I say we're through. In fact, I'm going to give Pinky a call in the morning. I think it's time she and I get together and have a little chat." Sylvia dashed into the house paying no heed to the gawking neighbors. She slammed the door behind her.

Jessy checked her watch. Where had the time gone? Once Billy's cruiser zoomed away, she sprinted toward the diner, the occasional street-light guiding her way. Later that night, all tucked in bed, she thought about Mundy Mike scaring the bejeebies out of Deputy Grizzle and smiled. The scene put a cherry on top of a spectacular day. "I can't wait to tell Rita May."

CHAPTER NINETEEN:

GOODER N' GRITS

Twenty-four hours had passed. Rita May glanced out the window as she spread peanut butter on another slice of bread. The station wagon stopped on the oyster-shelled road in front of the shack.

Clark ran to the window. "Mama and Papa are home."

The children's parents waltzed inside. The boys hung onto Davis, and the little girls encircled Lynette's legs. The mother eyed her oldest child. "Did they behave?"

"Yes, ma'am. I'm fixing sandwiches for their dinner. Marilyn's already been fed. She's in the crib with a bottle."

Once she washed her hands, Lynette seized a handful of cups from the cabinet. "I'll pour the milk."

* * *

After Rita May put the baby to bed and tucked the girls in for the night, she joined her father and the boys at the table. "Are you free, Papa, or will you have to go back to jail?"

Davis leaned on his elbows. A lit cigarette hung from his lower lip as if it belonged there. "Yeah, I'm free. The sheriff didn't have enough evidence to hold me, and that spineless wimp, Oliver Edson, ain't gonna be pressing no charges. The little weasel's smarter than he looks." He clutched Rita May's hand. "I did hear a rumor that he might be hightailing it back to Miami. Oh, yeah, I forgot. I've got a little present for you." He hunted through his pockets and retrieved a greasy black hairpiece.

The boys broke into roaring laughter and Rita May released her father's hand. "Not funny."

"Give me that disgusting thing." Flitting by the table, Lynette stole the toupee along with her husband's overflowing ashtray. She tossed the hairpiece in the trashcan and sprinkled the ashes and butts on top. "All in all a good day. Prayers answered."

Davis took a drag on his cigarette. "Jail was tolerable. At least I got a free meal, but I couldn't stay asleep. Cells were busting at the seams. Jabbering going on all through the night."

Lynette ran water into the basin. "Jails fill to the brim when people can't find work and families go hungry."

Gregory rocked backwards causing the front legs of his chair to rise. "Were there any real bad criminals in there?"

"Nah, mostly drunks sleeping off benders and bums in for panhandling." He huffed a final drag. "Give me my ashtray back, woman, or do you want ashes landing on the floor."

"It was filthy." She strategically placed the clean dish next to his hand. "Nasty habit."

Rita May scratched the blossoming hives on her arm. "Why didn't the police arrest Oliver Edson?"

"I guess scaring and chasing a teenage girl ain't a felony crime. Edson didn't hurt you or molest you, so the law won't put him in jail. As it stands right now, he won't even catch a slap on the wrist. I tell you that weasel's got friends in high places." He smashed the cigarette butt into the ashtray. "Lynette, any more of them sandwiches left?"

Lynette stood at the kitchen counter. "Yes. I'm fixing you one as we speak. By the way, did you overhear anything worth repeating down at the jail?"

"Let's see. I did hear about an upcoming town meeting. From what little I heard, I think people want to discuss how to keep the coloreds in their place. Seems nobody wants any part of this civil rights stuff." He pulled his feet out of his boots, one at a time. "Bedtime, kids."

* * *

On Sunday, April 8, toting her mama's sunhat, Rita May sprinted to the diner in her last year's swimsuit. Covering the areas where the suit was too snug, she wore one of her papa's T-shirts, which hung to her knees. With a folded old towel in her grasp, she sat at the picnic table, waiting on her friend. Five minutes later, Jessy rushed from the diner apartment lugging a beach bag and two fluffy towels.

"Hi, Rita May. Isn't it a perfect day? Daddy's busy fixing ham and cheese sandwiches, but we can go ahead and climb in the pickup."

The girls settled into the truck bed at the same time the back door creaked. Wearing a chartreuse cover-up that accentuated her tanned legs, Delilah pranced out of the building toting a multi-colored beach bag. Eli tailed her in his conservative beach attire, a navy-blue swimsuit and a white short-sleeved T-shirt.

The perky blonde hopped on the running board. "Hey, girls." She eased into the passenger side.

Rita May bent the brim of her straw hat. "You didn't say she was coming with us."

Jessy groaned and rolled her eyes.

When the truck reached the end of Bonita Beach Road, Eli wheeled into the public lot, a half-a-block from the beach. The girls couldn't climb out of the truck fast enough.

As she crossed the sand, Rita May spotted Jessy glancing back at Eli and Delilah. "Maybe they're just friends."

"Uh huh." Jessy unloaded her beach bag onto a towel.

Before running toward the surf, Rita May slipped her T-shirt over her head. She dropped it on the sand. When she reached the edge of the sand, she dipped her toe in the water. A ripple splashed her legs.

The younger girl waded in beside her. "If she knows what's good for her, Delilah better leave my daddy alone."

Rita May ignored Jessy's comment. After all, the beach was far more interesting. For the next few hours, the girls took turns swimming in the surf and constructing a sandcastle. After lunch, they cooled off by floating on top of the water.

Eli gathered the beach paraphernalia for the journey home right as the sun melted into the horizon. "Pack up, kids. Time to go."

The girls bunched together under an ancient quilt in the back of the pickup truck. On the ride home, Rita May focused on the scenery around her, releasing her hair from its confining ponytail, and letting the breeze tangle her curls. "Thanks for inviting me. It was a blast." The teenager shivered. "Can I have some more of that blanket?"

"Sure. I only want my legs covered," said Jessy.

Rita May chuckled. "Have you ever had a dream about Fizzle Grizzle?"

"Don't think so."

"I did last night, a funny one. Mundy Mike was sitting on top of the deputy, bashing his head in and smashing him flat as a super-sized pancake."

Both girls giggled. Rita May yanked the quilt to her chin. "Has anybody seen Mundy since that fight at Skip's house?"

"Not that I know of. When I think about the way he scared Deputy Grizzle, I can't stop laughing. Billy's face was white as a sheet. I bet he peed his pants." Jessy broke into the Grizzle song.

"Wish I could have been there. Hey, why don't we have a party at our next club meeting?"

"Okay. I'll bring the drinks. You bring something to eat."

"Yeah, and afterwards maybe we could go see Madame Zora. How much money have you saved up so far? I want her to tell me what's in store for me, you know, in my future. Don't you?" Rita May rubbed her cold feet together.

"I have fifty cents. If you still have a dime, we only need forty cents more."

"I'll manage the money somehow even if I have to steal change from Papa's pocket when he's asleep. Why don't we go Saturday after the meeting?"

"Sounds good to me."

* * *

Rita May halted her stride in front of the shack to observe the explosion of color the sunset left behind in the sky. Wincing at the redness on her shoulders, she twisted the knob and opened the door to the aroma of tomatoes and savory herbs.

Snapping beans into a pot at the table, Lynette glanced up from her task and smiled at her daughter. On the other end of the table, the boys played a card game of Go Fish, while Marilyn sat on a tattered blanket on the floor. The baby squealed at the sight of her big sister.

"Hey, pumpkin." The teenager bent to pat the child's curls. "Mama, it was the best day, but I got a tad sunburnt."

"Glad you had fun, but I really need your help now. Please, check on the girls. They're taking a bath; you know how they play more than scrub. When that's done, feed the baby. Once you get them all ready for bed, I'll fill the tub and sprinkle baking soda in the water. That'll cool you off. Meanwhile, I'll mix up a vinegar solution for later to help lift some of that redness out of your skin."

An hour later, Rita May, clad in a nightshirt, squatted into the seat across from the baby whom Lynette secured in a chair with a strip torn from an old sheet. The teenager prepared for battle. Giggling the entire time, the toddler slapped down bites of strained carrots. Combat finally ceased the moment Marilyn tasted a mouthful of sweet applesauce. However, the baby remounted her attack by later tossing a clump of mashed potatoes at her sister.

"I surrender." Rita May stared at the mess on the floor. After the cleanup, she wiped the baby's sticky hands and mouth, untied the toddler, and lifted her out of the chair. "Mama, I'm going to put this little monkey to bed."

Lynette smiled through tired eyes. "OK. Then it will be your turn."

* * *

The distinctive odor of vinegar inundated the front room causing the boys to scramble out the door. Holding her breath, Rita May lifted the nightshirt over her head and held it at her chest. Lynette dipped the end of a cloth into a bowl. She gently patted the pungent liquid onto her daughter's face, bare freckled shoulders, back, arms, and tops of her thighs.

Rita May carefully slipped the shirt back on. Both she and Lynette curved toward the door when tires crunched the gravel outside. A car door slammed. Davis lumbered inside with the boys in tow. He flung his cap onto a wall hook behind the door and then claimed a chair at the table's end. Bending over, he removed his boots.

Lynette pinched the back of her husband's shoulders. "Did you have a tough day?" She massaged his sore muscles, kneading the stiffness as if it was biscuit dough.

The weary middle-aged man tilted backwards. "The usual. Supper ready?"

"Go clean up. Soup's done and the cornbread needs slicing into wedges." She darted to the stove. Dipping a ladle into the steaming reddish-brown broth, she scooped chunks of beef and vegetables into deep bowls. "Seems you're a bit late tonight."

"Yeah. I checked out the meeting at the community center. The majority of folks doing all the talking were grousing about politics. I'm glad I don't have a dog in that fight. I'll stick to worrying about feeding my family. Anyway, we'll be settled in North Carolina by summer."

Clenching her teeth, Rita May felt a sharp pain in her jaw. *Sometimes he makes me so mad.*

* * *

On Saturday, the RJ Club meeting convened at one o'clock. Jessy furnished two bottles of Fanta Grape, and Rita May supplied samples of the yellow cake Lynette baked for Davis' birthday. Trying not to disturb a crumb, the redhead carefully parted the wax paper, unveiling two gooey chocolate-frosted slices.

Jessy took a bite from her slice. With her mouth full, she said, "As Grandpa Caleb says, 'it's gooder n' grits.'"

Rita May grinned. "Mama doesn't bake often, but when she does, it's to die for."

Even though the midday heat climbed to the high eighties, cooler temperatures prevailed under the banyan tree. The meeting lasted over an hour. When Rita May checked Jessy's watch, she said, "It's nearly two. We better go."

The best friends trooped south on the Tamiami Trail. After four blocks, the girls hung a right on Kentucky Street where they passed Villa Bonita, the classy hotel famous for its mineral springs. Several blocks down, the duo veered right at Nevada Street. One couldn't miss Madame Zora's pink and lime green eye-catching cottage in the middle of the block.

The girls stalled at the walkway. A brightly colored sign hung from two chains attached to a t-shaped post in the front yard. Painted on a picture of a giant blue hand were the words, Palm and Tarot Readings by Madame Zora, Princess of Bulgaria.

Rita May and Jessy approached the entrance in silence. Jessy rapped on the doorframe. Within seconds, the purple door opened. Wind chimes tinkled as if announcing the tall, foreign woman who appeared in the foyer, wearing a multicolored caftan that cascaded to the floor.

"I am Madame Zora, Princess of Bulgaria. How may I help you?"

Rita May swallowed hard. "Ah, we want our fortunes told."

"Then you may enter." Her voice was husky, her accent thick. "I have been given the gift of clairvoyance, a talent passed down through my family for ages. I can foresee the future."

"Okay." Rita May turned to Jessy. "I need your money."

The younger girl obeyed and gave her coins to the teenager.

Opening her hand, Rita May revealed four dimes, two nickels and two quarters. "Madame Zora, as you can see, we don't have enough money. We only have a dollar. Do you think you could read both of our fortunes and maybe give each of us fifteen minutes of your time?"

"Please." Jessy's eyes opened wide and round like the smiling moon painted on the woman's front door.

"Because I like you, I will give you discount. Follow me." Madame Zora drifted into a hallway appearing to float above the floor. Stopping at a doorway, she parted a curtain of suspended crystal beads. The girls blindly followed the woman into a dark room where colorful posters plastered the walls, a few depicting Madame Zora's homeland. Thick drapes masked the windows, impeding any trace of sunshine. The only light came from flickering candles placed around the room on small tables.

Passing an upholstered settee, Rita May stroked a red velveteen arm. "Wow, your place is really cool."

"Give me payment, please." Madame Zora peered at the girls from under fake black lashes.

Biting the fragile tissue inside her cheek, Rita May presented the money to the woman who sat in a top-heavy wingchair in the far corner of the room, her hands folded on top of a round table.

The Madame's silver-gray hair fell from under a lavender scarf wrapped around her head. She gestured toward an adjacent chair. "Sit."

Both girls squeezed into the smaller chair.

Madame Zora stared into the flame of a hefty candle centered on the table, her golden hoop earrings swinging from her earlobes. "Whose destiny shall I disclose first?"

Rita May nudged Jessy.

Clutching the younger girl's hand, the mysterious woman closed her eyelids as her cherry-stained lips uttered a sentence in a foreign language. She opened her eyes. "Your full name?"

Jessy played with a lock of hair near her cheek. "Jessica Rose Blanchard."

"Such a lovely name, Jessica Rose. Let's take a peek at what lies ahead for you." Madame Zora's sharp fingernail drew an imaginary line in the girl's palm. "Here is lifeline. You are lucky. You will have a long life, yet quite ordinary. My dear, do you see your heart line right here? Mmm, yes. You will find love early in life, but see there, how line splits in two." She licked her lips. "Your heart will break one day, but again you will love… this time a handsome stranger." Staring into the child's eyes, she smothered Jessy's hand in her own. "Your parents are content? Yes?"

Jessy lowered her gaze.

"Wait." Madame Zora touched her temple. "I sense trouble there. I am sorry. A person drives the loved ones apart. I speak truth, yes?"

"I guess so. Yes, ma'am." Jessy twisted a hank of hair between her fingers.

"Do you have questions?"

Jessy shook her head as she wilted against the back of the chair.

Madame Zora beheld the older girl. "And your name, my dear?"

"Rita May McAfee." Her heart hammered her ribcage.

Madame Zora grabbed the redhead's hands. The woman's finger, ringed with a magnificent opal, traced the lifeline on the teen's hand. "You, too, will live a long life, but a far more remarkable one. You will have many loves."

In her sitting position, Rita May fidgeted, unable to stop bouncing on the balls of her feet, her knees moving up and down. "Anything else?"

The woman met Rita May's glare. "You are restless, yes? You have questions for Madame Zora?"

Rita May licked the tiny bump on the corner of her lip. "Uh, will I have lots of money someday? Will I travel to faraway places?"

"The spirits do not hurry. Patience, my child." The exotic woman looked down; as if in a trance, she chanted in her native tongue.

Jessy scooted closer to Rita May.

Madame Zora lifted an ornate tin box, about the size of a pack of cigarettes, from a shelf behind her. "I believe the cards hold the answers." She set the container in front of the candle and waved her hands in the air near the lid. Next, using her index finger, the woman's blood-red fingernail tapped a repetitive rhythm on the box top. She slowly opened the lid dislodging a pack of Tarot cards; she shuffled the deck into two stacks. Once Madame Zora dealt four cards face down on the table, she chanted again.

Rita May licked her lips. "Are you casting a spell on me?"

"Be still." The woman inverted the first card. "The Four of Hearts." She tapped the card. "You will soon travel, my child."

Rita May smirked. That was old news. If her papa's plans came to fruition, her family would soon be moving to North Carolina.

Madame Zora repeated the motion fingering another card. "Ace of Diamonds. This card represents money, but sadly, your reward will come at a significant cost. I must warn you, Rita May. You shall reap what you sow, my child." When she flipped another card, her bracelets jingled. "The three of clubs. A wealthy suitor will enter your life." When she overturned a fourth card, Madame Zora winced. "Ah, my dear, this card can be a grave omen."

"What do you mean?" Heat rose in Rita May's face.

Jessy wrung her hands. "Is the Ace of Spades bad luck?"

The woman's fingernails drummed the table. "The tarot cards do not represent luck. One doesn't scoff at or dismiss the Ace of Spades. Each card tells a story, a prophecy. The order of the cards is important." She carefully lifted the Ace. Cradling the ominous card between her hands, she studied Rita May. "Some call it a sign of doom, in other words, an evil card, or even the death card."

Jessy got to her feet. "Time to go."

Rita May bit her bottom lip. Glancing at Jessy, she licked her mouth tasting blood.

Gently, as if the malevolence might tumble onto the table, Madame Zora set the Ace next to the other cards. She gave the older girl a wicked sneer. "Don't fret, Rita May McAfee. The spirits sometimes taunt us. You have nothing to fear. Yes?"

"I'm not scared of your stupid cards." Rita May rose too fast. A bit lightheaded, she held onto the edge of the table.

"There is more to tell, my dear."

"No, we're done."

Parting the hanging beads, the girls escaped Madame Zora's dark magic by bolting through the room and out the door into daylight. At the end of the front walk, Rita May doubled over clutching the hems of her shorts, her breath coming in spurts, words catching in her throat. "I don't believe any of that witch's…voodoo talk. Do you?"

Jessy shook her head. "No way. Madame Zora is a fake. She probably made everything up. Let's go."

The kids headed back to the banyan tree. It was half past four when they crawled inside their hideout. "She said those things just to frighten us," said Jessy.

Settling into a crevice in the roots of the tree, Rita May cracked the knuckles on both hands. "She didn't scare me, but when she put that death card down on the table, it was creepy. She must get a kick out of scaring kids."

Jessy wiggled inside next to Rita May. "She's no big deal. Anyway, I think we have more things to worry about than Madame Zora and her dumb cards. There's Mundy Mike and, of course, Fizzle Grizzle who plans to get rid of all the hobos."

"Grizzle can't get rid of those guys. Hobos decide to move on when they're good and ready. Do you think they're scared of some small town deputy? Even if Grizzle stuck one or two in jail again, they wouldn't stay locked up for long." At the onset of a leg cramp, Rita May pointed her toes. "I was wondering. Is Delilah still chasing your dad around like a puppy dog?"

"Yeah. Every day. I hate her guts."

"I don't blame you." A siren's wail caught the girls' attention. Rita May crooked her neck. "I can't see where it's coming from." She scrambled from the hideout. "It's a fire engine."

Jessy crawled out just in time to witness the hook-and-ladder truck brake and turn the corner onto Childers. Black smoked billowed into the sky.

Rita May turned to Jessy. "It's the diner. It's on fire!"

CHAPTER TWENTY:

ONE CARD SHORT OF A FULL DECK

The Bonita Springs fire engine parked sideways blocking both Childers Street and the Tamiami Trail. Three volunteer firemen worked to put out the blaze that engulfed the south side of Aunt Prissy's Kitchen.

Jessy hugged Eli's waist. "Are you all right?"

"Yes, Baby Girl, but the diner's a mess. Thankfully, everyone is safe."

"Did the firemen save Muffin?"

"Don't worry. I'll find her. She's probably hiding under your bed."

An inebriated Deputy Sheriff Grizzle staggered toward them. "Hey, Elijah. Would you like me to cart that young'un off to the motel down the street? It's the least I can do for you." His toothpick moved up and down when he spoke.

Jessy grabbed Eli's hand.

"No thanks. Go home and sober up, Billy. You've done enough for today. Tiny is standing right over there. I'm sure he'll give you a lift home, or if you'd rather, I'll call Pinky for you."

The deputy murmured something under his breath as he shuffled off toward his buddy.

Jessy stood in silence. *I hope he chokes on his toothpick.* Sensing a faint tap on her shoulder, she turned around and caught a glimpse of Rita May before she disappeared into the crowd of people that had congregated near the ballpark gate.

* * *

At eight-thirty that evening, Eli and Jessy dined at the Blue Crab, sharing a family-size portion of fried shrimp, corn on the cob, and French fries.

"The food is okay, but yours is better." Jessy dipped a bunch of fries into the pool of ketchup on her plate. Shoving three into her mouth, she tried to speak. "I'm glad the fireman found Muffin. Do you think she's okay by herself at the motel?"

"Finish chewing, please." He took a sip of his coffee. "Yep, y'all can snuggle together tonight. I've got to check on the diner one last time. Will you be okay if I leave you alone?"

"If there's a TV in the room, Muffin and I will be just fine."

"I guess you'll have to sleep in your T-shirt tonight, but I'll stop by the drugstore before they close. Besides a toothbrush, what else do you need?"

"Maybe a comb and an *Archie* comic book or *Betty & Veronica*." She sipped her Coca Cola.

* * *

At around nine thirty-five, Eli left Jessy in Room 6 of the Highway 41 Motor Court. Not particularly captivated by an episode of *Gunsmoke*, she stretched out on the double bed. She fell asleep with Muffin curled inside her arm. Sometime after midnight, her dad's keys clinked on the dresser.

"Hi, Daddy. You look tired."

Eli turned the knob on the TV. "There was a lot to do." He handed her a paper bag. "Here. Go brush your teeth and scoot under the covers. I'll find you some clean clothes in the morning. Hurry up now." His tone left no question about his disposition.

Ready for bed, Jessy tiptoed up to Eli who had collapsed in the gray swivel chair, his feet propped up on a matching ottoman. His weary eyes smiled when she kissed his cheek. "Night, Daddy."

"Night, Baby Girl." He closed his eyes.

* * *

Jessy awoke to an empty motel room. Not interested in Sunday morning television programming, she tried out the swivel chair and perused her comic book.

Soon Eli entered the room with a slight grin on his drawn face. "Hey there. I brought you something to wear. Mrs. Goodman was nice enough to loan me a few of Skip's things. Go on, take a quick bath, and get dressed. When you're done, we'll grab breakfast someplace. Are you hungry?"

"Yes, sir. I'm starving to death."

"Of course, you are." He smiled. "You know, Jess, we got lucky. The kitchen took the worst of the fire. We can go on home after we eat."

Eli chauffeured his daughter to a café on the other side of the river. She chowed down on scrambled eggs, bacon, and toast with grape jelly. He sipped on black coffee. His furrowed brow was an indication of his mood.

Jessy sipped tomato juice. "Why are you so sad? Didn't you say we were lucky?"

"Yes, I did. The insurance money will help, but in order to make major renovations in the diner, I'll need a bank loan. I have no idea when I'll be able to open for business again."

Once her father paid the check, Jessy begged him for more information about the fire. "Come on, Daddy. I'll be twelve in June and a teenager in a year. Please tell me what happened."

Outside the café, he helped Jessy up into the cab of the truck. He settled into the driver's seat, cranked the engine, and shifted gears. The truck idled in park. "The dinner rush had yet to begin. I think Delilah told me there were only five or six customers in the diner. Well, in walks Billy smelling of liquor. He started pestering her, and apparently, he wouldn't let up. I was in the storeroom when I heard Delilah shouting something about him going too far, stepping over the line, etc. About that time, I entered the service area and saw her slap the living fool out of him. Camilla soon got wind of the incident and came out to investigate as I led Billy right out the door."

"Wish I could have seen Delilah slap him."

"When I went back inside, Camilla was running through the diner screaming 'Fire.' I learned later that before the spat occupied all her attention, she had switched on the gas under a skillet to burn off some grease. Camilla blames herself. She thinks that she also left a dishrag too close to an eye on the stove. The bottom line is the fire quickly consumed the kitchen and smoke filled the diner. Luckily, I got everyone out while Delilah called the fire department at the payphone on the corner."

"The whole mess sounds to me like it was Deputy Grizzle's fault."

"Accidents happen, Jess. Nobody's responsible."

"Sorry, Daddy, but I hate the man. He's always showing up where he's not wanted—like one of those ugly Palmetto bugs."

"No, you don't hate him. Your mama taught you better."

At the mention of Margaret, her eyes grew moist. "Why isn't she home yet? We need Mama here with us."

Eli piloted the truck to the back of the diner. He shut off the engine. Wriggling closer to Jessy, he put his arm around her shoulders. "I don't have any answers right now, Baby Girl."

* * *

The summer months brought more business to Bonita Springs. With the growth of beach condominium and hotel construction in Naples, the traffic flow along Highway 41 increased. Once Eli received the insurance money for the fire damage, he hired a contractor to rebuild the kitchen and refresh both the inside and outside of the restaurant with a coat of paint. He also purchased a fancy display case, finally giving the cash register an appropriate home. Eli purchased new uniforms for the waitresses, the fitted aqua-blue knee-length dresses accentuating Delilah's curves and Mary Louise's popsicle-stick figure. Eli prepared to reopen an updated Aunt Prissy's Kitchen on June 4, 1956.

On the first day of the month, also the last day of the schoolyear, Jessy sat on her bed planning her summer schedule. The busy agenda included making jewelry on Wednesday afternoon at Sylvia Goodman's house, grabbing a few library books from the Lee County Bookmobile on Fridays, and showing up for RJ Club meetings on Thursdays and Saturdays at one o'clock.

On June 9, the club held an unprecedented induction ceremony. The unbearable heat in the cramped clubhouse motivated the kids to hold the event outside under the shade of the banyan tree. Rita May performed the ceremonial blood ritual as her brothers and Skip recited the standing oath.

* * *

A week later, Jessy sat on the curb in front of Lawhon's with her dad, awaiting the arrival of the five-thirty Greyhound Bus. When the vehicle came to a halt, several people stepped down into the daylight. Everyone in the vicinity stared at the woman who was last to step onto the pavement. At first, Jessy didn't recognize her mother whose raven hair hung loose on her shoulders. The beauty wore a black and white polka-dot dress and black patent pumps. A thick red patent leather belt cinched her waist showing off curves the child had never noticed.

In the evening, mother and daughter ate supper in a corner booth at the newly renovated Aunt Prissy's Kitchen. Jessy wanted the evening to be perfect. Earlier, when she discovered that Eli assigned Mary Louise to work in the service area, she exhaled a sigh of relief knowing he picked Delilah to handle the fountain customers. Swallowing the last forkful of salad, Jessy examined her mother's face. No dark circles surrounded Margaret's eyes.

Jessy touched her mother's sleeve. "I love your new dress."

"Thank you, sweetie." Margaret tendered a polite smile. "On sale at Burdines."

Jessy stabbed at a plateful of chicken and noodles. "I can't wait until you're home for good." She chugged from a large glass of milk. "I hope you're back by my birthday. I'm having a beach party and inviting all my friends. You can help me plan the games and food."

Placing her silverware on the edge of her plate, Margaret's expression altered. "This is important. I want you to listen carefully." She licked raspberry-tinted lips. "I was going to wait to tell you, but…" She dabbed her mouth leaving a lip print on the napkin. "Jessica, your father and I are getting a divorce. You will soon be splitting your time between the both of us, visiting me at least twice a year on weekends, plus some holidays and a month during the summer. Naturally, you'll stay in Bonita Springs during the school year."

Jessy's fork fell from her hand onto the plate. Her insides quivering and nauseous, she crossed both arms to cover her middle. "You can't do that. Divorce is a mortal sin." She searched her mother's face. "It's against the law for Catholics to divorce." She tasted the tears dripping into the corner of her mouth.

Margaret patted her daughter's hand. "Stop crying. You're not a baby anymore, Jessica Rose. Please calm down. You'll cause a scene." She cupped

Jessy's face in her hands. "I know this is all very upsetting, but I want you to know that your daddy and I love you very much. That is the most important fact to dwell on. The reasons behind the separation are nothing for you to be concerned about. Unfortunately, in life, unpleasant things happen, Jessy…even to Catholics." Margaret handed the child a tissue from her purse. "People change. Relationships change. Your father and I still care about each other, but we simply cannot live together. We disagree on too many important issues."

Jessy wiped one eye, then the next. "But I don't get it. Don't you love each other anymore?"

"It's a complicated situation, and you won't understand until you're older. We're much happier apart." She chuckled. "In fact, lately, your father acts more content than a bull in a barn full of cows. Surely, you can see it." Margaret's lips pursed when her head turned toward Delilah who stood at the cash register with a customer.

"I don't like Delilah either," said Jessy.

"Mmm. Well, your daddy better hold onto his hat. The girl's inching closer and closer all the time."

Clutching a crumpled tissue, Jessy leaned into Margaret and sobbed.

"Honey, this is the best thing for everyone. Your dad and I don't expect any problems. We want everything to go smoothly." She pulled a compact and a lipstick out of her shiny black purse. "By the way, I have a new friend I want you to meet. His name is Marshall Blakely. I know you'll like him. He's a bank manager in Miami Beach." She applied a new coat of red over her lips.

"When am I going to visit you?" Jessy blew her runny nose.

Putting her things back in her purse, Margaret said, "Later in August and possibly for Thanksgiving. You'll adore the area where I live and the Atlantic Ocean side of the state. The beach goes on forever when the tide is out."

"I don't want to hear anymore." Squirming away from her mother, Jessy bolted from the booth. She shoved both doors into the kitchen and ambushed Eli as he pulled a scalding apple pie out of the oven.

"Be careful. I've told you..."

She stood in front of him, her sad eyes giving her away. "Mama told me about the divorce."

He placed the tray on the stove, pulled off his oven mitts, and steered Jessy into the storeroom. Father and daughter embraced until she stopped crying.

* * *

Late into the night, no one saw Jessy crouched outside her bedroom door. She silently witnessed her parents hovering over the kitchen table. First Margaret and then Eli signed the document dissolving their fourteen-year marriage.

Afterwards, Jessy tiptoed into her own room, softly closed the door, and crept into bed, her body exhausted. It was as if each leg weighed fifty pounds. She heard her father make up a bed on the sofa. Soon Margaret shut the door to the master bedroom. An unnatural peace crept over Jessy's home, taking the place of past resentments, hostility, and outbursts of anger. The child pulled up the covers and snuggled with the cat. Although she wanted to cry, her tears had all dried up.

No more arguments would wake Jessy during the night.

* * *

On the second Monday in June, disturbing news created a buzz throughout the diner's breakfast crowd. Over the weekend, the State of Florida placed Gil O'Brien, the night manager at the Everglades Wonder Gardens, the man who regularly accepted the diner's leftovers, into a sanitarium. Rumor had it that the man's stay might be a lengthy one.

The episode triggering the manager's mental collapse occurred on Friday night. Due to excessive noise coming from the alligator pit, Gil checked on the reptiles he fed an hour earlier. To his shock, he witnessed the gators dining on something other than table scraps—the mutilated body of a Black man. According to town gossips, Gil lost his marbles that night, the State officially calling it a nervous breakdown. The Sheriff's Department later issued a statement indicating the dead body appeared unidentifiable.

Appeasing Jessy's undeniable curiosity, Billy and five of his buddies replayed the incident in explicit detail all morning long. The deputy spoke the loudest, his mouth full of one of Camilla's biscuits. "The guy in the pit was basically gator bait. Poor ole Gil. I hear he's a wreck. I mean the kid was always one card short of a full deck, but he's a decent sort. The corpse is nobody."

When Delilah topped off Billy's coffee, she added her two cents into the conversation. "It's a pity that no one has any idea who the victim was."

As Billy opened his mouth, his toothpick landed on his protruding belly. "I doubt we'll ever find out. The gators made a meal outta him." He picked up the toothpick and then slipped it between his lips.

Jessy hadn't moved a muscle during the discussion. Not able to finish her waffle, she squirmed off the stool. She passed the cash register where her father stood. "Daddy, was Mundy Mike the man in the pit?" Her voice trembled. "Please tell me the truth."

"No worries. The sheriff's boys found a man with a slight thin frame. Now does that sound like Mundy to you?"

"Oh, what a relief." She hurried back to her stool before a waitress could take away her unfinished breakfast.

* * *

The conversation at the afternoon meeting of the RJ Club centered on the identity of the mutilated man in the pit. Jessy smacked on a piece of Double Bubble. "Daddy said it wasn't Mundy." She blew a pitiful bubble.

Skip popped his own pink bubble, causing gum to stick to his lips. "It must have been Gator Breath, the skinny one. I just wonder how in the heck he got into the pit in the first place. I mean, the fence around it is really high, and there's barbed wire on top of it."

The kids unanimously agreed. If the man was Gator Breath, he must have been an acrobat in the circus when he was young. Jessy felt sorry for the man who suffered such an unspeakable death. Yet once the club meeting adjourned, she neglected to mourn his demise for another minute.

* * *

Four days later at nine-thirty at night, Mundy Mike surfaced again rapping on the diner's back door. Jessy's dad gave the hobo a paper sack full of day-old biscuits, a fried chicken drumstick, and a slice of apple pie.

It would be weeks before Jessy laid eyes on Mundy again.

CHAPTER TWENTY-ONE:
NO AX TO GRIND

Jessy spun halfway around on her fountain stool. "The Sunrise Special, please."

"Now there's a hearty meal. Are you sure you can handle it?" Although she spoke in a pleasant manner, Mary Louise rarely smiled.

"Yes, ma'am. Today is my birthday."

At that moment, Delilah, whose hair looked a little blonder than the day before, parted the swinging doors with one hip. "Happy Birthday, young lady."

To appease her father, Jessy remained polite to the floozy. "Thank you, ma'am."

Balancing a tray of dirty dishes in her arms, the waitress sashayed into the kitchen.

Mary Louise echoed Delilah's sentiment. "Happy Birthday, Jess." The unassuming waitress set a State of Florida paper placement on the counter. She placed a napkin and a set of silverware on top of Pensacola and a glass of orange juice close to Jacksonville.

Jessy twirled again, but paused to address the man sliding onto a neighboring stool. "Hi, Grandpa Caleb."

"Hi there! Aren't you the birthday gal? How old are you today? Ten?" He winked at Mary Louise.

"No sir, I'm twelve."

"Twelve. You can't be."

"I am." Jessy swallowed a swig of her juice.

Caleb planted a kiss on the child's cheek. "Happy Birthday."

"Did you and Grandma Betty remember to buy me a present this year?"

"Of course, we did. Your grandma wrapped a box with yellow paper and tied a blue ribbon around it. She left the box on the kitchen table next to another surprise."

The child's grandmother usually came through with a Nancy Drew Mystery Story to add to Jessy's collection. The surprise was sure to be either a pan of banana pudding or a key lime pie. "Did I tell you I'm having a party?"

Mary Louise caught Caleb's attention and lifted the coffee pot, her gaze probing his face. He lifted a finger in reply at the same moment he said, "Nope," in reply to his granddaughter.

Jessy swung her legs under the counter. "It's tomorrow at the beach at five o'clock. We're going to grill hot dogs, eat watermelon and cake, play games, and swim."

"Am I invited to this shindig?"

"Sorry, Grandpa. Only my friends and Daddy are invited."

"Oh, I see." Caleb carefully sipped his scalding hot coffee. "Mary Louise, I'm so hungry my belly thinks my throat's been cut. I'll have three eggs over easy, a slab of country ham, and a couple of biscuits, and oh yeah, hash browns."

The waitress jotted his order on a pad. She stuck the notebook in her pocket, grabbed a tray of dirty glasses, and then disappeared through the swinging doors.

Jessy added a few more party details. "And Camilla's baking a chocolate cake. She's going to write something on the...top." Her eyes cast downward.

"Sugar, what's wrong?" The elderly man bent toward the child.

"Mama used to decorate my cakes."

"Bless your little heart. It's a pity about your folks. Now, I have to tell you something about the Blanchard family. We live by one motto. When life knocks us down, we get right back up even stronger and wiser." Caleb grinned, his brown eyes twinkled under bushy white eyebrows.

Mary Louise interrupted Jessy's melancholy. Balancing two plates, the waitress placed the hot food in front of the child and her grandfather.

He folded a napkin into the neck of his T-shirt. "Boy howdy, I'm so hungry I could eat a whole pig."

Lifting her chin, Jessy spied Eli coming toward her carrying a saucer topped with a gooey cinnamon bun, a burning birthday candle stuck in the icing. Camilla poked through the parted doors when the breakfast crowd joined Eli, Delilah, Mary Louise, and Caleb in an off-key version of "Happy Birthday to You." Jessy blushed and blew out the tiny flame.

She wasted no time digging into the cook's best-selling homemade pastry. Still hungry, Jessy wiped sugar from her lips before she polished off the rest of her breakfast. She sniffed, expecting the glorious aroma of bacon, but instead a foul odor invaded her nostrils. Billy Grizzle, who often stunk like the trash bins behind the school on a ninety-degree day, slid onto a stool on the other side of Caleb. Several times, Jessy once heard Camilla refer to the deputy's overactive sweat glands as the reason he reeked during the heat of the day. Jessy pinched her nose and rotated halfway to the left.

The deputy grabbed the older man's shoulder. "How's life treating you?"

Caleb swallowed a mouthful of hash browns. "Fair to middling."

"I'm stuffed. See you later, Grandpa." Jessy hopped off the stool.

"Don't forget to come on by and pick up your presents." The old man swiveled toward the deputy. "I heard you flapping your gums over at that table there. Sounds like you've got a bone to pick with somebody."

"Uh, I ain't usually got no ax to grind, but I'm just saying that some things need to be taken care of around here."

Jessy waltzed toward the restaurant door and caught Caleb Blanchard's remark. "You don't say, Billy. You don't say."

* * *

Driving back from Mass on Sunday, Eli stopped for lunch at the Davis Bros. Cafeteria in Naples. He grabbed two trays, and stood behind a woman and her teenage son in the line.

He let Jessy charge in front of him. "So how many people have you invited to your party? Don't forget to count me and Delilah." He chose a miniature dish of lime Jell-O cubes from the options in front of him.

"Delilah?" Jessy asked a server behind the counter for a fried chicken leg.

"Yeah, she's very fond of you."

A young man, whose hairnet covered his eyebrows, handed Eli a plate of food—thick slices of roast beef and gravy, a serving of rice, and a doughy roll.

"Green peas and corn, please." Jessy faced her dad. "Are you going to marry her?"

"Whoa! I don't plan on ever marrying again. You're my first priority, Baby Girl."

Father and daughter carted loaded trays to the back of the seating area and found a corner table. Eli gobbled up a forkful of roast beef. "I do wish you'd try to like Delilah. She's fun, and I enjoy her company. I don't know what else to say, but it's easy, you know, comfortable."

Jessy didn't want to hurt his feelings. "Sure, Daddy. I'll try harder." Anyway, at the last club meeting, Rita May told her that it was okay to lie if it was absolutely necessary. The conditions of said lie, according to her friend, were as follows: one, you can lie to keep yourself out of trouble, or two, you can lie to protect someone you like. Jessy sipped cold milk through a straw in a carton that fit perfectly in her hand.

* * *

At four o'clock, Jessy and four of her friends squished into the back of Eli's truck. She proudly wore her new pink-and-white-striped bathing suit, a gift from her mom. Rita May donned her one and only swimsuit, and Clark and Gregory sported faded trousers shorn above the knees. Each child held a towel. Skip, whose mother dressed him in Beall's Department Store finery, wore a bright cobalt pair of swim shorts and T-shirt to match. He carried a fluffy blue towel under his arm. After the excitable kids calmed down, Eli insisted Skip squat on his inner tube to keep the rubber doughnut from blowing off the back of the truck.

The jam-packed Chevy pickup arrived at the end of an unpaved road, meeting up with three carloads of Jessy's classmates. The kids raced ahead to the sand, while Eli and Delilah lugged a cooler and bags of food to a deserted stretch of beach.

Jessy's dad dug a pit the size of Skip's inner tube. He lined the sandy ditch with layers of heavy-duty tin foil. Next, he poured charcoal briquettes on top. As he drizzled lighter fluid on the coals, he shouted, "Back up, kids," right before he tossed in a lit match. Sparks from the six-foot blaze floated upward until the flames dissipated. At that point, Eli laid an old oven grate on top of the pit. It took a half hour before the coals turned white.

Jessy's guests played in the surf while hotdogs sizzled on the grill. When charred patterns appeared on all sides of the wieners, Eli served them nestled in warm buns to the kids who crowned their dogs with ketchup, mustard, and relish. Icey cold glass bottles of Coca-Cola, chunks of watermelon, and Camilla's chocolate-iced yellow cake completed the feast.

After breakfast, Camilla and Mary Louise surprised Jessy with a Clue game. At the beach party, she received top-notch presents including two more games, several forty-five-RPM rock and roll records, a Hardy Boys Mystery Story, two Trixie Belden books, a Kodak Brownie camera from her mother, and a pink autograph book from Delilah. Skip gave Jessy a dainty pink bracelet that his mother had fashioned from tiny cockleshells. Rita May's gift was a small sack of hard candies with soft centers.

The birthday girl saved Eli's present until last. With a look full of expectation, Jessy opened the lid on the box exposing a diminutive cloisonné heart suspended from a silver chain. "It's beautiful. Thank you, Daddy. Please put it on me now." She hugged his neck.

"You might lose it at the beach. Why don't we wait until we're home?" He tucked the gift back in its box.

The kids played tag in the sand and later took turns balancing on top of someone's rubber raft out in the clear green-blue Gulf of Mexico. Although no one rode any waves that day, the long stretches of tranquil water allowed the group to hold swimming competitions.

As dusk settled on Bonita Beach, Eli splashed water on the fire pit. He dumped sand over the coals and scattered the ashes. Parents reclaimed their pink-skinned children while Eli and Delilah packed the truck. He drove Delilah and five heat-weary kids into the diner parking lot at a little past eight.

Before Jessy went to bed, Eli fastened the necklace around her neck. She vowed she would never take it off.

* * *

The town of Bonita Springs took immense pride in its preparations for the annual Fourth of July Extravaganza Parade. Red, white, and blue balloons and streamers draped telephone poles all over town. If you registered in advance and paid a fee, you could march in the parade alongside local politicians or merchants and wave at the curbside crowds from convertibles or elaborate floats. As always, the parade committee requested the Ft. Myers High School Band to lead the marchers a mile and a half down the Tamiami Trail at two o'clock in the afternoon, give or take, depending on whether or not a float mishap occurred.

Due to the local weatherman's blistering forecast, the manager of the L&S Grocery and Meats (or Lawhon's, as it was called) plastered a sign in his window that morning with the words Complimentary Fans Provided written on it. Earlier in the week, the Bonita Springs Chapter of the VFW gave each downtown vendor or storeowner a stockpile of miniature American flags to distribute among their customers on parade day. Some shopkeepers advertised Independence Day Specials and discounts. However, Isabel's Ice Cream Parlor outshined every one of them all by offering free mini-cups of red, white, and blueberry sherbet to perspiring parade spectators.

In the evening, citizens owning grassy lawns or lengthy driveways launched their own firecrackers. The ultimate patriotic display scheduled to commence at nine o'clock at Bonita Beach reclaimed its bragging rights year after year. To top off the Fourth's festivities, the well-publicized Stars and Stripes Dance couldn't begin until the last of the beachside fireworks sprayed into the sky or nine-fifteen, whichever came first.

Perched at the diner's counter, Jessy munched on a club sandwich. She waved at her grandpa who wandered into the diner. He responded in kind and joined the group of men seated at the center table with Deputy Grizzle. Upon Caleb's arrival, Mary Louise placed a pitcher of sweet tea and six tall glasses of ice on a tray then carried it to his table.

Jessy disregarded most of the talk swirling around that table. Not until Caleb posed an intriguing question to the deputy, did she show any interest. "Did the hobos do something to anger you? Or did they actually commit a crime?"

Billy cackled. "That's easy to answer. There I was waiting for Tiny to fill up my tank at the Shell station, when I seen them two boys lurking around. At first, I didn't pay them no mind, but soon the big one, that Mundy fella, started bothering this fine looking White woman who was sitting in her car, minding her own business. Can you believe it? He was asking her for money. That big boy gave me no choice. People can't go round begging for handouts like that, you know, pestering folks. I was sick and tired of that bum doing whatever he damn well pleased. I put a stop to it. There was just cause, which gave me the right to arrest both boys for loitering on private property."

Caleb scanned a menu. "I assume it was a temporary fix?"

"Yup, but I sure would like to make it permanent." Billy snorted.

Jessy shuddered, the deputy's wicked laughter having the same effect as the time Miss Rydell scratched her fingernails across the chalkboard.

The next time Mary Louise waltzed by, Jessy caught her attention. "Please ask my daddy to come here when he's got a minute."

The waitress called through the opening in the wall behind the soda fountain. In two minutes, Jessy's apron-clad father parted the doors into the service area. "What's up, honey? I'm awfully busy."

She stammered. "Um, I'm sorry to bother you, but I heard Mundy Mike got arrested."

"I know. We'll talk later. I've got burgers on the grill."

"I don't understand. Mundy isn't a criminal. Why did he have to go to prison?"

"He didn't go to prison. You have to commit a serious crime to be sent to prison, and no judge in Florida is going to jail a hobo unless he's committed a robbery or a murder." He vanished, doors flapping behind him.

Momentarily content, she sipped her Coke, but kept her sights on Billy Grizzle's table. By that time, a few more Bonita Springs' old timers and other celebrated coffee guzzlers had pulled up nearby chairs, seating themselves. They all howled at one of Billy's repulsive jokes prompting Jessy to roll her eyes and fake a gag by sticking her finger down her throat. She checked her surroundings. No one noticed a thing.

Her grandpa motioned to the pony-tailed waitress. "Sugar, when you have a sec?" He held up his empty glass.

"Coming right up." Mary Louise snatched a full pitcher off the back counter.

Caleb peered at the deputy. "So, Billy, let me see if I've got this right. You think you taught those boys a lesson?"

"Yessir, but I should've taken it one step further. I told you about the shit that big one had the nerve to say to me right there in Sylvia's front yard. Caleb, I swear I was this close to shooting the SOB."

To Jessy's regret, the jukebox began playing a Dean Martin tune, which drowned out the men's banter. For all she knew, Mundy Mike laid in a dark and lonely prison cell never able to ride the rails again. Jessy couldn't eat another bite of her meal.

As the lunch crowd dwindled, Jessy checked the clock. Since she volunteered to help arrange chairs in front of the diner, she hurried outside. Aunt Prissy's Kitchen allowed its customers the courtesy of watching the parade in folding chairs while enjoying glasses of free ice-cold lemonade.

Because Rita May had to babysit that afternoon, Jessy only confiscated two seats for herself and Skip. Anyway, she planned to see Rita May later. Their top-secret scheme to stay out all night came with perfect alibis.

Rita May had reaffirmed the plan. "Your dad will think you're at my house, and Lynette will believe I'm at yours. It'll be so much fun spending the night at the clubhouse and spying on people at the dance. We might even catch site of some necking."

Jessy looked puzzled. "Necking?"

"Hugging and kissing, dummy. You're such a child."

The girls had agreed to meet at the banyan tree at nine o'clock.

While seated in her chair outside the diner, Jessy glanced at her watch—one forty-five. She tilted her head and spied Skip racing toward her. "Finally." She pretended to grin when the boy sat next to her. "I'm gonna start calling you Turtle Boy because you're so slow. Sit down, Turtle Boy."

Gasping for air, he folded his arms in front of his chest. "Sorry...I got here as fast as I could. I had to help Mom sort a new batch of shells."

"You barely made it."

Jessy and Skip discussed last year's parade and their choices for best float, until the sight of an unkempt man across the street caught her eye.

"Look. There's another hobo. Oh, you'll never guess what happened to Mundy Mike. At lunch today, I overheard Fizzle Grizzle say he threw him in jail last night." She gave Skip a blow-by-blow description of the deputy's comments. "Why don't we go visit Mundy tomorrow?"

"Silly, the jail's in Fort Myers."

"Oh, yeah." Her lips formed a pout.

Dressed in navy trousers, a white shirt, and a red, white, and blue bowtie, Eli strolled outside to check on his customers; most of whom captured prime viewing spots. He paused at his daughter's chair. "I've got lemonade if you guys are thirsty. By the way, Jessy, the Lee County Sheriff's department released Mundy Mike and his friends at eight o'clock this morning. Odds are the hobos are riding the rails by now." He rushed back inside the diner.

Jessy made the sign of the cross. "Mundy Mike is a free man."

"Why did you do that?" Skip puckered his brow.

"Catholics do it before and after they pray. Mama used to make the sign of the cross when good things happened. Come to think of it, she also made the sign when she heard bad news. I've always thought it was a signal to God to show him we're paying attention."

Delilah trotted outside carrying a tray of beverages, catering to the patrons first. She gave cups of lemonade to the kids then squatted next to Jessy. "Did your daddy tell you he's taking me to the dance?"

"Yes." Jessy smirked. *Big deal.* She twisted several strands of hair between her fingers.

"I hope you won't mind going home alone."

Jessy's chin jutted forward. "I go home alone most nights. But tonight, I'm spending the night with a friend."

"Just checking. First, we're going to watch the fireworks on the beach and then go to Fort Myers for a burger before the dance. Would you like me to fix you a sandwich to save for dinner?"

Jessy shook her head at Delilah. "I'm having dinner with my friend, too."

The waitress sashayed inside and Jessy stuck a lock of hair between her lips. *Why did she speak to me like that? She's not my mother.*

Patriotic tunes filled the muggy July air. "Here comes the band." Skip stood blocking Jessy's view.

"Move over. Who do you think you are? The invisible man?" She waved a red and blue fan at her face.

The town commemorated the holiday in style. The parade lasted forty-five minutes and exceeded the previous year's success—not one misstep, not one calamity. To conclude the celebration, Mayor Harley Munroe postured himself in front of the pavilion. He recapped his re-election babble through a bullhorn followed by the band's patriotic salute, which included one stanza of "God Bless America." As the crowd slowly dispersed, a handful of people drifted back inside Aunt Prissy's Kitchen to cool off and to enjoy another round of lemonade.

Jessy stalked Skip back to his house where the kids spent the rest of the afternoon playing Monopoly in his air-conditioned living room. Around seven, Jessy accepted Sylvia Goodman's invitation to stay for fried pork chops, mashed potatoes, turnip greens, and warm apple pie à la mode. At eight-thirty, the kids climbed on top of Sylvia's baby blue Oldsmobile Super 88 parked in the driveway. Jessy and Skip lay on their backs in awe of the sparkling pinwheels and heaven-bound rockets shooting across the sky.

Jessy climbed off the car, and waved goodbye to Skip as she ran down the street and all the way home. Out of breath, she reached the diner a few minutes before the streetlight on the corner of Childers and Highway 41 switched on. The diner and the apartment were dark. Inside, she found an extra flashlight in Eli's dresser drawer and a cotton blanket in the linen closet. She entered the storeroom through the connecting door in her family's kitchen. Flipping on a light, she seized the bag of sugar cookies Camilla promised to leave on a table in the back. She locked up the diner and then stepped into the night with an armload of necessities, and let the streetlight guide her across the Tamiami Trail. A gust of wind rustled the palm trees near the highway causing her to take a deep breath. Dawdling in front of the banyan tree, she cleared her throat. "Rita May, I'm here." She crawled behind the tree and into a cavern that the giant roots created decades ago.

"Hey," Rita May responded, proudly showing her friend the bottle of RC Cola she'd stolen from the Shell station's soft drink cooler.

Jessy tucked the bag of provisions down behind a rather large root. She found another one to sit on, while the older girl lit a remnant of a chubby, round candle. However, because of a steady breeze, the flame flickered and extinguished. Several attempts to re-light the candle failed. Ignoring the darkness, the kids gazed at dwindling fireworks, finished off Camilla's cookies, and shared the soda pop. It took them nearly an hour to discuss the pressing issue of whether or not Jessy should let Skip kiss her on the lips. Given that there was no solution to the dilemma, she brought

Rita May up to date on the latest news—Mundy's capture and subsequent release from his shackles in a dark, damp prison cell.

At ten o'clock, music from the community pavilion drifted through the air, the melodies muffling the resonance of any residual skyrockets and firecrackers. The harmonious vocals of Patti Page and Frank Sinatra beckoned the holiday traffic, which sped up and down Highway 41.

Nestled in the banyan's roots, the RJ Clubhouse offered Jessy and Rita May a strategic view of the pavilion's dimly lit covered front porch where dancing couples could catch their breaths.

Two hours of voyeurism was enough for Jessy. She yawned. "I recognize a few people, but I don't see Daddy and Delilah. He could've changed his mind about dancing."

Rita May scoffed. "Maybe."

Jessy pouted. "Well, he could have. It's already midnight and there's no sign of them."

Her friend attempted to stretch her legs. "Don't fret, we'll see him in due time."

Jessy wiggled halfway out of the cavern. "Look over there. It's Billy Grizzle hugging and kissing on a new lady friend. I've never seen *her* before."

Rita May took her time climbing out after Jessy. "Maybe it's his wife."

"Nah, it's not Pinky. She's always reminded me of Skip's Bozo punching bag, heavy at the bottom, narrow at the top. Mama used to say Pinky Grizzle's backside could cover three seats in a church pew."

Rita May glared at Jessy. "Your mama sure likes to talk about people behind their backs. I bet she said something about my family and me, too. Didn't she?"

"Uh, no, of course not. Uh, I like Pinky; she's nice and smiles a lot." Jessy's face soured. "There's Daddy." Two distinct figures, fingers intertwined, huddled in a wicker loveseat. "Am I terrible if I wish Delilah would leave town and disappear?" Her body wilted on a large tree root.

"No. You can wish anything you want."

"I wish Mama and Daddy to fall in love again."

"Do you really think that'll happen?"

"You never know."

"Snap out of it and check out the couple on the other side of the door."

"Wait a minute. Daddy is kissing her. Gross, I can't watch." Jessy closed her eyes. "Tell me when they stop."

Rita May squeezed back into the hideout. They've gone back inside. Anyway, you gotta get over it. Looks like Delilah and your Dad are definitely a couple, and couples kiss and hug and a lot more."

Jessy followed her friend. "Yeah, so…"

"Maybe I need to tell you about the birds and the bees."

"I already know…about where babies come from…sort of."

"But has anybody ever clued you in on dating? Lynette told me everything. I'm ready for when the time is right."

Jessy shook her head.

"Well, Mama told me everything. I have to be choosy and not let some no-account boy feel me up and get me pregnant. I'm supposed to make sure the boy has money and, most importantly, to never fall in love if I can help it. You see, being in love puts us women at a dis…ad…vantage, but if I'm smart and use the gifts God gave me, rich men will buy me anything I want."

"Wow. My mama told me about kissing, but none of that other stuff."

"Lynette said if she had listened to her own mama, she might have married for money instead of love. She wouldn't be living in a broken-down shack taking care of six kids."

Jessy pondered Rita May's words and made a decision. *When I grow up, I'll only marry someone I love.*

* * *

The cars and pickups vacated the lot by midnight. The pavilion darkened, leaving an insignificant moon to render any light on the girls. Rita May's mention of a recent crush she harbored instigated a conversation about the number of cute boys in school.

Jessy stretched and yawned. "I'm sleepy. I think I'll go on home and get in my own bed."

"You go ahead, but I'm staying."

"Don't you think it's kind of scary out here right now?"

Rita May duplicated Jessy's yawn. "Quit acting like such a big chicken. You've got no reason to be afraid. I'm not scared." She giggled. "But come to think of it, it is really dark out tonight."

Jessy grabbed a section of her hair next to her ear and twisted the clump around her finger.

CHAPTER TWENTY-TWO:
DEAD AS A DOORNAIL

In the dark, no one could see the trunk of the banyan tree much less the hideout that existed behind it. As the occasional set of headlights sped down Highway 41, the dense canopy of arm-like branches camouflaged all the secrets of the night.

Jessy knew it couldn't be real, but she thought she heard her mother's voice saying "Don't you know that nothing good happens in the middle of the night?" The child poked her friend. "Wake up."

"What?"

"I heard something. Listen." she whispered. "Someone's coming."

Cowering next to Jessy, Rita May put a finger to her lips as deep voices pierced the peaceful night.

Jessy's heart raced.

The teenager strained to see. "Oh, my God." She gasped. "Four men wearing white robes and hoods."

Jessy explored the teenager's colorless face for an explanation. In response, Rita May grasped the younger girl's hand. Using her index finger, the redhead traced a *K* into Jessy's palm, repeating the gesture again twice.

Jessy held her breath, sweat dripped down the side of her face. Her shirt felt damp.

Upon the intruders' arrival, the kids sunk lower into their hideout. Within minutes, a small group had assembled at the front of the banyan tree. Because the massive tree and its roots obstructed most of her view, Jessy zeroed in on four pairs of shoes and one pair of scuffed brown boots, which looked familiar.

"If he won't budge, give him a shove," said an unmistakable twang. "Let's do this thing. I got to go home or my wife will begin to worry where in the devil I am and who I'm loving on." He chuckled. "Yeah, right."

"Move your big ole feet, boy," said a deeper voice.

Just then, a man wearing tattered shoes lost his footing. Stumbling to the ground, his face caught the moonlight. The girls swapped glances and froze. Mundy Mike knelt in the dirt, his hands bound behind him, a gag crammed in his mouth, tears streaming down his face.

The owner of a pair of dusty, black wingtips with extra thick heels sniffed as if he had a cold. "Hey, Billy, which limb looks the sturdiest? How about that big one there?"

Rita May squeezed Jessy's arm and mouthed the words *Oliver Edson*.

The deputy stomped the ground. "You dumb little shit. I should've left you behind tonight. Didn't I warn you not to call me by my name? You ain't got the sense God gave a goose." Billy gave another command. "Stick the crate right between the two big rocks." The beam of a flashlight highlighted a space closer to some lower limbs.

Clinging to her friend, Jessy closed her eyelids. *Dear God, please help Mundy Mike.*

"Stay put, big fella. I'm gonna slip this here noose around your thick ole neck." Tiny Vargas, a regular at Aunt Prissy's Kitchen, possessed one of those soft-spoken voices one could easily identify.

A hat somersaulted to the dirt. Jessy stared at Mundy's fedora as two men pulled the tramp off his knees. The hobo groaned.

Billy huffed. "Quit your bellyaching, boy and step up on the damn crate."

Mundy obeyed.

Afraid to utter a sound, both girls covered their mouths. Jessy felt sure the men in white heard her heart drumming inside her chest.

Billy barked at his captive. "You better say your prayers because it's now or never. You'll be meeting your maker soon." Someone snatched the gag from the hobo's mouth and tossed it to the ground.

The Black man stuttered as he spoke. "I…I ain't done nothing… nothing…to deserve this."

"Bullshit! You disrespected me, and right in front of Sylvia Goodman and her whole neighborhood. Now you got two minutes to confess your sins and ask God to let you into heaven. On the other hand, maybe you've been a big sinner, and it ain't heaven you're heading for. Honestly, I don't care, but if you're gonna pray, get on with it. Time's a wasting."

Mundy's plea vibrated deep in his throat. "Lord above, have mercy on me. Heavenly Father, I am a faithful man." He whispered another prayer. "And, Lord, I ain't a-scared of dying, no sir. I know for a fact I'm going to heaven, and I thank you for a good life. When I get there, I'm hoping to see my mama and Blue Boy, my ole hound dog. No sir, I ain't a-scared of dying." The dread in his voice and his twitching body declared otherwise.

"Enough outta you," said the fourth man.

Jessy smothered the scream inside her mouth. She knew firsthand Billy Grizzle kept a loaded pistol in his holster, and she spotted the barrel of a shotgun flush against Tiny's shoe.

The girls hunkered together, their bodies quaking, tears bathing their cheeks. The stench of the men's sweat overpowered the citrusy incense of the Allamanda bushes nearby.

"All right, boys. One, two, three." Billy Grizzle's mud-coated boot kicked the crate on its side, leaving Mundy Mike's legs swinging in midair.

Jessy froze. A droplet of blood trickled from Rita May's lip to her chin.

The banyan tree moaned as if in pain. For what seemed like hours, Mundy gasped in agony while his legs flailed in a contorted rhythm. Suddenly, the branch that held all the man's weight broke, the loud *crack* startling the girls who sat behind and below the crime scene. The gigantic tree shook so hard Jessy thought the monster might split in two. At that moment, one of Mundy's shoes fell to the ground. All movement ceased.

Billy snickered. "Unbelievable. That nigger must've weighed two hundred and fifty pounds. I do declare he's deader than a doornail now. Looks like his neck's done broke. Fetch the crate and let's go. Justice has been served, fellas."

"But boss…" Tiny scuffed the toe of his left shoe into the dirt. "Uh, are we just gonna leave him there?"

"Yep. Don't worry. One of his hobo buddies will find him soon enough and cut him down."

A cigarette butt fell next to the deputy's boot. Jessy rubbed her nose at the smell. She tried to swallow, but choked letting a puff of air escape.

Oliver Edson whispered, "Did you guys hear something?" His flashlight beam pointed to the tree trunk area and then moved along the end of the driveway.

Billy snickered. "Nah, you're imagining things. Probably a critter. Let's go." The murderers scattered. The victim dangled four to five feet from the ground, the frayed rope that held him wrapped around a tree limb.

When the hooded men left, Jessy let go of her tears. "He's dead. Mundy Mike is dead." She shielded her eyes.

Rita May gripped the girl's shoulder. "Stop your whining. Listen to me. Those men were Ku Klux Klan. Davis once told me that those crazy people could make a man flat out disappear. Nobody can ever know we were here. Got it?"

Sucking on a clump of hair, Jessy stared at the teenager.

"Swear to me, blood sister, you'll never tell anyone. We were never here. We didn't see anything. Understand? Swear on your daddy's Catholic soul."

"I swear." Jessy shivered.

Slowly, the girls crawled out of the cubbyhole behind the banyan tree. Rita May gaped at the hanging man, but Jessy studied the ground where Grizzle's smoldering cigarette butt lay. She slowly lifted her chin. The unrecognizable body didn't appear human. The rope had scored deep, severing Mundy's neck, his head almost separating from his body. Blood and mucous oozed from the vagrant's mouth and nose. Jessy veered away from the grotesque display. She vomited in the grass, and then wiped her mouth with the edge of her shirt.

Rita May clamped onto Jessy's wrist checking the girl's watch. "Five after three. We gotta go."

The younger girl whispered, "I want to go home." With the images of Mundy Mike's face clouding her thoughts, Jessy found it difficult to focus.

"No. We're heading down to the hobo jungle so I can tell Mundy's friends what happened. You'll see. They look after their own. We can spend the night at the camp and leave early in the morning."

CHAPTER TWENTY-THREE:
WHAT'S DONE IS DONE

When the girls reached the campsite, Rita May did all the talking. She informed the first few men she happened upon, including Pleasin' Pete, about Mundy's fate. The kids spent the rest of the night snuggled under a worn blanket near the fire. Neither girl slept, but no one uttered a word.

At dawn, Rita May led Jessy to the back of the diner and opened the screened door. "You don't look so hot. Go on inside and go to bed. Your dad's fixing breakfast for the whole town; he won't ever know what time you got home."

Jessy didn't move.

"Go on. I'll talk to you later."

Jessy stared at Rita May through vacant eyes. "My head hurts." The girl stepped inside the apartment, the green door softly shutting behind her.

* * *

The bedroom door creaked. Eli tiptoed next to Jessy who slowly rolled over on her side.

"Hi, Daddy." She winced when he kissed her cheek as if his touch hurt her skin.

"Good afternoon, sleepyhead. When did you get home? Are you ill? I'm guessing you stayed up too late at Rita May's last night." Eli patted her hand.

"Uh huh, but I have a bad headache."

"Hope you had fun."

She squinted trying to recall the previous night. "I guess so."

"I enjoyed myself for the first time in years. Anyway, I'm just checking on you. Are you hungry? I can bring you something. Lunch special is fried chicken."

"No, thank you." Jessy closed her eyelids and turned over on her stomach.

* * *

The following day, Eli drove his daughter to the local general practitioner. Doc Barnes dispensed a simple diagnosis. "Your girl caught the flu bug that's going around. Let her rest in bed until it passes. Give her plenty of liquids and an aspirin every four hours. She'll be right as rain afore you know it."

Back in her bed, Jessy slept most of the next twenty-four hours. For the next few days, she remained quiet, sleeping, watching TV, and reading library books. Not until Eli mentioned a Sunday beach outing, did her interest pique.

* * *

Another week passed. On Saturday morning, Jessy and Skip sat at the picnic table hunched over a checkerboard. Skip initiated a successful move then followed Jessy's line of vision to the baseball field where a game was underway.

Jessy looked down and made her move on the checkerboard. "It's Rita May. She's coming this way."

Skip yelled to the teenager. "Where've you been, string bean?"

Jessy smacked her lips twice. "Gee, I'm starving to death. I need a snack. Come on, Skip. It's your turn."

Rita May ambled toward them. "The usual—I've been home tending kids. Where have you been, Jess?"

"I had the flu. Come on, Skip." Jessy averted Rita May's gaze. "Have you been to the clubhouse lately? I might go over there this afternoon and read."

Rita May kicked at the grass under her feet. "I've been too busy to go to the stupid clubhouse."

Jessy paid attention to Skip's next maneuver then stared at Rita May. "Stupid clubhouse?"

The ginger-haired teenager held her arms stiff at her sides, gripping the hems of her shorts. "Uh, I'm leaving."

Skip looked up at Rita May. "You just got here."

"My family is moving away from here. Papa found a better job in Hickory, North Carolina taking charge of a huge warehouse. He'll earn lots of money. I'll have my own room in a giant, two-story house, and gobs of fancy dresses like the models in *Glamour* magazine."

"You're really leaving Bonita Springs?" Jessy's mood shifted as she eyed her friend.

"Yep, and I can't wait to say goodbye to this Podunk town."

"But you won't go until school starts, right?"

"We're already packing up. Leaving in a week."

"Wow." Skip scooted off his seat.

"Yeah. Sunday night."

Jessy inched off the end of the bench. She walked up to Rita May, but stopped short of hugging her. "If you'll stop by the diner tomorrow evening, I'll ask Daddy to cook something special for you. And we should have a goodbye RJ meeting at the hideout."

Rita May took a step back. "I doubt I can make it. Lynette's depending on me to help care for Marilyn while she packs."

"Please try." Jessy's voice cracked.

* * *

Davis heaved the old trunk onto the top of the station wagon. Steadying one side, he secured the chest with the rope he always used. Two over-stuffed suitcases and three dog-eared boxes took up the space in the back of the station wagon.

Rita May stood in front of her father. "Please. I just want to say good-bye to her. I promise I'll be right back. Come on, Papa."

"All right, but I need your help here. Don't dally. We leave at ten. Got to keep the little ones asleep."

Rita May sprinted to Jessy's back door in record time. Pressing on the stitch at her side, she knocked on the doorframe. The young girl appeared behind the screen and let Rita May inside. The two sat at the foot of Jessy's bed. For the next few minutes, Rita May scrutinized the compact space. *My new room will be so much bigger and better than this little boring place. I'll put movie star posters on the walls and have pretty curtains, maybe yellow or pink.*

Jessy hugged her teddy bear. "Are you packed?"

"Almost." Rita May avoided eye contact. "So has anybody at the diner mentioned what happened the other night?" She chewed on the inside of her cheek.

"When?"

"On the Fourth of July." Her heart fluttered.

"You mean the parade or after? I heard some people talking about the dance, making fun of the couples smooching on the porch. I really don't remember much."

"I'm talking way after that."

"After?"

"Don't you remember?"

"Remember what?" Jessy searched Rita May's face.

"Everything we heard and saw. What's wrong with you? I'm talking about Mundy, stupid."

"Mundy? Is he back? Have you seen him?"

A lump caught in Rita May's throat. "Yeah, dummy. We saw him. We saw him die."

"You're making that up just to scare me. Why would you say such an awful thing?"

"Listen to me, if you really don't know, then fine. But if you're faking, you better not ever tell a soul." Rita May glared at Jessy. "You know. Just forget it. I'm leaving, so it ain't gonna matter anyway."

All at once, Jessy teared up. "I don't want you to leave."

"Yeah, well, I have to." She chewed on a hangnail. "Uh, if you want, we can write to one another. You know, be sort of like pen pals. I'll promise to if you will."

Jessy sniffled. "Sure. After all, we're blood sisters forever. You first. Mail your letter to Aunt Prissy's Kitchen, Tamiami Trail, Bonita Springs, Florida. I'm gonna miss you, Rita May." Jessy reached out and hugged the teenager.

A minute was all Rita May could take, her friend's outpouring of emotion feeling claustrophobic. She left the girl weeping into a bed pillow. On the way home, Rita May wandered onto the vacant ballfield, stopping on top of the pitcher's mound. She contemplated Jessy's convenient memory lapse while scooping a rock off the ground and pitching it toward home plate.

"Jessy's such a baby. She can't face the fact that Mundy's dead. Who cares anyway? What's done is done." *Served Mundy right. If he had hopped on the train and left town, he'd be alive right now.*

As she continued her hike toward the shack, Rita May envisioned her new life in North Carolina. She was sure she'd be going to a good school where parents cared about their kids' education. Because her family would soon become rich and all, she didn't see any more tenant housing in her future. Wasn't it funny how things worked out? She never thought she wanted to leave Bonita Springs, but since Davis promised her life would be better for it, she considered the move a plus, a stepping-stone to her future. *We'll live in a big ole house, while the high and mighty Blanchards will still be living in that dingy little apartment in the back of the smelly diner.* Rita May couldn't help but enjoy the moment.

When she reached the shack, she put both hands on her hips and faced in the direction of the town. She shouted, "Goodbye, Bonita Springs. I hope I never see you again."

PART THREE

CHAPTER TWENTY-FOUR:
LIE LIKE A RUG

The weekend trip to Beaufort had shaken Rita's confidence. Exhaustion seeps through her bones. For the first time in years, she feels her age and the vulnerability that comes along for the ride. With her carryon put away, Rita plods downstairs to Harrison's office. A stack of mail sits at the corner of his desk. She thumbs through the envelopes. One letter stands out from the rest, the artistic handwriting giving it away. She hides the envelope under her shirt and heads to the kitchen where she tucks Jessy Tate's correspondence inside her purse. Taking a deep breath, she wanders into the family room.

Standing at the mini bar, she pours pinot noir into a black opaque wine glass, one in a set of six hanging from a rack. Her hand trembles. Burgundy liquid spills onto the bar. Rita's thoughts jumble together. *I've worked too hard to let anything upset my life now.* She freezes noting Harrison's presence in the hallway. "Honey, would you like a drink?"

He breezes into the room wearing navy plaid pajama bottoms and a U.S. Naval Academy T-shirt, a laptop under one arm. "Definitely. Bourbon and water, please."

Rita pours from a half-empty bottle of Knob Creek.

Harrison collapses into a leather recliner. "I'm beat. The trip and Mama wore me flat out. If I didn't have to refine this speech, I'd go straight to bed."

"Can't it wait?" Rita hands the glass to her husband as she sinks into the sofa. She props her bare feet on the glass coffee table.

"Nope. Roger expects my final edits by morning."

Sipping wine, she flips through a copy of Architectural Digest in a lame attempt to concentrate on something other than her immediate dilemma. She tosses the magazine aside. "I'm going to run a bubble bath."

Harrison's eyebrows arch above his glasses. "How's your headache?"

As usual, lying comes easy. "Practically gone." She finishes the rest of her wine and sets the glass on the wet bar. On her way through the room, she stops and leans over to kiss Harrison's mouth, the sort of kiss that had always bought her anything she wanted. "Don't work too late."

She slowly ascends the staircase, her legs heavy like concrete. In the master bathroom, Rita runs hot water into an oversized tub. After adding lilac scented bath beads, she presses the button launching the Jacuzzi jets in motion. Rita peels off her clothes and then dips into the tub of churning bubbles. Resting her head on a bath pillow, she adjusts the speed letting the warmth relieve her aching body.

She relaxes until Harrison disrupts the mood by wandering into the bathroom.

"Have you shriveled into a prune yet?"

Rita sighs. "Hope not." For a few fleeting moments, everything was fine. She flips the switch in the tub to the off position.

* * *

Two hours later, she lies in bed with her husband. At the first sound of a modest snore, she sneaks downstairs to retrieve the letter in her handbag.

Rita slides her thumb under the envelope's flap and unfolds Jessy Tate's mundane stationary.

April 3, 2008

Dear Rita May,

Thanks to my psychiatrist, but no thanks to you, I have recalled our Fourth of July nightmare and the horrific scene of the crime. When I close my eyes, I see Mundy's legs swaying in front of me, and I gag at the memory of his face and Billy Grizzle's disgusting voice.

Why did you keep it from me? I told you I was dealing with anxiety issues. You just didn't care. Although we were frightened children at the time, one of us should have informed an authority figure. My brain blocked the trauma; yours did not. You have no excuse.

If you help me now, I'll forgive your complacency. I won't be satisfied until Mundy Mike's relatives learn how and why he died. Ask your husband for advice; he has clout. Maybe he can recommend an investigator.

Please don't ignore me, old friend. I swear to you I won't let this die.

Jessy

Rita tears the letter into shreds dropping the pieces in the trash. *So what if she remembers. I know Jessy. She's a quitter, always has been. When things become too difficult, she'll latch on to another pathetic cause.* A nightlight guides her way back up the stairs.

* * *

In the morning, Rita sacrifices her usual run to compose a response and polish off a pot of strong coffee.

April 7, 2008

Dear Jessy,

As I've told you numerous times, I'm an extremely busy woman. Unlike you, I don't have the luxury of lounging around the house during the day. I work for a living and am constantly on call due to Harrison's re-election campaign. As a politician's wife, I have responsibilities and social functions to attend and here I am using my precious time to address your absurd claim.

This is the last time I'll speak of the summer of 1956. The fact you remembered the hobo's death has no relevance. It's been fifty years. It's too late to do anything about it now, and definitely too late to raise the dead. Disclosing such an incident will only cause harm to a lot of people. I'm warning you. Don't do it. You swore to me back in 1956 and I'm holding you to that promise. If you expose our unwitting participation in ancient history, you will live to regret it.

I won't answer your emails or phone calls. I'm done.

Rita

* * *

Several weeks ago, Rita sent out invitations to the most influential people in Harrison's congressional district, as well as to a few wealthy D.C. businessmen known for their political give-and-take generosity. The elegant requests stated, "You are cordially invited for cocktails at seven on the Twelfth of April. Dinner to Follow."

It's almost *showtime*, and the redheaded hostess flits around her upscale home. Everything must be perfect. Due to the last-minute addition of another foursome requested by Harrison's campaign manager, Rita gives explicit instructions to the caterer.

At around seven o'clock, chauffeur-driven Lincoln Town Cars swing into the Rhodes' circular drive and deposit stylish couples bathed in affluence. Three Jaguars and two Mercedes abut the curb on the street.

Mrs. Harrison Rhodes feigns composure, tugging at her sleeves that hide the splotches of pink lotion covering her itchy arms. She sashays up to the handsome butler whom she'd hired for the evening. Promising a political favor to his boss, Rita successfully pirated the handsome young man away from Isabella Weinberg, the first lady of Virginia.

"Ethan, I would love a champagne cocktail."

"Yes, ma'am, coming right up. By the way, I hope I'm not being too forward, but Mrs. Rhodes, you're undeniably the most striking woman in the room tonight." Tall, dark, charming, and handsome, Ethan had the right look, the look of a young Harrison Rhodes.

"Why, thank you. Your presence tonight is a godsend." She centers a vase of white lilies on a Chinese chest in the foyer. Wearing a revealing, emerald-green floor length sheath, which compliments her reddish locks and creamy complexion, Rita admires herself while passing the hallway mirror. Satisfied, she hurries to the patio, her black high-heeled sandals *clicking* across the hardwoods. She smiles at the dramatic effect she has paid for—miniature white lights placed above the pool area, her home and the lawn. *What more could a woman want?*

Harrison sneaks up behind his wife embracing her waist. "Darling, you've done a remarkable job. By the way, have I told you how amazing you look tonight?"

"Oh, sweetie, you lie like a rug." She glances back at her husband.

The butler surfaces carrying two flutes of champagne on a silver tray.

"Thank you, Ethan." She reaches for both glasses. "And here's yours, Congressman Rhodes."

Grasping the flute, he kisses her cheek.

Each time the doorbell rings, Harrison and Rita welcome another wealthy guest into their home. The couple shakes hands at the same time radiating polite charm and false enthusiasm. By eight-thirty, any remains of the beef tenderloin, roasted fingerling potatoes, and sautéed asparagus have vanished. In addition, the partygoers consumed both dessert choices—a raspberry cream tartlet and a white chocolate mousse.

At nine, Rita rests in a wicker patio chair and sips on a cocktail, a pleasing expression on her face. By throwing this party, she single-handedly kicks Harrison's re-election campaign into high gear. As she surveys her guests through a glass window panel, she recalls what she said to her husband the previous evening. "These people have more money than God with never-ending bank accounts and multiple reasons to fund your campaign. I predict a prosperous evening, Mr. Congressman."

Everyone assembles in the living room for after-dinner drinks, awaiting Governor Weinberg's *few* words. At last, he finds a spoon and gently strikes the side of a highball glass. "May I have your attention?"

Rita saunters inside. Glancing around the room, she soon grabs the hand of her personal politician. A strategically placed porcelain bowl, a cobalt and white Asian antique, sits in the center of the coffee table with the expectation of contributions. Staring at the half-empty bowl, she grits her teeth. *These big shots better not let us down.* She downs her last sip of champagne.

The southern silver-tongued governor has difficulty making his point. Finally, after a comment pertaining to the upcoming election and the Democrats' predicted win, he gestures to his left. "Tonight is all about Harrison Rhodes. Let's hear it for our congressman."

Reserved applause encourages Rita's husband to sidle up next to the governor's left. Governor Weinberg continues. "My friend, Harrison, a moral and intelligent young man, will continue to lead us into the future; I have no doubt. Right now, he needs our support, financial and otherwise. Let's not disappoint him tonight." The room explodes in a round of adulation.

Rita slinks back onto the patio where the butler materializes at her side. She accepts another drink. Their eyes lock. "You win the contest," she says.

"I do?"

"For the most attentive."

"And what do I win for my efforts?" He brushes her arm. "I can't help myself. You are irresistible."

She smiles as if she's keeping a secret. "Why, thank you. You realize that Isabella will never forgive me for stealing you away from her."

"The decision was mine." Ethan winks. "When Mrs. Weinberg proposed the arrangement, I jumped at the chance. I had seen you once before, and I needed to see you again. So what's my prize? I'm dying of curiosity, Mrs. Rhodes."

She steps closer, recognizing the scent of his cologne. *He is adorable. Such an inviting mouth.* Her heart pounds faster at the prospect of acting on impulse. Anticipating the risk, the idea excites her even more. In the past, she indulged in illicit affairs, but none since Harrison walked into her life. *Do I dare? Time spent with this good-looking waiter might do me good.* She whispers in Ethan's ear. "I'm sure we can work something out."

"Your husband, ma'am." Ethan nods at Harrison who is trying to obtain Rita's attention.

Standing at the French doors that lead into the house, Harrison mouths the words, "Come here."

Rita waves a reply and hands the young man her glass. She speaks in a soft, low tone. "Give me a call in a day or two." Strutting toward her husband, she senses the butler's leer.

* * *

In spite of after-party fatigue, Rita makes love to Harrison in their king-size bed. Afterward, he snores in a trance-like state. She lies awake weighing the pros and cons of a liaison with the sexy butler. Unfortunately, the faces of Jessy Tate and Mundy Mike intrude on her deliberations. Rita's spacious bedroom has become crowded.

CHAPTER TWENTY-FIVE:
GOING WHOLE HOG

Strolling back from the mailbox, I stop to pick a piece of trash off the lawn. Although the morning fog has dissipated, the afternoon air remains heavy. Clutching a handful of bills, letters, and a flyer, I pass through the kitchen. Here comes Lulu from the other side of the room chasing an imaginary critter. She skids along the tile, the home plate slide landing the kitty head-first into her water bowl. I cradle my baby, wiping her fur with a dishtowel. "You silly cat."

Midway through sorting the mail, a pale green envelope mono-grammed with an *RMR* peeks from the pile. I rip off the end, scan the contents and then crumple the single sheet of stationary. I feel my jaw tighten. "I should have known." I chuck the wad into the trash.

My cheeks feel hot. I linger in front of the kitchen window eyeing a wren nibbling seeds on the bird feeder. I was such a fool believing the two of us would stay friends forever. The reality is I don't really know Rita at all; perhaps I never did. For years, I listened to her self-important drivel about the wealthy people she'd met on the road to success, especially the men she used and tossed aside. If you look at her life, one would say she got her wish. She rose above what she labeled her *unfortunate childhood.* Yet I wonder how many people she manipulated along the way in order to achieve her dreams. I suspect Harrison Rhodes has no idea whom he married. He's only met the façade.

Gray clouds shroud the sky and a flash of lightning nearby blinks the lights in my home. On autopilot, I pull the kitchen window down. Thunder rolls overhead, and a noisy shower waters my oregano and thyme, herbs I planted next to the patio.

I snatch a wine glass from the cabinet. The longer I dwell on Rita, the more infuriated I become. Generally, I'm not inclined to hold onto anger, even when Phillip admitted his fling during his foolish mid-life crisis. My inner rage faded once he pleaded for forgiveness; I let the initial sting of betrayal pass. It was easy to grant him absolution, no strings attached. Easy because I loved him.

I remove the half-opened bottle of Chardonnay from the refrigerator and pour the cool liquid into the glass. After a few sips, I make a conscious decision to pity Rita May McAfee Rhodes, my self-centered friend, who in my meager opinion, has slipped over the edge of egocentric into the quicksand of full-blown narcissism. I grab my phone off the counter. I should call Dr. Priest. I forgot. He's in London on vacation. Wiggling onto a kitchen stool, I punch my daughter's number.

"Jasmine Interiors, Gretchen speaking."

"Hey, honey, how's business?"

"Hectic, which is good."

"Is by any chance Mimi working with you today?"

"No, she's got classes and she mentioned a stop by *The Signal* office to speak to her editor. Why don't you try her cell?"

"I will. How are you doing? Any word from Conner?"

"No, and I don't expect there will be. We have a mediator now who is supposed to keep us out of court. Can't wait for everything to be settled."

"Of course, you do. Please call me when you've got time and you feel like talking."

"Mom, I have to go."

I try my granddaughter's cell with no luck and I leave a message for her to call me back.

* * *

Due to Mimi's technological expertise, my rejuvenated jewelry business is growing and keeping me quite busy. She skillfully engineered my website and taught me how to maintain the user-friendly pages.

Staying up late at night with insomnia seems to produce creative brainstorms. Just this past week, I introduced five seashell designs incorporating beautiful yet simple semi-precious stones. These new pieces granted me more inventory and pushed productivity to a higher level. I fulfilled a seven-day record-breaking twelve orders.

I sit arched over my worktable adding the final touches to a pair of earrings by inserting teeny opals inside coquina shells. After crimping a wire into place, I attach the creations to an imprinted card that advertises *Jessy's Jewels* on the top of my logo—a pink-hued conch shell.

My hobby and part-time business affords me a semblance of sanity, gives me a reason to get up in the morning, and supplies a little extra money. My days are active, and some nights, I sleep; some I don't. If sleep does abandon me or I suffer an occasional nightmare, I try an over-the-counter sleep aid. Old standbys, Xanax and Ambien are drugs in the past, but I keep a bottle of white wine in the fridge or a bottle of red on the counter. I figure a little anesthetic now and then won't hurt.

The upcoming weeks promise to keep me out of trouble—nine orders to fill, a neighbor's party on Sunday, and a local Spring Arts and Crafts Festival the following weekend. Maisie Dean, whom I met at a Christmas craft show, invited me to share a display table at the festival. I feel blessed to have a new friend. For at my age, they are hard to come by. Maisy and I meet at Windstar Stables two mornings a week and ride our horses over meadows owned by the stable.

Contemplating my next creation, I rummage through a jar of miniature shells. The right one surfaces to the top. The lavender shade of this coquina sparks a pleasant childhood memory of Mother and me gathering seashells at the beach. I hesitate before continuing my task, the frequency of such memories rare. I close my eyes to remember—toes in white sand, damp hair, warm sunshine, our laughter, and Mom's beauty. At a young age, I lived in a home where Margaret Blanchard used her addiction to perfect the art of distant mothering. If Dad hadn't raised me in such a loving environment, there's no telling how screwed up I'd be.

I try and refocus on threading a crystal bead onto a wire, but recollections cloud my mind. I imagine myself as a child clinging to the infrequent hours of Margaret's happiness. For me, those treasured yet fragile moments are like the shells I string on delicate thread, spaced apart and easily shattered.

The front door squeaks. "Hey, Gran, it's me."

"Hey there. I'll meet you in the sunroom." I turn off the lights and leave my work for tomorrow.

Mimi cruises toward me in the hallway, her wavy brown hair brushing her shoulders. "Ooh, I love your blouse," she says when she gives me a hug. "You ought to wear that shade of blue more often."

I remove my glasses and kiss my granddaughter's fair-skinned cheek. "There's bottled water and Diet Coke in the fridge."

Mimi plops in a wicker chair, setting her backpack on the floor. She bends over getting a closer look at the vase full of flowers on the coffee table. "No thanks, Gran. These are pretty and they smell wonderful."

"Lilies of the Valley. I bought them yesterday at the outdoor market when I was running errands. One of my favorites. I'll be right back." I head for the kitchen and straight for the fridge. An open bottle of pinot grigio sits in the side door. I grab the wine before stealing a glass from the cabinet.

Upon my return, I set the wine on the coffee table, sink into the sofa and pull my bare feet under me. "So, have you finished the school piece on Civil Rights?"

"Yes, ma'am. *The Signal* published the article in February. I'm sure I mentioned it."

"You probably did. I guess I forgot."

"I'll email you a copy."

"Please do."

Mimi slides out of a pair of flip-flops. "It's so cool. My editor loved the articles so much that he promoted me. Gran, you are now in the presence of a staff writer responsible for contributing to a new continuing series."

"How exciting! Will your subject matter remain the same?"

"More or less. The Civil Rights issue is relevant and race is such a hot topic. Due to all my research, I've discovered that history does more than shape the present and forewarn the future. It not only aids our perspective of others, but in how we view our own circumstances as well. Gran, would you mind if I picked your brain? I bet you have plenty to share."

"You have no idea." I taste the wine. "If you have the time, I have a true story to tell you about a disturbing time in my own history. It's a fact that children learn what they see and hear at home. For instance, if a child's mother and father are bigoted, the child might become an adult who leans toward the parent's belief system. In the fifties and sixties, most southerners saw the issue of race and Civil Rights as a shock to their way of life. No one wanted to see change. Even as a child, I felt the tension of it all. However, I was luckier than most. My parents believed in treating all people equally."

"I understand. Most of the research I've done is factual. You could bring a personal spin to it. Did you know anyone who opposed racial equality where you lived as a child?"

"Oh, of course. I grew up in a small town and spent most of my time in a popular diner. Folks from all walks of life with different opinions dined there." I take a deep breath. "Mimi, you already know about the years I suffered nightmares and anxiety attacks. Right?"

"Yes. You've been dealing with that like forever."

"According to Dr. Priest, a blocked memory of a childhood trauma was the cause. Due to no fault of my own, I harbored a secret most of my life. When I was twelve, I witnessed a murder, a hate crime. The shock of seeing that incident erased the event from my memory."

"How awful! And you never had a clue?"

"No. Apparently, the anxiety was the direct result of the trauma. Your grandfather's recent death compounded my stress, which resulted in my having to visit my psychiatrist again. Thank goodness, therapy and hypnosis reawakened my memory. I can now recall what happened."

"So this is a positive?"

"Oh yes." I swallow the last of the liquid in my glass. "I still have strange dreams sometimes, but nothing so terrifying. I haven't experienced a panic attack in months."

"Do you still see your therapist?"

"Uh huh, but not as often. I actually have an appointment on Wednesday for a progress report. Today, depending on your time schedule, I'd like to tell you about my experience. I suggest you take notes. The subject matter is right up your alley."

"I'll make time. I'll record you, if that's okay." Restless in the chair, Mimi shifts to the floor and wrenches her recorder from her pack.

"Are you sure, you're not thirsty." I make my way toward the kitchen for a refill.

"I'll take a Diet Coke if you've got it."

Minutes later, I set Mimi's beverage in front of her. "During most of my life, I couldn't remember much about those two crucial years. The nightmares and flashbacks made no sense to me. Now, it's clear." I relax in my late husband's recliner.

"What a revelation, huh? I can't imagine what you went through."

"Once I explain, maybe you can help me decide what to do with my story. I've considered going public, but I need a partner in crime." When I take a sip of wine, I taste a hint of pears.

Mimi drinks through Diet Coke foam. "I'm on the edge of my seat."

"You see, I didn't forget the event on purpose, but the guilt I'm experiencing at present, which I suppose is a kind of penance, is unbearable. My apologetic prayers aren't enough to ease my conscience. Oh, and my childhood friend was with me at the time. She watched those men kill the hobo, too. Regrettably, Rita and I don't speak anymore. I digress. Let me start from the beginning, but if I drift off into tangents, please reel me back in."

Mimi burrows into her purse to remove a pad and pen. "I'll keep the recorder running and take notes. I don't want to miss a word."

"Great idea."

Mimi strokes the kitten that appears at her feet. "Hey, little Lulu."

I relay the account with as little emotion as possible. When my mouth becomes too dry to continue, I stop. At five-fifteen, my granddaughter leaves and I mosey back into the den where I collapse on the sofa. Reliving the past again and consuming three glasses of wine depletes one's energy. Sometime later, Lulu leaps on top of me, a reminder of her perpetual starvation.

* * *

On the Wednesday drive to Dr. Priest's office, I clamp onto the steering wheel and squeeze until my chalky white fingers become numb. At the thought of Rita's unwillingness to help me, a dull ache pinches my neck. I should try one more time. It would make things much easier if she would change her mind. Although Mimi agreed to write Mundy Mike's story, the chances are slim anyone will publish it. If, and that's an enormous if, the best-case scenario unfolds, then I'll inform Rita.

The parking lot appears full, but I get lucky and guide my car into a vacant spot. Checking myself in the visor mirror, I rub the space right between my eyebrows and decide that it's time for a little Botox. I pull a favorite tube of lipstick from my purse and smear on a liberal coat of Pink Camelia. "The best I can do." Once out of the car, I suck in my gut before I lock the doors.

Today, Chelsea's candle smacks of strawberries. I settle into an empty seat in the waiting room. A magazine article has my attention until the receptionist calls my name.

"Nice to see you." Chelsea props open a door leading to a narrow hallway where Dr. Priest stands at attention at his threshold.

He reaches for my hand. "Jessy, you're looking well."

I trail him into the office and to his desk. "Hanging in there. Did you enjoy your vacation?" I pick the chair directly across from him.

Once he sits, small talk precedes a fifteen-minute summary on my progress. "I hope you appreciate how much you've accomplished. By facing your fears, you're on your way to leaving a lifetime of distress, anxiety, and depression behind." Dr. Priest winks at me. "I might have to present a clinical paper on your case."

"You deserve all the credit for my improvement. Somehow releasing those demons also tempered my grief and liberated me in a sense. I spend half of my time revitalizing my business, the other half on a mission to right the wrong I witnessed." Of course, I do not mention the fact that some nights I spend hours dwelling on shame and contrition. I'm definitely going to Confession tomorrow.

"Is the pursuit a healthy one?"

"Yes, indeed. I'm finalizing plans to travel to Bonita Springs in June. Besides visiting my father, I intend to research the KKK's presence, concentrating on the summer of 1956 in the Bonita Springs area. I've convinced my granddaughter to tell the story of Mundy Mike in her college newspaper. As my Grandpa Caleb used to say, 'We're going whole hog.'"

* * *

It was good to see Dr. Priest, but I don't consider the session productive. I regret my earlier decision to meet Gretchen for lunch, but brush off my so-so mood when I see her seated in the front booth at Terésa's, a nearby café we like to frequent. We sip on Chardonnay and munch on idyllic Cobb salads.

I bite into a chunk of fresh avocado. "Lately, I'm feeling empowered. I have a goal."

"I can believe it. I'm so proud of you. You're definitely on top of your game, but perhaps you ought to take a step back. You don't have to make any drastic changes right away. You've experienced a great deal with Dad's death and your recollection of the past." Gretchen extends her hand. "Please don't be in such a rush."

I squeeze my daughter's hand. "You don't understand. The story can't wait. Sure, it's all stressful, but what I felt before, the anxiety of not knowing, was a hell of lot worse. More importantly, there's a family somewhere who deserves to know the truth."

* * *

"Hold on a sec, Mimi. Let me put you on speaker. Okay. Here's the plan. We'll stay at Dad's, research local sources, and we might have time to enjoy the sugar white sands of Bonita Beach. My treat. What do you say?" I string a wire through a tiny hole in a seashell.

"I'd love to go. Haven't laid eyes on Great Grandpa Eli in over five maybe six years."

Using a tiny pair of pliers, I crimp the wire. "You won't recognize him. He aged overnight. I'm hoping he'll let me quiz him on the old days at

Aunt Prissy's Kitchen, his beloved diner. His long-term memory is exceptional; short-term is a different story."

* * *

On the last Sunday in June, Mimi and I board a Delta Flight scheduled to land in Fort Myers at 3:48 p.m. Since I confessed all my sins to my parish priest a few weeks ago, there will be no more wallowing in Catholic guilt. At least, I'll give it my best shot.

Seated in the center seat of the plane, I become a little claustrophobic and flip through the provided Delta magazine. "Mimi, did I tell you that Manuel is meeting us at the airport? While we're at Dad's house, he and a friend are going to hike a section of the Appalachian Trail in the much cooler North Carolina Mountains. He'll return on Thursday." I'm running off at the mouth.

Mimi smiles as she hunts for the perfect playlist on her new mobile phone, which she told me also acts like an MP3 player. "I'm sure he could use a break."

So far, thank God, the plane ride is boring. I've often viewed flying as an expensive necessity. Personally, I'd rather keep my feet firmly on the ground. My sweet granddaughter listens to music, her headphones surely muting any ambient noise. She strikes a rhythm on her tray table, her hot pink fingernails marking time to a melody I'm positive I've never heard.

The flight attendant slides her beverage cart next to our row. "Would you like something to drink, ladies?"

I nudge Mimi and she shakes her head. The young man next to me asks for coffee. I offer the attendant a ten-dollar bill. "Red wine, please."

Although not exactly the best merlot I've tasted, the crimson liquid works enough magic to relax the tension in my neck. My mind wanders. Nine months have whisked by since Phillip passed, yet I still miss all the shades of him—at his best, a hot white and at his worst, a faded gray, with hues of boring beige in between.

Thoughts of my late husband feed my conscience. I long for the smell of his beachy cologne, his powerful voice, his wry sense of humor, and above all, his smile. The last time I sat on this flight to Florida, he sat to my right, furiously working a crossword puzzle. I clearly remember him pausing his momentum and informing me that he was *in the zone*. The lovely retrospective, however, does not offer me any peace of mind.

I guess I dozed off because the Delta captain's voice awakens me. "Ladies and Gentleman, we are approaching Southwest Florida International Airport. Please secure your seat belts and slide your tray table into its upright position."

A trip to see Eli Blanchard is way overdue. No matter my age, I crave my father's approval and steadfast love. He's my rock and I'm his Baby Girl. The airplane glides onto the tarmac; at the same time, a shiver runs up my spine to the nape of my neck. I squeeze my granddaughter's arm. "I just had the weirdest sensation…like a feeling of impending doom."

CHAPTER TWENTY-SIX:
CAN OF WORMS

Returning to the southern tip of Florida, one immediately remembers the density of tropical air. Climbing out of the Jeep, the back of my blouse is damp and sticks to the vinyl seat. The weather-beaten cottage stands before me. I assess the condition of the structure where my grandparents called home for most of their lives. The roof needs repair and the peeling clapboards cry out for a coat of paint. I'll ask Manuel to get a few estimates.

Toting the bags inside, my dad's live-in home health-care worker announces, "We're home, Eli." Mimi and I bring up the rear.

Dad shouts, "I'm in the den."

We tread down a hallway where family photos plaster the walls on both sides. I enter the TV room, the main living space in the three-bedroom, two-bath cottage, if you don't count the screened-in porch. He's in his wheelchair; a warm smile crosses his face.

I squat to embrace the elderly man. "How are you doing, Daddy?" I hold on tight, his gentle touch welcoming.

"Fair to middling." He catches sight of my granddaughter. "And, who is this lovely young lady?"

"It's me, Grandpa Eli, Mimi."

"No way. You're an adult." His grin widens when she stoops to peck his cheek.

I grab his wrist. "Daddy, you're too skinny. You should fatten up, put some meat on your bones."

"Just trying to maintain my girlish figure." He chuckles and angles the wheelchair toward the kitchen. "Manuel, please fetch us a pitcher of iced tea and set the tray out on the porch."

"Coming right up."

My father coughs into a handkerchief he pulled from his pocket. "How was your flight?"

I sigh. "Just the way I like—uneventful. Let us unpack, and we'll meet you on the screened porch in ten minutes."

"Okey dokey." He rolls in front of the TV. "Hurry up. I want all the news."

I lead Mimi to the guestroom where we kick off our shoes and begin. The antique dresser has narrow drawers, so we must squish our clothes inside. I giggle at the sight of the ancient rosebud lining that covers the inside of the drawer.

Mimi gathers her hair into a ponytail. "Boy, it's hot in here."

I spy Manuel in the hallway toting an olive-green duffle bag. I stop him before he goes into the kitchen. "Ready to leave already?"

"Yep. I stocked up at Publix yesterday so you should be set. By the way, there's a copy of Eli's routine and medication schedule on the refrigerator door. Don't forget, you have to make him eat. He doesn't have much of an appetite. Call me if you have any questions." Manuel cocks his head to one side as a car draws near to the house. "There's my ride. You girls have fun."

Mimi and I join my father, his wheelchair backed into a corner on the screened-in porch. "It's shaking out to be a right pleasant evening." He slurps his tea.

On cue, nearby palm trees snare a western breeze and a scarlet hibiscus shimmies near the side of the porch. I glance at the ceiling fan, weary from age, one blade suffering from some fatal mishap. To my right is the can't-miss wall thermometer, its dial constant at a clammy eighty-plus degrees. A bead of sweat dribbles between the cups of my bra.

"I'll be right back. I have to make a call." Mimi dashes outside into the yard.

"Boyfriend?" Eli raises his eyebrows.

"Nathan. The latest crush." The sweetened tea cools my throat.

"Oh, to be young." My father chuckles in baritone.

I nod at the ceiling. "So who ate the fan?"

"Long story." Dad's booming laughter transports me back to my childhood.

"Come on, tell me." I smile at my father, who over time has morphed into the spitting image of my Grandpa Caleb, accent and all, the epitome of an *old codger* in southern colloquialism.

"It was late, say eleven o'clock, about six months ago and somebody forgot to latch the porch door. Of course, Manuel blamed it on me." He clears his throat. "But I'm not always the last one to bed around here. Well, around two o'clock in the dead of night, Randy, the granddaddy of a nearby long-standing family of raccoons, comes a-calling." He inhales and sips his tea. "He was looking for food, I guess, and made a mess of things out here."

"Wait. How did you know it was Randy?"

"The old boy has one cloudy blind eye. You can't mistake him."

"Didn't Manuel hear him?"

"Nope. He slept right through the racket, but not me. I got the broom from the kitchen and snuck out onto the porch on my walker. The critter didn't hear me at first. Then we saw each other. We stared at each other until I swung at him a few times. Hells bells, that old fella kept running me in circles. I kept on missing him, and I…ah…eventually hit the fan." He chuckles. "At that moment, Randy panicked. If I'm lying, I'm dying now. Cause damn if he didn't open the blasted back door by himself and skedaddle into the night. Since then, haven't seen the old guy. I reckon I scared the tar outta him." Dad and I fall into hysterics.

A little later, I broach the dreaded subject. "By the way, how's your health, Dad?"

He clears his throat. "I'm…uh…fit as a fiddle. Most mornings, I do my exercise by puttering to the end of the drive and back, and I touch my toes a few times. These old bones don't act up as much in the hot weather. Not like in the wintertime, when I do good just to get out of bed. Glucose numbers are down, too. Hell, I'm going to set a record and live to be a hundred." A grin froze on his face.

He didn't fool me.

* * *

I run my hand over the dated kitchen countertop, feeling several cracks in the Formica. Grandma Betty used to stand at this very counter rolling pie dough or dreaming up a new mouthwatering dish. In fact, my dad depended upon quite a few of Betty's recipes when he took over Aunt Prissy's Kitchen, the diner in Bonita Springs.

For our light supper tonight, I open up the card table out on the porch, clean off the dust, set the table, and put a basket of Ritz Crackers and a bowl of fresh fruit in the center. The three of us enjoy tuna salad on romaine leaves with sliced homegrown tomatoes and sweet tea. Credit the giant water oak and its hovering limbs for temperatures staying ten degrees cooler than any other part of the house.

At twenty past eight o'clock, my dad bids us goodnight and wheels into his room. Mimi and I tackle lightweight kitchen duty. I lift a soapy plate out of the sink. Rinsing the porcelain under a steady stream, my fingers slide over the petite daisies painted around the rim.

"I had forgotten about this china. It's Mother's." I give the dish to Mimi.

Snatching a clean dishtowel from a nearby drawer, she wipes the plate dry. "Expensive?"

"Not back then, but maybe now. She loved this pattern, but I never knew why she didn't take the set with her to Miami Beach." I scrub a bowl with suds. "So, how does Dad appear to you?"

"Kind of feeble." My granddaughter places the plate in the cabinet above her.

"I agree. He's awfully thin and pale."

"Honestly, it's hard to see him this way. The last time I saw a picture of him, he looked different, energetic, I guess. Is that the last of the dishes?"

I yank several paper towels off the roll. "Yes. I'll wipe the counters and we're done. Would you mind putting the card table away? Just set it over in the corner next to Dad's TV. Meet you on the porch."

For the rest of the evening, Mimi dictates the topic of the conversation, apprising me of her young and busy life—everything from college classes to a possible new car to Nathan Caruso, a fellow journalism major and new love. We call it a night around ten.

At ten-thirty, I lie on top of cool sheets staring at the ceiling. Mimi scribbles in her journal for a few minutes before tucking the notebook under a pillow.

She turns off the lamp. "It sure is hot in here. The window's open, but it's like there's no air in the room."

"I know."

"So, Gran, do we have an agenda tomorrow?"

"Not really, but I don't plan to spend the entire day doing research. Don't know how long we can leave Dad by himself."

"If you're not ready to fall asleep, I'd love to hear more about your friend, Rita May. She also witnessed the hanging, right?"

"Uh huh. I was twelve when she moved away from Bonita Springs. We wrote letters and emailed each other until about two years ago when communication became sporadic. Presently, the friendship is nonexistent, which I blame on her selfishness." I exhale a lengthy sigh. "The thing is… Rita was always like that. Looking back, I realize I made excuses for her, which I suppose made it easy to overlook the narcissistic behavior." Lying on my side and facing Mimi, my vision adjusts to the dark. "Through the years, what began as an aspiration to escape her past became an obsession. My self-absorbed friend truly believes money and status will bring happiness." I cover a yawn with my hand. "Think I'm getting sleepy."

Mimi sits up in her bed. "It would be great if y'all were on speaking terms. I could throw in a paragraph or two from her own words, you know, get her side of the story. It's totally up to you. I mean, we certainly don't need her. You and I can do this all by ourselves."

"Yes, we can." I roll over and face the wall. "Night."

* * *

At Eli's request, I construct bacon, egg, and cheese sandwiches on toasted English Muffins for our breakfast. I take the last bite, finish chewing, and sip coffee. "Daddy, before I go back to Atlanta, I'm going to ask Manuel to get a few estimates on a house painter and someone to patch the roof. I'm also going to give him a check to purchase two ceiling fans—one for the porch and one for the back bedroom. It's an oven in there and very uncomfortable." I set my cup on the wicker table.

The prickly old man shakes his head. His napkin falls into his lap. "Okay, but that's money wasted. My cottage is perfectly fine. I don't even feel the heat anymore."

"Well, we do. Glad it's a little cooler on the porch. I think I'll sleep out here on the chaise tonight."

"You go ahead, but I don't want to hear a peep about Palmetto bugs. How about you, Mimi? How did you sleep last night?"

"Not great. I felt like I was in a tomb. No air."

Dad smirked then chuckled to himself.

Mimi gathers our plates. "Gran, when we're out today why don't we purchase a couple of rotating fans? At least they will push the air around a little."

"Good idea."

"I'll take care of these few dishes before we go." She heads to the kitchen.

"Dad, will you be okay by yourself for a few hours? Mimi and I have some errands to run in downtown Bonita Springs.We should be back by one."

"Of course, I will. Hell, Manuel comes and goes whenever he pleases. Besides, I have your phone number if I need you."

* * *

Mimi pilots Dad's Jeep Cherokee southward on Old Highway 41. When we draw near the downtown area of Bonita Springs, my heart bangs inside my ribcage. This is crazy. Silently and slowly, I count to ten as Mimi drives past a gas station where a farmer is selling vegetables and fruit under a canopy.

I point behind us. "Did you see those peaches? We have to stop on the way back." I gulp more water. "If the fruit is good and ripe, I'll make Grandma Betty's cobbler recipe. You'll love it. Nothing better with a scoop of vanilla ice cream." I seem to be jabbering at warp speed.

Mimi studies me. "Are you okay? We don't have to do this today. We can postpone it." She steers the car across the bridge. Renovated buildings reside among newer construction on the far side of the Imperial River.

"Yes, we do." My breathing is heavy. "There's the Liles Hotel and the cottages that originally belonged to the Imperial River Court. Back then, the buildings sat closer to the riverbank. Do you see the band shell on the green? That's where the old ballfield used to be."

We cruise by Reynolds Street. "Let's park in front." Flipping the visor mirror, I brush hair off my face.

Mimi swerves into an empty spot. "This is such a cool little town."

"There's the banyan tree." My pulse races.

"Gran, it's enormous."

I unbuckle the seatbelt, silently begging God to give me strength.

Mimi switches off the ignition and looks over at me. "I researched the internet for banyan trees and found that the monster tree has another more sinister name." She cracks the car door.

Whispering, I count to ten again.

"The strangler fig. I mean it's so appropriate, right? I read that apparently, the banyan tree swells in size attaching itself to a host tree and eventually strangling the smaller growth to death. Think I'll use the term in the article." She exits and the door closes behind her.

"An excellent idea." Once I obtain my bearings outside the car, I force one foot in front of the other. Mimi is up ahead. I stop first where the branches of the massive growth shield the sunlight. My pulse calms and I gaze at the tree's expansive limbs; several stretch outward and touch the dirt, but many are more than six feet off the ground. Gnarled roots grip the base and spread like giant claws into the mixture of sand and dirt.

"In the past, I could barely drive by this monstrosity. Today is the first time I've been able to get close." I swallow a mouthful of air. "I had no way of knowing why it affected me like that."

Mimi ducks under a swag of drooping moss while admiring Mother Nature's gigantic relic. "It's almost peaceful. It's hard to imagine a murder here, someone hanging from these limbs. It doesn't seem real."

Rays of sunshine peek through the leaves above us, creating silhouettes on the ground resembling the paper patterned cutouts my mother and I made when I was a child, the doily-like creations she called jinkies. Walking away from the tree, my granddaughter and I stroll down the sidewalk where the shops tempt us. Mimi leads me into a boutique where a local artist sells his watercolor seascapes. Twenty minutes later, a thunderclap in the distance spurs us back toward the car.

"See that vacant lot on the corner. Aunt Prissy's Kitchen stood right there." Opening the passenger side door, I recall being twelve years old and running down Childers Street, Rita May and Skip by my side.

Out of the blue, charcoal clouds stream over the landscape toward the east and the sky spits raindrops on my head. Mimi and I jump inside the Jeep. Escaping just in time, we manage to evade the deluge as it douses the streets of Bonita Springs.

I rub a taut muscle at the back of my neck. "It's as if I never left." I buckle the seatbelt. "Let's stay on the highway, and go left at Dean Street."

"You're in charge." She cranks the engine.

In typical coastal Florida fashion, the rain subsides within minutes, leaving little evidence, apart from the steam rising off the highway. We drive by the Shangri La Resort and proceed to the Bonita Springs Elementary School, where a historical marker protrudes from the grass in front of the property. My granddaughter turns the Jeep's steering wheel, skirts the curb, and idles the engine.

"I remember the school building being a lot larger. When I was eleven, Rita May and I used to meet on the playground during recess. We were best friends, blood sisters. I miss *that* girl." I chug the last of my water. "There's a hardware store a block down on the other side of the street. They'll have fans. Tomorrow, we'll do Fort Myers. After we check on Dad and fix lunch, I think I'll drive down to the beach. A walk on a never-ending stretch of sand will do me a world of good. Are you game?"

"You're on." Mimi shifts into drive. "Let's don't forget those peaches."

* * *

Lounging on the porch daybed, I lose myself in the next chapter of my novel. Dad disappears into his room for a nap and Mimi sits to my right glued to her laptop.

I open my eyes. I must have dozed off. According to my watch, it's five twenty-three. Sliding my feet into flip-flops, I gather my book and phone and find Mimi in the kitchen making a pitcher of sweet tea. She drops ice into a glass and pours.

"Mmm. I'd love some of that, please." I pull a glass from the cabinet. "Want to help me with the cobbler? Like maybe peel and slice the peaches while I work on the crust?"

"Sure, Gran. I'll look for the peeler. Is there an apron around?"

"Check the hook on the back of the pantry door." After I pour my tea, I ferret through an under-the-counter cabinet. "Wow. Look at this ancient milk glass baking dish. I guess Pyrex lasts forever."

For the next hour, my granddaughter and I recreate a recipe from my memory bank, one I prepared during summer months when Gretchen was a little girl. While the dessert bakes in the oven and the delectable aroma permeates the old cottage, Mimi and I discuss the possibility of a pre-dinner stroll on the beach.

In forty-five minutes, I remove the cobbler and set the dessert on hot pads near the stove. I hear my dad, pushing his walker down the hall. "Hey, Daddy, we're going down to the beach. Be back in an hour."

"You two have fun. *NBC Nightly News* is on. I like that Brian Williams. He's one smart fella."

* * *

Mimi flips burgers on Dad's charcoal grill, and I toss a salad with a homemade vinaigrette. Again, we dine on the screened porch. After supper and an initial cleanup, I scoop the still warm cobbler into three dessert bowls, and cap each one with a scoop of vanilla ice cream. I carry the bowls on a tray while Mimi brings a cup of instant decaf to my father. She drinks iced tea, and I sip from my glass of pinot noir. I must replenish Manuel's wine stock.

A taste of warm fruit and flaky crust melts in my mouth. "Okay, Daddy, let's talk."

His eyebrows scrunch together. "Baby Girl, don't you think you've had enough wine tonight? One before supper and then two more at mealtime. So this is your fourth glass."

"No. I count three, but it's really none of your business." My jaw clenches.

Mimi takes another bite.

Dad clears his throat. "Jessica, are you aware that the alcoholic gene doesn't merely trickle down the limbs of your mother's family tree? It gushes. Your grandmother, Florence English, died of liver disease. I don't want the same thing to happen to you."

I refuse to get into this with him. "I'm fine." I place the glass on the coffee table.

"All right. All right. What's on your mind?" He corrects his posture and slurps coffee.

I compose myself. "Do you remember the summer of my twelfth birthday? And the hobo named Mundy Mike who appeared at the diner's back door?"

"Vaguely." My father's eyes narrow into slits.

"Because it took me several years of nightmares, anxiety, and extensive therapy to retrieve my memory, I can now recall that summer and what happened on the Fourth of July, the incident that haunted me most of my life." I clasp my hands together in my lap.

His dessert is almost gone. Scraping the bowl, he spoons in one last bite. "Mmm, mmm. The first decent peach cobbler I've eaten since Delilah passed. God rest her sweet and shiny soul."

I wring my hands. "Daddy, I was there…at Mundy's hanging."

In mid-sip, he ingests too much coffee and chokes. Clutching a napkin, he covers his mouth. "A hanging? What in blazes are you talking about?"

"Back then, Rita May and I made a clubhouse in the roots of the banyan tree. We hid and witnessed Mundy Mike's murder." I inhale. "And, it might end up being a waste of energy, but I'm seeking answers." I exhale waiting for my father's reaction.

He doesn't blink, but sets his cup on the table. He swats at me as if he would a bothersome fly. "Stop right there! We're not discussing this. Anyway, it doesn't matter. Happened a lifetime ago." Sweat dampens his forehead. He rotates his chair to the right, surveying his back yard. "Look out at that. I think they call that a strawberry moon."

I scoot to the edge of my chair. "Please listen. While Mimi and I are visiting, we're going to look into KKK involvement that took place back in the fifties in Lee County and any info about hobos in southern Florida at that time. She plans on writing an article about Mundy Mike and his murder."

A stern expression crimps his brow. "Damn it, Jessy. You're opening a dead and buried can of worms. I'm telling you to leave well enough alone."

With legs crossed, I dangle my right foot up and down. "Sorry, but I can't do that."

After a deep sigh, Mimi interjects. "Grandpa Eli, when you owned the diner, did you ever overhear rumors of any Ku Klux Klan activity in Bonita Springs?"

Dad wheels his chair away from the screen. "Nope. Can't say as I did." He mumbles to himself.

I curve a strand of hair behind my ear. No one speaks until I break the awkward pause. "We've hardly put a dent in the effort to date, but we will. I'm determined to share the story and possibly generate some interest, and who knows, maybe we'll find a connection to Mundy's family."

Eli kneads the rubber handrails on his wheelchair. His knuckles whiten. "You don't realize what you're doing." Perspiration outlines his lips. "I'm off to bed."

"Dad, do you know if Billy Grizzle is still alive?"

His gaze shoots right past me. "Yeah. He's in one of those nursing homes for old folks who are on death's door. I hear he's got maybe six months. Cancer, I think. Why do you want to know?"

"Because he and his buddies murdered Mundy Mike."

Eli mutters to himself. "Hearsay…can of worms." He presses the button on his wheelchair and zooms off the porch into the cottage.

Carrying a tray full of dirty dishes, Mimi stops in the doorway between the porch and the house. "Wow, Gran. Sounds like you struck a giant nerve."

CHAPTER TWENTY-SEVEN:
DIGGING UP BONES

The trip to Fort Myers consumes an hour on I-75. We stop for lunch at a Chick-fil-A and then have no problem locating the Lee County Courthouse.

Dressed in white shorts and a hot pink T-shirt, Mimi scrambles to exit the car first. "If we find stuff we can use, I'll snap a million pictures and take notes."

Inside the historic structure, I plod behind her as she hurries up the stairs to the archives. "I'm glad you're helping me, honey. I can't do this alone."

Although our initial investigation stalls at the office of the Clerk of the Circuit Court, an obliging receptionist suggests we try the Lee County Regional Library. After a short walk, we hit the jackpot. In the reference section, our investigation unearths page after page of newspaper articles preserved in microfiche and sheets from actual newspapers sealed in clear plastic for protection. Records of civil rights activists marching and picketing during the 1950s give credence to the general civil unrest that eventually engulfed the larger cities in the southern states. On the other hand, documented incidents or accounts in rural areas and small towns are scarce.

Mimi's single-minded dive into county records pays off. "Listen," she says in a low voice, "Uh, June something, 1956. Oh, man, the ink has faded. Lee County, Bonita Springs. Deputies arrested two unidentified Negro males for loitering and harassing a White woman at a local Shell station."

I whisper in her ear. "Mundy Mike and his buddy Pleasin' Pete."

Minutes later, the tip of Mimi's finger draws an invisible line under an account of an unknown vagrant found mutilated to death in an alligator pit at the Everglades Wonder Gardens. "Does that ring a bell?"

"Oh, my God, yes. Local officials couldn't identify the body. My friends and I figured it was Gator Breath."

Mimi giggles. "I love the hobo names." She retrieves her camera from her purse and snaps several pictures. "It's not much to go on, but at least it's something."

Due to stiff legs and a numb backside, I rise and stretch. "I doubt we'll find any direct reference to Mundy Mike's murder. When he evaporated into thin air, I never heard anyone speak of him again. I'm guessing crimes committed by the KKK were seldom reported for fear of retribution, among other things."

Mimi and I peruse newspaper and magazine articles and timeworn reference books not paying attention to the time. She sighs. "We've been at this for over an hour, but we could spend days here. There's more than enough documented historical data about the KKK in the south, particularly in Florida. Information like this creates the picture you want to paint, the backdrop of the story."

"I agree. Oh, look. This is good. Turn on your recorder." I read aloud. "Apparently, after the Florida Legislature passed an anti-mask ordinance in 1951, the Klan retaliated with more cross burnings, floggings, and hangings from the Florida Panhandle to Miami." I remove my glasses and wipe the lenses using the edge of my blouse.

Mimi picks up where I leave off. "At the time, the press in the northern states labeled the KKK, *The Florida Terror*." Mimi stops, reaches for her camera, and takes another picture. "Gran, did you ever hear anyone speak of this when you were a kid?"

"Not really, but I never paid much attention unless it directly involved me. Kids are narcissistic little beings, you know. For that matter, the adults I remember were very careful not to talk about reality or anything controversial in front of children."

Mimi smirks. "The old *See No Evil, Hear No Evil* thing." She offers me a piece of gum.

"No thanks." I check my watch. "It's time we head back."

Mimi and I collect our notes before we circumvent the stacks of books and leave the library. The blazing sunshine dictates donning sunglasses as we make a beeline to the Jeep.

I shimmy behind the steering wheel. "We'll try downtown Bonita Springs again tomorrow. The Historical Society might have something we can use."

Mimi climbs inside. "It's almost five. We should stop by the store. Any dinner ideas?"

"Why don't we eat out tonight? Dad used to love Joe's Shrimp Shack."

* * *

Grumbling the entire time, my father rolls down the ramp in his wheelchair. "Why do we have to do this? A cheese sandwich would've sufficed." He turns back to the cottage. "Did you lock up?"

"Yes, sir." Mimi helps him into the Jeep. "Why are you fussing? You love seafood."

"Oh indeed, I do, but I'm not used to getting gussied up, and I'm not all that hungry. Money and time wasted. The Braves game is set to start soon."

"Gussied up?" I grin at my father who took a comb to his slicked back silver hair. Sporting a navy blue short-sleeve shirt and beige slacks, his image is a brief reminder of the young man who once escorted his daughter to Mass on Sunday mornings.

Mimi drives and Dad spouts directions from the shotgun seat. I sit in back letting the breeze from the side window tousle my hair. When the Jeep nears the beach, I taste salt in the air.

* * *

The next morning, after we eat breakfast, Mimi and I travel back downtown. Ebony clouds chase us into a parking space in front of the Liles Hotel. Standing outside the car, I clutch an opened umbrella avoiding the water pellets striking the pavement.

The aroma of strong coffee welcomes us inside the reception area, where bookshelves and office machines line the back walls. A woman sits behind a raised counter, her ash blonde hair shaped into a pixie cut. Spying over a pair of granny glasses, she bounces toward us. "Hello, ladies. May I help you?"

"Hi, my name is Jessy Tate, and this is my granddaughter, Mimi Stewart. We're looking for the Historical Society."

"Their office is upstairs, but I'm sorry it's closed today. It's a volunteer organization so their schedule varies."

"Shoot. We're doing a little investigating into the past. Digging up bones, you might say."

The woman acted genuinely interested. "I'm Opal. Lived here my whole life. I bet I can steer you in the right direction. Would you like a cup of coffee? Got a fresh pot."

Mimi and I decline the offer.

She points to the corner of the room where chairs encircle a cocktail table covered with brochures. "Y'all have a seat. I'll be right back." She emerges from behind the counter grasping a coffee cup. The woman squats into one of the club chairs, but stands when her cellphone jingles. She fumbles inside her shirt pocket. "Sorry, I have to take this." Her pitch raises almost an octave. "Good morning, The Historic Liles Hotel…No, ma'am, we're not a working hotel, but a historical landmark. The hotel presently houses city government offices and the Bonita Springs Historical Society, which has exhibits on both floors. Uh, no problem." She slips the phone back in her pocket. "I'm sorry. Where were we?"

I clear my throat. "We're here to do some research for an article my granddaughter plans to write."

"You look sort of familiar. Are you from around here?" She leans back in her chair.

"Yes and no. I was born in Miami, but spent most of my childhood years here in Bonita Springs."

Opal bites her bottom lip and frowns. "Wait a sec. There was a Jessy in my class at school. You're not Jessy Blanchard, are you?"

"Yes. Jessy Blanchard Tate."

"I do declare. I sat behind you in the sixth grade. I'm Opal Grizzle Goodman."

I inspect the woman's face for a sign of recognition. "Hi, it's…ah… how are you?"

"I can't believe it's you, Jessy. Did you hear I married Skip Goodman? Didn't you date him in high school?"

"Yeah, my junior year. Sweet guy. How is he?"

"He's retired and we've got six grown kids and losing count of the grands."

I swallow hard. "And your mom and dad?"

Opal's grin flattens. "Mom passed nearly ten years ago, and I don't speak to my father." She squirms in her seat.

"My dad said that Billy lives in a convalescent facility."

"Yeah, but I don't have anything to do with him. We haven't spoken in years. He is a vile human being."

I go blank. I can't form a word much less a sentence.

Mimi bails me out. "We're visiting Great Grandpa Eli and investigating Ku Klux Klan activity in Florida in the fifties and sixties. We're lucky we ran into you because we have a strong suspicion your father might be able to help us due to his affiliation with the organization back in the day."

Opal cocks her face to the side. "May I ask why the sudden interest?"

I lick my lips. "In the summer of 1956, I accidentally witnessed a murder, a hate crime perpetrated most likely by the Klan. When we've exhausted our inquiry, Mimi has agreed to write the story in her college newspaper. The victim, a Black man, must have family somewhere. I'm hoping for answers and, in due course, some sort of resolution, if possible."

"Involving a crime committed ages ago?"

"To me, time is irrelevant."

"Why did you wait so long to do this?" Opal puts her elbows on her knees.

"Unfortunately, my subconscious blocked the trauma until recently."

She waves her hand. "Hold on a minute. I've gotta make a call." The woman punches a number on her phone and waits. "Hey, are you busy? Do me a favor and don't move a muscle. I've some people for you to meet. You and I have the opportunity to help two lovely ladies in their quest to open Pandora's Box."

Turning toward my granddaughter, I recognize her expression of pure delight, so like the youthful pictures of my mother, Mimi's namesake.

Opal lurches from her chair, its wooden legs scraping the floor. "That was my brother, Andrew. You probably don't remember him; he graduated three years ahead of us. He's a huge history buff who can put you on the right track. He's also a retired lawyer and currently a member of the City

Council. First, let me lock up the hotel. Then if you have time, follow me to Andrew's house. By the way, he legally changed his name to Turner a long time ago, due to obvious reasons. Turner is our mother's maiden name."

Billy Grizzle's daughter secures the Liles Hotel while Mimi and I hop in the Jeep. We tail her beige Acura to the Surfside Golf Resort right off the Bonita Beach Road. Due to our proximity to the beach, my window stays open. I take a whiff of sea air. "Isn't life funny? Here I am in Bonita Springs and Opal Grizzle has offered to help me. In school, she was a bully—everyone hated her. I suppose that demonstrates that anyone can change for the better."

Opal's car brakes at the resort entrance. My former enemy leans through her car window to press a code on a security pad. The wrought iron gate opens, and we cruise in behind the Acura, entering the affluent subdivision. Both vehicles come to a halt at the end of a winding driveway where a stucco Spanish-style mini-mansion sits surrounded by a low-maintenance tropical landscape and a lush green lawn.

Andrew welcomes us at the doorstep. Thank God, the man bears no outward resemblance to his despicable father. In fact, the genes must have skipped a generation. He doesn't favor his mother, Pinky, either, but Opal certainly does. Andrew is fit and attractive with a full head of frosty gray hair, broad shoulders, and a six-foot frame. Time being gentle on the man, tiny laugh lines surround his mouth and eyes, adding character to chiseled looks. Dressed in khaki shorts and a Tommy Bahama shirt, he wears the costume of a wealthy Florida retiree; a golf tan puts the icing on a very appealing hunk of cake.

I want to know Andrew Turner. I extend my hand, spouting polite introductions and shamelessly inspecting his ring finger. No evidence, not even a tan line.

"Pleasure to meet you. Let's go on into the great room. May I offer y'all a glass of iced tea?"

"No, thanks."

Mimi's answer duplicates mine.

Opal sits on an ottoman in front of a masculine chair upholstered in leather, the color of milk chocolate. "I'll have a glass if you've offering." Her brother exits the room and her posture stiffens. "I have no problem discussing my dad and his sordid past, but I'm not a hundred percent sure about Andrew. Through the years, our family has endured its fair share of scrutiny. My brother might not jump on your band wagon right away, but I think he'll come around."

"We appreciate any help y'all have to offer." Mimi settles into an upholstered wing chair.

I sink into the sofa, the smooth leather chilly under my legs. "I'm afraid what I'm going to tell you about your father might come as a shock."

Opal sets her jaw. "No, you don't understand. Our father can't surprise us anymore. You see, he wore his sins as if they were badges of honor. When I was a child, I prayed my mom would have the courage to leave him. Bless her heart, she waited until Andrew and I left home to cut those ties."

Grizzle's son re-enters the room and hands Opal a glass of tea. He sits next to me on the sand-colored sectional. "Ladies, the floor is yours."

Pure irony. I sit here conveying my story to the daughter and son of the man I deem to be pure evil. I end the account with, "I'm hoping I can answer the long overdue questions the hobo's relatives must have."

Opal gulps her beverage. "If I'm making the decision, I wouldn't hesitate. Who cares about the consequences? Our father admitted his past involvement in various heinous activities, but there's never been anything linking him to a murder in Lee County. If he did take part in killing the hobo, he deserves a conviction, or at the very least to be publically humiliated. Andrew, you've been too quiet. Give us your opinion."

"I agree, Sis, but…" He opens his mouth to speak but hesitates pressing his lips together.

"Are you afraid of dirtying the precious family name a little more?" Opal chomps on a chunk of ice.

"Not at all. It's just…displaying our family's dirty laundry once again."

I unconsciously brush Andrew's hand. "I sympathize, but imagine the hobo's family never discovering how he died."

He rubs his forehead. "You're right. I'm being selfish. If you want answers, I recommend you question our father face to face. If you can convince him to admit his guilt, I'll help you in any way possible."

I fidget with a loose button on my blouse. "Thank you, Mr. Turner."

"Please, call me Andrew." He pauses. "I warn you. Billy is obstinate and as mean as a snake. There's no guessing his reaction. Although relatively harmless at this stage of his life, he's unabashedly proud of his past, and he never wavers in his racist viewpoint. Above all, he still loves to hear himself talk."

"I can handle it." I check Mimi's reaction. Her smile is wider than mine is. Glancing at Andrew, I'm glad I chose the black Capri pants and white sleeveless blouse today. The simple outfit compliments my figure. "May we speak to your father tomorrow morning, say ten-thirty?"

"I'll call ahead and meet you there. Before you leave today, I insist you ladies have some tea." He exits the room, shortly returning with a pitcher and four glasses filled with ice.

Andrew dominates the remainder of the morning, sharing his familiarity with the history of the KKK in Lee County, his sister interjecting a word here and there. He mentions an organization that has monitored the association's activity for the last fifty or sixty years. "The Freedom Watchdogs have an office in Fort Myers." Andrew strolls over to a mahogany desk in the corner. When he returns, he offers me his business card.

"Thank you." I stick the card in my purse. "I'm afraid we've taken up way too much of your time."

"Not at all. Why don't you and Mimi join me and my sister at the club for lunch?"

I blush when I stare into his eyes. They're blue-green, the color of the Gulf of Mexico on a clear day. "Are you sure we're not intruding on your plans?"

"Come on, ladies. Meet me at the Surfside Golf and Country club." When he beams, both cheeks dimple.

"We'd love to," says Mimi. "I just need directions."

"Just follow my car. It's not far at all." Opal struts into the kitchen carrying the tray of empty glasses.

* * *

Within a half an hour, we sit dining in the front room of The Pelican's Roost, the window table commanding a view of a private beach not far below. Andrew insists on treating us to delicious seafood salads and glasses of expensive Sauvignon Blanc.

After lunch, Mimi thanks our host and catches up with Opal. They chat like old friends. Andrew and I shadow the women outside to the parking lot. Standing alongside the Jeep, I thank him again.

He jabs both hands into his pockets, his coy expression reminiscent of Phillip when he and I first began dating. "Um..."

"Yes?" With my back to the door, I'm motionless.

"Staying in Bonita for the rest of the summer?"

"Oh no, just a few more days." My heart quivers like I'm fifteen and flirting with the boy whose locker borders mine.

"Jessy, may I treat you to dinner tomorrow night?"

As Andrew opens my door, I smile and say, "Yes, I'd love that." Once inside the Jeep, I strap on our seat belt as he walks away.

Mimi looks sideways at me. "Why the silly grin, Gran?"

"Andrew asked me out to dinner. I said yes, but I'm wavering. I really shouldn't go on a date." My chest tightens; the sensation is familiar. "It's too soon, you know, after Phillip."

Revving the engine, Mimi frowns. "No, it's not."

"I still feel married. I'm not ready."

"It's dinner. That's all. You have nothing to lose, and you might actually have fun."

Staring at the lofty pines zooming by, my mind spins. A single flash of Mario Ricci sneaks into my head. Aside from my harmless yet perpetual Dr. Priest fantasy, I remained true blue to my husband throughout our marriage. However, once Mario began the flirtation, I changed, allowing the unthinkable to happen, going against everything I believed in. I became an unfaithful wife and *the other woman*, a disparaging term that has always disgusted me. Although I only weakened once, one night, one passionate yet regrettable night, it remains the worst night of my life. I'll never know if Phillip forgives me, but I know I can count on God's absolution. However, my conscience won't let me off the hook. I can't forgive myself.

Would an evening with Andrew be another mistake? In any case, I never understood why Mario Ricci zeroed in on me. I try to keep myself fit and minimize the wrinkles, but at sixty-two, it's all a losing battle. I'm no Rita May McAfee Rhodes. I don't let doctors tighten and tuck me so that I no longer resemble myself. A little Botox occasionally...that's it. When I study myself in the bathroom mirror, my vision is twenty-twenty. Like a used book, my binding is in need of repair, pages worn and yellowed, but well read by my late husband.

However, during the last year of his life when Phillip lost interest in everything, including me, our lives mutated into one of monotony and emotional separation. Because of his disinterest, I believed no one would ever desire me again. Then along came Mario enticing me into becoming one of his neighborhood conquests. Insecurity is no excuse for adultery.

Now, from out of this past year's fog comes Andrew.

Mimi interrupts my contemplation. "Aren't you excited? I wonder if Billy Grizzle will admit his crime."

I gaze at my lovely granddaughter as the channels switch in my brain. "I am excited. Although I'm dreading the actual confrontation, I can't wait to find out what the devil has to say for himself."

CHAPTER TWENTY-EIGHT:
WORRYWART

As the campaign to re-elect Congressman Harrison Rhodes shifts into overdrive, Harrison's manager boasts of recent monetary contributions and strategic endorsements from prominent supporters. However, the congressman remains skeptical. He needs to see positive numbers, which equates to a boost in the current polls. He must add off-the-schedule public appearances to his already-busy calendar. To strengthen the campaign, Harrison requires additional deep-pocket support from a number of heavy hitters and lobbyists.

During Rita's summer teaching hiatus, she reduces her client list, allowing the campaign effort to monopolize her time. One night in June, the couple attends a dinner at the Ritz Carlton Hotel in Washington, D.C. sponsored by the local Democratic Party. Red, white, and blue banners crisscross tabletops and adorn the stage behind the main table. Place cards denote the seating hierarchy, including the guests of honor—the congressman and his wife.

Rita counts her drinks. *Two so far. I better eat something.* She seeks nourishment at a buffet table and polishes off several cocktail shrimp. Scanning the room, she spots Harrison leaning against the baby grand piano in the corner of the room doing his best schmoozing at three potential voters and a fellow politician. She sidles up and slips her arm into the crook of his until a waiter carrying a tray of beverages passes by. Rita surrenders to the impulse and grabs a martini.

Harrison's expression sobers as he whispers, "Rita, you've had enough."

She leans in closer. "No, I haven't."

"I don't want you to embarrass yourself."

"No, you don't want me to embarrass you." Rita licks the tiny bump on her lip and smirks. "Quit being a worrywart. I'm fantastic." She walks away, a far cry from fantastic. Although the Valium she swallowed earlier had eased her nerves, the recent letter from Jessy Tate plays on Rita's mind.

Later at dinner, she picks at the cherry tomatoes in her salad. She manages a bite of her filet, but ignores the yeast roll and whipped potatoes. She excuses herself. On the way to the ladies' room, she plucks her phone from a designer bag and punches numbers. Her voice is hushed. "Are you free tomorrow? Three o'clock? Great." During this immediate crisis, which she blames on Jessy Tate, Rita deems time spent with her new lover and his magic hands essential to her well-being. Given his skill level, no pill in her secret stash could alleviate the tension in her body any better. She tucks her cellphone back into the clutch purse.

Rita returns to her seat at the same time Harrison steps to the podium. *I don't give a damn about Jessy Tate. I'm Rita Miller Rhodes, wife of that spectacular Black man, the future President of the United States.* She consumes the other martini, one she pilfered from a waiter on her way back to the table.

* * *

Cold water runs into the bathroom sink. Rita squeezes toothpaste onto her toothbrush then glares into the mirror. "Okay God, it's time to talk. If Jessy Tate spills her guts about something that happened fifty years ago, it will ruin me. If you'll help me, I'll stop seeing Ethan, uh, the day after tomorrow. You go work a miracle and extinguish Jessy's obsession with ancient history. On the other hand, you could just make her disappear, give her a lengthy disease, or cause a dreadful accident, which would incapacitate her. If you can swing it, I'll be the perfect politician's wife—loyal, loving, and faithful." She brushes her bottom teeth, spits, and stops. "By the way, since I haven't bothered you lately, you owe me."

Harrison cracks the door. "How many people have you got in there?"

"You startled me." Rita twists the faucet handle to the off position.

"You're talking to yourself again. Should I be worried?"

She smirks. "Just thinking aloud." She bites her lip. As Harrison vanishes into the bedroom, Rita tastes blood.

CHAPTER TWENTY-NINE:
COMIN' UP A CLOUD

The drive from Eli's cottage to Bonita Beach takes almost a half-an-hour, the morning traffic easing along at an adequate pace. At ten twenty-five, we roll into the circular drive at the Waving Palms Convalescent Center. Set four blocks from the beach, the pelican gray clapboard structure, once an old family estate, shows an urgent need for some tender loving care. At first whiff inside the reception area, one experiences a combination of distinct smells—talcum powder, Pine Sol, and regrettably, urine. In a weak attempt to mask the unpleasant odors, the center also stinks of cheap air freshener.

Dressed in navy Bermuda shorts, a pale-yellow Polo shirt, and brown Timberlands, Andrew paces back and forth in front of the reception desk. He stops when he notices me. "Hey." Scraping a hand through his hair, he rocks in his shoes, heels to toe and back again. "Ah…he'll be here shortly."

I find a chair. Mimi patrols the corridor. The clock on the far wall ticks down until a middle-aged woman in coral scrubs struts up to Andrew.

"Mr. Turner, if you follow me, Deputy Grizzle will see you and your friends in the sunshine room."

Mimi and I shadow Andrew to the sun porch where all the vinyl covered furniture matches, the décor depicting a tropical theme, the room infused in a bird-of-paradise pattern. I park next to my granddaughter on a nearby couch, the vinyl creaking under my weight. She holds my hand. My stomach gurgles.

"I'm sorry. I'm a bit queasy." I clasp my hands together to keep them from trembling.

A male attendant pushes a wheelchair transporting a shrunken old man into the room. Andrew hesitates and then inches toward his father. Billy Grizzle, the former Deputy Sheriff of Lee County, Florida, scoffs. "Well, well. It's my ungrateful son. What do you want?" He inhales, coughing several times. Each cough produces a loud scary rattle inside his chest. His gaze centers on me. "Who are you?" His eyes, though surrounded by creases of aged skin, possess the same intensity and invariable darkness I will never forget.

Andrew squats to his father's level. "Jessy Tate and her granddaughter, Mimi, have questions for you regarding Klan activity back in the 1950s." He eases into a chair nearby.

The old man grunts. "Shoot. I'm an open book. What do you wanna know?"

I clasp my hands together. "Uh, I don't expect you'll remember me, but my father is Eli Blanchard."

Billy sneers and retrieves a toothpick from his pajama shirt pocket. He sticks the wooden pick between his teeth. "Sure, I do. You're the spoiled brat who bothered everyone at your dad's diner."

I chew on my lip. "I'm interested in your past, Mr. Grizzle."

"It's Deputy, if you don't mind. Go ahead and ask away. I got nothing but time." Billy juts his chin forward with a sinister grin.

My throat is parched and I find it hard to swallow. "Mimi, please see if there's any bottled water nearby."

Andrew pops from his seat. "I'll go. Anyone else?"

No one speaks. He disappears into a hallway.

I'm breathing too fast. Oh, God. I can't have a panic attack. Not now. Staring at the floor, I dig my fingernails into the sofa cushions. When I look up, Andrew returns with two bottles of water. "Thank you." I quickly gulp down half the liquid in the bottle. Mimi ferrets through her handbag for her recorder and lays the device on the seat between us.

Another sip of water and I begin. "Deputy, do you recall any African-American hobos in Bonita Springs back in 1956? In particular, a large fellow named Mundy Mike?"

"Nah. Don't think so."

I grip the half-empty bottle. "Late at night on July 4, 1956, a friend and I hid in the base of the giant banyan tree in town. We witnessed first-hand the hobo's gruesome lynching committed by you, Tiny Vargas, Oliver Edson, and another unidentifiable man. I saw you kick the crate out from under Mundy Mike's feet; I saw him struggle for his life." My heartbeat resounds in my ears.

Billy picks at a hangnail on his thumb. "Give me a minute."

Andrew's lips tighten. "Dad, think."

Billy glares at his son. "If me and my friends did render our own brand of justice a time or two, who cares? I'm damn proud of the work I did. No regrets." He coughs several times clutching his ribcage.

Mimi and I lock glances. She points to the recorder on the sofa. "By the way, Deputy Grizzle, we are taping this interview."

"I don't give a rat's ass what you do. Hell, videotape me. I'll even put on a funny hat and do a jig for you, if that's your thing. Don't you get it? I ain't ashamed of anything I've done."

I squeeze my sweaty hands into fists. "Do you admit your involvement in the crime, Deputy Grizzle? Did you hang Mundy Mike until his neck broke?"

"Let me see. Mundy Mike, the big ole boy. Oh, yeah. You're right. I was part of that posse. I don't deny it."

I feel Mimi's hand at my back as I inhale. "Were you in charge? Did you instigate the attack?"

Billy opens his mouth to answer, but suffers another coughing spell. He removes a handkerchief from his pocket and wipes bloody sputum off his mouth. "Water. I'm choking here."

I stiffen. I have no pity for this hateful man.

The attendant lingering in the hallway heeds his patient's call, bringing him a lidded travel mug, the word *Deputy* written on its side. Billy guzzles the liquid. The attendant retreats to his post and Billy lifts his chin. He leans backward, the crumpled handkerchief in his hand. "Lady, I'm dying as sure as I'm sitting here. I got no reason to hide a thing. If I do spill my guts, I want somebody to write a book about me. You know, what's the term? Oh, yeah, immortalize me. After all, I've led an interesting life up until now. So, missy, we got a deal?"

I squint at the man who makes my flesh crawl. "Okay, Mimi will only agree to write your story if you admit you murdered Mundy Mike. Did you have orders to lynch him, or was it your idea? You hated him after he embarrassed you in front of your girlfriend, Sylvia Goodman."

Billy's wheelchair squeaks when he repositions his pajama-clad legs. "Yeah, I hated him, but if I had been in charge, I'd have just run him and his buddies out of town. If I recall correctly, our own Grand Dragon, gave the order to capture that nigger and string him up by the neck until he croaked. The boy was a nuisance to the community."

Andrew curls forward, his elbows on his thighs. "Give us the name of the man in charge of the local KKK."

Billy chuckles. "I told you. The Grand Dragon."

Andrew frowns at his father. "His name, Billy."

"I'll save that juicy tidbit, if you don't mind. Another time, another place." He resumes picking his teeth.

My empty water bottle tumbles to the floor. "Who are you protecting?"

"I may be a lot of things, lady, but I ain't no snitch." Billy plucks a Bic lighter and a pack of cigarettes from his pocket. "Y'all mind if I smoke?"

Not waiting on a reply, he tucks the toothpick into his pocket, flicks the lighter, and says, "They let me light up here on the sunshine porch. If I try to smoke anywhere else, they're on my case. I don't go outside. Too damn hot." He inhales a drag and blows an unbroken stream toward the ceiling. Leering at me, he coughs several times. "So you're Elijah Blanchard's daughter. You always were a nosey girl."

I fan the smoke from my face.

"I bet you're bunking at your Grandpa Caleb's old place."

"I am."

"If I was you, I'd ask Elijah. He just might have the answers you're looking for." Billy sucks on his cigarette. Finally, he nips off the end between his thumb and middle finger, and tosses the butt to the floor. "You tell him, his old friend, Billy, says hello. Don't forget now."

Wheeling himself backward into the hallway, he says, "I'm done. Think I need a swig of oxygen. Breathing is getting tougher by the minute." He takes an uneasy breath. "Hey kid, take me back to my room." The attendant scurries behind the wheelchair and rolls Billy Grizzle away.

I can't get out of there fast enough. Clinging to my purse, I turn to Mimi as we walk toward the exit. "What a strange thing for him to say about Daddy."

Andrew catches up to us in the parking lot. "Please ignore my father. He gets a kick out of upsetting people."

"I'm sure he does."

"Gran, he just wanted to see your reaction." Mimi unlocks the Jeep.

Andrew faces me and jangles his keys. "Is there anything else I can do?"

"You've done way too much already. I can't thank you enough for your time and for arranging the interview with your father. I'm sure there will be more questions for Billy down the road, but right now, Mimi and I need to go check on my dad and fix his lunch."

"Will I see you tonight?"

"Oh, yes, yes, of course. Do you have the address?"

He nods. "I'll pick you up at seven-thirty."

Once inside the car, I rest my head against the seat and consider Billy Grizzle's words. Mimi maneuvers the Jeep out of the parking lot and onto the Bonita Beach Road. Evergreens line both sides of the road, standing like soldiers at attention. In a manner of minutes, a strong gust of wind sweeps the treetops and gray clouds span the sky.

I fondle the cloisonné heart attached to the chain at my neck. "Comin' up a cloud."

"Beg your pardon?" Mimi lowers the radio's volume.

"*Comin' up a cloud* is a Grandpa Caleb expression. He'd say the phrase when a storm appeared out of nowhere."

* * *

After a lunch where the discussion centered on who among the Atlanta Braves players could be a contender for the upcoming All Star Game, Dad retreats to his room. Mimi hunches over the kitchen table, tapping on her laptop. I wander onto the porch with a book in an attempt to concentrate on anything other than Billy Grizzle. Slipping off a pair of sandals, I unwind on the daybed, the intermittent showers outside providing an ideal backdrop. Unfortunately, reading is pointless, my brain running at full tilt.

I must have fallen asleep because a loud noise awakens me. "Mimi, what are you doing in there?"

"Creating a masterpiece."

I wander into the kitchen where several pans, a large bowl, and mixing utensils cover the counter. I spend the rest of the afternoon helping Mimi prepare a cake. Afterwards, we tackle a cheeseburger casserole and a tossed salad for supper.

At around six forty-five, I model five different outfits in front of my dad and Mimi. Everyone agrees on the turquoise sundress and strappy sandals. Back in the bedroom, I sit in front of the tiny dressing table, which once belonged to Grandma Betty. Taking a deep breath, I apply another coat of black mascara on my lashes. "Why am I so nervous about this silly date?"

Mimi watches me from her twin bed and giggles. "Because this a *first* date, Gran. I mean, you never even looked at another man except Grandpa Phillip. It's time for you to do a 360-degree turn for me."

I stand and twirl several times, dismissing Mimi's innocent comment. "Should I take a wrap?"

"Yes, ma'am. Restaurants keep their thermostats way too low. Wow, you're gorgeous, by the way. Yep, my grandmother is positively smoking." Reaching for Mimi's hand, we share a smile.

I flinch at the *crunching* of shells in Dad's driveway. "He's here. Will you grab my shawl, please? It should be hanging in the closet. Mimi, I wonder what your Grandpa Phillip would think of me going out on a date."

Mimi lays the wrap beside me. "He's smiling down on you from heaven. I know it." We hug before she opens the door. "When you're ready, make a grand entrance."

Sitting on the edge of the bed, I hear Dad's laughter rise from the other room while I tug at my shoe straps. I begin to perspire as my guilty conscience rears its untimely head. Once it pops into my psyche, it's hard to ignore. "This is stupid." Tossing the pashmina over my shoulders, I strut into the living room where Dad and Andrew are discussing the upcoming mayoral race.

"Wow." My date stands, his expression revealing his satisfaction. "You look lovely."

My father beams at me. One might think it was my senior year in high school and Chad Hammond, the quarterback of our football team, stands waiting to whisk me off to the prom. "Beautiful, Baby Girl."

"Thank you, gentlemen." Although I'm a bit shaky, Andrew and I glide to the door. I peek over my shoulder. "Don't wait up."

A humid breeze leftover from the earlier storm tousles my hair, and I attempt to smooth wayward strands in place. Andrew opens the passenger door to his Nissan Pathfinder. I shimmy inside on leather seats. I buckle my seatbelt as he shuts himself inside the shiny, black SUV. "Where are we going?"

"The best seafood place in town." He winks. "I understand the crabs crawl right out of the Gulf and walk into the restaurant through the back door."

He laughs at himself. Obviously, his nerves incite him to gab and crack jokes. In contrast, my jitters inhibit me. It takes me about ten minutes to insert a comment here and there, but soon, the casual banter between us becomes effortless. Andrew drives into the crowded lot of the Conch Restaurant and Oyster Bar. He brakes at the valet's kiosk and gives a young man the car key.

He reaches for my hand on the way inside. Despite the overstated ambiance, the restaurant is lovely. The host checks a seating chart and orders a nearby waiter to lead us to a table in the back. My date chooses the wine, and we toast my promise to revisit Bonita Springs in six months. The evening unfolds and my apprehension fades. Like reading a captivating work of fiction, I'm eager to flip the page.

At the end of the delicious meal, he cradles my hand in his before he pays. We walk out hand in hand and linger in the parking lot next to his car. I face him. He moves closer. His warm breath brushes my face. Just for a moment, a pang of guilt returns.

"Would you like a nightcap?" The profound hue of his eyes might be enough to weaken my resistance.

"Uh, no thank you. I have to pack and it's late. We leave in the morning."

He places a kiss on my lips. Tender yet provocative.

On the drive home, remaining in the moment, I wish time to stand still. I immerse myself in the timbre of Andrew's voice, but I'm not really listening to what he's saying.

He wheels the car into Dad's driveway. "Earth to Jessy." He interrupts my thoughts.

"Sorry. It's the whole Ku Klux Klan mess. My next step is to quiz Dad about what Billy said today, see if he ever heard rumors. It's not going to be easy. You're familiar with the old adage, *squeezing blood from a stone?*"

Andrew opens the door for me. His eyes meet mine, and I read his mind. I take a step toward him certain he can hear my heart thumping to an erratic beat. He pulls me toward him. This time, the kiss is deeper, longer.

His hands gently squeeze my shoulders. "Thank you for a wonderful evening. I sure wish you would stay in town for another week or two. There's a lot to do around here. I could show you the sights of new Bonita Springs."

"Dinner was lovely. I'd love to do it again sometime in the future. If you come to Atlanta, I'll treat you to one of our fantastic restaurants." I dig inside my purse for a business card.

Once I give him the card, he lifts my chin with his finger. "Please keep in touch."

"Of course."

Andrew slides his hands up my face into my hair. He kisses me. I let myself melt in his arms as his tongue parts my lips. For a brief moment, I resurrect an emotion I buried long before my late husband died. I linger too long. After a breath, I drift back from his grasp and whisper, "Night," and tiptoe inside Dad's darkened screened porch.

"Gran, I'm over here." Mimi calls to me from a nearby wicker chair.

I collapse on the daybed next to her.

"Okay, let's have it. I want details. Let's go."

I placate my granddaughter's curiosity and confess to most of it. However, I can't admit how the last kiss made me feel.

A half an hour later, I slip on a nightshirt. Mentally preparing myself, my mind wanders. When I question Dad on the subject of Mundy Mike tomorrow, my words must be deliberate. Yet I don't wish to upset him again. A tender heart with an empathetic soul, Eli Blanchard finds the good in mankind while staying a bit naïve about reality. Surely, he never knew how wicked Billy Grizzle was. Although the deputy did his best to unnerve me today, I'm positive Dad will ease my mind.

Lying in bed, I can't help but dwell on Andrew's kiss and my surprising reaction. I ask Phillip for forgiveness. Again.

CHAPTER THIRTY:
CAT'S OUT OF THE BAG

It's six o'clock. Venetian window blinds permit shades of gray into the room, suggesting an overcast day. In spite of the new fan oscillating from the top of the dresser, the air in the bedroom is oppressive.

Dishes clink and a cabinet door closes in the kitchen. Swinging my feet to the floor, I yank the bedsheets off the bed and then stuff them into the pillowcase. Mimi's bed lies stripped, and a packed bag sits next to a stack of folded sheets. Sniffing the irresistible aromas of coffee and bacon, I shower and dress.

My stomach rolls as I finish packing. I know better than to believe the cause of a digestive upset is anything other than stress much less hunger. I firmly shut my suitcase as Mimi calls, "Come and get it."

Eli sits at the end of the table, a section of the morning newspaper spread in front of him. Printed on the dingy white cup he loves are the words *Off the Hook* under a sketch of a wiggling rainbow trout. Dad brings the cup full of hot coffee to his mouth. "Hey, lazybones. I thought you were gonna sleep through the day."

"Morning, Daddy." I pick the chair to his left.

He flattens a crease in a folded page. "When does your flight leave?"

"One something. We've an hour and a half or so before we have to leave for the airport."

Mimi sets a plate of bacon, two scrambled eggs, and an English muffin in front of Eli.

"Thanks, sugar. I'm sure gonna miss this special treatment."

My granddaughter fades into the kitchen, and returns carrying two more plates.

"Thank you." I place a cloth napkin in my lap.

Dad tastes his breakfast. "Mimi, looks like you inherited my cooking skills."

Sitting next to me, she spreads strawberry jam into the nooks and crannies of her muffin. "Well, maybe your talents plus my dad's. Breakfast was always his specialty. He used to fix a feast every Sunday morning."

I meet her unhappy glance. It's the first time she's mentioned her father to me in months.

Mimi sips her juice. "So, Grandpa Eli, have you checked your blood sugar and given yourself a shot this morning?"

He scowls, his white brows forming a V between his eyebrows. "Yes, child. I have a good idea how to take care of myself. I've been pricking my finger and injecting myself with insulin for thirty years." He scratches the top of his head. "So Manuel *is* coming home today?"

I stab at my eggs. "Anytime now."

Eli snaps the opened paper in place in order to view an entire page. He chomps a hunk off his muffin. "I'll be glad to see him…used to having him around."

"Daddy, um, after Mimi and I clean up the kitchen, we'd like to have a talk with you. I promise we won't discuss your health." I wink at my granddaughter.

Once she and I clean up the breakfast dishes, we all relocate to the screened porch, where the thermometer already reads eighty-five degrees. The disfigured fan spins above us, its knocking rhythm predictably inconsistent, and its circular motion futile. Dad continues a rant about an article in the newspaper about new construction in old Bonita Springs. A neighbor's dog barks in the distance. Uncomfortable in the wicker chair, my gaze strays to the yard where a redheaded finch lands on the edge of the birdbath. He hops into the concrete bowl furiously splashing in yesterday's rainwater.

When Eli takes a breath, I interrupt the flow of his conversation. "Dad, yesterday, Mimi and I met Andrew Grizzle at his father's rest home. I questioned the deputy about the murder."

"What is wrong with you? Are you *trying* to stir up trouble? What can you possibly gain by rocking that particular boat?" The crease between my father's brows deepens.

"I needed to hear Billy admit it, and he did, by the way. He came right out and said he took part in killing Mundy Mike. Once Mimi writes her article revealing the crime and Billy's part in it, we think it will go viral. We're hoping to generate enough interest that will cause Mundy's family to step forward. We'll have to wait and see if Lee County or the State of Florida holds the deputy accountable. Because he's dying, he'll never see the inside of a prison. It's too bad. Billy Grizzle is an evil monster. Surely, he will burn in hell."

Eli lifts his chin and bristles. "I don't know what viral means, but I disagree with you. Monster? Nah. I mean Billy is no angel and never had much of a conscience, but I wouldn't go so far as to say that. Anyway, like I said before, all that stuff is ancient history. Stories change. People change. Now let's talk about something else."

I grit my teeth. "No, sorry. We need to discuss this. You see, he admitted everything. However, there's an important fact he declined to divulge—the name of the man who gave the order to kill Mundy Mike. Billy suggested I ask you; he said you have all the answers."

His face turns beet red as he fixates on his yard. "That moldy old birdbath sure could use a good scrubbing. Manuel kept telling me he would clean the damn eyesore. The grass looks straggly, too. He needs to get on the stick and do some work around here."

"Dad, please tell me if you have some information. I need to know."

Eli's body slumps in his wheelchair, his body curving toward me. At last, his eyes meet mine. "Daughter, you do not *need to know*." His expression is stern as if he's scolding an insolent eleven-year-old child. "Some secrets should stay buried."

"If you have knowledge that could help, why won't you tell me?"

"Because you're hitting too close to home."

Mimi squirms in the seat next to Eli. She touches his hand. "How so?"

"It's complicated." He clears his throat. "Back in the fifties, people handed down their belief systems and opinions from generation to generation like family recipes. You accepted and trusted whatever your parents and grandparents said and did, at least most things. It's funny. You see, everything was political. White vs. Black. Democrats vs. Republicans." He chuckled. "Kind of like nowadays."

He licks his lips. "But, back then, many southerners were adamant about keeping things at status quo. They sought to stop integration no matter the cost, believing that giving freedom to one group meant denying the freedoms of another. Me, I held different views. Hell, I loved and trusted Camilla, our cook. She was part of the family." He coughs. "Ah, if I'm gonna be flapping my gums, shouldn't I have something to wet my whistle?"

Mimi leaps from her chair heading toward the kitchen. "I'll get you a glass of tea." In a few minutes, she skips back onto the porch with Dad's beverage.

He takes a swig. "I've always considered myself a fair man and abided by the golden rule. Early on, I adopted a live-and-let-live attitude. Hell, if someone asked for my help, I was there no matter who they were or the color of his skin."

"Of course, Daddy." I repeatedly tap the heel of my foot against the chair leg.

"Now in those days, old timers hated big city rules."

My fingers toy with a piece of torn wicker under the seat of the chair. "So Billy created his own rules?"

"Not only Billy. In 1956, the State of Florida and the Federal Government got serious. Desegregation and separation of church and state were hot topics, and locals didn't particularly agree with the rhetoric. To some folks, government interference came awful close to socialism and communism—seems a rumor saying MLK was a communist just added fuel to the fire." Glancing back at the window, my aging father presses his lips together. "All that's in the history books. I think I'm done. Said enough for now."

"But you haven't told me…"

Dad gulps half the liquid in his glass. After setting down his tea, he runs a trembling hand through his hair. "You're not going to let it lie, are you?"

"No, I'm afraid not."

Leaning forward then back again, he clears his throat. "Okay. Okay. I do remember a group of redneck locals who were hell-bent on causing trouble. They often met at the diner to bitch, moan, and share opinions. I heard chatter about taking matters into their own hands, exacting their own brand of segregated justice. At the time, I didn't give their yakking too much credence."

"You overheard that on a regular basis?"

"Honey, more than a body should have. For instance, Billy and several other guys were downright jubilant about the bombing of Reverend King's house."

I wring my hands. "Doesn't shock me in the least." A knot forms in the pit of my stomach.

"It gets worse, Baby Girl." He exhales into a long, heavy sigh.

A metallic taste rises in my mouth.

His voice quakes. "I'm just gonna come out and say it." He clears his throat. "My father, your Grandpa Caleb, was a member." He swallowed several times. "He organized and led the local chapter."

"The local chapter of what?" I'm terrified of his answer.

"The Klan."

I gulp air, choking on my words. "Are you serious? You're telling me that my own grandfather was not only a member of the KKK but also a leader and gave orders?"

"Now, do you understand why I didn't want you snooping where you didn't belong? I didn't want you talking to Billy." My father's chin rests on his chest. He squints at his arthritic hands.

Heat rushes to my face. "Is there more?"

He shuts his eyes. When his lids open, he bows forward placing his forearms on both knees, his hands together as if praying. "On the morning of that Fourth of July, my father confided in me and swore me to secrecy. He mentioned the possibility of a lynching that was to take place soon, but I promise you, I had no idea the name of the targeted individual or the date—not until Billy bragged about the whole thing later on." Dad rotates toward me. "And you. Why didn't you tell me you were there?"

I bolt from my chair and shout at him. "I was a child, Daddy—a frightened child. Witnessing the murder traumatized me." Tears run down my face.

Dad clears his throat again. "Mimi, fix your grandmother a glass of iced tea."

I stoop to my father's level, my fists clenched into balls. "I don't want any damn tea, Daddy. Have I got this right? You knew of a scheme to murder an innocent man and you didn't do a thing about it. You kept the secret all that day, and you still took Delilah to a dance as if nothing was wrong? How could you?"

Staring into his lap, he wilts. His voice is barely audible when he says, "It was easier to sit tight and keep quiet. I had customers who were KKK supporters."

"Why didn't you report the murder to the State police? To somebody?"

He shakes his head.

I stand up, arms stiff at my side. "You're as disgraceful as Billy Grizzle."

Tears stream down the sides of his face. "You don't understand how life was back then. I couldn't defy my own father." He hangs his head.

I stumble backwards into the chair.

Mimi interrupts. "Uh, Grandpa Eli. Um, do you remember Mundy's full name?"

"Mike Mundy Limba Patterson."

My mind goes blank. "Are you keeping any other secrets…family secrets?" Perspiration glazes my upper lip and the back of my hairline.

He sobs into his hands.

"I'm glad we're leaving." Ripping the cherished keepsake from my neck, I squeeze the locket and silver chain inside my fist. "I'm ashamed to be a Blanchard, ashamed to be your daughter. You are a coward." I throw the necklace at my father and then turn to leave. I hear him mumbling. "What did you say?"

"You sound like your mama. She called me a coward, too. That's why she deserted me."

I swiveled back around. "I thought she left because of Delilah."

"No. Delilah never entered into it. If Margaret hadn't left, we would have stayed together. I'm convinced of it." Eli rubs the top of his thighs. "She somehow discovered your grandpa's Klan affiliation. She couldn't tolerate his actions, or my apathy." He pauses. "Can you ever forgive me?" My father extends an open hand; he uses the other one to yank his handkerchief from his pocket and wipe his tears.

I turn away and march into the kitchen.

Mimi pursues me. "Can I do anything?"

I shake my head. Running cool water, I splash a handful on my face and use a paper towel to blot my cheeks. Manuel's voice carries as he says goodbye to his friend out in the driveway. I rush to the guestroom and grab my carry-on and purse. Charging through the screen porch and out the door, I don't look back at the cottage once occupied by Caleb Blanchard.

* * *

On the Delta flight, Mimi sits to my left, her earplugs securely in place. I sip Merlot from a plastic cup. Although physically exhausted, I can't relax while my dad's words echo inside my head. The man whom I loved and respected is a stranger, not the father I revered, the honorable man I idolized. No, not anymore. He is a coward and a fraud. I punch the button flagging the flight attendant's attention. I crave a refill.

The captain announces his approach to Atlanta on the intercom. As I tilt toward my granddaughter, she unplugs her ears.

"Since the so-called cat is out of the bag, I want you to write the article anyway you wish. Expose the whole story. Do more investigating if you have to, but write every sordid detail. When you're done, I'll give it my blessing. I don't care if the repercussions ruin the precious Blanchard name; it's the right thing to do." I sigh. "Oh, and I meant to ask you, did you catch Mundy's full name?"

"Yes, ma'am, I recorded every spoken word."

CHAPTER THIRTY-ONE:
SQUEAKY WHEEL

One day after another uncelebrated Fourth of July, I receive an email from Andrew Turner.

> *Jessy,*
>
> *I pray you are well. I think of you often and hope to see you soon. Even though we were together only a short time, I thoroughly enjoyed your company. Please tell me you're coming back to Bonita Springs for a visit. I'd love another chance to wine and dine you.*
>
> *Andrew*

I respond in an instant.

> *Glad to hear from you, Andrew. Thank you. I am doing well. Hope you are, too. Keeping busy creating jewelry and enjoying daily rides on Nutmeg. Yes, we did have a lovely time together, didn't we? I'm sorry to say, I don't plan a return trip anytime soon. I won't go into detail now, but right before I left, I learned Eli was cognizant of your father's activities. Mimi is*

hard at work on the story, and when her paper publishes the piece, I will email you the link. Take care.

Jessy

* * *

Using miniscule tweezers, I flip a delicate seashell onto its back. I secure the angel wing in place with diminutive alligator clips fastened to a magnifying glass. I drill a tiny hole at each end. Threading nylon cording through both openings allows the slender rope to cross the inside of the shell. I string three pearl beads on each side of the cord and drape the creation on top of an elongated piece of newsprint. "Where's my sketchbook?" Somewhere on my worktable under pages of artwork and notes, my cellphone vibrates. I check Caller ID before I answer. "Hey, how are you?"

"Gran, may I come by? Six o'clock? I have news. How about I pick you up and we'll go devour a meat lover's pizza and top it off with ice cream sundaes. My treat." The enthusiasm in Mimi's voice is infectious.

"Sure, come on by, but instead, I'll put burgers on the grill. How's seven o'clock instead?"

* * *

I shove a spatula under a charred ground beef patty sizzling on the grill and place it on the bottom half of Mimi's bun. I slide the other hamburger onto my plate. "The fixings are on the island in the kitchen."

"I'm starving to death." She opens the French doors into the family room.

I switch off the gas grill before going inside. "Will you grab the potato salad out of the fridge, please?" Topping off my half-glass of Zinfandel, I remind Mimi of the beverage options.

She hesitates for a minute before choosing. "Diet Coke."

After adorning our burgers, Mimi carries our plates out to the patio; I gather the beverages and utensils. We settle around the glass-topped wrought iron table. An open turquoise umbrella provides enough shade for what's left of the sun in the western sky.

"So you've got news?" The first bite of my overloaded work of art tastes delicious. The second causes a tomato slice to slide off my bun onto the plate.

"I have a draft ready for you to review, but there's more to come." She bites into her burger.

"Can't wait to read it." I dig into a mound of potato salad, my mother's recipe.

"I have a professor who's into genealogy. She showed me a cool website where you investigate people who have been missing a long time. I found out all about Mundy Mike."

"You did? That is wonderful. Tell me."

"Mike Mundy Limba Patterson came from the Beaufort area of South Carolina, and his Gullah family originated in Sierra Leone, Africa. The info I found said that his family began life in America as slaves on plantations in the area. At the end of the Civil War, some freed men and women travelled north and found work; others became caretakers or housekeepers in homes where they had served. Young men acquired farming jobs, eventually owning family farms of their own. The trail of info dead-ends there. Don't worry, Gran, the minute the first article hits the internet, relatives will begin to come forward. My editor is counting on it."

"I agree. Someone will claim him soon enough. I hope you know how proud I am of the work you've done."

"I wrote the piece for both of us, Gran." She grinned at me. "It's your fault, you know. I can't get that poor man and his murder out of my mind." Mimi attacks her burger again. She swallows. "Did your friend, Rita, ever respond to you?"

"No, and I don't expect her to. Oh, By the way, there's pie."

"Ooh, key lime?"

"You bet."

"I love you, Gran." Mimi polishes off the last bite on her plate.

* * *

I linger on my front porch watching my granddaughter back her car out of the driveway. Out on the curb, lightning bugs circle the mailbox, taking me back to childhood summers—playing tag with Skip Goodman in the grass behind the diner or the ongoing pleasure of beating him at checkers until the streetlights popped on. Those are the pleasant memories. "Wow. Skip Goodman and Opal Grizzle."

I lock the door and stroll into the kitchen. The bottle I want is in the cabinet above the microwave. I pour Frangelico, Phillip's favorite cordial, into an appropriate glass, the hazelnut aroma flooding my senses. A draft of Mimi's exposé awaits on the counter. I tuck the folder under my arm, slide into my husband's recliner, and then place eyeglasses on my nose. The title of the piece is "A Revelation after Fifty Years—Justice for a Hobo named Mundy Mike." My granddaughter's article reads like a historical drama and a murder mystery rolled into one. Evoking passion, empathy and sorrow, her words spring from the pages. The last paragraph is the perfect summary.

In our quest for answers, it was never our intention to cast a shadow on anyone's family, including our own, but only to open an investigation into an innocent man's death. My grandmother, Jessy Tate, and I hope that by bringing this unforgiveable incident to light, someone will claim Mike Mundy Limba Patterson from Beaufort, South Carolina as a family member. Even though this heinous crime was committed in 1956, we want the justice system to hold the guilty parties responsible.

We also wish for this article to inspire Jessy Tate's childhood friend to step forward and admit her part in witnessing the murder. Doing so would offer additional credibility to this article.

Gripping my phone, I punch in the numbers.

Mimi's young voice sings with expectation. "Hi, Gran. And the verdict is?"

"Honey, it's terrific, and I love the hint of a follow-up. You've heard about the squeaky wheel getting the grease. Well, my sweet girl, you're pushing a big ole noisy wheel."

"Fingers crossed. Although I mentioned Billy Grizzle and Caleb Blanchard, I'm saving the answer to the million dollar question of *who done it* for the sequel using Billy's own words. Do you wish to make any edits?"

"Not a one. I can't wait for part two. The more exposure, the better." The last of the cordial crosses my lips.

"I'm supposed to give the final copy to my editor in the morning."

"Good. Uh, is your mother nearby?"

"Hold on."

"Hi, Mom, isn't she amazing?" For several minutes, Gretchen brags about her daughter's accomplishments until she alludes to the upcoming divorce. Apparently, Gretchen's private detective discovered that her husband had participated in several affairs during their marriage.

"Gretchen, are you all right?"

"Yes, I'm okay. It was a shock, but then again, on some level I always knew."

"I think you're the strongest woman I know. You'll get through this ordeal and find happiness again."

"In time, I'm sure I will. By the way, have you spoken to Grandpa yet?"

"No, and I don't want to discuss it."

* * *

The Signal publishes Mimi's article on July 25, 2006. Within twenty-four hours, the *Atlanta Journal-Constitution* requests Georgia State University's permission to reprint the piece on August 1. Reporters beg to question me. Screening my calls allows me a tiny semblance of power, which by the way,

I enjoy. Due to my instant notoriety, I've received an added bonus. Jessy's Jewels continues a surge of record-setting sales.

At least once a day, Gretchen or Mimi pleads with me to call Dad. I refuse and delete another pitiful voicemail from Elijah Blanchard. My family doesn't understand me, yet my logic is simple. My father committed the most grievous sin of all. He tarnished my childhood memory of a perfect father. His offence is unforgiveable.

I'm the one who placed him on top of that pedestal, which over time grew moldy and cracked with age like the dilapidated birdbath in his yard. Eli Blanchard didn't just lose his balance and tumble off that crumbling hunk of cement. I stood behind the man and pushed.

CHAPTER THIRTY-TWO:
THAT DON'T HOLD WATER

By July, Harrison Rhodes remains stuck in a dead heat with his counterpart, Steven Bookings, for a U.S. Congressional seat representing the Commonwealth of Virginia. In August, the polls nudge Harrison two points ahead in the race. The increase, however, isn't enough to satisfy his campaign manager.

The congressman and his wife have plans tonight, another Friday evening fundraising affair. Harrison fine-tunes his bow tie. Brushing off a tuxedo jacket, he admires himself in the full-length bedroom mirror. He beholds a decent and handsome man who rose above mediocrity to become the first Black U.S. Representative of Congress in his district.

"Damn, you look good, Congressman Rhodes," he says as his cellphone pings. He scans the text then calls out, "Rita, the limo is on its way. You've got five minutes."

She responds from the adjoining room. "No problem."

Lingering at the dressing room door, he leers at his wife as she spritzes cologne into her cleavage and under the back of her hair. She slips her caftan over her head and folds the garment over the back of a chair. "Honey, please hand me that dress hanging on the hook behind the door."

Harrison obliges and zips her into a sequined black cocktail dress. Rita's trim body shows not a bulge or a bump, her ginger-tinted curls cascading onto her shoulders.

"You're gorgeous, woman." He tracks her into the bedroom.

"Thank you, darling, and by the way, you're not half bad yourself." She lightly strokes his hair.

"I adore you." He pulls her to his chest and plants a soft kiss on Rita's cheek. Rotating on his heels, he struts to the landing and hurries down the staircase. "The limo's in the driveway."

"Shoes. I can't find the right pair. Two minutes."

He waits at the bottom of the stairs as she leisurely descends, three inches taller in heels, her skirt skimming the top of her knees showing off never-ending milky white legs. Harrison beams. *That magnificent creature belongs to me.*

* * *

The boring party at the Ashworth's home drags on into its second hour. Because her feet ache, Rita buckles into a nearby loveseat. When Harrison drifts into view in the company of two other tuxedoed men, she blows a kiss to him. He gives her a brief smile before checking the messages on his phone.

Minutes later in the first-floor bathroom, Rita reapplies a raspberry stain to her collagen-plumped lips. She rejoins the party, worming her way across the room until she spots Beverly Ashworth, wife of a prominent contributor and deep-rooted Democrat, and this evening's hostess. Rita steals a glass of champagne from a waiter and makes a beeline toward the buffet.

Standing near Beverly and two other impeccably gowned women, the redhead interjects herself into the conversation. "…and I'm also interested in fighting for women's issues. During Harrison's second term, I plan to spearhead a crusade that promotes free childcare for single mothers."

When her uninterested audience exhibits no response to the comment, the hostess sprouts an artificial smile and abruptly switches topics. Rita's fingers tighten her grip on the stem of her glass. She scours the room and spots Harrison chatting up a threesome, which includes a past governor, an unknown woman, and a current state senator. She recognizes the shawl laying over the crook of her husband's arm. *Thank God. He's ready to leave.* Rita chugs her champagne, sets the glass on a table, and gives Beverly a reserved hug. "Thank you for hosting tonight. Harrison and I are extremely grateful for yours and Melvin's support."

Beverly tilts her nose a little higher. "Yes, well, I'm fairly certain we don't have a choice, now do we? He *is* the Democratic candidate."

Stunned by the remark, Rita sneers at the woman. "Yes, he is." She turns and aims herself in Harrison's direction. Biting her lip, she weaves through the crowd until she reaches him. He expresses his gratitude to the host for the dinner party while placing Rita's pashmina around her shoulders. The couple turns toward the door.

He leans close to her ear. "I saw you speaking to Beverly. The look on your face was priceless. Unfortunately, no matter what she said, you must let it go."

She snatches his hand. "Already have."

The chauffeur opens the limousine's rear door letting the couple step inside the glossy, black Mercedes-Benz. Harrison pulls his phone from his pocket and checks his messages again.

Rita stares out the window until she cracks the silence. "So how do you think it went?"

"Oh, very well. I'm beat though. Aren't you?"

"Yes, definitely."

He continues perusing one message then another. His demeanor shifts with an election-winning smile. "Honey, you're not going to believe this. Mama called. It seems a Georgia relative of hers saw an article in the

Atlanta Journal referring to, of all people, my Uncle Mike. Someone has come forward with detailed information about where and how he died. Mama is skeptical though. She uttered her usual *that just don't hold water* opinion. I'll call her back in the morning after I try and check the online article for veracity. You never know. It could just be a hoax."

Rita feels the color drain from her face.

CHAPTER THIRTY-THREE:
THE DEVIL'S BEATING HIS WIFE

Rita lies awake waiting to hear Harrison's gentle snore. In a few minutes, she slithers out of the sheets and creeps downstairs into the kitchen where her laptop sits charging on the counter. She balances on a stool and taps the mouse until a search engine appears on the screen. She types *AJC.com*.

The article headlines a column on the second page. "Oh, my God," she whispers. Rita's pulse vibrates through her body. *Jessy Tate has finally done it—taken steps to destroy me. She's always been jealous of my happiness.*

A wave of uncertainty rushes over her. Rita stops reading Mimi Stewart's words. *Did I ever utter Jessy's full name in front of Harrison?* She nibbles a cuticle on her thumb. *No. I wouldn't do that. There's no way he can place me at the banyan tree listening to Billy Grizzle's command and cringing at the sound of Mundy Mike's neck cracking in two.*

She shuts her eyes to reject the horrific scene, but the images are as clear as the crystal pendeloques hanging from her expensive dining room chandelier. A dull ache dances up the back of her neck. *Everything is fine. Yes. Fine. I'll agree with Harrison. The ideal timing of the story is a plus for his campaign. I'll mention how pleased I am that his mother will have closure about her brother.* She shuts her laptop.

Back in bed, insomnia plagues her. At three o'clock, Rita again steals downstairs to examine the article one more time. She re-reads the last sentence twice.

If anyone has any connection to or information about Mike Mundy Limba Patterson, please contact me via my email address: MimiStewartArticle@newsthesignal.com.

* * *

Harrison sips coffee and scans the article. Emitting a sense of importance as he sits behind an oversize desk, the congressman phones Beaufort, South Carolina. He listens to his mother's voice, her raspy breathing worse than the last time they spoke. He massages his temple.

Anyika Rhodes wheezes into the phone. "Rabbit, I had a dream that the devil, in the form of a crazy White man, killed my brother. Also, years ago, my fortunate teller, Lady Odah, told me an evil monster did Mike in." She coughs. "I just never figured on the Klan. Lord have mercy. That devil, he sure does get around. I can't imagine how scared my brother must have been."

"Uh huh. Listen, Mama. You and the family must sit tight. Tell everyone we're not ready to go public. So don't go talking to any reporters. My campaign manager and I are working on an appropriate response. I'll call you back when we have a plan in place." Harrison presses the delete button on his phone and scrawls a rough note on a legal pad. Setting the pen down, he props his feet on the top of the desk. *I'm a damn lucky man to have this fall into my lap.*

He pushes a number on his phone and drums a rhythm on his desk with recently manicured fingernails. "Roger, we've caught a huge break." He briefs his campaign manager on the gist of the story and the family connection. "Call Jim and the rest of the staff to investigate the piece in the *Atlanta Journal-Constitution* about a black hobo named Mundy Mike. The article ran over the weekend. My official reaction will show how incensed I am at finding out that someone kept the murder a secret, etc., etc. Roger, if we tag the piece exploiting my name, the story will go viral and the Associated Press will devour it. It's free media exposure."

"That's fantastic. Great timing, huh?"

"You bet. It's just what we needed. To accentuate the positive, we'll bring my sweet old Gullah mama front and center. She'll love spouting her two cents to the world, but I won't permit her to speak to the media until you or I have coached her properly. Let's contact the journalist ASAP."

Roger agrees. "I'll call the gang. Meet us at headquarters in an hour. I'll begin drafting your response right away. After we speak to this reporter, Mimi Stewart, we'll schedule the press conference. Timing is everything. I'll keep you posted."

Harrison leans back in his leather chair. "Okay. Send me a draft as soon as possible. Talk to you later." The connection dies. He can't help but smile. This news is more than timely; the story creates the kind of pure gold publicity that shouts *give me more*. He reviews the article again absorbing each paragraph. At first, he skims past the name of the woman who unwittingly attended the murder of his uncle, but on second perusal, the name, *Jessy Tate*, flickers recognition. He shuts off his computer and snatches his suit jacket off the coatrack.

"Jessy Tate. Where have I heard that name?" He passes by his secretary. "See you around three."

* * *

At five until six, Harrison sits at the desk in his office reviewing Roger's draft, a red pen in his grasp. His phone rings. "Mama, I told you I'd call you back."

Ani inhales oxygen in mid-sentence, her voice piercing Harrison's ear. "Rabbit, I'm beside myself. I've read this thing at least twenty times. This college girl, Mimi Stewart, wrote it. Apparently, when her grandmother, Jessy Tate, was a child, she saw four men hang my brother 'til his neck snapped into. Strange thing though, she didn't recall the murder until a psychiatrist hypnotized her."

"You have to listen to me. Calm yourself and don't speak to anyone about this, not to Mimi Stewart or the press. However, you *can* practice your reaction. You should be sorrowful, but above all, shocked at the way Mundy died. Mama, you have no idea how much this unexpected account of Uncle Mike's death will benefit my re-election campaign. I need your help. Will you do as I say?"

"Oh, yes, of course I will." She wheezes at the end of an intake of air.

"We have to stay on top of the narrative before all hell breaks loose."

"All right, son. I trust your judgment."

He disconnects and phones Roger. "I've edited the draft, so you should receive the markup any minute. I'll give the official response in the morning. I just spoke with my mother and asked her to squelch her opinion for the time being. She can't wait to share her outrage with the world. Once I let her, she'll steal the show."

Harrison checks the time—six-fifteen. He locks his office, rides the elevator to the basement lot, and squishes his long legs into the sports car he parked in a reserved space. The congressman zooms out onto the street in his black Corvette repositioning his earplug. He says, "Call Rita."

The line rings and she answers, "Hey, baby."

He detects music in the background. "Where are you?"

"Uh, I'm in my office working on my book."

Harrison hears the *tinkling* of ice stirring in a glass. "Really? It sounds like cocktail time."

"Just having a glass of water. I've completed two chapters, but they need reviewing. I should be home by…uh…nine, nine-thirty tops. By the way, Dolores made her famous tortilla casserole. You go ahead and eat."

"Okay, but I might stop off at the Monocle first."

"You should. Have a martini or two. Love you."

He dismisses the fleeting notion that Rita wasn't alone. Dark clouds hover above the skyline as the congressman steers three blocks to his hangout. Thunder rumbles in the distance.

When the Corvette veers in front of the upscale tavern, a young pony-tailed man dressed in black rushes to Harrison's car. "Congressman Rhodes, how are you tonight, sir?"

"Excellent. And you, Dane?" He hands the set of keys to the valet.

"No complaints. Thank you, sir."

Inside the bar, a fellow representative beckons from the corner of the room. Harrison's gaze travels beyond his colleague to an attractive woman perched between two other recognizable politicians. The two well-dressed men encircle the chocolate-haired beauty who sits posed on a barstool wearing a lavender knit dress, which accentuates every asset. Crossing her legs, she takes a sip of a burgundy tinted wine. Harrison moves toward the trio, but can't resist pressing the flesh as he glides through the patrons in the bar.

One at a time, Stan White and Paul Adams, old buddies from Harvard Law, shake Harrison's hand. The three men catch up for a few minutes, making light of each other's jobs.

"And you, Stan, are you still working for that pushy lobbyist?" Harrison captures the sexy brunette's stare.

"Yeah. It never ends." Stan turns to the brunette to his left. "Harrison, have you met Angelina Chavera? She's an attorney on Senator Deloria's staff."

A confident aura surrounds the young woman, her magnetic eyes drawing the congressman in. "We've met, haven't we, Harrison? Olivia Clemons introduced us at a party last year. You're looking well. What's your re-election forecast?"

"Pure sunshine, not a cloud in the sky." He returns her smile. "How've you been? You look amazing."

In no time, Harrison and the Latina beauty become engrossed in each other, enough to exclude the rest of the group for over two hours. When he pays the bar tab, he notices the time on his Rolex. "Eight forty already? I'm afraid I'm going to have to run along. How about we get together for coffee sometime soon so I can persuade you to switch sides. I'd love to have you…on my staff."

Angelina reaches inside her clutch. "Coffee sounds like a great idea. Give me a call." She offers him a business card; their hands accidentally touch causing a static electric twinge. "One can never tell about the future." She smiles with her eyes. "Come on, one more drink?"

"All right, but just one more. You're not driving, I hope. In fact, I'm going to call for a car. May I give you a lift home? I promise you, the valet will keep your car safe overnight."

"That's very sweet of you."

Although the situation is ripe with seductive innuendo, Harrison isn't prepared to go any further tonight. *Rita should be home by now.*

* * *

The redhead shuts off her phone. "Come on. We don't have long."

"Long enough." Ethan embraces Rita and kisses her neck.

The congressman's wife escapes reality again inside Room 103 at the Southside Suites in Forestville, Maryland. At exactly eight fifty-two, Ethan zips up the back of her dress. She turns to him. "This was lovely." She brushes his cheek with a quick kiss. "I'll call you." Grabbing her purse, she dashes out of the room. She exits via the hotel's rear door, hustling to the car where a broken streetlight bulb aids and abets her infidelity.

* * *

At nine thirty-five, she drives into the garage with no sign of Harrison. She enters the house and heads upstairs. Because Ethan's scent still clings to her skin, she immediately sheds her clothes on her way to the master bath. A shower is mandatory.

Rita May McAfee Rhodes had one goal in life—to rise above her miserable childhood circumstances. Attaining money and status, whatever the cost, kept her motivated. At eighteen, a brief and impulsive marriage briefly sidetracked her and produced an unplanned pregnancy. Divorced and broke in Hickory, North Carolina, Rita worked as a cocktail waitress until she figured out a way to give her kid a decent life and, of course, make money for herself. She found a wealthy childless couple who agreed to pay her fifty thousand dollars for her one-year-old daughter. The deal, however, required her to give up all parental rights.

After relocating to Charlotte, she waited tables while attending community college, taking classes in science and nutrition. Keeping her goal in sight, Rita enticed her teacher, Herbert Burstein, a middle-aged biology professor, to chuck his twenty-year marriage, to take a loan out to pay for Rita's tuition to the University of North Carolina-Charlotte, and to buy her a new 4,000-square-feet home in the suburbs for the two of them. Five years into a loveless relationship, Rita divorced Herbert citing irreconcilable differences. With her settlement, she obtained a college degree and certification, attending extra classes to garner a license to practice as a nutritionist. Within six months, she opened her own consulting business.

Three years later, Rita acquired a teaching position at George Mason University in Fairfax, Virginia. She married Jeff Barnes, who was ten years her senior, but from old Virginia money. She loved him enough to stay married for twenty-six years. He died at sixty-eight of a heart attack, but left Rita fixed for life. Six months later, she plunged into the Washington D.C. singles scene. Enter Harrison Rhodes, the new and amended model of the man of her dreams.

Rita lingers in the shower, fixating on Jessy Tate's disastrous plan. "I have to stop this runaway train." Even if her concern is premature, she must be ready in case the shit hits the fan. The redhead mentally rehearses her story. *Jessy Tate has a vivid imagination. By June of 1956, my father, a successful lawyer, had moved his family to Charlotte, North Carolina.*

Harrison's footsteps resonate from the first floor. Rita towel dries her hair and eavesdrops on a phone call, her husband's baritone echoing throughout the house.

"I told you…Don't worry. I'll have Ms. Stewart call you, but…yes, Mama, your words might appear in the *AJC*'s Sunday edition." His deep sigh implies exasperation.

Rita's thoughts scramble. *What will I do if it all spins out of control?*

* * *

At eight-fifteen on Friday morning, Harrison remains preoccupied. His thoughts center on the effect his Uncle Mike's murder will have on his future. *I'll email Miss Stewart shortly and light the fire.* Stroking his face, he glides the razor down his cheek. Warm water from the bathroom faucet dribbles into the basin. He feels Rita slink behind his six-feet frame, the redhead's silk caftan bonding to her naked body.

He places the razor under running water. "Again, thank you, darling. It was a perfect beginning to my day."

"My pleasure." She floats back to the bedroom. Peeking through the window blinds, she shudders. "How can it be raining and the sun is still shining?" She collapses onto the bed. Lying on her side, her body curves toward the wall, her caftan falling off her shoulder. "What's that saying… something about the devil and the rain?"

Blocking the threshold, his bathrobe sash loose at his waist, he gawks at Rita's birthmark, the crescent on her shoulder. "The one about the devil beating his wife with a frying pan?"

"Yeah. Another ridiculous southern saying I've never understood." She rolls to face him.

There's something in the way her cheek rests on her arm. In a *déjà vu* minute, the congressman evokes a memory, a conversation he and Rita shared months earlier regarding a telephone call.

At the time, he asked, "Who were you talking to anyway?"

"An annoying old friend who recently lost her husband. She uses me as a sounding board."

"An old friend?"

"Jessy Tate...she lives in Atlanta."

CHAPTER THIRTY-FOUR:
MAMA DIDN'T RAISE NO FOOL

Harrison throws the towel behind him. His brow furrows; his eyes turn cold.

She sits up and hugs her knees to her chest. "What's wrong?"

He widens his stance. "Do you know someone named Jessy Tate?"

"Who?" She grips the sheet. "Why?"

"Rita, don't lie to me." His accusing glare stabs at her composure.

She swallows. "I don't think so."

"Jessy Blanchard Tate from Atlanta is the woman who witnessed my uncle's murder in 1956. Didn't you tell me you had a friend named Jessy Tate in Atlanta?"

"Did I? Let me see. Yeah, I once knew a Jessy, but that was a long time ago. I swear I don't know anybody who lives in Atlanta. I must have misspoken." *I'm talking too fast. Slow down.* She takes a breath.

He approaches the bed. "Why are you lying? Wait. In the article, Jessy Tate mentions a friend who witnessed the lynching. Are you that friend? It's you, isn't it?"

She moves to the end of the mattress and lunges at her husband's arm. "I didn't know how to tell you."

He pushes her away. "I'm waiting."

Rita's body slumps in surrender. "Okay, yes. I lived in Bonita Springs, Florida when I was a kid. I befriended Jessy Blanchard for almost a year, but I, too, blocked the incident from my mind. I didn't remember the lynching until she reminded me. I was confused, but I never put two and two together until that night in Beaufort when your brother spoke of Mundy Mike. I didn't want you to learn of that violent crime that way." She fakes tears. "I was biding my time. I knew you and your family would be hurt by the horrific incident."

"You're lying. According to Mrs. Tate's account, this friend came from an unfortunate background, the daughter of a seasonal farmer, a citrus fruit picker. If you *are* the friend she is referring to, everything you've told me about yourself is a lie."

Bitterness taints her speech. "Jessy Tate is the liar. Always has been. Why would you believe her instead of me?" Her tears quickly recede.

He takes two steps backward, his face forming a scowl. "I'm going to postpone my response to Ms. Stewart's article until I have the whole story." His steely eyes match his posture. "I demand that you tell me the truth. Now."

Talking a mile a minute, she tucks her hands under her thighs. It takes a half an hour for her to explain herself and acknowledge her defeat. Without divulging too much, she conveys a few aspects of her life as Davis McAfee's daughter travelling from town to town, picking vegetables or fruit, living in deplorable housing, and taking care of the brats her father forced upon her mother. At the end of the soliloquy, she again admits to witnessing the hanging, but pleads innocent of any malice.

Harrison collapses into a club chair, a weary look on his face. "You've blindsided me. How did you do it? I investigated you and none of your genuine background came to light."

"You did *what*?"

"Yes. Because I'm a member of Congress, it's necessary."

"Well, I suppose I'm too smart for any investigator, and I usually manage to get what I want. I abhor any reference to my pathetic childhood, so I legally changed my name to Miller ages ago. In reality, it's easy to become someone else if you pay the right people. I even obtained an additional social security number." She plucks a tissue from the box on her bedside table. Dabbing at phony tears, she stops to blow her nose.

He grits his teeth, his jaw quivering before he speaks. "You've been lying to me from the moment we met." Harrison's steely glance darts back and forth from Rita and back to the bedroom window. "At the very least, you could've shown basic decency by telling me that you connected the dots from my family to a hobo from your past. My God, you witnessed the hanging of a Black man and never told a soul. I understand about Jessy Tate and her lost memory. After all, the event traumatized her. On the other hand, you apparently weren't; your memory is intact. It is inconceivable to me how you could keep the murder a secret all this time."

The pretense vanishes as she crawls off the bed. She stands with both hands on her hips, her voice stronger. "It's not my fault. I made a choice to leave my past and become a new person. It was my only chance at survival."

"Deceit is always the wrong choice, Rita." Harrison heads toward the dressing room.

* * *

A half an hour later, dressed in an impeccable suit and a power tie, Harrison grips his brief case and pauses at the bedroom door. Rita sits on the edge of the bed, the look in her eyes unyielding.

He clears his throat. "I'm done. We're through. You need to be out of my house by the end of the day. Call somebody to pick up your belongings."

Rita watches him as he moves to the other side of the room. She touches where her lip is bleeding. "Are you serious? You're saying our marriage is over because of one little mistake. What about everything that we meant to each other? The good times. The love we shared. Can't you just get past this blip? One mistake. Come on. You've never made a mistake?"

"Of course, I've made mistakes. I'm looking at my latest and greatest one sitting right in front of me. However, Rita, you and I are different. I'm an honest man. I admit my faults and I don't lie." He chuckles to himself. "I find it interesting that you've not uttered a single word of regret. I *will* move on or get past this, as you say, because I don't dwell on my mistakes. Now that you've made a fool out of me, I see the real you, and honestly, I don't like what I see. Your beauty is fading; your charm is all a façade, and your speech, that's probably false, too. You're not real, Rita. You're a fake inside and out." He smirks. "Funny though. Mama pegged you the instant the two of you met. She said you were white trash." He ambles into the hallway and stops. "Your dishonesty has killed any affection I felt for you. You see, my deluded wife, like a lovely painting or sculpture one might acquire, you are easily replaceable." He straightens his posture. "Don't worry. I won't allow your name to be mentioned in Mimi Stewart's article."

"What if I..."

Adjusting his tie in the wall mirror on the upstairs landing, he interrupts her before she can finish the question. "Oh, and you should use your Visa cards today because they won't be any good tomorrow. Regarding the divorce, I'll be fair. You'll receive your share, your entitlement under the law, but no more. If you cause me any trouble or try to sue me for any additional money or property, I'll obliterate you. Are we clear? I want you gone. Give Roger your temporary residence so he can forward your mail. My attorney will contact you soon."

Harrison takes a deep breath and slowly descends the stairs. He strolls into the kitchen, but hesitates near the sink, twisting the solid gold ring off his finger. He drops it into the trashcan. After pulling his wallet from his pocket, he removes a business card. He brings it to his nose permitting Angelina Chavera's cologne to flood his senses. *Chanel.* He smiles. *My mama didn't raise no fool.*

* * *

The garage door whines as Rita rolls onto the bed and turns on her side. Clutching her pillow, she cries out. "I can't believe this is happening. What do I do now? Look at all the time I wasted on him. And to think I actually thought he was so special." She turns over on her back.

After an hour of blaming everyone but herself, she sits up. "I've got to stop this. There's no time. I've got plans to make." Rita springs from the bed, and she darts into the bathroom. She considers the evidence in the mirror. "And thanks to God and that bitch, Jessy Tate, I have to start over yet again. Maybe this time I'll find some fat cat who has tons of money and clout, one who will love me unconditionally." Seething with rage, she shouts into the mirror. "Damn you, Congressman Harrison Rhodes, and your low-class Gullah family."

CHAPTER THIRTY-FIVE:
REAP WHAT WE SOW

Mimi skims the notifications on her laptop. The computer's clock reads nine twenty-three. She spots an email from Congressman Harrison Rhodes. The subject line reads *Mundy Mike*.

She reviews the message. "This is great." Feeling shaky and her mouth suddenly dry, she seizes a bottle of water. She chugs a drink as she prints a copy of the email. Pulling herself together, Mimi struts into her editor's office, email in hand.

His grin grows wider as he reads. "Wow! This is major. Call the congressman's assistant or campaign manager and schedule an interview ASAP. We need him on the record. You can use his quotes in the second part of the series. Oh, man, the AP will gobble this up. Whoa, this is prime time stuff." He stands and drums a rhythm out on his desk. He licks his lips. "Okay. Okay. This is the plan. Ah, tell his people that we'll accommodate him, go to his office, or interrogate him on the phone. Do whatever he suggests, and call the AJC. They're expecting a sequel, but I believe it will be more extensive than originally planned."

Giggling to herself, Mimi hurries back to her desk. Without wasting a moment, she responds to the email and then phones Harrison Rhode's assistant. After a one o'clock meeting is set, Mimi phones her grandmother.

* * *

I blink into an oversized magnifying glass attached to the table, while looping an end piece of wire into a hollow bead. My cellphone vibrates.

"Hi, Mimi."

"You better sit down. This is big." My granddaughter's voice quivers. "It's the coolest thing…"

"Slow down. Take a breath."

"Congressman Harrison Rhodes emailed me early this morning. Uh, he saw the article. Mundy Mike was his long lost uncle."

"Are you serious?" My mind spins. "Wait a minute. Mundy Mike is related to Congressman Harrison Rhodes, who just happens to be married to Rita May McAfee."

"Yeah. Way too much of a coincidence."

"Not merely a coincidence, but probably one reason Rita didn't want the story to go public. She somehow discovered the connection and kept the information from her husband, knowing the truth would reveal her past. To Rita, it's the worst that could happen." A tightening sensation grips my chest. "I ought to call her. She didn't ask for any of this."

Mimi *clicks* her tongue. "It's not your fault, Gran."

"Yeah, maybe, but here I am trying to do what is right and because of my interference, I may have ruined Rita's life."

"We have no idea if she told her husband or not, but the woman did refuse to help you. I don't pity her at all."

"Her letters revealed how happy she was and how much she loved him. Now I've destroyed her perfect life. Rita will have to begin again at sixty-four years old. All the plastic surgery in the world won't keep her young forever."

"Let's concentrate on the plus side. I have an interview with the charming congressman this afternoon." Mimi giggles.

"I'm dumbfounded. Call me later and give me a play-by-play. Bye."

I leave my work undone and stroll into the kitchen. A half-empty bottle of pinot noir sits on the counter. There's a clean glass in the dish drainer. I pour and take a sip. The wine warms my throat as I punch in Rita's number on my phone. The call streams to voicemail.

"It's me, Jessy. I realize now why you didn't want me to dig into the past. Why didn't you clue me in on the connection between Mundy Mike and Harrison? We might have found a better way to approach the situation, one benefiting everyone involved. I'm truly sorry if the article hurt you in any way. Let's talk it over. We used to be good at solving problems together."

* * *

It's three-thirty and my granddaughter phones again.

"The interview exceeded all expectations, and he is such a super guy, like up close and personal."

"And Rita?" I stroll onto the patio.

"Congressman Rhodes and I chatted for about twenty minutes or so, and at first, he didn't mention his wife. When I asked him for permission to include his family in the article, he paused. Then he said he needed the next aspect of his statement to be off the record." Mimi clears her throat. "He said and I quote, 'You may include my mother and my family in Beaufort, South Carolina. However, my wife's name will not be mentioned in the article in any context.' Of course, I agreed to his terms."

I drop into the nearest chair. "Rita confessed. He knows everything."

* * *

Rita switches on her phone. She prolongs packing long enough to toss back a few shots of whiskey. Taking a minute to read and delete phone notifications, she spies a message from Jessy. As she listens, she bites down on her sore lip. She sucks a huge breath before she shouts, "You did it, Jessy Tate.

It's all on you," and heaves the empty glass at the bedroom wall. She returns the call, but the voicemail greeting answers.

"Hello, you've reached Jessy's Jewels. Please leave a message, and I will return your call as soon as I can. Have a nice day."

Rita kills the call and pours another drink before she tries again. This time, she delivers a dissertation. "Jessy, I know why you did this. You've always been jealous of me. Obviously, my happiness means nothing to you. In order to massage your conscience and ease your useless guilt, you stuck your nose where it didn't belong. Now you've ruined my happy marriage. Well, the joke's on you, old friend. I'm a survivor and stronger than you could ever be. I won't let your actions damage me. Goodbye, Jessica Blanchard Tate."

* * *

The next morning as I listen to my old friend's message, her vindictive words automatically cure me of any responsibility for her. I stare out the kitchen window. "We reap what we sow, Rita May." I carefully sip hot coffee from my favorite mug while spying on several gray doves scurrying through the grass. I dismiss the sudden ringing of my phone. A minute later, a *ping* sounds. I take a deep breath for I know who left the message. "Sorry, Dad, forgiveness is not on the menu today."

* * *

In a few days, the Associated Press picks up the original Mundy Mike story and publishes the article in thousands of newspapers across the country, in anticipation of the juicy sequel set to unfold soon. When the *AJC* runs the second part of Mimi's exposé in the Sunday edition, the segment quotes Congressman Harrison Rhodes and includes a paragraph of emotionally charged words quoted by Ani Rhodes. Later that evening at a press conference broadcast on all major television networks, the dapper congressman renders a heartfelt speech.

On Monday, *Good Morning America* interviews Ani Rhodes on the front porch of her Beaufort home. The congressman's mother, wearing her hair pinned into a tight bun, sports a bright pink dress. As she tweaks the oxygen prong in her nose, she lets her accent, quick wit, and colloquial delivery captivate the television audience.

Prim and proper, she clasps tiny hands in her lap. The petite woman smacks her thin lips. "I figured my brother didn't just up and vanish into thin air. Always knew Satan did the deed and Mike's bones would be laying in the ground somewhere. He was a big, strapping man, six feet and five, a pleasing wide grin from ear to ear. God rest his sweet soul."

Toward the end of the fifteen-minute interview, the reporter states, "It must have been hard for you to learn of the Ku Klux Klan's involvement in your brother's death."

Ani inhales a whiff of oxygen. "Lord, have mercy. Nobody wants to meet his maker that way—hanging from a tree, life oozing outta him."

* * *

Due to all the publicity, my cat and I spend the summer in a rental cottage three hours away in the mountains of Cashiers, North Carolina. Circumstances dictate I suspend my business for the time being. Mimi keeps me current on the third and final series installment of the story commissioned by the newspaper.

In September, both *Good Morning America* and the *Today Show* interview both of us. By the end of the month, the media firestorm surrounding Harrison Rhodes finally cools down. However, while making his way down the campaign trail, the congressman reignites the spark of interest every time he resurrects his Uncle Mike's ordeal.

In November, Congressman Harrison Rhodes easily defeats the competition and wins his Virginia seat back in the U.S. House of Representatives.

* * *

Rita quits her job at George Mason, pays off the office lease, and within a month relocates to California. Once she receives a divorce settlement, she legally takes back her maiden name, the name she abandoned for over thirty years, and opens McAfee Health and Nutritional Counseling in San Diego, her anonymity secure.

One evening in December, Rita attends the annual Nutrition and Wellness Conference held at the San Diego Convention Center. While browsing the exhibits, she introduces herself to Timothy Bannon, a chiropractor who owns a conglomerate of health and wellness practices in Los Angeles. The tall and tanned white-haired gentleman emanates wealth and class. When he asks Rita to dinner, she accepts the invitation without a moment's hesitation. After all, the attractive chiropractor checks all the right boxes.

CHAPTER THIRTY-SIX:
A SINGLE THREAD

I spend the last of our crisp November days creating jewelry in my Atlanta studio. Unfortunately, intermittent bouts of insomnia still plague me. One morning, still in my bathrobe, I sip my first cup of dark roast in the living room where I carefully unwrap the contents of boxes labeled *ORNAMENTS*. Although, I promised Mimi I would decorate for Christmas this year, I'm not looking forward to it.

"I need more coffee." I scuff into the kitchen, stopping at the patio doors as the cat snakes through my legs. "Lulu, we've got to feed those starving birds, don't we?" The kitty stares through the glass door and squeaks at the winged creatures scrounging for food on the frosty lawn. I bend over to stroke her fur and she meows. "You're right. It's time I called him." I pour coffee into my cup then find the familiar name on my phone. I press the number.

"Dr. Justin Priest's office, Chelsea speaking."

"Hi, it's Jessy Tate. Does he have any openings soon?"

"Let me see, Mrs. Tate."

I wait on hold. Soft jazz plays in the background.

The receptionist's deep southern accent always makes me smile. "His schedule is booked until next week except for the last time slot tomorrow evening at six."

"I'll take it. Thanks."

* * *

Pushing open the door, a whiff of stale vanilla lingers in the reception area. Chelsea spots me and ushers me inside Dr. Priest's office. He sits at his mahogany desk holding a phone to his ear.

Justin motions to me. "Yes. I will. Can we discuss this tomorrow?" In less than a minute, he cuts the call short. Walking up to me, the doctor offers me his hand. "Jessy, how are you doing?" His pale blue button-down shirt complements his eyes.

I hang my jacket on the coat rack before clasping his warm hand. "Not bad. I assume you've heard." I plop into the chair in front of the desk.

"Yes, and I saw your stint on *Good Morning America.* You did a super job."

"Thanks, but I'm glad the hoopla is over. We're waiting on the State of Florida to make a decision on Billy Grizzle."

"How are *you* doing?"

"Pretty good, but I'm still battling this annoying insomnia. Although the dreams have almost disappeared, my brain won't settle at night. I suppose it's good that I'm not popping pills." I set my purse on the floor.

He opens his laptop. "I examined your file and re-read my notes about your visit to Bonita Springs. When you returned from your trip, you spoke about the truths that you and your granddaughter uncovered. However, you refused to talk about your father as it pertained to his betrayal, as you called it, and the toll it took on your relationship with him."

"Well, here's an update. I haven't spoken to him since." I dig down inside my handbag for a pack of mints.

"Has he called you?"

"Daily and leaves pathetic voicemail messages."

"And you have no intention of speaking to him?"

"Nope. Not interested." I toss a wintergreen mint in my mouth and stretch my neck left to right.

"Jessy, that's the answer to your sleep problem."

I pick at a stray thread from my jeans.

"It's an unresolved issue. You've adored your father your entire life, and he disappointed you. Search your heart and forgive him. Carrying that level of resentment, not allowing the man his flaws, this will continue to eat at you. Forgiveness can give you peace of mind."

"You make a lot of sense, and my daughter, Gretchen, agrees with you. I'll tell you the same thing I say to her. I can't do it. I won't do it."

The session, which ends at seven, fails to give me the answers I desire. Dr. Priest means well, but he doesn't understand. Walking to the car, I blink at the glare from the parking lot lights. I wiggle into my SUV, and because I'm expecting a call from my friend, Maisie, I switch on my phone. There's a message from Manuel marked *URGENT*. A boulder descends into the pit of my stomach.

"Jessy, call me. Eli…he's in the hospital."

Although the inside of the Explorer takes several minutes to warm up, I'm burning up. I roll down a window. "God, take care of him." I inhale a lungful of outside air before I make the call. It rings and rings. Finally. "Manuel, tell me."

"Today at your dad's doctor appointment, he received results from last week's bloodwork and CT scan. I guess there's no easy way to say this. It's liver cancer, Jess. Stage IV. Looks like he's been living with it for months and suffering in silence. Bottom line, he's gravely ill."

"How did he keep it from you?"

"I really don't know. He was losing weight, but he never mentioned any pain. Your father is a stubborn old cuss."

"Where is he now?"

"He's in a private room on the Oncology Floor at NCH North Naples Hospital. The doctors insist he stay a while for more tests, but you know him, he's fighting mad and demanding to go home." Manuel's tone is somber. "They don't give him much time…a month or two. Hard to tell."

I exhale slowly. "Uh, I need to get myself together. I'll call you back."

The connection dies, but I hold the phone to my ear for another minute before it slips from my hand. I clutch the steering wheel. There is no way to stop the tears. "Oh, my God." I repeat Dr. Priest's words. "Search your heart and forgive him." Sobbing, I crank the ignition and phone my daughter. "Honey, I…"

"Hi, Mom. I'm kind of busy with something here. Can I call you back?" Her voice is cool and clear.

"No, you can't. I need you now, Gretchen. Your grandfather is dying."

* * *

My daughter and I wait at the baggage carousel at the Southwest Florida International Airport. I see her suitcase on the conveyor belt. After the bags circle one more time, I rescue the pale blue one I bought several years ago. Once we tow our luggage through the airport, we stand together at the curb.

Beads of perspiration cover my forehead. "Where did this heat come from? It's December for goodness' sake and eight-thirty in the evening for that matter. I'm burning up." I remove my lightweight sweater, gripping it in my clammy hand. The Jeep surprises me as it swerves to the shoulder and idles.

Manuel hops out. "All aboard, ladies." He stows the bags in the rear compartment.

Gretchen hugs Manuel and is first to question. "How's he doing?"

He smacks his gum and slips a key into the Jeep's ignition. "Not good. Sorry to say he's not doing well at all. Since I've been taking care of Eli, he's always reminded me of an old balloon with a tiny hole, air slowly seeping out of him year by year, a tiny bit of life at a time, but still able to float through the air. When he received the diagnosis, it felt like the puncture expanded, the hole increased in size. Now, the air is leaking out way too fast." Manuel pauses to catch his breath. "At least Mr. Eli's home in his own bed now. He's just too weak to do much but lie there and sleep. A Hospice nurse visits every day. It's her job to manage his pain, but the morphine destroys any appetite he has left. By the way, we told him you were coming."

The Jeep speeds down the highway as twilight fades to blackness. Gretchen and Manuel converse in the front seat. I sit in the back staring at the headlights coming toward us, allowing my doubts to consume me. I have no idea what to say to my dad.

Why can't I excuse *his* actions?

Forgiveness isn't always hard. When Phillip fooled around, I forgave him. Although, in the end, I suppose karma got its way, dictating the turn of events. Phillip achieved the perfect unintentional revenge by dying, his death obliterating any remote possibility of my one-night stand ever becoming anything more. For that, I am beyond grateful. On the other hand, I still wonder if Phillip ever forgave me for leaving him to die alone. If I'd been faithful, I could have called 911, or at the very least, hold his hand and share his last moments.

The drive eats up too much time. Manuel decelerates at the end of Dad's driveway, where an unfamiliar white Toyota invades the space to the left of the mailbox. He navigates the rest of the way, parking the Jeep on the other side. I glance at the yard. A floodlight from a neighbor's house spotlights Dad's moldy birdbath.

Gretchen and I trail Manuel to the screened porch where a stocky middle-aged woman opens the door. "Hello, Mrs. Tate. I'm Wanda Pickens, your father's nurse."

"How do you do?" I gesture to my left. "This is my daughter, Gretchen Stewart. Uh, how is he?"

Manuel hauls the luggage into the house behind the nurse who shepherds us inside, her lilac scrubs *swishing* as she walks.

"The pain meds cause him to drift in and out, but when I told him you were on the way, Mr. Blanchard's spirits rallied a little. I'm off now. Manuel has my number."

"You'll return early tomorrow?"

"Yes, of course. I'll be knocking on your door promptly at nine. We have several items to discuss and I have forms for you to sign—the hospice process, the status of your father's health, and details of his managed pain care." Carrying a briefcase and a tote, Wanda ambles to her car.

Flinching at the slamming of the screened door, I crumble into a wicker chair.

"I'll make a pot of coffee. Want some, Mom?" Gretchen wanders into the kitchen; her voice trails behind her. "Or would you like a glass of wine?"

"Nothing, thanks." Hugging my handbag, I can't seem to move.

In minutes, my daughter strays onto the porch and sets a mug of coffee on the glass top table. "I'm going on in to see him or you can go first, if you wish."

I focus on the wrinkles on my hands. "No. You go, but please switch off that overhead light. I have a splitting headache." The light dims. The porch instantly cools. Gretchen's footsteps recede to the back of the cottage.

The ceiling fan rotates at low speed, the broken blade hindering the others. My vision wanders to a corner near the screen where a spider web glistens in the outside floodlight's reflection, its artistic weave swaying to the fan's revolution. A frantic beetle fights to escape the silky netting, his wings fluttering. The poor defenseless creature barely holding onto a single thread, his struggle like someone hanging from a rope, clinging to life with each breath.

I set my purse on the table. In two steps, I'm on tiptoes swatting at the web. The beetle becomes free to flit through the air. Within a minute, I slink down the hallway where Gretchen's gentle words echo from Daddy's room.

"Hi, Grandpa, do you know me? I'm Gretchen, your granddaughter. It's been a few years, hasn't it?"

The closer I get, the harder my heart beats. I enter his room. I feel as though I'm trembling. Gretchen teeters on the edge of a threadbare wing chair, one of my mother's. I look about the room and inhale. It smells of inevitability. I exhale hearing my father before I see him, life leaking from his body with his every breath.

His appearance alarms me. Six months ago, he looked elderly and somewhat feeble, but today there's nothing left but skin and bone. This shell of a man lying in front of me can't possibly be my father, my hero, the one who held me in his arms when Mama left us, his words whispering in my ears. "Baby Girl, *I'll* never leave you."

Uncertainty creeps over me. Why do loved ones disappoint us? My father, the strong parent I worshiped my entire life, is no longer worthy of adoration, a mere mortal with faults. Does he deserve my forgiveness? And Phillip? Did he forgive *me*? I never got the chance to ask him.

I stroke my father's cheek, and his paper-thin eyelids open. "Hey, Daddy."

He manages a weak smile, but the effort slowly fails. He squints as if he's in pain. "Jessica Rose, you're…," his words breathy and faint, "…sorry. I'm so sorry. Please forgive me."

Tears blur my eyes. "It's all right. Shush, Daddy." I pat his hand. "I'm here."

He stares at me and says something inaudible. I tip closer to his ear, kiss his cheek, and lower my voice to a whisper. "I love you, Daddy. Everything is okay."

"But...Jessy...do you forgive me?"

I speak slowly, like my father does when he answers the phone, not fast with my words all jumbled together, but one word at a time. My heart feels huge as it thuds inside my chest. "I. Don't. Know."

A lone tear drips down his cheekbone.

I can't give him the one thing he wants from me. If I do forgive Dad, my psychiatrist promises I'll be free of guilt. The gnawing inside will disappear. If I don't absolve Eli Blanchard of his sins, Justin Priest says the regret will devour me. Sadly, the war between my head and heart demands more time to find some sort of peace. However, time is short.

I inhale. When I pry the words from my mouth, my voice cracks. "I forgive you, Daddy." I exhale as if all my breath escapes into the room.

Next, I must learn to forgive myself.

Like everyone else, I am flawed and human. I am, after all, my father's daughter.

The End